BATTLE BEYOND THE VEIL

An Urban Fantasy Where Angels and Demons Collide

Cassie Sanchez

Silver Labs Press

For the readers who step into strange worlds with open hearts, who chase light through shadows, and who trust me to guide them into a new world. This story is yours as much as it is mine.

Author's Note

This book uses angels, demons, and biblical concepts as inspiration, but it is not meant to be a literal or doctrinal representation. I've blended tradition elements with creative freedom to build a world that fits the story, the characters, and the fantasy genre.

If you come from a faith background, please know that none of these choices are intended to challenge or contradict personal beliefs— only to create an engaging fictional world.

Content Warnings: Violence, death, firearms, and themes involving suicide (not depicted in detail)

Pronunciation Guide

Archangels

Michael

Gabriel

Raphael (RAH-fye-el)

Chamuel (SHAM-you-el)

Jophiel (JO-fee-el)

Ariel (AH-ree-el)

Azrael (AZ-ray-el)

Characters

Kyden (KYE-den)

Zahra (ZAH-ruh)

Adinah (ah-DEE-nuh)

Demon Princes

Apollyon (uh-POL-ee-on)

Mammon (MAM-un)

Satan - aka Marach (MAH-rak)

Asomodeus (az-MOH-dee-us)

Beelzebub (bee-EL-zuh-bub)

Belphegor (BEL-fuh-gor)

Leviathan (luh-VY-uh-thun)

Ancient Relic

Atar'zul (AH-tar-zool)

PROLOGUE

A *war rages, one human eyes cannot see. It's not a battle of flesh and blood, or at least not human blood. You should be familiar with this statement—it is, after all, the first sentence in the most famous book ever written: "In the beginning, God created..."*

But what about the time before—the time of the angels? God created warriors. Which begs the question: Why? Who was there to fight before time began? Perhaps He knew all along there would be a war, one that first started with betrayal.

This is how the legend has been told through the generations, finally written down as a warning to all.

Apollyon, second-in-command to God Himself, wanted what he could not have, and he betrayed his first love, craving a throne for himself.

The Celestial War began, and Heaven split in two.

Those who remained loyal to God battled their brothers and sisters who had chosen Apollyon and his prideful ways. Little did Apollyon and his followers know that they had chosen the losing side and soon realized their folly when fire from Heaven's throne shriveled their wings until nothing but stumps remained.

A fierce battle occurred between the archangel Michael and the betrayer Apollyon. Sweat and blood dripped under their halos and down their faces as the fighting continued, the Heavens quaking with each collision of their swords.

With a desperate slash of his blade, Michael sliced the halo from Apollyon's head. Michael's golden blood mixed with Apollyon's, now stained black with sin. Their combined blood dripped onto the broken halo and cursed the once-holy crown.

Apollyon, wounded and bleeding, was cast down to the Abyss along with his fallen warriors.

Not one to take defeat, the demons continued to fight the angels, an endless war between good and evil, valor and deceit.

But as with all things magical and powerful, a balance was needed. God created humans, favored beings that inhabit the earth. Only a select few are granted a talisman, a way to see beyond the veil into the spiritual realm. Only they, the Vaelatori, can protect the legend of the halo and the prophecy tied to it.

This is my purpose in this dark hour. The demons have come, and the halo is missing. I have taken parts of the prophecy and hidden them, leaving clues where only the Vaelatori can find them. Neither the angels nor the demons know of the prophecy, and we must keep it that way.

Or else all will be lost.

—Bahram, the first Vaelatori,

The Prophecy of the Atar'zul

From loyal blood and fallen grace,
the crown was forged from war's
cruel fate. Its form was neither
cursed nor blessed, but watched by
eyes that never rest.

Guardians shaped from mortal clay
concealed the relic and held darkness at bay. Their purpose pure—to
guard the lore, from hands of peace
and those of war.

When halo's gleam was again exposed, it drew the eyes of the op-
posed. Of all the sins it was power
they craved, and altered the crown for
the depraved.

The angels bowed to twisted might,
and shattered all they held as right.
Once steadfast and pure, their will
now bent to shadow's lure.

Yet hope remains, though dim and
slight. A mortal must bleed to feed the
light—bound to an archangel's heavenly might, to turn the tide against
the night.

A sacred bond, united and pure,
shall cleanse the crown of dark allure.
From shadow's grip and sorrow's
chains, the angels rise in light's refrain—redeemed through blood and
solemn vow, they seek the grace they
once let down.

CHAPTER ONE

KYDEN

The sun beat down mercilessly, creating wavy lines of heat along the street while humans scurried like ants, drawn to the vibrant stalls where vendors hawked their wares with the promise of a bargain. Pungent spices, cooking meat, and body odor combined into an unpleasant fragrance that tickled Kyden's sensitive nose. He soaked in the busyness of Hillah, Iraq's bustling marketplace while enjoying a cup of Turkish coffee at an outdoor café—no one the wiser an angel dwelled among them.

Kyden sat in the shade with his back to the wall as he eyed a grunt scuttling through the busy streets in search of its next prey. The lesser demon, oblivious to humans, skulked by the café, its yellow eyes sifting through the people. Kyden slowly slid on his sunglasses so the demon wouldn't see his unique amber eyes, a trait all angels shared, except for the archangels, whose eyes shimmered gold. If anything was to reveal Kyden's presence, his eyes, although pleasing to humans, were a dead giveaway to a grunt demon.

The demon twitched its nose and continued down the street.

The green, scaly beasts originated from the Abyss, a demon-filled realm ruled by Apollyon, one of the princes of hell. Six other princes bowed down to him and helped wreak havoc over the earth.

Kyden glanced at his watch, the hands pointing to 11:55. Any minute now, he should receive a call with further instructions. While he waited, he saw another demon that was about four feet tall. It wore an armored chest piece and spiked gauntlets, and lumbered next to a man walking across the street. The demon whispered in the man's ear while another lurked near a vendor selling produce.

The slimy minions couldn't physically harm a human, but they caused enough damage by manipulating emotions for their dark purposes. The grunts were witless and easy to kill, unlike the Fallen, once-angelic warriors until the Celestial War.

Kyden rarely allowed his thoughts to wander to that time—one of the darkest since the creation of humankind. After the dust had settled and the blood cooled, he had hung up his sword. With humans now occupying the earth, he had a new purpose—that of Protector.

But as with all best-laid plans, he'd chosen to wield his sword once again. Through the centuries as a Slayer, his taste for hunting and killing demons grew. The role of Protector no longer appealed to him, and as far as he was concerned, humans were on their own. He found them fickle and self-serving.

And then there were the daemonkin. These people craved wickedness and had aligned themselves with demons, becoming slaves to the Fallen, delighting in doing their bidding. And if a Fallen couldn't find a compliant subject, then possession was their next course of action, since Fallen, like angels, were forbidden to kill a human. The cost—the obliteration of their essence—was more than either side was willing to pay.

A cab driver slammed on his brakes and honked at a white van monopolizing the narrow street. Kyden crossed his ankles and leaned back in his chair, stretching out his long legs as he watched the two drivers yell at each other. The van inched forward, forcing the cab to reverse down an adjacent alley while people gathered in the streets, regarding the spectacle.

Kyden's phone vibrated, and he flipped it open. "Right on time," he said.

Despite the advances in technology, angels used archaic flip phones to prevent the other side from tracking their whereabouts. Many of the Fallen had infiltrated cell phone and tech companies, but thankfully, the angels had their own computer geniuses, a skill Kyden had chosen not to learn. He preferred sharp, pointy objects that could slice through a demon, leaving a sulfuric mist in its wake.

Yells and honks continued as the van progressed forward.

"What's going on?" the man, who called himself Shane, said.

"Traffic jam." Kyden shifted his legs out of the way as a waitress placed another cup of coffee on the table. He smiled his thanks, causing her to blush. She dipped her head and moved to another patron.

His human appearance, the one most like his true form, was tall and muscular. He was, after all, a warrior. Unlike some of the other Slayers, he kept his dark hair short and no matter how often he shaved, his jaw was always lined with what the humans called a five o'clock shadow. He wore his normal clothing—a T-shirt with an '80s rock band logo and a pair of button fly jeans along with his black combat boots.

His best friend and fellow Slayer, Titus, constantly made fun of him for his love of the eighties. That decade, in Kyden's opinion, had the best music and movies. But what did Titus know? He spent his days surrounded by computer monitors. Granted, the angel was brilliant and his skills were invaluable, but any style Titus had was lacking.

A loud thump had everyone in the café turning. The cab driver had stepped out of his car, his face mottled red, and slammed his hand against the side of the van, which featured a green and black image of an Egyptian scarab. Kyden scanned the painted logo but couldn't find a company name. The driver of the van leaned out the window, pumping his fist and yelling obscenities.

"Right. Anyway, I assume my tip paid off?"

Kyden tore his gaze from the spectacle and twirled a coin on the table. "What's so significant about this dig site? This isn't the normal type of information I pay you for."

"The archaeologist is very close to finding an important artifact—one that could make your job considerably more difficult," Shane said.

"I fail to see how archaeology has anything to do with terrorism."

"It doesn't, but trust me, you'll find this information extremely valuable."

Kyden had first met Shane when he'd been tracking a Fallen stirring up terrorist activity in Europe. Kyden, impersonating a Europol agent, was investigating the latest bombing in a subway station in Paris when someone had bumped into him. He later found a burner phone in his pocket.

The message had been to the point: *Assassination attempt, Turkish President, two days.*

Kyden had unsuccessfully tried to discover the identity of the mysterious person. Since he had been close by, he trusted his gut and flew to Istanbul, where he had found the leader of a terrorist organization planning an attack on the president. The man, possessed by a Fallen named Raghav, had put up quite the fight. Kyden had used up most of his self-control to not kill the human host.

The rule grated on Kyden's nerves, especially when inherently evil humans deserved wrath, like the daemonkin. But Elohim, his Father and Creator, was full of grace and mercy—gifts most humans, in his mind, didn't deserve.

Since Kyden couldn't kill a human, the only way to free them from a demon was a blast of Divine Light. Using this magic was risky as too much light could harm the human, but if done properly it didn't leave any lasting marks, at least on the outside. The Divine Light, however, tormented a demon, causing it to abandon its host—it also drained power from the angel, making them vulnerable.

Kyden gritted his teeth, remembering how Raghav had once again escaped the edge of his blade by summoning a horde of grunt demons. The grunts had surrounded Kyden, giving the betrayer the opportunity to disappear. Losing Raghav stung more than the wound on his upper arm from the demonic blade the Fallen wielded, leaving a permanent scar.

So far, his snitch, whoever he was, hadn't led him astray. Kyden had stopped three assassination attempts and two bombings throughout Europe and the Middle East. Shane had even warned him about a group of rioters in the United States. Who the man was and what connection he had with terrorist organizations remained a mystery, but Kyden had to give Shane credit for having courage, an attribute Kyden respected, since he assumed Shane put his life on the line every time he warned him of impending doom.

He'd grown to trust Shane over the last two years, which was why he currently sipped a steaming cup of Turkish coffee while watching an irate taxi driver yell at the driver of the van, the heat causing droplets of sweat to drip down his back. Thankfully, the coffee was excellent.

The van with the scarab image disappeared down the street, and the people returned to their daily routine. "What's so special about this artifact? You mentioned life and death the last time we spoke," Kyden said.

"Powerful people are looking for it and could use it to harm…" A noise sounded through the other line, followed by Shane's muffled words. When he returned, he whispered, "I gotta go. I can't give specifics, but you're smart. You'll figure it out. Hopefully."

Kyden frowned as the line went dead. Shane's usual confident tone had sounded strained, like he was worried or scared.

He continued to spin the coin as he pondered Shane's words. How could an ancient relic, buried for thousands of years, be used to harm anyone? He wasn't convinced of the artifact's relevance, but Shane had given him just enough information to make him curious.

The coin spun faster on the table. He'd give Adinah, another Slayer Angel, fifteen more minutes to arrive before he flew to the dig site. Iraq, after all, was part of her territory, but according to Shane, time was of the essence. Of course, knowing Adinah, she'd show up with two minutes to spare. If anyone pushed the boundaries, it was her. They had fought and worked side by side for over a century. Besides Titus, she was the closest thing he had to a friend.

Twelve minutes later, a woman wearing a lightweight cream top, green cargo pants, and brown hiking boots strode through the crowded café.

"Sorry I'm late," Adinah said, sliding a chair back and tucking a strand of blonde hair behind her ear.

"Technically, you're not late."

Adinah snorted. "I know you were checking your watch before I walked in, grumbling under your breath."

"I don't grumble."

She waved her hand as if shooing away a fly. "We may have a problem."

Kyden removed his sunglasses. "What kind of problem?"

Adinah leaned forward, sneaking a glance over her shoulder. "I checked out the company you told me about—Excavate International. The head archaeologist is none other than Dr. Hugh Neeman."

"Do I need to care who that is?" Kyden asked, spinning the coin until it was a metallic blur.

Adinah's gaze flicked to the coin and then back to him. "Dr. Neeman is renowned for his discoveries. His primary interests are biblical artifacts, namely those with supposed magic."

Kyden snorted. "Okay, so a modern-day Indiana Jones. Who cares?"

"Who?" Adinah asked.

"Indiana Jones. Don't you watch movies?"

She rolled her eyes. "You're so weird." With inhuman speed, she plucked the coin from Kyden. "That's annoying, by the way." He arched an eyebrow as she pocketed the coin. "Dr. Neeman's been searching for the Atar'zul."

He tilted his head. "Apollyon's halo?"

Adinah gave him a tight smile. "The very one."

Every once in a while, the halo would pop up in history. The last time was during King Nebuchadnezzar II's reign. The spiritual battle during the siege of Jerusalem had been bloody. The defeat still made Kyden seethe.

"According to my snitch, this archaeologist is very close to finding the halo," he said.

"How does your guy know this?"

He shrugged. "I didn't ask."

Adinah narrowed her amber eyes. "I think Neeman might have been successful."

"Why do you say that?"

"Supposedly, so-called 'raiders' disturbed the site," she said, using air quotes.

He leaned forward, resting his arms on the table. "Was anything taken?"

"Unknown. I did a quick flyby, and the place was covered in green mist."

Kyden pushed back from the table, stood, and tossed a few bills next to his empty mug. "I guess that's my cue."

CHAPTER TWO

ZAHRA

Zahra Jenkins hid in a tomb, sucking on a Dum-Dums lollipop and mentally tackling her mountain of color-coded tasks. At the top of that list: one last update to her boss with the bad news.

She sat on a stone bench staring at ancient scripts carved into the wall depicting the reign of King Nebuchadnezzar II. Flickering torches transported the guests back in time to 570 BC while artifacts placed throughout the exhibit told a story of domination and conquest.

All the artifacts except one.

A loud crack echoed through the tomb as she bit into her lollipop. For the last two years, she'd worked tirelessly curating pieces from the Mesopotamian era for Boston's Gallery of Time Museum. All the sleepless nights and damage done to her teeth from her addiction to lollipops were about to pay off, with or without the missing artifact.

She simply needed to explain that to her boss, Mr. Rousseau.

Zahra exited the tomb and strode through the exhibit hall. If the gala was a success, then her goal of being promoted to head curator was finally within her grasp. There were only two people in her way: Mr. Rousseau and Brandon Hayes, the other associate curator and her competition.

She paused in front of a statue of the king who had conquered much of the known world during the Babylonian Empire. A smudge on the nameplate caught her eye, and using the hem of her shirt, she quickly wiped it clean.

If everything went according to plan, this exhibit would showcase her talents as a curator and, hopefully, acquire the funding the museum needed. And when Mr. Rousseau retired in a few months, the job would be hers.

If everything went according to plan.

Zahra finished her rounds, making sure everything was in its perfect place. She'd gone over the layout a hundred times and felt confident the artifacts she and Brandon had acquired would impress the esteemed guests invited to the gala this weekend.

There was only one piece missing—the coup de grâce of the entire event that had made for a nonstop nervous stomach, especially as opening night grew closer.

She rubbed her temple as she recalled the numerous back-and-forth emails with Dr. Hugh Neeman regarding the Atar'zul—a supposedly magical relic stolen from the Jewish temple by King Nebuchadnezzar II. Zahra didn't believe in anything magical, let alone artifacts, but when she'd received word via her personal email a week ago claiming the infamous halo had been found, excitement had made her rush to her boss's office.

"We've got it," she had said, entering his office without knocking.

Mr. Rousseau arched a brow at her impropriety. "What have we got?"

"The Atar'zul. Dr. Neeman found it."

Her boss smiled, a rare occurrence, and she hoped his face wouldn't crack from the expression. "Do whatever you can to get it here by the gala."

"Yes, sir." She'd turned to leave, but Mr. Rousseau stopped her.

"However you managed to get Dr. Neeman to donate it to us—well, I'm impressed."

Little did anyone know the famous archaeologist also happened to be her father.

Everything she'd accomplished until now had been based on her merit and hers alone. But with her dream of climbing to the role of head curator before she turned thirty within her reach, she'd broken her rule.

Just this once, she had thought.

She hadn't blinked twice about making her absent father feel guilty, expressing how important the Atar'zul was to the museum's collection—and her future.

Convincing him to send the relic had been another hurdle, but one she jumped over as if her life depended on it. And in her mind, it did. There were many antiquity collectors who would spend an obscene amount of money to sponsor the Atar'zul and the museum itself, practically guaranteeing Zahra that promotion.

Only after she agreed the piece would be behind glass with extra security in place, the kind requiring lasers sounding an alarm if anyone opened the case without proper clearance, did her father agree to bring it with him.

With him, she thought once again, digging out another lollipop from her pocket. Her father arriving with the Atar'zul had not been part of the plan. No one knew of her relationship to Dr. Neeman; not the archaeology world, nor her boss, coworkers, or the board of directors, and she would like to keep it that way.

Her dad had made a name for himself with his dangerous digs in the Middle East. When Zahra had mentioned Dr. Neeman attending the gala, the museum board had dollar signs flashing in their eyes. Having his name on the program as the guest of honor for the gala would bring in many interested sponsors looking to provide money for grants and other needed programs for the museum.

"Miss Jenkins," her boss said from behind her.

Zahra turned and removed her lollipop from her mouth with a loud smack.

Mr. Rousseau arched a gray eyebrow at the hand now hidden behind her back. Although he was in his early seventies, his mind and body were as sharp as someone in their forties. In some ways, he reminded her of her father.

"Hello, Mr. Rousseau. What can I help you with?"

"Have you heard from Dr. Neeman or Excavate International on the status of the Atar'zul?"

"No, sir. I've been trying to get ahold of them, but I'm not having any luck. No one at the dig site is answering the phone or replying to our emails." After confirming her father's arrival with the Atar'zul, she hadn't heard from him since, but this was normal for him. History had taught her she could never rely on the man and had therefore always concocted a Plan B. "The replica is almost finished."

Mr. Rousseau walked to the empty case and laced his fingers behind his back. "I promised a lot of important people we'd have a complete exhibit."

Zahra fisted her hands. "The 3D-printed model Carl has created looks exactly like the Atar'zul. We'll have a placard indicating it's a replica—this isn't abnormal for exhibits such as these."

Mr. Rousseau slowly turned. "I'm well aware of what is normal and what is not, Miss Jenkins. Keep me apprised if you hear anything."

"Yes, sir," Zahra said to Mr. Rousseau's retreating form. She rubbed her temple again, swearing when her lollipop stuck to her hair. She threw the sucker into the trash can, the hard candy banging loudly in the cavernous room. "Thanks a lot, Dad," she murmured.

Her parents had divorced before she was born, and when she was old enough she'd taken her mother's maiden name as her own, to spite the man. From that moment forward, no one knew her as Zahra Neeman.

She hadn't seen him since her high school graduation, and that was from a distance. The last time she'd actually spoken to him face-to-face was during her sixteenth birthday when he'd piqued her interest in competitive shooting. She'd been a natural, and he'd immediately signed her up for classes at a nearby gun range.

Zahra came to a stop when she noticed Brandon Hayes, her coworker and competition, leaning against the wall with his hands in his pockets. His sandy brown hair was styled off his face, and his navy-blue suit fit his frame perfectly. His gaze swept from her brown boots, up her legs to where her pencil skirt stopped below her knee, to the cream sweater and finally to her face. She inwardly cringed at the unease his lingering look caused.

Three months ago, on one dark and lonely night, and after too much wine, she'd found herself in Brandon's arms. They'd both admitted it was a mistake, especially now that they were in competition for the promotion. Thankfully, they'd remained—well, she wouldn't call it friends, but at least friendly acquaintances.

Zahra tucked a strand of hair behind her ear. "Hey, Brandon."

"Hi." He pushed off the wall and glanced down the hall to where Mr. Rousseau had disappeared. "You ready for this weekend?"

"Despite not having our honored guest nor the most important piece, yes. Now we just need people to show up."

The corner of Brandon's lip lifted. "They will. Even though we're a team on this, you made it all happen. I'll keep trying to reach Excavate International. Maybe I'll have more luck."

Zahra forced a smile. Brandon hadn't been pleased when Mr. Rousseau assigned her as the project coordinator for the Nebuchadnezzar exhibit, but he'd gotten over the slight fairly quickly. He'd been supportive, and she had to admit they worked well together.

Silence filled the hallway, and she cleared her throat. "Yeah, well, I better get some work done."

He touched her arm as she moved past him. "What are you doing tonight? I thought maybe we could have dinner to celebrate the big event. Despite the whereabouts of the Atar'zul, Mr. Rousseau seems quite impressed." A flicker of emotion flashed through Brandon's eyes but disappeared as quickly as it came.

"Thanks, but I can't. I need to visit my mom. Besides, we said we'd keep things professional, remember?"

His eyes slipped to her mouth. "I know what we said, but that night with you was one of the best I've had in a long time." His hand slid down her arm and gripped her fingers, causing her ring to dig into her skin.

Her cheeks heated, but she released his hold and took a step back. Getting involved with a coworker was never a wise thing to do, especially when said coworker was gunning for her job.

"Maybe another time. After the event, or something," she said, forcing a smile and keeping her voice light.

Brandon shoved his hands into his pockets and nodded. "How is your mom?"

"Oh, you know. She has good days and bad days. Anyway, I'll see you later." The last thing she wanted was to discuss her mom's declining health with Brandon. She turned and walked toward her office, feeling his gaze on her the entire way.

Zahra had three places she cherished above all others. One was the coffee shop down the street, which served the best flat white lattes in all of Boston. Another was the shooting range where she liked to blow off steam. And the last was her office, with its hodgepodge of mismatched furniture, shelves lined with books, and trinkets from some of her early travels.

Her worn leather office chair squeaked as she reached into her bottom drawer for another lollipop. She'd smoked throughout college, but had quit a few years ago. Dum-Dums had become the habit to replace the cigarettes. At least lollipops wouldn't give her cancer, or so she hoped. Who knew these days.

After the awkward conversation with Brandon, a cigarette sounded a lot better than the root beer–flavored sucker. He hadn't asked her out since that night, and she thought his timing odd. She wasn't sure how much he'd overheard of her conversation with Mr. Rousseau, but she suspected he'd heard enough. The competition was moderately friendly, and she figured Brandon could get a head curator job anywhere. She, on the other hand, needed the job to remain in Boston to stay close to her mother. Granted, there were other museums, but the Gallery of Time had become a second home for her. She hated the thought of leaving all her hard work behind.

She fiddled with the ring on her right hand, one she hadn't taken off in four years. She remembered the day so clearly when her college boyfriend, Jake Callahan, had given it to her.

They'd been in between classes and a light rain fell, making his brown hair look almost black as water dripped down his face. She'd been laughing at a joke he'd said when he'd gone still.

The next thing she knew, he was on one knee holding a silver ring with a lapis lazuli stone—her favorite.

"Marry me," he had said, his wet eyelashes framing beautiful gray eyes.

The laugh withered in her throat like grass scorched by the sun during the last days of summer. Her answer would change both of their lives, and their relationship would never be the same again.

A knock on the door brought Zahra back to the present, and she forced the hurt that had marred Jake's face from her mind. She barely rearranged her expression before Alexis, her roommate, best friend, and the Education Director of the museum, walked in. She plopped herself down on one of the two mismatched Victorian chairs across from her desk. Zahra winced as the creak of wood sounded in protest. Alexis did nothing halfway, including sitting. She didn't gently place her butt on a chair but sat with enthusiasm and vitality.

They'd met on Zahra's first day at the museum and hit it off immediately. Alexis was looking for a roommate, as apartment prices in Boston were ridiculous; Zahra's mom had just moved into Glendale Assisted Living and Memory Care. The timing couldn't have been more perfect.

Zahra's time with Alexis was the pinnacle of her social life. Between her job and visiting her mom, she barely had time to go to the shooting range, where she competed in precision and practical shooting competitions. The practice and competitions helped clear her mind, and if she was being honest with herself, also kept her father close. Even though she was angry with him, she still loved and missed him.

"I just saw Brandon wandering the halls," Alexis said, a skeptical look in her deep brown eyes.

Zahra often joked with Alexis about how she hated her because of her looks. She didn't, of course, but a part of her envied her lush lashes around her eyes, the natural curl in Alexis's silky black hair that hung to the middle of her back, and her perfect olive skin. Zahra resembled her mother with dark blonde hair and a petite build, standing at five-foot, four inches. The only traits she'd acquired from her father were hazel eyes and a love for historical artifacts.

"Yeah, he asked me to dinner," Zahra said.

"Dinner, huh?" Alexis asked with her brows raised. "Well, at least he's easy on the eyes. That man can definitely fill out a suit."

Zahra shook her head, not wanting to give her friend any encouragement. Alexis's flirting skills were impressive, to say the least. She offered Alexis a lollipop.

Alexis shook her head. "We're both twenty-five, not three. You probably have a juice box in your lunch."

Zahra pointed her sucker at her best friend. "Those are delicious and you know it."

Alexis rolled her eyes. "Anyway, I have a class arriving in about ten minutes. I wanted to pop in to see if you needed any help with the gala."

"Not unless you can make an ancient magical artifact appear out of thin air."

Alexis winced. "Still hasn't shown up, huh?"

"Nope. But other than that, everything is ready to go. Oh, and the caterer is making dim sum."

Alexis fist-pumped the air. "Yes! I love those things."

Zahra chuckled. "Yeah, well, I'm a giver. Just take it easy at the bar this time."

Alexis pushed out of the chair. "No promises there, my friend." With a wave over her shoulder, she darted out of Zahra's office.

Zahra checked her messages throughout the day, even having her assistant, Meredith, make phone calls to Excavate International for any news on Dr. Neeman or the mysterious Atar'zul. She organized the paperwork on her desk as the light in her office dimmed. Fall had washed Massachusetts in reds and golds, and dusk made its appearance early as the sun dipped below the Boston skyline. Zahra checked her email one last time, hoping for a note from her father. As expected, nothing.

Chapter Three

Kyden

Kyden and Adinah flew toward the outskirts of Hillah, where the ruins of the ancient city of Babylon dwelled. Their silver wings flapped in magnificent arches, and dust swirled around their feet when they landed. Most humans weren't aware of the spiritual realm interwoven with their own. If they could see beyond the veil, they'd either faint or run away screaming at the two warriors with their bronze armor glinting in the sun, golden halos encircling their heads, and glowing eyes.

The dig site reminded Kyden of a garden maze, except it was comprised of dirt and rock instead of foliage. Striated trenches cut through the valley with planks crisscrossing to allow the archaeologists a way to navigate the ruins.

"It's fascinating seeing parts of ancient Babylon like this, isn't it?" Adinah asked.

Kyden only grunted. Based on what he could tell, Dr. Neeman and his team had been working near the famous Hanging Gardens.

He'd been to the ancient city only once, but remembered its beauty and magnificence. At least in the human realm. In the spiritual realm, the evil spewing through the city, especially near the palace, had created a stench Kyden had a hard time forgetting.

Unwanted memories fought through his carefully constructed wall, taking him back to that dark time when King Nebuchadnezzar II and his army attacked Jerusalem.

Kyden had been a Protector Angel, his charge a Levite priest. During the attack, a horde of grunts had charged the temple, forcing Kyden to fight them off. When he returned, the priest was dead, and the holy temple engulfed by flames.

Filled with rage and a suffocating sense of failure, he had pursued the demons and humans who had stolen treasure from Elohim's earthly temple.

Demons had crawled throughout Babylon, the Fallen possessing influential leaders surrounding King Nebuchadnezzar II, who himself had been possessed by Mammon, the Prince of Greed. The Slayer Angels had been unprepared for the attack and many of Kyden's fellow angels were injured. The battle had raged for days until the archangel Raphael had ordered them to retreat.

A trail of dust brought Kyden back to the present. The van he'd seen earlier with the scarab logo drove toward the dig site entrance where police cars were parked. Digging equipment was strewn across the area as if a tornado had swept through the land. Tents were ripped and trunks lay on their sides, their contents spilling onto the sand, revealing the treasures within.

To the human eye, the destruction looked like raiders had attacked the dig site. In the spiritual realm, grunt demons roamed throughout the site, leaving behind a green mist clinging to the ground like an odorous fog. The grunts hadn't noticed the two angels yet, too distracted by whatever they were looking for.

Kyden continued to scan the area. "I don't see any Fallen."

"I can't sense any either," Adinah said, tucking in her wings as they strode down the hill.

A demon clung to the back of a police officer, its talons digging into the man's shoulders while it whispered in his ear. The officer barked at his employees and disregarded the fear of a nearby archaeologist, who tried to explain what had happened.

When they neared, Kyden cleared his throat. The grunt ceased whispering to the police officer and turned, its yellow eyes widening.

It screeched and leaped from the human's shoulders. The police officer shook his head as if to clear it, while the other demons who lingered nearby scattered through the dirt maze.

The demon, standing about four feet tall, wore a brown leather chest piece with spiked gauntlets covering its sinewy forearms. The helmet only allowed Kyden to see its eyes and mouth with an extended lower jaw full of sharp teeth.

Kyden drew his sword. "Tell us what you're looking for or meet your end." With another screech, it scampered off across the wrecked camp.

"I'll go north," Adinah said, pointing to where half the grunts ran. "Oh, and Kyden, we need at least one alive."

Kyden smirked. "I'll see what I can do." Using his angelic speed, he caught up to the grunts fleeing to the other side of the dig site. A few reached for their weapons but never drew them as his celestial blade whipped around and sliced through them. Sulfur filled the air, and more green mist spewed along the ground before slowly dissipating. Kyden focused on the grunt who had been influencing the police officer as it darted into the ruins of the ancient palace. He unfurled his wings and soared into the air, landing seconds later in front of the fleeing demon.

The grunt slid to a stop with its axe drawn. "We weren't doing anything. Leave us alone," it said in its gravelly voice.

Kyden stepped closer, his sword hanging loosely at his side. "By the looks of the mess you and your filth made, you were definitely doing something. Tell me what you were looking for, and I'll let you live."

"Nothing," the demon said. Its clawed fingers tightened on the handle of its axe as it glanced at Kyden's sword.

Kyden circled the demon, mindful of his wings in the narrow passageway that was once part of the aqueduct system leading to the famous Hanging Gardens of Babylon.

He'd always wondered what the Abyss was like where grunt demons were made, where Apollyon himself ruled. The memory of fighting and bleeding in the streets of Babylon with its carnal lusts, twisted truths, and debauchery was as close to the Abyss as the angel would get.

The echoes of that long-ago battle that had left him bitter and bruised scratched against the walls of his memory, seeking light. He grabbed the demon by its shoulder. "I thought your kind was better at lying."

The grunt swallowed and glanced behind it, where screeches filled the air. Adinah fought the remaining demons, leaving green smoke in her wake.

"There's nowhere you can run." Kyden tightened his grip on his sword. "I'll ask one more time. What were you looking for?"

The demon's narrow lips pulled back, revealing jagged teeth. "Just a trinket, nothing of importance."

"Who's your Fallen?" Kyden asked, circling the pathetic beast.

The grunt's yellow eyes widened, and it quickly shook its head before muttering under its breath. Darkness shimmered on the ground, opening a portal to the Abyss.

Kyden was out of time and patience. "Very well."

The demon shrieked and raised its axe to block Kyden's sword, but the celestial steel cut through the weapon and the demon both like a hot knife through butter. Kyden flapped his wings once to dispel the sulfuric smoke and strode back to the congregated people.

Adinah met him near the tents. "Where's the lead grunt?"

"Dead," Kyden said.

"Seriously? I told you to leave one alive. How are we to get any answers?"

"It wasn't going to tell us anything." Kyden examined the men and women huddled in a circle. "Where's this Dr. Neeman?"

Adinah shook her head. "Back at the safe house, I did a quick search on the internet for his picture, but I haven't seen him among the other archaeologists."

He scanned the police officer. "Time to get some answers of our own."

"I'll stand guard just in case a Fallen makes an appearance," Adinah said, gripping her sword.

Kyden nodded and then closed his eyes. In seconds, his wings and armor disappeared, as did his long-sleeved shirt, black leather pants, and boots. In its place was a police uniform. He darkened his hair and skin and approached a young archaeologist, who stood alone and away from the others, chewing on her thumbnail.

"Miss, can I ask you a few questions?" Kyden asked in perfect Arabic while lifting his hand.

Her gaze drifted to the glamoured police badge he held. "I don't speak Arabic."

"No problem," Kyden said, switching his language to English with a heavy accent. "Can you tell me what happened here?"

"I honestly don't know. When we finished last night, everything was fine. Then this morning, the place looked like this." She swept her arm at the chaos.

"What part of the site were you excavating?"

"A section of the palace near the Hanging Gardens. We'd found most of the artifacts, but Dr. Neeman wanted us to go over the area one more time, saying he'd discovered some new information."

"Where is Dr. Neeman?" Kyden asked, looking over his shoulder to where the police officer questioned the other archaeologists. He didn't have much time before the officer would notice him.

"He's not here. I thought he was going to stop by before going back to America, but he didn't, which is unusual."

Kyden arched a brow. This man was getting more and more interesting. "Can you show me where his personal tent is?"

The woman looked at him and shrugged. "Sure." She led him to a large tent at the end of the dig site. The torn canvas flapped in the breeze, revealing the interior.

"What a mess," she said. "Dr. Neeman's is the worst from what I've seen."

"Thanks. I'll have a look around. Why don't you return to your coworkers so they don't worry?"

She bit her lip. "Okay. Please let me know if you find anything."

"Will do." Kyden waited until the woman joined the others before removing his glamour. Adinah was already inside the tent with her hands on her hips.

Demon residue stained the entrance of the tent and the furniture. A cot on the far side of the area was flipped onto its side, and feathers from a shredded pillow floated through the air. He walked to the middle of the room and looked down when his boot crunched on the handle of a small shovel.

"Whichever Fallen was in charge must have daemonkin working with them to cause this much damage," Adinah said, standing next to him. Trunks were open with the contents scattered, and a desk was overturned with the drawers emptied.

"You're probably right."

"I usually am."

"I thought you were keeping watch," Kyden said, glaring at her over his shoulder.

Adinah's lips curved into a smile as she examined a map hanging by one corner on a dented white board. "I was, but I got bored. There's not a demon in sight for miles since big bad Kyden scared them all away."

Kyden snorted. "The demon said it was searching for a trinket. I'm assuming, based on our combined information, that trinket was the Atar'zul." He knelt next to a large pot lying on its side with burnt pieces of paper lining the bottom.

"That seems to track. There's a lot of demon residue in this area," Adinah said, pointing to the overturned desk.

He walked toward the desk and empty drawers, searching for any clues, and frowned when he noticed a glossy piece of paper. He picked it up and turned it over. "Looks like Dr. Neeman was invited to an event at the Gallery of Time Museum in Boston."

Kyden lifted a brow when Adinah snatched the invitation from his hand. "'The Mysteries of King Nebuchadnezzar Revealed.' The gala is in two days."

"I want you to get any information you can about Dr. Neeman. Also, call Titus and bring him in on this," Kyden said, and walked out of the tent.

Adinah followed him. "And what are you going to do?"

"I'm going to Boston." He unfurled his wings and lifted his head. "You know how to reach me." With a mighty flap, he launched into the air, leaving ancient Babylon in the dust where it belonged.

Chapter Four

Zahra

Zahra gnawed on her lollipop as she swerved through traffic on her way to the museum. She'd stayed up too late and had overslept. Now, every red light seemed to mock her tardiness.

After work yesterday, she'd visited her mother at Glendale Assisted Living and Memory Care. She hadn't been lying to Brandon about having other plans—seeing her mom was something she did every Tuesday and Thursday evening and once on the weekend.

Nancy Jenkins, age sixty-one, had moved into Glendale a year ago when her symptoms had worsened and Zahra couldn't trust her mom to live alone. Zahra had offered to move in, but with working full time, she couldn't give her mother the care she needed.

After months of taking her mother to different doctors due to a variety of behavioral changes, namely her speech and memory, the doctors finally diagnosed Nancy with an advanced case of frontotemporal dementia. Many of her symptoms had been overlooked, and the guilt Zahra felt for not having pushed harder or being more insistent about getting her mother to the doctors threatened to swallow her whole.

Even though there wasn't a cure, a part of Zahra still clung to the notion that if she'd done something sooner, then maybe her mother wouldn't be deteriorating as fast as she was.

Zahra honked her horn at a driver going ten miles below the speed limit. "For the love of all that's holy, the pedal is on the right!" she shouted as she sped by.

Sadness and exhaustion were two emotions she did not need, especially with the gala's opening night looming. Normally she could compartmentalize the situation with her mom and the rest of her life, but no matter how many pep talks she'd given herself while getting ready for work, she still couldn't get the confrontation with her mother out of her mind. She'd replayed the conversation over and over last night and then tossed and turned, unable to fall asleep, finally deciding to read until three in the morning.

"Zahra! Happy birthday, dear," Nancy had said as Zahra approached a table with three other residents. They were playing a card game Zahra wasn't familiar with.

The nurse who'd escorted Zahra to the common room had said, "Happy birthday. Any fun plans?"

"It's not my birthday," Zahra whispered, and then turned to her mom. "Thanks, Mom," she said, forcing a smile.

She'd kissed her cheek and then pulled up an extra chair.

Her mother looked over her shoulder. "Where's Jake? Of all the boys you dated, he was my favorite."

Zahra winced as the other people at the table looked at her expectantly. Jake, who had been adopted at a young age, never knew his biological mother and, as far as he was concerned, didn't need to know. Nancy had developed a tender heart toward Jake, and ever since the disease had taken residence in her mind she couldn't seem to grasp they were no longer together.

Zahra rarely felt like she disappointed her mother, but when she'd ended things with Jake, she'd seen the look in her mother's eyes.

Zahra cleared her throat and directed the conversation to safer ground. "What game are you playing?"

"I have no clue, but Barb is cheating, as usual," Nancy had said.

Barb's watery eyes widened as she gripped her cards, the veins protruding from her bony hand. "How many times do I have to tell you I'm not cheating?"

Nancy rolled her eyes and whispered to Zahra, "She always cheats." She picked up the empty box of cards and began chewing on it.

"Oh, Mom, don't do that." Zahra grabbed her mom's arm to retrieve the box.

Nancy shoved to her feet and gripped her hand with a strength Zahra didn't know she still had. "You will not tell me what to do, Zahra. You're just like your father, chasing dead things instead of being with the living!"

Nancy turned and stormed away but before she got a few feet, she stumbled into another table and began laughing hysterically. The nurse ran over, steadying Nancy before she fell, and gave Zahra a sympathetic smile. "I'll just get her back to her room. Wait for me up front."

Zahra had nodded, blinking back the tears. Her mother's outbursts had become more frequent and more aggressive. Her mother's obsession with chewing on whatever she could get her hands on had surfaced a month ago, and her coordination had worsened, not to mention her memory.

Thankfully, her mother still remembered her name, but it was only a matter of time.

Zahra stood and returned to the lobby to wait for the nurse, deciding she needed to talk to her father about his ex-wife's health. If he'd ever return her calls or emails. She couldn't help the worry that nagged at her. She was accustomed to the man ghosting her, but when there was an ancient relic involved, she thought he'd be more responsive. After all, his first love, it seemed, was items long forgotten, hidden in the sand.

Zahra had never forgiven him for leaving them for his career and now, when "for better or worse" should have meant something, the care of Nancy fell on Zahra's shoulders. Not that she minded. She loved her mother and her mother loved her—they had a wonderful relationship, becoming the best of friends. But Nancy's heart had always remained with her father despite his leaving. Maybe things would have been different if he had valued his marriage over his job.

The nurse finally returned and sat next to Zahra. "Your mom is having a bad day, but she's resting now."

"She seems to have a lot of those lately," Zahra said.

"Unfortunately, with this disease, the bad days will start outweighing the good." The nurse squeezed her hand. "I am sorry, but rest assured, we are taking wonderful care of her."

Unlike me, Zahra had thought as she sped into the museum's employee parking lot and grabbed her laptop bag and purse. "Of all the days to be late," she grumbled, swiping her security badge over the sensor, waiting for the door to click open.

When she strode into the museum offices, her assistant, Meredith, sprinted for her as if she'd been lying in wait like a tiger lurking, ready to pounce. She grabbed her arm and dragged her into her office, locking the door behind her.

"Meredith, what the hell is going on?" Zahra said, rubbing her arm. The woman had a firm grip.

"Why aren't you answering your phone? I've been trying to reach you."

"What are you talking about? My phone hasn't rung." She dug the device out of her purse and then cursed, the screen showing *Do Not Disturb*, something she rarely did just in case Glendale called. She had set it last night before finally falling asleep and had forgotten to turn it back on.

Zahra sat in her chair and pointed to the one across from her desk. "Take a breath and tell me what's going on."

Meredith straightened her skirt and sat, inhaling deeply. Zahra unwrapped one of her lollipops and shoved it into her mouth. The skin on the inside of her mouth was turning raw from the suckers she'd eaten in the past hour. She needed to find a healthier habit than Dum-Dums, otherwise she wouldn't have any teeth left by the time she was thirty-five.

"It's about the programs. I proofed them and everything, but when I picked them up this morning, well..." Meredith slid the program for the gala across Zahra's desk.

Zahra picked it up and scanned it. When her eyes fell on *Project Coordinator*, she shot to her feet. "That conniving son of a bitch!" Brandon Hayes's name was listed where hers was supposed to be. In fact, as she scanned over the program, she realized her name wasn't mentioned anywhere. Fury coursed through her, making her hands shake.

"I'm sorry," Meredith said, wringing her fingers. "I don't know how this happened."

"One guess," Zahra said, gripping the program as she marched out of her office in search of Brandon.

Meredith was on her heels. "He's not in right now, mentioned something about off-site meetings."

"Of course he's not here, the slimy weasel." Zahra tried calling him, but his phone went straight to voicemail.

Zahra trudged back to her office, needing to find the energy to pivot. "Do we have time to reprint?" She inwardly winced at the cost and wasn't sure she could justify it to her boss or the board.

Meredith shook her head. "I already asked. Their main printer went down and the formatter is out sick."

"Of all the rotten luck." Zahra rubbed her temples and then looked up. "What about labels? Could we print them and stick…"

Meredith grimaced and slid a program with a label across Zahra's desk. "I already tried. It looks really cheesy."

Zahra held it up. She was right—the cover-up looked ridiculous. She crumpled the program into a tiny ball and threw it in the trash can.

"Do you really think he did this on purpose?" Meredith asked.

Zahra arched a brow. "I find it hard to believe the printer *accidentally* left my name off the program."

What really irritated her was that not only did it look like Brandon was in charge of the event, his contact information was there as well, so any sponsors or donors would communicate with him directly. The more money and support he obtained for the museum, the higher the chances of him getting the promotion.

Meredith wrapped her arms around herself and stared at Zahra's dragon-shaped lamp. She was pretty with her long blonde hair and pixie-like features. Zahra was surprised Brandon hadn't hit on her yet. Then again, maybe he had. A part of her wanted to ask, but Human Resources would probably frown at her for questioning her assistant regarding personal matters.

"I'm so sorry, Zahra. Is there anything I can do?" Meredith asked.

"Get me the RSVP list again, please."

Meredith nodded and left her office.

All Zahra had to do was sell the hell out of her exhibit to the right people before Brandon could. Brandon was charming but wasn't nearly as passionate about Babylon and all the pieces they'd collected. Plus, she could lay on the charm if she needed to.

Two hours later, after Zahra had made more phone calls than she'd thought possible, she finally leaned back in her chair and opened the wrapper to a blue raspberry lollipop. A knock sounded on her door.

"Good afternoon, Miss Jenkins," Mr. Rousseau said, his eyes sliding to the white stick jutting from her mouth. Zahra smiled and removed the sucker, placing it on the wrapper.

"You're an interesting person," he said with his brows furrowed and lips pursed.

"Thanks?" She seriously doubted her boss was complimenting her. She was about to bring up the program *mistake* when he placed a small brown box on her desk.

"You received a package from Baghdad. Looks like it's from Excavate International, but based on the size, I'm assuming it's not our missing relic." Zahra's heart sank. Her boss was correct—the box was way too small to contain the Atar'zul.

Mr. Rousseau eyed her. "Despite this crown object…"

"Atar'zul, or Forsaken Halo," Zahra interrupted. She was about to say more but snapped her mouth shut at her boss's narrowed eyes. "Sorry."

"As I was saying, despite the missing artifact, you and Brandon have performed admirably. Myself and the members of the board are impressed. I've no doubt the museum will be in capable hands once I retire." He stopped at the door, glancing once more at the unopened package. "See you tomorrow night."

A lead ball dropped into her stomach as disappointment flooded through her system. She cut through the tape sealing the box and lifted the lid. A note lay inside atop a velvet pouch. Opening the pouch first, she sighed in disappointment as she removed a silver necklace and held it up to the light. The twisted design reminded her of a feather, the thin strands intricately woven into a beautiful necklace. She turned it over to look for an inscription or clue, but there was nothing. Closing her eyes, she took a calming breath and reached for the folded piece of paper.

I'm sorry. For everything.
Love, Dad

Zahra examined the brief note, his usually neat handwriting messy, as if he'd written it hastily. Another wave of disappointment rushed through her, followed quickly by a rush of anger. He'd promised her he'd show up at the gala, knowing how much this exhibit and event meant to her. She had secretly hoped that he'd walk through those doors tomorrow night with the Atar'zul in his calloused hands.

But why was she surprised? Her father had broken promises in the past. Biting back a curse, she crumpled the note and threw it in the trash can. After dropping the jewelry box into her bag, she yanked on the zipper, which broke.

She huffed out a disgusted laugh. "Could this day get any worse?"

Chapter Five

Kyden

Kyden adjusted his tie as he waited to enter the Gallery of Time Museum. A red carpet lined the steps toward the entrance like a river of blood pouring from a gaping wound.

A rather negative image, Kyden thought as the line moved forward. Wearing a blue suit, he felt underdressed, especially compared to the elderly couple in front of him with their tux and evening gown. When he'd grabbed Dr. Neeman's invitation, he hadn't realized the importance of this event nor the affluent guest list, based on the limousines hiding Boston's wealthy residents behind tinted glass.

Kyden observed a grunt demon clinging to an older man. The woman on his arm looked young enough to be his daughter. The man displayed his diamond ring and fancy watch as much as he touted the woman, who wore a bored expression, her bright red lips settled in a seductive pout.

The demon probably belonged to Asmodeus, the Prince of Lust. The seven princes of hell had minions everywhere despite the princes' locations in the world. Based on recent intelligence, Asmodeus lived in Paris. Kyden's territory was Europe, namely Great Britain, but he'd run into quite a few of Lust's Fallen and their grunts in the area.

Two princes occupied North America: Mammon, the Prince of Greed, and Leviathan, the Prince of Envy. Apollyon, the Prince of Pride and leader of the other princes, never settled anywhere for long, roaming the earth to wherever his evil heart desired. The Abyss, Apollyon's true home, was a realm all its own, which demons used as a portal to get from one location to another.

Kyden likened the portal to the movie *Stargate* with Kurt Russell. He'd tried to explain this notion to Titus, who had laughed for longer than was necessary.

Traveling through the Abyss portals wasn't faster than an angel's flight, but the magical tunnels allowed the demons to go wherever they wanted. Granted, many of the prince's Fallen had possessed people who owned personal jets, which allowed them to travel around the globe with ease. An angel was still faster, not bound by earthly physics. One of the many advantages angels had over their counterparts.

A whistle sounded in Kyden's ear, causing him to flinch.

"Is that Bill Guerin?" Titus's voice sounded through Kyden's earpiece.

He turned and scanned the crowd.

"To your left. He played professional hockey."

"You do understand the mission, right? We're looking for archaeologists, not hockey players," Kyden said.

"Seriously? Who would you rather hang out with? A hockey player or someone who plays in the dirt?"

Kyden refrained from rolling his eyes as he inched closer to the front of the line. "Neither."

"You're such a curmudgeon, you know that," Titus said.

"Well aware. Anyway, from your vantage point, do you see anything interesting besides famous athletes?" he added, attempting to keep his friend focused. If he suspected anything unusual, Kyden would have Titus enter through the back of the museum and plant bugs in the employees' offices.

A sigh sounded through the earpiece. "Besides a handful of grunts, no. I don't see any Fallen in the area, nor our archaeologist."

"I better not have worn this suit for nothing," Kyden said, once again tugging on his tie.

"Quit fidgeting. You look dapper."

Kyden had glamoured himself from the spiritual realm so a Fallen wouldn't notice him. If they were close enough, they'd be able to sense an angel in the vicinity, but Kyden had centuries of practice making himself invisible to demonic eyes.

As he observed the various grunts with their unsuspecting prey, his fingers itched for his sword, but now was not the time for battle.

"Name?" the guard said as Kyden approached the entrance. Tall stone pillars stood on each side of the entrance, topped with fire dancing from copper bowls.

Kyden showed the guard his invitation. "Sam Malone," he said, using his alias—a favorite character from the TV show *Cheers*.

The guard arched a brow at him and then scanned the list. Kyden subtly waved his hand and the guard blinked. "Thank you, Mr. Malone. Enjoy your evening."

Titus snickered through the earpiece. "These aren't the droids you're looking for."

Kyden glared over his shoulder at the indistinct van parked on the opposite side of the street, though a part of him was proud of Titus for referencing the *Star Wars* movies.

Kyden slipped his invitation into the inside pocket of his sport coat and stepped into the past as he entered ancient Babylon. He frowned at the carved images on the wall and the towering statues, one of King Nebuchadnezzar II himself. Someone had even recreated a smaller version of the Hanging Gardens. A few details were off, but whoever curated this exhibit knew their Mesopotamian history.

A woman dressed in brightly colored silk robes, with black kohl lining her upper eyelids, handed him a program. Under *Guest of Honor* was a picture of Dr. Hugh Neeman standing near the ancient ruins of Babylon, a grin brightening his face. He wore a long-sleeved button-down; the kind found in a sporting goods store, with brown khaki shorts and leather boots. The sun glinted on a silver chain around his neck as he pointed to a discovery over his shoulder.

Kyden had ventured into the online world and briefly researched the archaeologist—in-depth searches were tasks he left for Titus. For some reason, many of Dr. Neeman's important finds were sent to the Gallery of Time instead of museums like the Smithsonian. Boston was known for its history, but most of that was United States history. It was odd for Neeman to favor this museum.

Another name was on the program, a Brandon Hayes, project coordinator for the exhibit that had garnered such wealthy, and according to Titus, famous patrons.

The head curator was Mr. Rousseau, an older gentleman with silver-and-brown hair, who stood talking with Hayes and another assistant curator, Zahra Jenkins. Based on Titus's research, both Hayes and Jenkins had worked on gathering the pieces for the gala. Strange that only Hayes's name was on the program.

Kyden eyed Mr. Rousseau. He reminded him of the butler from the *Batman* movies. Kyden grabbed a glass of champagne and meandered around the room searching for Dr. Neeman. He strolled through the lobby, steering clear of the grunt demons who shadowed unsuspecting humans, but there was still no sign of the archaeologist. He entered the exhibit hall where the replica of the Ishtar Gate surrounded the door like a blue, gaping maw.

He paused his search at an artifact he'd seen personally during the battle that had occurred in Babylon. Behind glass, sparkling from the light in the case, stood the intricate breastplate King Nebuchadnezzar II had worn as he destroyed Jerusalem, another one of Elohim's sacred treasures taken from the temple.

Kyden gritted his teeth. He could honestly say he despised Mammon. Normally, angels didn't fight a prince of hell since they weren't powerful enough. Only the archangels could accept that challenge. But Kyden and another angel, Aradan, had the opportunity during the battle.

It hadn't ended well.

Kyden quickly turned from the painful memories and walked straight into a woman who clumsily spilled champagne on his chest.

"Oh shit. I'm so sorry..." She looked up and her eyes widened. "Tall," she whispered. Shaking her head, she stepped back, a flush brightening her cheeks. "Sorry about running into you. And spilling my drink on your suit. I'll have the museum pay for the dry cleaning."

Kyden tilted his head as the woman continued to babble, patting his chest with her napkin. She'd pulled her dark blonde hair into an elegant twist, and the emerald green gown made her hazel eyes shine.

"It's really no problem," he said, holding her wrist. Pieces of wet napkin clung to his stained button-down shirt.

Her eyes drifted from his to her hand pressed against his damp shirt. "What a cluster—" She put some distance between them, seeming to finally realize she'd been pawing a stranger, and mumbled more curses under her breath. A human wouldn't have been able to decipher what she'd said, but Kyden's supernatural hearing picked out each unique expletive.

"Wow. Is it wrong that I'm slightly impressed?" Titus's voice said through the earpiece. Kyden refrained from rolling his eyes.

The woman forced a smile and held out her hand. "Hello, I'm Zahra Jenkins, Assistant Curator."

"Sam Malone," Kyden said, and shook her hand.

"Nice to meet you, Mr. Malone."

"Sam is fine." He tucked his hands into his pockets and scanned the exhibit hall. "This is a really thorough exhibit. I, uh, also have a thing for ancient Babylon. Big fan. Of...the era." He inwardly grimaced. Most of the Slayer Angels wouldn't characterize him as charming. In fact, that characteristic would be last on the list if someone described him. Thankfully, Titus was quiet, his commentary having ceased for a minute as he broke into the museum's computers to see who else was on the guest list.

"So, Sam, based on your accent, you're obviously not from around these parts."

He forced a chuckle. Having spent so many years in Britain, he'd adopted their accent and sayings. "I've recently arrived in Boston and was intrigued by the description of the exhibit. I make it a habit of financially supporting museums of this caliber."

Kyden and Titus had decided ahead of time that his cover would be a wealthy donor who gave generously to museums and other organizations that educated people.

"I don't remember your name on my list," Zahra said.

Kyden smiled. "I received a last-minute invitation from Mr. Rousseau. My travel plans suddenly changed and the schedule worked out."

"Well, I'm glad I ran into you first. Literally," she said, a slight pink forming in her cheeks. "Is there a particular piece you're interested in?"

Kyden rubbed the back of his neck, feigning embarrassment. "Actually, I'm a huge fan of Dr. Neeman. I noticed on the program that he's one of the honored guests. Can you introduce me?"

"I'm sorry, but Dr. Neeman was unable to make it."

He tilted his head. Zahra's shoulders had visibly stiffened when he'd mentioned the archaeologist's name. "That's a shame."

"There are some other archaeologists I can introduce you to…"

Her sentence trailed off as her gaze drifted over his shoulder. Her nostrils flared and her hands fisted on her hips. Kyden turned to see a man striding toward them. His slick hair and even slicker smile made Kyden clench his teeth. A demon lumbered beside him, its yellow eyes narrowed in concentration.

The man extended his hand. "Hello, I'm Brandon Hayes."

Kyden glanced at his hand and then plastered on a smile. "Sam Malone," he said, squeezing Hayes's hand until the man winced. He maintained eye contact, intentionally not looking at the grunt, whose nails dug into the human's arm.

"Good grip," Hayes said as he flexed his hand.

"Mr. Malone is interested in a few of the pieces, so if you'll excuse us," Zahra said, stepping between Hayes and Kyden, and threading her arm through his.

Kyden arched a brow as the two curators glared at each other. He did not have the desire to get caught up in office drama, but since Hayes was the project coordinator, maybe he had some information on the missing archaeologist.

"I was curious, Mr. Hayes, if you've heard from Dr. Neeman. I was hoping to meet him."

A flicker went through the man's eyes, disappearing in a flash. The demon's lips curled into an ugly grin. Yellow, pointed teeth jutted out as if the grunt wanted to bite the man.

Kyden inhaled deeply, reaching for self-control and forbidding himself from drawing his sword to cleave the demon in two.

"I've been in touch with him. There was a slight delay, but hopefully he'll arrive within the week," Hayes said.

Zahra's mouth dropped. "Why wasn't I told you spoke with him?"

"With everything going on, it must have slipped my mind." Hayes turned toward Kyden. "Can I show you some pieces or…"

Zahra forced a smile at Kyden. "Will you excuse us for a minute?" She grabbed Hayes's arm and led him away.

"Sure. Take your time," Kyden said, and wandered to another exhibit. "Titus," he murmured, "do a background check on Brandon Hayes."

"Already on it," Titus said through the earpiece.

Kyden engaged his amplified hearing while pretending to read the placard on one of King Nebuchadnezzar's goblets.

"First the programs and now you're blatantly lying about Dr. Neeman contacting you," Zahra said between clenched teeth.

Hayes's jaw pulsed, and his eyes narrowed. "I told you. The programs were an accident."

"Accident my ass, you pathetic, slimy worm," she said.

The demon had maneuvered up Hayes's back, whispering in his ear. He grabbed her arm and pulled her closer. "Watch it, Zahra."

Kyden cleared his throat and stepped toward Zahra's side.

"Miss Jenkins and I still have unfinished business, so if you'd kindly unhand her." Kyden inched closer, towering over the other man. "Now."

Hayes scowled from Kyden to his hand, his knuckles white as he gripped Zahra's arm. Kyden slid a glance at the demon and flared his eyes. The unholy beast jumped off Hayes and scampered across the hall in search of its next prey. Kyden gritted his teeth and scanned the ballroom. If a Fallen was nearby, the grunt would inform him of his presence.

Hayes took a deep breath and straightened his suit jacket. "I have other donors to meet with. Mr. Malone," he said, dipping his chin. He smiled smugly at Zahra before striding across the exhibit hall.

"Asshole," she muttered, glaring at Hayes while rubbing her arm.

Kyden was inclined to agree. He wasn't necessarily a violent angel, unless demons were involved, but he had the sudden urge to smack the arrogant look right off Hayes's face.

The woman continued to glare at her coworker. "Miss Jenkins?" he said.

"Zahra," she said, still focused on Hayes.

"Is everything okay? I mean, despite your coworker being a manipulative wanker."

She forced a smile. "I have stronger words than wanker, but I'm fine."

Kyden smiled. It was time to move on and away from this somewhat volatile woman. "I've monopolized your time, and I'm sure there are others who would love to hear your passion for this exhibit."

Zahra rubbed her hands down her dress as if trying to wipe away the confrontation with her coworker. "I'm happy to…"

Kyden held up a hand. "It's fine. I actually see Bill Guerin. I'm a huge fan of ice hockey." A snort sounded through his earpiece. "If you hear from Dr. Neeman, will you contact me?" He handed her a business card with his name and cell phone number.

Zahra took the card and slid it into her evening bag. "Absolutely. Plus, I owe you a clean shirt."

Kyden smiled and dipped his head. "Cheers." He turned and strode toward a hallway leading away from the exhibit. "Titus, meet me at the back door. I want to check Hayes's records regarding Neeman."

Chapter Six

Zahra

Zahra pressed her palms against the sink vanity and forced herself to take calming breaths. Her frustration with Brandon over the programs had amped up to pure rage when he lied about speaking to Dr. Neeman. There was no way her father would talk to him before speaking to her. Watching the weasel maneuver among the other donors with that calculated smile made her want to throw something heavy at his head.

A bright side to the evening was meeting the alarmingly attractive Sam Malone. There seemed to be a fierceness hidden behind the fitted blue suit, one that had made her pulse race. Especially when he towered over Brandon, coming to her rescue when her slimy coworker had grabbed her arm. She'd never admit to needing help, but the knight-in-shining-armor gig definitely made butterflies flutter in her stomach.

Sam looked to be in his early thirties, but his unique amber-colored eyes seemed almost ancient, like the pictures of warriors in one of her many history books. He wore his black hair short, which complemented his angular jaw and high cheekbones. The man definitely came from an excellent gene pool.

Sam hadn't been the first guest to ask about Dr. Neeman's whereabouts, but the way he'd stared at her, as if he could see into her soul, had made her jumpy. Granted, her skittishness could also have stemmed from the fact that she'd pawed the man after spilling champagne on his very muscular chest.

Just hours before, she'd once again tried to contact Excavate International, but the receptionist kept transferring her to the number in Baghdad. No answer, and the voicemail box was full. The fact that she couldn't reach the actual dig site was worrisome.

She thought back to the hastily written note from her father.

I'm sorry. For everything.

Had her father finally gotten himself into the kind of trouble he couldn't get out of? The worry of not knowing coiled in her stomach like a snake primed to strike.

The door to the bathroom opened and Alexis stormed in. "What an absolute bastard," she said, her brown eyes filled with anger.

"My thoughts exactly," Zahra said, pushing away from the vanity and straightening her dress. She hadn't told Alexis about Brandon's sabotage of the programs until right before the event. Obviously, her friend was still as outraged as she was.

"What are we going to do?"

Zahra smiled at her friend, her comrade in arms. Her saying "we" meant the world to her. Alexis was fiercely loyal, and if Zahra asked her to kick Brandon in the balls, she would do it, and with a running start.

"Mr. Durand of Durand Enterprises is my concern now. If I can get his support, all of Brandon's manipulations will be wasted." Zahra had come up with this plan while tamping down her anger. The only donor she needed to charm was Laurent Durand, one of the wealthiest men in the United States and parts of Europe. He had a reputation for collecting unattainable artifacts like the Atar'zul.

Zahra's nails dug into her palms, and she bit back a curse. She was too late. Laurent Durand, CEO of Durand Enterprises, talked with Brandon, while a pretty woman standing next to Durand jotted something on a business card and handed it to Brandon. With a victorious gleam in his eye, he tucked the card in his pocket, shook hands with Durand, and strutted away.

No, she thought. She could still salvage this. Brandon might schmooze with his charm, but his knowledge of this exhibit didn't match hers. She'd show Mr. Durand and his impressive bank account who to put his faith in.

She set her shoulders and walked toward the billionaire. Durand Enterprises had their corporate fingers in everything from politics to technology, and now archaeology, namely ancient Babylon. Zahra wasn't sure why and didn't care.

As she made her way across the ballroom, the hairs on the back of her neck stood at attention, sensing the weight of someone's stare. She scanned the area, and her eyes met Sam's, his intense gaze boring into her.

Zahra forced away inappropriate thoughts regarding the mysterious man and focused on her primary target. Laurent Durand was of average height and had dark brown hair with streaks of gray woven throughout. The tuxedo he wore fit him perfectly, and a gold ring covered in diamonds sparkled on his finger as he spoke to some other patrons, one of whom Zahra thought was a movie star.

"Excuse me, Mr. Durand?" Zahra asked.

Laurent Durand turned and deep brown eyes behind wire-framed glasses traveled from her face to her toes and back up in a slow caress that made her inwardly cringe.

"I'm Zahra Jenkins, the assistant curator of the museum."

"Pleasure to meet you, Miss Jenkins." Durand lifted her knuckles to his lips. "How many curators does the Gallery of Time have?" His teeth practically glowed when he smiled.

Zahra chuckled. "Three, actually. Mr. Rousseau is the head curator. Myself and Brandon Hayes are the assistant curators."

Durand flicked his gaze to the woman next to him, who quickly checked her notepad and then nodded. "From what I can see from just the lobby, this is a most exquisite exhibit."

"I'd love to give you a personal tour. I believe there were a few pieces you were interested in," Zahra said.

"Sounds lovely." He nodded toward the Ishtar Gate leading to the main exhibit hall. "Lead the way."

Zahra glanced at the two men behind him, both with stern faces and eyes that constantly scanned the area, earpieces tucked away like secret service agents.

"Don't mind them," Durand said.

She stopped in front of each exhibit, explaining its importance to Mesopotamia and the Babylonian Empire. Durand seemed fascinated by the pieces, asking thought-provoking questions and adding tidbits of information she didn't think most billionaires knew.

They paused in front of an ancient drawing. "I'm not familiar with this piece," Durand said.

She smiled. "Dr. Neeman recently found this drawing along with a partial inscription. We're still hoping they can find the rest."

The image was of an extremely tall man with his back turned, a robe concealing most of his frame. Another person, smaller in size, stood next to him. They both held a circlet. Light flowed from the simple crown as if driving back the darkness.

Durand leaned forward and read the inscription. "*...though dim and slight. A mortal must bleed to feed the light...*"

"We think the taller person is King Nebuchadnezzar II, and one of his priests is handing him his crown," Zahra said.

Durand frowned and leaned back. "I've researched the king and have acquired many of this time period's artifacts, safely stored in my personal collection. I don't recall this one, though. You said Dr. Neeman found it?"

Zahra nodded. She glanced over his shoulder—and her heart jolted to a stop and then thumped right out of her chest. Her lapis ring clung to her finger like dead weight and blood rushed in her ears as a face she hadn't seen in years came into view. Jake Callahan strolled toward her, his gaze directed to the floor, his head tilted as he listened to the woman next to him.

Zahra knew once he looked up she'd see the most gorgeous gray eyes ringed by thick lashes. Eyes that had once gazed upon her with love and adoration, but after that awful day in the rain when she'd crushed both of their hearts, those same eyes had hardened into stone.

His brown hair was longer than when she'd last seen him, which made it even more alluring as it skimmed the tips of ears, and of course styled to perfection. How many times had she run her hands through those soft locks as he kissed her senseless?

She took a step back as her gaze shifted to the woman on his arm, almost as tall as Jake's six-foot-three frame with her stiletto heels. Her elegant burgundy silk dress draped over one shoulder and fit her like a second skin. She looked like a model, a goddess with a beaded evening bag.

Zahra's breath came in short, choppy bursts. What was he doing here at her museum? She'd always wondered if, and secretly hoped, she would see him again. In fact, she had concocted a speech explaining why she had broken things off, why she was such a coward. But all that preparation evaporated like steam as the corner of Jake's lip lifted.

"Miss Jenkins?" Durand asked, gently gripping her elbow.

"Oh, um. How about some champagne?" she asked, desperately searching for a way out as Jake and the goddess slowly moved in her direction. Why were they coming this way? Of all the rotten luck. A server passed by with a tray of bubbly courage, and she snagged two glasses, offering one to Durand. Her gaze drifted back to Jake as if a magnet pulled her in.

When he finally looked up, his eyes immediately met hers, and his lips parted. He removed himself from the woman next to him and walked toward her.

"Ah, Jacob, there you are," Durand said, following the direction of Zahra's stare. "I'd like you to meet Zahra Jenkins. She's one of the curators at the museum."

She briefly shut her eyes and gathered her composure, reminding herself to be professional. "Hello, Jake," she said, lifting her chin and forcing a smile. She spun her ring around so the stone faced her palm and shook Jake's hand quickly, letting go as if her skin had burned from his touch.

"Hi, Zahra. I was hoping I'd see you tonight." His gaze drifted across her face as if trying to sort out a puzzle.

Her brows crept up her forehead. "You were?" She was shocked to see him, but he didn't seem surprised at all. Needing to calm her spinning mind and take control of this conversation she said, "And how do you know Mr. Durand?"

Jake shoved his hands into his pockets. "He's my boss. I work in his acquisitions department."

"Damn valuable too," Durand said with a smile. "He's the reason I'm here, actually."

She snapped her head toward Durand. "He is?"

Durand arched a brow. "He said this museum was a hidden gem in Boston. Naturally, I had him come with me. Do you two know each other?"

Jake was about to answer when she said, "We were acquaintances in college." Guilt swarmed in her gut at the hurt that flickered across his face.

Jake's eyes narrowed slightly. The woman standing next to him cleared her throat. He tore his gaze from her. "Zahra, this is Gabriella Romano. Gabriella, this is my *college acquaintance*, Zahra Jenkins."

"Pleasure to meet you," Gabriella said, giving her a once-over before her blue eyes drifted across the other patrons.

"Miss Jenkins was giving me a wonderful tour of the exhibit. Care to join us?" Durand asked.

Based on Zahra's luck, Jake and his goddess would join them. She gulped an inappropriately long drink of her champagne.

"Wouldn't miss it," Jake said, the corner of his lips curving.

Zahra tore her gaze from his mouth and gave Mr. Durand a winning smile. Turning toward the center of the exhibit hall, she said, "This is one of my favorite rooms. Many of the pieces were discovered by Excavate International in Iraq." She led them into King Nebuchadnezzar's throne room while trying to ignore the weight of Jake's stare along her bare back.

Blue marbled columns, gold veins weaving delicately through the stone, lined the majestic room. Bronze arches with carved images of lions linked the columns. Strategically placed pedestals showcased ceremonial artifacts, and next to the throne in a glass case lay the replica of the Atar'zul.

Durand placed his hands behind his back and examined the relic, his brows drawing together.

Zahra fiddled with the stem of her champagne glass. "We were expecting to have the original piece, but we've had a difficult time getting ahold of the excavation company."

The billionaire arched a brow. "Mr. Hayes said you'd have the piece within a few days."

"Did he?" She forced a smile, imagining unique ways to torture her coworker. "Well, one can only hope."

Jake's shoulder brushed hers as he leaned closer to the glass case. "Is the crown supposed to be broken?"

Zahra held her ground, sandwiched between the two men while trying not to shiver when Jake touched her. "Based on the information we have obtained, the Atar'zul has always been cracked. We're not sure how it was damaged."

Jake rested his hands on his hips and gazed around the throne room, his lips curled into a smile. "This is quite impressive, Zahra."

"Thank you." Any warmth from his praise chilled when Gabriella covered her yawn with her perfectly manicured nails. If it weren't for trying to secure the funding from Durand Enterprises, she would have turned on her heel and marched, albeit seductively, from the room.

"I agree with Jacob," Durand said. "Very impressive, Miss Jenkins. I'll be even more impressed once the Atar'zul arrives."

"Did I hear the word Atar'zul?" Sam Malone said, his eyes shifting from the relic to her.

Zahra tilted her head as the man appeared unexpectedly from behind one of the columns. She smiled and introduced them. "Laurent Durand, this is Sam Malone. He's also interested in Mesopotamian artifacts."

Sam held out his hand. "Mr. Durand. What a privilege to meet you."

Durand hesitated for a moment, shook his hand quickly, and smiled, taking a step toward the case holding the Atar'zul. "The pleasure is mine, Mr. Malone."

Sam smiled. "Miss Jenkins has done a fabulous job recreating ancient Babylon, hasn't she?"

"Indeed, she has," Mr. Durand said, his attention on the artifact. He summoned one of his bodyguards and spoke quietly to him.

Jake crossed his arms, his gaze darting between her and Sam, and a thrill traveled along Zahra's spine. Her ex might have a goddess on his arm, but she had Sam. Well, technically she didn't, but Jake didn't know that.

Was she acting petty and immature? Yep, and she'd deal with the shame of that behavior later. She didn't want Jake to see her in this situation, proving he'd been right about her all those years ago. His words still lingered in her mind like a festering wound.

"You keep pushing people away, Zahra, and all you'll be is alone," Jake had said, raindrops dripping down his face. When she had tried to give the ring back, he folded her fingers over it. "Keep it. You never know, maybe you'll change your mind."

She'd done the same with her father, granted she didn't believe he actually loved her. He barely knew her. And she hated to admit it, but she had treated her mom the same until her mom's health had taken a turn for the worse.

Zahra shook away the memories and touched Sam's forearm. "How rude of me. Sam, this is Jake Callahan and Gabriella Romano."

Zahra couldn't help but appreciate their attractiveness as Sam and Jake shook hands like two alpha males in a standoff. Even though Sam was taller, Jake had filled out since college, and she wasn't sure who would come out the victor. It seemed Gabriella appreciated the scenery as well since her gaze skimmed down Sam's impressive form, and her red lips curled into a seductive smile.

"Why don't I show you the reproduction of the secret passage discovered by Dr. Neeman during his time at the dig site? It's rumored to have led directly to the famous Hanging Gardens," Zahra said, threading her arm through Sam's and pointing to an area behind King Nebuchadnezzar's throne.

Sam frowned at her hand on his arm and then at her face. She widened her eyes, trying to beg him telepathically to play along. He glanced over his shoulder to see a scowling Jake. When he looked back at her, he arched a brow as he put two and two together, then mouthed, *You owe me.*

Twenty minutes later, they exited the replica of the Hanging Gardens and entered the crowded lobby. Other patrons immediately surrounded Mr. Durand, all wanting an opportunity to shake hands with a billionaire.

"Your hard work definitely paid off," Jake said, as he glanced around the room.

"Thanks," she said. Any satisfaction she'd felt at making him jealous evaporated when he smiled at her, as if he really was proud of all she'd accomplished.

Gabriella grabbed Jake's hand. "Look, there's Spencer Wyatt. I must say hello." Jake simply nodded, his eyes fixed on Zahra's.

Sam took Zahra's empty glass and said, "Why don't I get you another drink?"

She tore her eyes from her ex and smiled sweetly. "Yes, please."

Mr. Durand approached them after Sam had walked away. "Well, I've seen all I need to. Miss Jenkins, it was a pleasure meeting you." Durand nodded toward Jake. "Jacob, see you in the morning."

Both Zahra and Jake watched the billionaire stride through the throng of people, who parted in his wake as if he were Moses splitting the Red Sea, with his bodyguards trailing behind him. The noise seemed to lessen as Jake turned toward her.

She took a step back, not realizing how close she stood to him, and tripped on the hem of her dress.

Jake grabbed her arm and steadied her, his eyes sparkling with mischief. Memories of how they first met during her freshman orientation assaulted her. She'd literally run into him, focused on the map of campus and not paying attention to where she was going. He'd gently grabbed her arms and smiled down at her—the same smile he was giving her now.

Once he made sure she wouldn't fall on her ass, he said, "I'm sorry about the shock of me just showing up," he said, shoving his hands into his pockets. "This was rather last minute."

The warmth of his touch still lingered on her arm. She tried to ignore it and said, "Pretty sure you have a phone in that fancy suit of yours."

Jake dipped his chin and chuckled. "You're still direct, I see, and as beautiful as ever."

"I don't think your hood ornament will appreciate that sentiment," Zahra said, folding her arms around her waist. Where was Sam with her champagne?

"My hood ornament?" He pressed his lips into a straight line as if trying to suppress a laugh. "And where did your eye candy run off to?"

She opened her mouth but snapped it shut when his laugh made the butterflies in her stomach swarm.

"Anyway, we haven't talked in years. Besides working at the museum, what else have you been up to?" Jake asked, a kind smile on his face.

She huffed out a laugh. "This museum *is* practically my life, but I still go to the shooting range, plus I visit my mom a couple times a week."

"How is your mom? I've always had a soft spot for her."

"She's not great. She was recently diagnosed with frontotemporal dementia. It's pretty aggressive, so I had to move her to Glendale Memory Care." She picked at the skin around her thumbnail. "I hated leaving her there, but I couldn't work and take care of her."

Why was she telling him all of this? Jake had always been easy to talk to. He listened so intently, making conversations effortless to the point she would reveal things she usually guarded like a door she didn't remember unlocking until it was standing wide open and revealing the hidden secrets inside.

Jake's shoulders sagged. "I'm sorry to hear that. Would it be all right if I visited her while I'm in town?"

"Of course," she said, a reluctant smile forming. "I think she still likes you more than me."

Jake chuckled and the sound sent a shiver down her spine. "I doubt that."

"So, it must be amazing working for Durand Enterprises," she said, filling the silence.

"It's been a wild ride. I've traveled the world and have had so many opportunities." His words exuded excitement, but his expression remained flat. "Living in Vegas is interesting, but I miss New England—the food, the weather." His eyes scanned her face. "The scenery."

Her cheeks burned, and a crack broke through her heart. She hadn't realized how much she missed him until he was standing in front of her looking even more handsome than she could remember. Her lungs tightened and the need for air had her stepping away. She glanced around the room, seeing her boss speaking with some loyal patrons. "It was nice seeing you again, Jake. Excuse me."

"Zahra," Jake said as she walked away. Just her name on his lips made her chest ache, unwanted tears filling her eyes at what could have been. What would her life have been like if Jake had been by her side tonight, celebrating her dreams coming to fruition? But it was her fault he wasn't, her fault she was alone.

She continued across the ballroom, nodding and shaking hands with other guests, forcing herself to not turn around, wrap her arms around him, and apologize for everything.

She joined Mr. Rousseau as the mayor and his wife excused themselves.

"How do you think the evening is going, Miss Jenkins?" Mr. Rousseau asked, a satisfied smile on his wrinkled face.

She still hadn't discussed Brandon's treachery regarding the programs—a conversation that would have to wait until Monday. "I've heard a lot of positive feedback. I showed Mr. Durand all the pieces, explaining their history. He seemed pleased."

Mr. Rousseau smiled. "He was very impressed with both you and Brandon."

Zahra gritted her teeth as Brandon joined their conversation, appearing out of nowhere.

"Who's impressed with me?" Brandon asked, winking at Zahra.

Would it be frowned upon if she plucked his eye from his skull? Probably.

"I was just telling Miss Jenkins how Mr. Durand was impressed with our exhibit. He's invited us to his restaurant, The Indulgence, on Monday evening. Won't that be wonderful?" Mr. Rousseau beamed and patted each of them on the shoulder before joining the chief of police near the bar.

Brandon crossed his arms and gazed out over the exhibit hall. "We pulled off quite the event, didn't we?"

Zahra's mouth dropped and anger flushed through her system, making the blood pulse in her ears. She stared in disbelief while he pretended he hadn't intentionally stabbed her in the back.

She kept her voice low as her anger boiled. "You can try to fool everyone with your charming bullshit, but based on my interaction with Mr. Durand, that promotion is mine. I'd start looking for another job because I *will* fire your ass."

She didn't allow Brandon to reply as she spun on her heel and walked across the room. She'd done all she could tonight and was ready to take off the dress and throw the torture devices on her feet in the trash.

She found Alexis near the exit saying goodbye to some guests. "Hey, I'm heading out. Want a ride home?" Alexis asked.

"I'm leaving soon too. Just need to check on a few things. I'll meet you back at the apartment."

"Sounds good. And I want the skinny on those two very hot men you were talking to earlier," Alexis said, resting her hands on her hips. She continued when Zahra didn't answer. "You know, extremely tall, black hair, and broodily handsome and the tall, brown hair, and sophisticatedly handsome."

Zahra chuckled. "Broodily handsome is from England and likes museums. Sophisticatedly handsome is my ex, Jake Callahan. We dated in college." Sadness cinched her heart. She thought she was over him but one look into those gray eyes and the feelings she'd buried reawakened like ghosts with unfinished business.

"Why haven't I heard about him before?" Alexis held up her hand when Zahra opened her mouth. "This sounds like a sweats-on-the-couch conversation, not a fancy-gown-in-a-ballroom one. Let's take this back to our apartment."

"Deal," Zahra said, and forty minutes later, after checking with the rest of the staff, she hopped into her car and drove to their apartment. Alexis waited on the couch with an open bottle of red wine and two glasses.

"You're the best," Zahra said.

"I really am," Alexis said, already having ditched her dress, opting for a tank top and shorts.

Zahra quickly changed into leggings and a baggy sweatshirt. On the drive home, her mind had again drifted to her father and his whereabouts. The uncertainty and worry exhausted her, and she was tired of keeping the secret of her father's identity. She had a choice—to invite her friend into her world or keep her at a distance. Jake's words from years ago plagued her.

You keep pushing people away, Zahra, and all you'll be is alone.

"There's something I need to tell you," Zahra said, joining Alexis on the couch.

Alexis tucked her long legs underneath her. "Okay. But I have a full bottle here, so first, tell me about this Jake."

Zahra took a deep drink of wine and then explained her relationship with Jake. She finished her glass. "When he proposed, I panicked, thinking about all the things that could go wrong."

Alexis swiped at her eyes and poured more wine. "That's utterly brutal."

Zahra leaned back into the cushions and stared at a water spot on the ceiling. "I've had this apology speech planned for if I ever ran into him again. But seeing him tonight...Well, of course I couldn't remember a damn thing. Anyway, he seems to have moved on with his goddess."

"Oh, I saw her, as did every man at the event. Maybe she'll sprain an ankle wearing those wickedly high heels." She shrugged. "So what else did you want to tell me?"

"You know who Dr. Neeman is, right?"

"The famous archaeologist—modern-day Indiana Jones is what the archaeology magazines call him. Too bad he wasn't here tonight. I would've loved to have met him."

Zahra placed the wineglass on the table and took a deep breath. "Dr. Neeman is my father."

Alexis sputtered her wine and patted her chest. "Your father?"

"Yep," she said, making the P pop.

"Okay, I'm confused. Why would you keep this a secret? He's amazing."

"*That* right there is why I didn't tell anyone. People would have unrealistic expectations of me. Plus, I wanted to earn my promotions based on my work, not who my father is." Zahra fiddled with the hem of her sweatshirt.

Alexis rubbed her bottom lip with her thumb and stared at her glass. "Makes sense," she finally said. "Does anyone else know?"

Zahra shook her head. "No."

"I'm honored you told me."

"Besides my mom, you're my only family."

Alexis gave a watery smile. "Are you worried that you haven't heard from your dad even though he was supposed to attend tonight?"

"A little. He sent me a necklace and a note apologizing for everything. He's sent cryptic gifts before and not shown up when I needed him, so I wasn't worried. But now I'm not so sure."

"I bet he's okay. You know those adventurous types. They often lose themselves in their work." Alexis patted Zahra's leg and smiled.

She hoped Alexis was right. The note still bothered her, though. "Of course, everyone was asking about him, even Mr. Tall, Dark, and Broody."

"Yes, let's talk about him. Holy hot, is all I have to say."

Zahra laughed and then smacked her forehead. "Dammit!"

"What? What's wrong?"

"I forgot to apologize to him." Zahra rubbed her forehead. Alexis waved her hand as if saying *get on with it.*

"Okay, don't laugh, but when Sam introduced himself to Mr. Durand, I wanted to make Jake jealous because of the goddess."

"Loathe the goddess," Alexis said, pouring more wine.

"Right? Anyway, I sort of implied Sam and I knew each other better than we did. I made a fool of myself, touching him and giggling."

Alexis's eyes widened. "You don't giggle. Ever."

"I know. It was sick and wrong." She took another sip of wine. "Anyway, he'd gone to get champagne, and I forgot to look for him before I left."

"Well, he certainly isn't hard on the eyes. You should definitely call him up and get to groveling." Alexis winked.

"You're shameless," she said with a laugh, and rose to her feet. "This day has been too crazy and I'm exhausted. I'll see you in the morning."

Zahra sat on the edge of her bed and opened her purse, removing the necklace her father had sent. The silver filaments of the twisted feather sparkled when she held it up to the light. She rubbed her thumb over the pendant and stared at a flickering streetlight.

Where was her dad, and was he okay? His note had been so cryptic. What exactly was he apologizing for? Not coming to the event, divorcing her mom, always being gone? Or was it something else? The list of wrongs continued to pile up.

A shadow slinked by her window, and she jumped, dropping the necklace. "What the hell?" She slowly approached the window and peered down the street.

Empty.

Shaking her head, she returned the necklace to the velvet pouch and dropped it into the drawer of her nightstand. Her jaw cracked when she yawned. The last few days had exhausted her, and she longed to fall into a deep, dreamless sleep.

Unfortunately, her luck didn't change. She tossed and turned as visions of shadowy creatures lurked in the darkness while familiar gray eyes tormented her.

CHAPTER SEVEN

KYDEN

The door slid open on the unmarked van and the smell of coffee immediately had Kyden reaching for the steaming cup. He'd been stuck in this tin can for the last three hours, bored out of his mind. His knee bounced up and down at an unnatural speed with the need to stretch his wings and feel the cool Boston air wash across his face.

"Is it possible for angels to be addicted to caffeine?" Titus asked, shutting the door behind him and settling into a chair across from the computer monitor.

Kyden shrugged and took a long drink, wincing through the burn on his tongue. Technically, this was only his fifth cup today. As it was two in the afternoon, he was pacing himself pretty well.

Titus chuckled and clicked a few keys on his computer. "Anything new at the museum?"

The phone taps and bugs he and Titus had installed the night of the gala had worked perfectly, but so far there had been no mention of Dr. Neeman. According to Mr. Rousseau's staff, the archaeologist was still missing. Kyden asked Adinah to monitor the dig site and the surrounding area for any news of Dr. Neeman's whereabouts.

Kyden had hoped someone would have said something by now, but no one spoke about the archaeologist or the Atar'zul. The only interesting tidbit was that Brandon Hayes hadn't shown up to work yet, followed by some choice adjectives from Zahra.

"Nothing to report. What do we know about Hayes?" Kyden asked.

Titus's fingers tapped on the keyboard. "How much do you want?"

"I don't need his entire backstory. Just whatever is related to this case."

Titus clicked a few more times while Kyden sipped on his coffee. If angels could be addicted to caffeine, then he definitely was.

"Well, there's the usual: school, jobs, that sort of thing. But based on his financials and my computer wizardry, it looks like our friend Hayes has a bit of a gambling problem."

Kyden leaned forward and peered over Titus's shoulder. "That causes people to do desperate things and would explain the grunt clinging to him."

"Not surprising," Titus said.

"What about Laurent Durand? He showed interest in the Atar'zul."

"Durand's a little tougher to learn more than the basics on. He graduated from Princeton with honors and then received his master's in business. He has a knack for buying corporations and built a name for himself early in his career. From there, his businesses and earnings skyrocketed." Titus scratched his jaw. "The firewalls on his computers are impressive. Granted, he has ties to tech, along with politics and investments, not to mention he's a collector of rare artifacts; the more lore attached to the relic the better."

Kyden chewed his thumbnail. The lack of demons surrounding Durand surprised him. Normally, billionaires with their need for power and money would have a grunt or two clinging to them. Durand had come across as pleasant, if not a little arrogant, and his interest in the exhibits had seemed genuine.

Kyden leaned back in his chair, savoring his coffee and crossing his ankles, thinking back to the gala. He'd spoken with all three curators, and was proud of himself for not punching Hayes, but hadn't discovered anything regarding Dr. Neeman or the halo. He'd left the event after noticing a group of grunt demons scurrying out and following them, calling Titus to meet him at the front of the museum. The grunts had bolted along the street and disappeared down an alley. The only time they moved with such purpose was when their Fallen was summoning them.

Titus and Kyden had trailed the sulfuric scent until they ran into the harbor, where the trail vanished. Both angels shed their glamour and took to the skies, but found nothing. By the time Kyden had returned to the museum, Zahra had left.

A loud crunching sound echoed through the speakers.

"What *is* that woman eating?" Titus asked, wincing at the noise.

"A lollipop."

Titus raised his eyebrows.

"That's her fourth one. How she has any teeth, I don't know. From what I gathered from her file, she used to be a smoker."

"Ah," Titus said, lowering the volume on the speaker.

Titus had done a brief background check on Zahra but nothing raised any suspicion. She'd been born to a single mom in Dover, New Hampshire, and had attended the University of New Hampshire, graduating with a degree in Museum Science, later getting her master's. Her mother was diagnosed with dementia, which seemed like the reason Zahra accepted the job at the Gallery of Time in Boston instead of choosing a more prestigious museum.

The sound of a door opening followed by the clicking of heels compelled them both to lean forward.

"Zahra, we got a call from *Archaeology Today*, and they want to interview you and Brandon regarding the Babylonian exhibit."

A final crunch sounded, this one more violent than the others. "Thanks, Meredith. I'm available at the end of the week. Not sure about Brandon. Has he come in yet?" Zahra asked. Papers shuffled and her chair squeaked.

"Not yet. I tried his home number, but nothing."

Zahra mumbled something, and Titus turned up the volume.

"I'm sorry again about the programs. I double-checked the proof I sent to the printer."

"It wasn't your fault," Zahra said.

"Maybe tonight you can swing Mr. Durand to your side. I heard the boss saying that he was impressed by the tour you gave him."

Zahra sighed. "That's my plan—to charm the pants off him. Well, not literally, but you know what I mean."

Meredith giggled. "Don't work too long. Dinner is at seven. Have you picked out what you're going to wear?"

Kyden tuned out the two women as they talked outfits until Zahra's phone rang. The sound of a door closed, then, "Hello, this is Zahra Jenkins."

"Hello, Miss Jenkins. This is Lorraine Ortiz from Excavate International."

Kyden set his mug down. Hopefully, they'd finally get some information. Zahra's chair squeaked as if she were leaning forward, physically preparing herself for the conversation.

"Finally. I've been trying to reach someone—"

The woman on the line interrupted her. "I'm sorry for not getting back to you sooner. Events at the Hillah dig site have been, um, sensitive. We didn't want to report anything until we had credible information."

"What do you mean 'sensitive'?" Zahra asked, her voice laced with worry.

The woman hesitated and cleared her throat. "We've filed a missing person report for Dr. Neeman. He hasn't checked in nor have we received any communication from him. As you are his primary contact at the museum, we thought you should know."

"He's done this before though, hasn't he?"

"Yes, but never for this long. Plus, an important artifact is missing, which is very uncharacteristic."

"Are you talking about the Atar'zul?" Zahra asked.

"I'm sorry, at this time I cannot divulge anything else. As he was expected to attend your gala, this is simply a courtesy call. Have a good—"

"Wait. Please, if you hear from him, will you call me?"

There was a pause. "Of course, Miss Jenkins. Goodbye."

The line went dead and silence filled Titus's speakers. After a minute, Zahra whispered, "What have you gotten yourself into this time?"

Kyden leaned back and rubbed his thumb along his bottom lip. "Is it odd that the company called her?"

"Seems strange. Might need to question her again? She seemed more than willing to talk with you at the gala." Titus focused on the computer screen, but his lips pressed into a flat line as if caging in the laugh that wanted to spew forth.

Kyden sighed. "She was simply trying to make her ex jealous." During the gala, when Zahra had suddenly become very interested in his arm and smiling up at him like the Cheshire cat, he'd known what she was attempting. He had almost pulled away, but the desperation flowing through her hazel eyes caused him to play along with her ruse. That brief glimpse of her vulnerability created a crack in his figurative armor and a sliver of compassion had wormed its way through.

His eyes narrowed as he stared out the window. Wisps of clouds surrounded by blue sky called to him. "Looks like I need to be a guest at that dinner party."

"Looks that way. Shouldn't be too hard for you though, Mr. Charming," Titus said, restraining a chuckle.

Kyden lingered in the shadows cast by the glow of the streetlamp and waited for Zahra to arrive. He'd researched The Indulgence, a Michelin three-star restaurant, discovering they of course had a dress code. For the second time in a matter of days, he tugged at the tie around his neck.

"You're fidgeting," Titus said through the earbud.

Kyden grunted and was about to respond when a car arrived on the opposite side of the street and familiar golden-brown hair peeked out from the open door. Zahra spoke to the Uber driver, shut the door, and watched him drive off. She tilted her head back and stared at the restaurant on the top floor.

She wore a black cocktail dress with spiked heels, pointy enough to be an effective weapon. As she waited for traffic to clear, a limousine pulled up in front of the building. One of Durand's bodyguards hopped out and opened the passenger door.

Laurent Durand unfolded himself from the car. Zahra raised her hand, dropping it as another man stepped out. From what Kyden had researched, Jake Callahan had been Zahra's serious boyfriend throughout college and then left New Hampshire for Las Vegas to intern at one of Durand's smaller companies.

The next person emerging from the limousine was the woman on Callahan's arm at the museum. Kyden shifted his gaze to Zahra. She pressed her lips into a straight line and glanced up and down the street as if searching for an escape.

"Cue the gallant rescuer," Titus said, restraining his laughter.

"Are you going to jabber the entire night?" He crossed to the other side with his angelic speed so as not to be seen, and walked toward her. As he approached, she mumbled under her breath, "Oh, grow a spine."

"If you didn't have a spine, you wouldn't be breathing right now."

"Lame," Titus said. Kyden gritted his teeth, desperately wanting to tell his friend to shut up.

Zahra jumped. "What the f—" She pressed her hand against her chest and glared at him. "You scared me. What are you doing here?"

"My hotel is down the street. I was heading to Bull Finch Pub. Care to join me?"

She tilted her head. "The *Cheers* bar? Doesn't seem like a spot a Brit would hang out at."

Kyden shrugged. "I think it's brilliant. Very iconic of the eighties."

"Makes sense since your name *is* Sam Malone." Then she laughed, and said, "What, are you going there because it's 'where everybody knows your name'?"

Kyden sighed. Now the *Cheers* song would be stuck in his head all night. Figures. "Looks like you're going somewhere fancy."

"The Indulgence." She pointed to the top of the building.

He whistled and leaned his head back, scrutinizing the restaurant fifty floors up. Zahra glanced across the street, where her ex was disappearing inside the building.

"Imagine my surprise when I returned with your champagne and couldn't find you," he said.

Zahra winced. "Sorry about that. I had work stuff to deal with." She focused on the glass doors now closing, a look of sadness filling her eyes.

Kyden crossed his arms. "I take it that man meant something to you? Husband? Fiancé?"

Her head turned so quickly he was surprised he didn't hear her neck crack.

"Why would you ask that?" she asked, her voice higher than normal.

"Let's just say I noticed an increase in..." He paused, pretending to think of the right word while tapping his chin. "Attention."

Her cheeks reddened as she blew out a breath. "Yeah, sorry about that too. Jake is an ex-boyfriend. Someone I haven't seen in years."

"How about a deal?" he asked. "I'll be your date for tonight. I'm sure my presence will make Callahan squirm."

Zahra's brows lifted. "I couldn't ask you to do that."

"The Indulgence is known even across the pond—there's a six-month waiting list to get in."

"What's the catch?" Zahra asked, her eyes narrowing.

"You'll call me when the Atar'zul arrives at the museum. I'd love to see the actual piece." He didn't want to come across as desperate, but he needed to get into that restaurant. He could change his appearance and go as a waiter or delivery man, but he wouldn't have access to the conversation. Not like he would as Zahra's date.

Zahra swallowed and glanced once more at the imposing building. As if finally making up her mind, she said, "I can't compete with the goddess, but with you, at least I won't be a total loser."

Kyden arched a brow, not understanding the goddess comment, but didn't feel like gathering more information than necessary. "So do we have a deal?"

"We do," she said, holding out her hand.

Kyden shook it and led her across the street.

Titus's voice drifted through the earpiece. "Well played, Casanova. Once you get up there, I'll start recording."

CHAPTER EIGHT

ZAHRA

Zahra removed her sweater and focused on the ticking floor numbers, wondering at her good luck—finally. When she'd witnessed Jake getting out of the limo with Gabriella, she'd wanted to run in the other direction. Sam Malone showing up out of nowhere was almost too good to be true, and she wouldn't look a gift horse in the mouth. She'd observed Jake's reaction at the museum when she'd flirted, albeit horribly, with Sam. At least she could hold on to some dignity during this dinner. Having Jake with his girlfriend and Brandon, her backstabbing coworker, sitting at the same table would have been unbearable, especially by herself.

Plus, after the call she received from Excavate International earlier, a friendly person at her side was desperately needed. She hadn't been able to talk with Alexis before getting ready for dinner, and despite her estranged relationship with her father, worry twisted through her gut on a constant loop.

She slid a glance from the corner of her eye and found Sam leaning against the elevator wall, observing her with his unique, amber-colored eyes. She tugged at her cocktail dress that now felt too short and wondered if she should have gone with the sensible pantsuit she'd originally pulled out of her closet. But considering she hadn't stepped foot in a fancy restaurant since—well, she couldn't remember when—she opted for fun and flirty.

Sam wore a dark gray suit with a black button-down and a black and silver tie that he pulled at while twisting his neck.

"Does your pub have a dress code I'm not aware of?" she asked as he continued to fidget.

"Pardon?"

She pointed to his tie. "You seem awfully dressed up, is all."

"I just came from a meeting." He lowered his hand and shoved it in his pocket. "What did you mean by 'goddess'"?

She rubbed the back of her neck. "The woman Jake was with at the gala resembled a goddess."

"Ah." With a slight shrug he said, "I suppose we should get some particulars straight about our 'relationship.'"

She nodded. "Right. Let's see. We met at the museum and...yeah, that's all I got."

Sam snorted. "That works. Just follow my lead."

"Have you done this before?" she asked, frowning up at him.

He slid her a glance from the corner of his eye. "This is my fifth fake date this week."

"Ha. Hilarious." She chuckled and then frowned. "Wait, are you serious?"

He smirked. "Of course not. I do have a job, you know."

Her laugh morphed into a gasp as the elevator doors opened, revealing blue marble floors that sparkled under the ornate chandeliers. Flickering candles sat atop mahogany tables, and floor-to-ceiling windows overlooked the Boston skyline.

"Wow," she said, stepping into the luxurious room. "Have you ever seen a view like this?"

"A few times," Sam said, resting his hand on her lower back and steering her into the restaurant.

She tried to hide the shiver as the warmth of his palm seeped through the silky fabric of her dress.

"Where is everybody?" Sam asked.

"My boss said it was a private dinner."

The room dripped with sophistication, from the paintings on the wall to the white linen tablecloths. In the center was a circular bar, the polished wood and brass shining to perfection.

Jake leaned against the bar, speaking with Mr. Durand and her boss. His broad shoulders filled out the gray suit, its perfect fit hinting at the strength hidden beneath the elegance. She had hoped the excitement of the gala and the champagne had exaggerated how handsome he was.

She was wrong.

The butterflies fluttering in her stomach on the elevator transformed into a swarm of bees as the corner of Jake's eyes creased when he laughed at something Mr. Durand said. She pressed her hand to her chest where an ache had formed.

He'd been about to take a sip of his beer when his gaze met hers. He slowly lowered the bottle as his gaze traveled from her face to her ridiculous red heels and back up.

Sam leaned down and whispered, "What goddess?"

She tore her eyes from Jake and smiled up at him. One point for her. She scanned the restaurant, noticing Brandon had yet to arrive. Another point in her favor. Sam had just become her good-luck charm.

"Ah, Miss Jenkins. There you are," her boss said as she and Sam approached the group.

"Hello, Mr. Rousseau."

Jake pushed off the bar. "Zahra, you look…" He cleared his throat.

"Stunning," said Mr. Durand, giving her a grin.

Jake shook his head and took a long pull from his beer. Gabriella, who'd been scrolling on her phone, finally looked up.

If looks could kill, Zahra would be a corpse.

"Thank you. And I hope you don't mind, I brought my friend with me. This is Sam Malone."

Sam shook Mr. Rousseau's hand. "We met at the gala. Quite the event—I was very impressed, especially with Zahra." He gave her a quick wink.

Mr. Durand interlaced his hands behind his back. "Ah yes, I remember you." His gaze slid between Jake and Zahra. "The more the merrier, I always say." He then looked at Mr. Rousseau. "Are you expecting Mr. Hayes to join us?"

Mr. Rousseau's brows furrowed, and he glanced at his watch. "He should have been here by now. For some reason, he didn't come to work today."

"Is that normal for him?" Mr. Durand asked.

"No, not really."

Sam fiddled with his ear. "I wonder if someone should check on him? Does he have family nearby?"

Zahra tilted her head. She had only just met the man, but even that comment seemed out of character.

"That's very thoughtful," Mr. Rousseau said. "I'm sure he's fine. He possibly took the day off after the gala's success. But not our Miss Jenkins. She's quite the workaholic."

"She's always been very driven," Jake said, smiling at her, even though the smile didn't reach his eyes.

Heat filled her cheeks. She didn't want to acknowledge the satisfaction or the flutter in her stomach his comment had made.

Gabriella reached for Sam's hand. "It's lovely to see you again. We didn't get much of an opportunity to talk the other night."

Sam stepped closer to Zahra, avoiding Gabriella's touch. "I was a little preoccupied." He glanced at Zahra and smiled.

Zahra wanted to cackle in victory, but maintained a dignified level of self-control that surprised her. She could kiss Sam for all the envious tension he created in the room, but she quickly pushed that image away. He was doing her a favor, and she needed to keep things professional.

"Now that we're all here," Durand said, pointing to a large round table near the window offering an extraordinary view of Boston's skyline and the harbor in the distance.

"Thank you again for this meeting, Mr. Durand," Mr. Rousseau said, placing his napkin in his lap. "Despite the misprint in the program, Miss Jenkins is the project coordinator and can answer any questions you have about our exhibit and its amazing pieces."

Her boss's praise startled her so much she nearly dropped her sweater before draping it over the back of her chair. Too bad Brandon wasn't there to witness it—just so she could gloat. "Thank you, Mr. Rousseau."

Mr. Durand tilted his head. "I hadn't realized you were the one in charge of that fabulous display. But I should have. Your tour and knowledge of the artifacts were very thorough and entertaining. I have a feeling we'll be working together soon," he said, lifting his martini glass in a toast.

"I look forward to it," she said, unable to hold back her grin. She caught Jake staring at her, his lips slightly parted. He shifted his gaze and took a long pull from his beer.

Gabriella leaned toward Sam and asked, "So, Sam, what brings you to Boston?"

While Sam told her about his desire to meet Dr. Neeman, Zahra felt Jake's stare and snuck a glance at him. His eyes traveled across her face, a wrinkle between his brows, as if he was attempting to get inside her head. The expression was one she knew well from when they dated. She took another sip of her wine, staring at him over the lip of her glass. He smiled and the pain and loss of their broken relationship squeezed her heart. Once again, she rubbed her sternum as she focused on everything in the room besides him.

"Zahra, why didn't you mention you were the project coordinator the other night?" Jake asked, resting his forearms on the table, forcing her gaze back to him. "You did such a fabulous job and should be recognized for your endeavors."

Mr. Rousseau cleared his throat and adjusted his tie.

"I was simply keeping things professional," she said with a saccharine smile.

Sam snorted as he sipped his beer. She kicked him under the table while trying to suppress a laugh. Her level of professionalism that night with the man sitting next to her had been truly abysmal.

Mr. Durand arched a brow and studied her. She used all her willpower not to fidget under his intense scrutiny. Thankfully, dinner was served, and the conversation shifted to the famous Hanging Gardens of Babylon, one of the Seven Wonders of the Ancient World.

Sam seemed content to let the discussion flow around him while she, Mr. Durand, and Mr. Rousseau discussed plans for adding on to the museum. The project was an ambitious endeavor, but with Durand Enterprises' support, plus a few other donors, the likelihood of success was high.

She tried not to look at Jake, but he had made some interesting points regarding the expansion. Gabriella caught her staring and smirked when she gripped Jake's hand. He frowned as he glanced from his hand to Gabriella. Shaking his head, he reached for the salt and pepper.

Zahra turned her chuckle into a cough when Gabriella's head shot up, her eyes like fiery darts. Sam's knee nudged hers, and he gave her a look that said, *Keep it together.*

Once they finished dinner, Mr. Durand dabbed his mouth with his napkin and leaned back in his chair. "Tell me, Zahra, what are your thoughts on the legend of the Atar'zul?"

She fiddled with the stem of her wineglass. "Most legends tell an enchanting story, but as for the Atar'zul being magical? I highly doubt it."

"What exactly is this Atar'zul?" Jake asked, leaning forward.

Zahra shifted in her chair. "As the myth goes, the Atar'zul, also known as the Forsaken Halo, was created during a war between the angels and demons."

"And what makes this relic magical?" Gabriella asked, circling the rim of her wineglass with her French-tipped manicure.

"According to legend, the halo can drain the power of an angel or a demon," Mr. Rousseau said, his eyes sparkling with mischief.

"Halo as in the gold circle you see above angels' heads in paintings?" Jake asked.

"That is correct," Mr. Rousseau said.

Jake arched his brows and glanced at Zahra, who shrugged. She'd seen pictures of the Atar'zul and could understand why some called it a halo. To her, it looked more like a circlet that kings or princes wore.

Mr. Durand tapped his finger on the table. "What if I told you the myths were true?"

"Surely you don't believe in such things," Sam said with a chuckle.

Zahra glanced at him, her brows furrowing at his white knuckles as he gripped his beer bottle.

Mr. Durand smiled. "I've dedicated my life and resources to re-searching rare and powerful objects, Mr. Malone. I have found there's always some truth within the legends. The last time there was any record of the Atar'zul was during King Nebuchadnezzar's reign, until recently when rumors circulated the archaeological world with Dr. Neeman's work in Baghdad." He sipped his martini, his dark eyes pausing on Zahra. "I'm curious if you've heard from our missing archaeologist."

She was about to answer and shift the topic into safer territory when Mr. Rousseau said, "Besides Miss Jenkins receiving a package from Baghdad, we haven't heard anything from Dr. Neeman or Excavate International, which is odd."

Mr. Durand adjusted his glasses. "A package, you say?"

Zahra fisted her hand on her lap and forced a smile. "It was nothing. Just a correspondence from an old acquaintance."

Mr. Durand's focus drifted from Zahra to Mr. Rousseau, his eyes narrowed as if attempting to solve a puzzle. "You must have quite a few acquaintances in the Middle East."

"In our line of work"—she nodded to her boss and continued—"we know many people across the globe. Anyway," she said, with a slight wave of her hand. "The legend of the Atar'zul is fascinating. Based on research from scholars and archaeologists, the halo originally belonged to Lucifer but was cursed by the mixing of demonic and angelic blood, and then it was lost for centuries."

"Lucifer as in Satan? Like, the devil?" Jake asked, his gaze bouncing around the table as if waiting for the punchline to a joke.

Mr. Rousseau sipped from his wineglass. "Yes, the Prince of Pride himself."

"Actually, a few years ago a transcription of an ancient ritual was unearthed in Asia. Supposedly, Lucifer and Satan are two different princes. One is pride, but I'm not sure about the other one," Zahra said, a twinge of satisfaction coursing through her at the pursed expression from her boss.

"The Prince of Wrath," Sam said, staring into his beer bottle.

Zahra raised her brows. "How do you know that?"

He looked up and a muscle twitched in his jaw. He cleared his throat. "I've done a little research on this as well."

"Oh. Right, anyway, in this ritual supposedly Satan had his followers call him by a new name."

"Why?" Jake asked.

"He didn't like being confused with Lucifer," Mr. Durand said. When everyone stared at him, he added, "I actually own the original scroll with the ritual you mentioned."

Zahra leaned forward. "Really? I'd love to see it sometime."

Mr. Durand tipped his martini glass toward her. "I'd be happy to show you my collection."

Jake leaned back in his chair, a wrinkle forming between his brows. "You mentioned pride and wrath. Are we talking about the seven deadly sins?"

"The very ones," Mr. Rousseau said.

"So what's Satan's new name, then?" Gabriella asked.

Zahra didn't want to admit she was curious too, and was surprised Gabriella had stayed with the conversation as long as she had.

"According to the scrolls, his new name is Marach," Mr. Durand said, giving her a small smile.

The man definitely seemed to boast in his knowledge of historical artifacts. She couldn't blame him though, based on what she'd learned about his collection.

"Like I said, it's a fascinating tale if you believe in the spiritual realm, which I do not," Zahra said.

"With all the artifacts and history you've discovered, I'd think you'd believe more in the paranormal," Mr. Durand said.

"I'm a science girl. I need to see it, touch it, to believe in something," she said.

"I tend to lean more Zahra's way as well," Jake said. "There's just not enough evidence in my mind to warrant that belief." He looked at his boss. "No offense, of course."

"None taken," Mr. Durand said with a wave of his hand. "And how about you, Mr. Malone? What do you believe?"

Sam crossed his ankle over his knee and draped his arm on the back of Zahra's chair. Jake's eyes narrowed at the move. "Saint Augustine said, 'Faith is to believe what we do not see.'" Sam shrugged, even though his gaze resembled stone. "I happen to agree."

"Well, time will tell," Mr. Durand said, once more lifting his drink and taking one last sip. He took hold of Zahra's hand and kissed it. "You've been fascinating company this evening. Don't you agree, Jacob?" He slid a mischievous glance toward her ex, whose eyes widened briefly. "A woman with looks and brains. So refreshing."

"Umm, thank you, Mr. Durand," Zahra said.

"Mr. Malone, a pleasure," Mr. Durand said, and shook Sam's hand, quickly letting go and striding through the restaurant to the elevators.

Sam frowned at his hand. A ringing sounded from his pocket and he pulled his phone out.

"Wow, I didn't know they made flip phones anymore," Jake said, eyeing the archaic device.

"I miss the days of no cell phones." Mr. Rousseau buttoned his suit jacket. He clapped her on the shoulder. "Well done," he whispered, and followed Mr. Durand to the elevator.

"Let's go, Jacob," Gabriella said, holding out her hand.

Zahra arched her brow as Jake's shoulders stiffened.

"You go ahead. I'll meet up with you later," he said, the muscle in his jaw twitching. Gabriella lifted her chin and glared at Zahra then turned and marched toward the elevators. He addressed Sam. "Can you give me a moment with Zahra?"

Sam slid her a look and she gave a slight nod. "Sure. I need to make a call anyway."

She watched him walk past the bar to the windows, sensing Jake's gaze on her face.

"I'd love to catch up. Can I call you?" Jake asked, walking around the table toward her.

"What about your girlfriend?" She pointed to the obviously very ticked-off woman getting in the elevator with Mr. Durand and her boss.

"She's not my girlfriend."

"She certainly acts like your girlfriend."

"She works in Laurent's office here in Boston." Jake leaned closer, his eyes intense. "But the question you should be asking yourself is do I act like *her* boyfriend?"

She opened her mouth, then shut it. Unless his entire personality had changed in the last four years, then no, he didn't act like they were together. In fact, he had barely talked to her the entire evening. He hadn't even touched her, which was unlike him.

"Things are really busy at work and..." Her voice trailed off as he draped her sweater over her shoulders, his fingers gently brushing her collarbones. She couldn't help the tightening of her stomach at his familiar touch.

He turned her around and tucked a stray hair behind her ear. "I'm simply asking for coffee or a drink."

She bit her lip and glanced around the restaurant. Sam kept his back to her but his shoulders were tense. He shoved his phone in his pocket and walked toward her and Jake.

"Something's come up, and I need to run," Sam said.

"Oh, okay," she said. Based on his expression, whatever happened wasn't good. "Is everything all right?"

"Yes, just an important business matter I need to deal with." He looked at Jake. "Will you make sure she gets safely to her ride?"

"Sure." Jake crossed his arms and watched Sam stride past the tables, bypassing the elevator and opening the door to the stairs. "He's an interesting guy."

"That's a lot of stairs to run down," she said, eyeing the closing door.

Jake made a noncommittal sound and grabbed his suit jacket from the back of his chair. "My boss sure seems to like you. He couldn't stop talking about the gala and how true to history it was. I, of course, had no idea what he was talking about since I negotiate deals for a living."

She tucked a lock of hair behind her ear. "I'm glad he liked it. Anyway, you don't need to see me down. I can manage on my own."

"Well, I'm not taking the stairs like your friend, so you'll have to stomach riding in the elevator with me," Jake said with a smirk.

Zahra licked her lips and walked toward the elevator, stabbing the Down button harder than necessary. The thought of being in a cramped space with the man who seemed capable of breaking her resolve with a few smiles and friendly words—maybe she *should* take the stairs. She looked at her shoes and shook her head. After the success of the evening, she didn't want to trip and fall to her death.

The doors snicked shut and she put more space between them, quickly pulling out her phone and summoning her Uber.

Jake stood on the other side of the elevator, drumming his fingertips on his folded arms. "I'm not going to bite, Zahra."

"Don't you dare say, 'Unless you want me to,'" she said, feeling her cheeks burn.

"The thought had crossed my mind." One corner of his lip slipped into a smile. "I like that I still make you blush."

She refrained from fanning herself. "Don't flatter yourself. It's hot in here, that's all."

"Indeed it is." He laughed when she almost dropped her phone.

She inhaled a calming breath, wishing the elevator would speed up. Never had fifty floors taken this long. A shiver flitted across her skin, making her antsy.

"You haven't changed a bit," he said, breaking the awkward silence. "Back when we dated, I couldn't keep my eyes off you, and now...You really are stunning."

"Thank you." She dipped her chin, keeping her eyes fixed on her shoes, summoning the courage to finally apologize. "I've had this speech lodged in the back of my brain for years." She glanced up at him. "I'm sorry for how I ended things. I was..." She searched for the words but came up blank.

He moved across the small space and grabbed her hand. "You don't need to apologize. We were young and I..." He frowned and turned her hand over, noticing the ring he'd given her when he proposed. "You kept it," he whispered, lifting his eyes to hers.

The elevator dinged and she yanked her hand from his. When the doors opened, she almost fell on her face as she tumbled out. She quickly regained her composure and walked through the lobby, her heels clacking on the shiny surface. Jake caught up to her with his long strides, a question forming on his face as his eyes shifted again to the ring on her finger.

She needed to move the conversation in a safer direction. "Your not-girlfriend looks really pissed," she said, nodding toward the parked cars where Gabriella stood, her arms crossed and toe tapping.

"Nice dodge." He dipped his chin as if giving her a reprieve and then looked to where she was indicating. "Anyway, Gabriella always looks like that. RBF, I believe, is what my sister calls that look."

"How is Chloe?" Zahra had always liked Jake's older sister.

"She's good. She and Daniel still live in New Hampshire. They had a baby girl last year, which makes me a very proud uncle."

A smile lit up his face, and she had to catch her breath. His eyes were alive with the love he felt for his family. She could imagine him playing with his niece, pushing her on the swings.

Stop it, she scolded herself.

"Chloe always asks about you, by the way. She was thrilled when I said I was coming to Boston to—"

Zahra's phone dinged, alerting her to the Uber's arrival. "Yes. Well, have a great night," she said, only thinking of escape.

"I'm going to call you, Zahra. We need to talk."

She clicked her teeth and pointed at him. "Right," she said with more confidence than she felt. She couldn't slide into the backseat of the car quickly enough as the heat from his lingering stare ignited a flame she'd thought had burned out years ago.

CHAPTER NINE

KYDEN

Kyden took the steps two at a time and pushed through the door leading to the roof. He realized how strange it had been for him to use the stairs, sensing Zahra and Jake watching him, but Titus had told him to hurry. With a quick scan of the skies, he jumped off the ledge, free-falling into the night air. Wings erupted from his back, and a wave of power coursed through him as he shed his glamour.

The cool Boston air brushing against his face cleared his mind and his purpose. He'd hated leaving Zahra with Jake, especially after seeing the vulnerability in her eyes, but she seemed resilient and would be fine. He had a mission to finish, one that was getting more complicated by the minute.

Titus waited for him with his arms crossed, leaning against the brick wall of a two-story townhouse.

"What did you find?" Kyden asked after he landed. He walked alongside Titus to the front door.

"See for yourself," he said, leading the way.

Sulfur and blood immediately infiltrated his senses as he entered the living room. A trail of demon spawn floated through the room and into the kitchen. When he found Hayes, he refrained from muttering a few choice swear words. Hayes was bound to a chair, blood oozing from various places on his body, namely his face and hands. Fingers were missing. One of his eyes was brutally absent, and looking at the angle of his right leg, someone had shattered his kneecap.

Titus stood next to him. "I've already alerted the police. Based on the temperature of the body, he hasn't been like this for long. I must have just missed whoever did this."

"Why would demons torture him?" Kyden asked. Grunt demons couldn't physically hurt a human. Torment them emotionally and mentally, yes, but never take a life. A Fallen could influence someone with evil intent, like a daemonkin, or possess a person not sealed by Elohim's grace, then use them for their nefarious purposes. But the question still remained: Why Hayes?

"Maybe his gambling debts finally caught up with him?" Titus stepped closer to the mangled body and examined the killing wound—a slash across his neck.

"Let's look around before the cops arrive," Kyden said, leaving the kitchen and heading down the hall to the bedroom, removing his sword from his back. He didn't sense any demons, but better to be prepared.

Before the Celestial War, all angels wielded celestial swords, but when Apollyon's angels rebelled, their blades lost favor with Heaven, changing from celestial to demonic. Their weapons were still capable of injuring an angel, but they weren't as powerful as celestial steel.

Police sirens sounded, and Kyden sheathed his sword. So far, his search had turned up nothing of importance. He stopped at Hayes's office, where Titus was sifting through drawers. A laptop sat on the desk. Why wouldn't the demons take the computer if they wanted information badly enough to torture the man? Then again, they were evil and enjoyed abusing humans.

"Grab his computer. We're out of time," Kyden said.

They could have remained in the home when the police arrived, staying invisible in the spiritual realm, but just in case grunt demons returned, it was better for them to leave now. Kyden didn't want a Fallen alerted to the fact that angels had discovered the crime scene.

They both shot to the sky, landing on a nearby roof when a police car skidded to a stop in front of Hayes's home.

Titus's phone buzzed. He pulled it from his pocket and frowned at the screen. "Adinah found something and wants to go back to the dig site."

"Tell her to wait for me," Kyden said.

Titus raised his brows. "You're flying back to Iraq now?"

He tilted his head back and sighed. Angels needed little sleep, but he'd been awake for days, and flying over the Atlantic Ocean wasn't his idea of restful. However, if Adinah discovered something regarding Dr. Neeman or the missing halo, then sleeping would have to wait.

"Let me know what you find," he said, nodding to the laptop Titus had shoved into his bag. He rose to his feet and flared his wings. With a mighty thrust, he launched into the moonlit sky, leaving a crack in the concrete where he had previously stood.

Kyden touched down on the outskirts of Baghdad and shifted into his human form. Adinah sat in a rusted chair outside a dilapidated house, wearing black cargo pants, a ribbed tank top, and sunglasses, despite the sun barely emerging over the horizon. "That was fast. I hung up with Titus less than two hours ago."

Kyden's combat boots kicked up dust as he strode toward her. He twisted his head and cracked his neck. "You look comfortable."

"I was." She unfolded herself from the rickety chair, lifted her glasses, and rested them on the top of her head.

"Please tell me there's food in there," he said, walking past the poor display of outdoor furniture and up the wooden stairs. He held open the door that had seen better days.

"Of course. I picked up a few of your favorites, as I knew you'd be grumpy. What do they call that now? When someone is hungry and mad?"

"Hangry." Kyden followed Adinah into the old home. On the outside, the place looked like it was one stiff breeze from falling down. But the inside told a different story. The smell of coffee wafted from the stainless-steel kitchen where four chairs surrounded a sleek table covered in papers. Two leather couches filled the living room, and on the wall was a seventy-inch plasma television—one of Titus's newest finds. And even though angels required little sleep, there were two bedrooms in the back, both with king-size beds and their own bathrooms with showers that had four different nozzles.

As spiritual beings, angels didn't need human comforts, but after a battle or flying across the world, they had to recharge their power. Might as well do it in style.

Kyden took a bottle of water from the fridge and chugged it down before opening a box of donuts. He sighed and grabbed a chocolate glazed pastry while pouring himself a steaming cup of strong coffee.

"You're the best," he said, finishing the donut in two bites.

Adinah sat on a barstool and rested her arms on the gleaming counter. "I don't really understand why you like those so much. Of all the after-flight snacks, why donuts?"

He snagged a glazed one with sprinkles and waved it in front of her. "These are classic."

She rolled her eyes and grabbed a file folder. "While you were off playing Mr. Romantic, I researched Neeman's background."

"Mr. Romantic?"

"Titus told me about your fake date," she said, smirking.

Kyden scowled at her, reminding himself to punch Titus the next time he saw him.

Adinah continued, "There is of course all the normal stuff—graduated with a master's in archaeology, traveled the world with various companies, making a name for himself, until finally settling in the Middle East with Excavate International."

"We know all of this," he said, leaning against the counter and taking a sip of coffee.

She glanced up and frowned. "Eat another donut."

He arched a brow and then motioned for her to continue.

"I decided to go back farther, to his upbringing, that sort of thing. And guess what I found?" A smug smile spread across her face.

Besides Titus, Adinah was one of the best with computers and could find almost anything. She had been key in creating a system to track demon activity while also keeping tabs on the humans that were of interest. The only issue was if the angels had the skill to rework the system, then the demons did too. There were some Fallen who'd possessed certain people in the computer and cell phone industry and had access to the same information the angels had.

"Please, do tell," Kyden said.

"I found some obscure documentation from Neeman's family tree. It seems our famous archaeologist is also a descendant of the guardians of the Atar'zul."

He lowered the mug slowly. "Are you saying...?"

"Yep. He's a Vaelatori." She slid the paper with Neeman's lineage across the counter. "It's all in the report."

"I thought the line had died out during the Roman Empire."

"According to this, a young captive named Batya had found favor in King Nebuchadazzar's court, and somehow stole the halo and hid it. Batya married while in captivity and had children. The lore of the halo was never written down, not until later, when one of Batya's great-great-great-great—"

"I get it."

"So impatient," she mumbled. "Anyway, someone in the line documented the importance of the Atar'zul and the history of the Vaelatori in scrolls. Somehow, Neeman learned of his heritage, and my guess is he's spent his time in the Middle East searching for the scrolls and the halo."

"This changes things."

"Yes, it does. And now we know why the dig site was attacked by demons. Not only was a Fallen looking for the Atar'zul, but also Neeman's research."

Kyden remembered the details of Neeman's tent, recalling the overturned pot with burnt papers. "I have a feeling Neeman burned his research. He must have known someone was after him."

"And if he is a Vaelatori, then he'd have a talisman, right? He'd be able to see into the spiritual realm," Adinah said.

Vaelatori, the protectors in the line of Branok who guarded the Atar'zul, were given an angelic feather that morphed into a pendant, allowing them to see demons and angels. That way, if demons were following them, they would not be caught unaware, and could seek safety inside a church or other holy building.

"Yes. I wonder if he had an angel protecting him. And if so, where are they now?"

The corner of Adinah's mouth curved into a smirk. "You just need to make a phone call."

He gripped the mug and the handle cracked. The last angel he wanted to speak to was the leader of the Protectors. "I'll owe you one if you talk to him."

"You big baby."

Kyden placed his mug in the sink. He longed for a shower and a nap, but those creature comforts would have to wait. "Let's go."

Within seconds, Kyden and Adinah appeared at the dig site. They shifted from their angelic form into humans dressed in plain clothes, becoming visible to the natural world. The demon spawn that had covered the area before had dissipated, but a few grunts still lingered around the site.

Kyden strode down the hill and found the new team leader. It seemed Excavate International still had a job to complete despite missing their most valuable archaeologist.

A woman named Carol led them to the tent that had been Dr. Neeman's and sat behind a desk with her hands folded on top. "What can I help you with, Mr."—she glanced at the card he'd given her—"Walker?"

Kyden crossed his ankle over his knee and smiled, attempting to put the woman at ease. "Excavate International sent us to gather Dr. Neeman's research. It may contain information regarding his whereabouts."

Pebbles skittered outside the tent, and Kyden gave Adinah a nod. She pulled her phone from her pocket. "Excuse me, I need to take this."

Carol couldn't see or hear what happened next, but the sound of a sword sliding free from its scabbard accompanied by the scream of a demon filled Kyden's ears. Adinah would keep the nosy grunts away while he interviewed the archaeologist.

"It looks like you came a long way for nothing. I'm surprised corporate didn't let you know," Carol said.

"Let me know what?" he asked.

"Dr. Neeman's journal containing his research on the Atar'zul is missing too. There's a chance he took it with him when he left for the evening, but now that we haven't heard from him in days..." Carol bit her lip and shook her head. "I really hope he's okay."

Kyden squeezed his fists until his nails left marks in his palms. He had hoped he and Adinah had caught a break after discovering Neeman was a Vaelatori, that maybe his research would be waiting for them in his tent.

"Is there anything else you could tell me about the last week, anything unusual?" Kyden asked.

Carol tapped her chin, her focus on an ancient map hanging on the wall. "Two days before the dig site was attacked, Dr. Neeman had me mail a small package for him. He was acting odd."

"Odd in what way?"

"He seemed more jittery than normal. He was always happiest during a dig, but he kept glancing over his shoulder. Even started mumbling to himself."

"Really? And where did you mail the package?"

"To the Gallery of Time Museum in Boston. I remember that specifically, since he was supposed to attend an event there."

Kyden leaned forward. "Do you remember who it was sent to?"

"The label said Z. Jenkins. Why? Do you think the package has something to do with this?"

"I'm not sure." He recalled Zahra saying she received a package from an acquaintance in Baghdad. Why not say it was from Dr. Neeman? It seemed his charming museum curator was hiding something. "What was the size of the package?"

Carol demonstrated with her hands. "Not large at all. Probably the size of a jewelry box."

A few minutes later, he strode from the tent and shifted into his angelic form, meeting up with Adinah. Their steps cut through the vaporous fog of demon mist clinging to the ground.

"How many did you kill?" he asked.

"Eight. They were quite interested in your conversation."

"Good." Kyden waited until they crested the hill. "Where do you think Neeman might have gone?"

"If he needed to get out of the city fast without leaving a trail, then traveling by bus is probably the safest bet. Jerusalem is about an eleven-hour bus ride. Kuwait, seven."

He glanced skyward. "Call Oz and see if there's an increase in demon activity in Jerusalem and send him a picture of Dr. Neeman. My guess is Neeman went to Kuwait—shorter bus ride."

"Agreed."

Their wings materialized on their backs and bronze armor formed along their chests and legs, along with their golden halos resting on their foreheads. With a mighty flap, Kyden and Adinah shot into the air and headed south toward Kuwait.

They flew toward the bus station but veered when dark smoke curled from a line of buildings on the outskirts of the city.

They landed a few blocks from a fire-engulfed home. Kyden rested his hands on his knees and inhaled deep breaths.

"You okay?" Adinah asked.

"Yeah—just burned a lot of energy flying over the Atlantic. Could've used a bit more time to regenerate my power." He took one last deep inhale and stood to his full height. "Are you familiar with this area?"

Adinah nodded. "If memory serves, there's a Christian safe house around here."

"Dr. Neeman might have gone there for protection," Kyden said.

He followed Adinah's lead, frowning as they neared the home where flames and green mist swirled. People loitered in the streets, soot dusting their faces as they looked on.

A buzzing came from Kyden's pocket. A familiar voice said, "Watch your back."

Kyden frowned at the phone as the line went dead.

"Who was that?" Adinah asked.

"My snitch. The one that got me on this case in the first place. He said to watch our backs." Kyden glanced over his shoulder but didn't see any demons.

Adinah raised her brows. "How would he know that?"

"He has connections to some unscrupulous organizations in the Middle East. So far, he hasn't led me wrong."

Sirens sounded in the distance as they walked toward the destroyed home, standing just outside a group of people.

"Did the family get out?" one onlooker asked.

Another nodded. "Yes, they were unharmed. It doesn't look like anyone was in there when it started to burn."

Kyden turned from the flames and scanned the area. Demons were nearby; he could sense them now. "Split up."

Adinah dipped her chin and strode in the opposite direction, heading for a side street. Kyden drew his sword, thinking about the call he had received from Shane. Demons had obviously started that fire based on the green mist surrounding the safe house, a home he'd wager had been Dr. Neeman's destination. Did his snitch have some connection with the supernatural realm, and if so, how? He'd have to think about it later as a chill crept along his skin.

A Fallen was nearby.

A gunshot sounded, and Kyden took off at a sprint toward an alley. He rounded the corner and froze.

Dusty hiking boots stuck out behind a crate and blood spattered the wall. A man stood still, his back toward Kyden, holding a gun. He slowly lifted it, aiming the weapon at his head.

"Stop!" Kyden said.

The man twitched and slowly turned. His eyes were solid black, torment twisting his face. The gun was still pressed to his temple. His head tilted and lips curled into a malevolent grin. The Fallen possessing this man was going to end his life.

"You are unwelcome here," a deep, gravelly voice said.

"Leave your host and fight me, you filthy coward."

The man's eyes narrowed, his finger moving to the trigger.

Kyden had a split second to decide his next course of action. He raised his palm and a blast of Divine Light hit the man square in the chest.

A scream sounded from two different sources as the holy light forced the Fallen out of his human host. The man's body fell to the ground, unconscious but alive.

The demon folded over, scorched nubs of bone protruding from his back where his wings used to be. His skin no longer held an angelic glow but was sallow and drawn, as if he couldn't absorb sunlight and was constantly malnourished. Although the Fallen were more human-looking than the demon grunts, they'd lost the beauty and grace of the faithful angels who remained loyal to Elohim and Heaven.

The Fallen swore and stood, facing Kyden.

"Raghav," Kyden said through gritted teeth. The scar on his arm burned from where Raghav had cut him during their last confrontation. But what was the demon doing here? His master was Marach, the Prince of Wrath, who resided near Russia.

He glared at Raghav as he edged toward the toppled crates, fearing the worst.

"You're too late," the demon said.

Dr. Neeman lay on the ground with a single bullet hole in the middle of his forehead. Kyden closed his eyes, the suffocating sense of failure returning once more.

A laugh sounded from behind him. Keeping one eye fixed on Raghav, he recognized Darsh, a female Fallen, emerging from the other side of the street. Her lips curled back, revealing pointed teeth, and her sickly green eyes brightened. Her smile melted as Adinah landed across from Kyden, the ground cracking under her feet.

"You're a long way from home," Adinah said to Darsh, twirling her sword.

Darsh tightened her grip on her axe. "Russia's weather is miserable this time of year." Her presence brought even more questions to this case, and now with Dr. Neeman dead, finding answers was going to be almost impossible.

Kyden and Adinah stood back-to-back, swords ready. Fallen wouldn't betray a prince of hell, which made Kyden smile. He didn't need to leave them alive for questioning. But killing a Fallen was as difficult as killing an angel. Removing their head was the only way to guarantee the ultimate death, which is why both angels and Fallen wore protective armor around their necks.

With a mighty flap of his wings, Kyden shot toward Raghav, swinging his sword. The demon blocked, then spun out of the way. Blades crashing together sounded behind him as Adinah engaged Darsh. He needed to trust Adinah could handle herself, as fighting Raghav would take all his concentration, especially since using the Divine Light had drained some of his power.

Raghav parried and lunged the other way. Sparks flew as the demonic blade grazed Kyden's chest piece. Kyden stabbed, slicing through the demon's leather pants. Black blood bubbled to the surface and Raghav hissed.

The demon used the narrow alleyway, running along its side, trying to maneuver behind Kyden. With a flap of his wings, he spun, his right wing blocking the strike.

Kyden resumed his attack, feinting to the left with his sword while grabbing his dagger. Raghav lunged forward, and Kyden twisted, sinking his weapon into Raghav's shoulder. The demon growled and backed away, holding his wounded arm.

"I remember you being stronger," Kyden said, provoking the demon. "Faster too."

"I remember you being smarter," Raghav said, and raised his fist. The sound of claws scraped the cement, followed by screeches echoing along the alleyways surrounding them.

Kyden shifted his gaze to see at least fifteen grunts charging from the other end of the alley. "Always hiding behind your minions."

"You'll soon be answering to me, seraph." With a mock salute, Raghav called power from the depths of the Abyss and smoke and shadow enveloped him. Cutting through the haze, the grunts attacked.

The fight with the lesser demons only took minutes. Kyden returned his sword to the scabbard on his back and strode through the green mist toward Adinah. Black blood bubbled on the ground at her feet.

Adinah winced as she wiped her forehead. Gold blood dripped down her forearm, disappearing behind her gauntlets.

"You all right?" Kyden asked.

She nodded. "I left a mortal wound. Not sure how long before she regenerates."

"Good work." He moved back to where Dr. Neeman lay in a pool of blood.

Adinah knelt next to him and pulled the collar of his shirt back. "His talisman is missing."

He thought back to what Carol had said earlier about mailing a package to Zahra, which was the size of a jewelry box. He growled his frustration. "Zahra has the talisman. I'd bet my wings on it."

"Why would Neeman send it to her?" Adinah asked as she searched the dead archaeologist's pockets, removing a slip of paper. She handed it to him.

It was a receipt from a post office in Baghdad. Whatever Neeman had mailed, he'd done it a week before the gala.

"Would he have mailed the halo to her as well?"

He paced along the alleyway. "I don't think so. According to her coworker, he was in contact with Neeman and awaiting the Atar'zul."

"And where is this coworker?"

"Dead." He rested his hands on his hips. This couldn't be a coincidence. Plus, in his line of work, he didn't believe in coincidences. Brandon Hayes had been tortured to death and now Dr. Neeman murdered in an alleyway. The connection was the halo. The only thing that didn't make sense was why Zahra Jenkins had received a package from the archaeologist.

"What are you going to do now?" Adinah asked.

"Looks like I need to have another date with Miss Jenkins." Dust and smoke swirled as Kyden shot into the air, using his anger and frustration to propel him across the ocean and back to Boston.

Chapter Ten

Zahra

Yellow tape blocked the entrance to Brandon's office when Zahra arrived at work Wednesday morning. Mr. Rousseau and Meredith lingered in the hallway whispering while a woman and a man searched the office.

"What's going on?" Zahra asked, adjusting her grip on her laptop bag.

Mr. Rousseau stepped away from her assistant. "Mr. Hayes was found dead in his apartment."

Zahra pressed a hand against her chest, trying to process what her boss had just revealed. "Dead? But...how? Why?"

"They suspect foul play and will ask the entire staff questions once they're finished searching his office."

"And who are 'they'?"

"Detectives." Mr. Rousseau tucked his hands into his pant pockets and glanced over his shoulder to Brandon's office. A male detective rifled through the open drawers while a woman dressed in dark jeans and a blazer scanned the bookcases. She turned and caught Zahra watching.

"I'm Detective Reyna Flores," the woman said, ducking under the tape. "And that's my partner, Detective Graham Coleman. Is there a place we could talk in private?"

"We have a conference room down the hall," Mr. Rousseau said. "Miss Jenkins, please escort the detectives while I meet with the museum director."

"Sure," Zahra said, her mouth as dry as the desert. She led the detectives to the conference room and sat in one of the black leather chairs surrounding a rectangular table. A chill ran down her spine, and she wrapped her arms around herself. "I can't believe he's dead." The thought looping through her mind had finally escaped her lips.

"How well did you know Mr. Hayes?" Detective Coleman asked. His blue eyes, framed by glasses, stared at her as if trying to unearth some hidden treasure. He leaned against the wall with his arms crossed, his muscles straining against the fabric of his tan button-down shirt.

"Well enough. We worked together on the Babylon exhibit."

"Oh right. That big gala the other night. The chief of police went, said it was quite the *to do*. His words, not mine," said Detective Flores. She sat across from Zahra and rested her hands on the table.

"Yes, I saw him but didn't get a chance to speak with him."

"Did your relationship with Mr. Hayes escalate into something more?" Coleman asked.

Zahra uncrossed her arms. "Why would you ask that?"

Coleman arched a brow. "We checked out his social media—found a picture of you two together at some event. You two seemed more than coworkers."

She was hoping this line of questioning wouldn't surface, but knew better than to expect good luck. She'd been able to keep her and Brandon's affair quiet, but it looked like that secret was about to see the light of day.

"There was one night last year when things escalated beyond friendship, but it's been platonic ever since."

"Bad breakup?" Flores asked.

She tilted her head. "Am I a suspect?"

Detective Flores raised her hands. "No one at the museum is a suspect, at this time." She added the last part as if someone could eventually end up on their list of offenders. "We need to be thorough in our investigation. I'm sure you can understand that."

Zahra tucked a piece of hair behind her ear. "Of course. This is all just..." She licked her lips and shook her head. Alarming, scary, surreal—none of the words she could formulate seemed to encompass what she was feeling.

"Did Mr. Hayes have any enemies?" Detective Flores asked.

Zahra shook her head. "Not that I'm aware of."

"Mr. Hayes had a gambling problem. Did you know that?" Detective Coleman asked, his gaze hard.

Flores glanced over her shoulder and rolled her eyes. "Don't mind his grumpiness. He hasn't had enough coffee this morning."

Detective Coleman huffed and crossed his arms.

"We have some in the break room, if you'd like a cup," Zahra said.

The corner of the man's lip lifted. "I'll take you up on it." He raised his hand as Zahra rose to her feet. "I'm sure I can find it."

The door clicked shut and an uncomfortable silence filled the room. Detective Flores looked around, her gaze stopping at various art pieces along the wall. Finally, Detective Coleman returned with Mr. Rousseau and Meredith on his heels.

Flores took out her notebook while everyone sat at the table. "When was the last time you saw Mr. Hayes?"

Zahra and her boss both answered Saturday night at the gala, but Meredith, whose face had drained of color, bit her lip.

"Miss Shaw?" Flores asked as she scrutinized Zahra's assistant.

"Sunday morning," Meredith whispered.

Detective Coleman arched a brow. "And where was this?"

"At his home." She hung her head while sneaking glances at her and Mr. Rousseau. His pursed lips displayed exactly what Zahra was feeling.

Her assistant had slept with the man who tried to sabotage her career. Zahra's nails dug into her palms, hoping the pain would silence her before accusatory words flew from her mouth.

"And how long have you two been in a relationship?" Detective Flores asked.

Tears formed in Meredith's eyes. "We weren't in one. It was just that one night. We were both in a festive mood, and one thing led to another."

"And what exactly were you celebrating?" Coleman asked, resting his arms on the table.

"The success of the event and..." She winced when she looked at Zahra, who leaned back and crossed her arms.

"And what?" Flores prompted.

"Brandon had bragged about securing a sizable donation from Mr. Durand—one of our largest donors," she clarified as Detective Flores wrote his name in her notebook.

"Backstabbing son of a bitch," Zahra whispered, and then pressed her lips together, realizing she'd said the words out loud.

Detective Flores glanced around the table. "There seems to be some tension here regarding Mr. Hayes. Care to elaborate?"

Her boss tugged at his collar. "Mr. Hayes and Miss Jenkins were both in line for a promotion. Mr. Hayes decided to play dirty."

"You think?" Zahra asked.

Mr. Rousseau shot a glance at the ceiling as if searching for patience.

"How did Mr. Hayes play dirty?" Detective Coleman asked.

"By intentionally removing my name from the program as project coordinator, therefore putting him in a position to gain favor with our regular donors. It was *my* work, *my* knowledge, and *my* connections that made the exhibit successful, and he took credit for it. And then slept with *my* assistant," Zahra said, choosing to ignore Meredith's muffled sobs.

The detectives glanced at one another. Zahra squinted at the notes Detective Flores wrote in her notebook.

Great, she thought. Now she definitely looked like a suspect.

Mr. Rousseau cleared his throat. "Can you tell us when Mr. Hayes died?"

Detective Flores flipped a few pages. "Time of death was Monday evening."

"Where were you, Miss Jenkins, during that time period?" Detective Coleman asked.

Zahra's eyes widened, and unease coiled in her gut.

"Now wait a minute," Mr. Rousseau said, lifting a hand. "Are you implying Miss Jenkins had something to do with this?"

"I'm not implying anything, just asking a question. And I'll ask the same of all of you." Coleman took a sip of his coffee, and Zahra hoped he burned his throat.

Mr. Rousseau rested his arms on the table and glared at Detective Coleman. Zahra had been on the receiving end of that stare only once and did not envy the man, even if he was acting like a brutish jackass. "Zahra and I were at dinner at The Indulgence with Mr. Durand. I'm sure you can call his assistant to corroborate."

Detective Flores raised her brows. "That's quite a swanky place. Or so I've heard."

"And what about you?" Detective Coleman asked Meredith.

"I worked all day Monday and then went home." Meredith swiped at a wayward tear rolling down her cheek.

Coleman narrowed his eyes and jotted down something in his notebook.

"How did he die?" Zahra asked.

Detective Flores arched her brow and glanced at her partner, who shrugged as if to say *why not*. "Someone tortured him to death."

The museum closed early and the employees were sent home due to the news of Brandon's death and the ensuing investigation. Meredith had tried repeatedly to talk to Zahra, but she didn't have the margin nor the control over her emotions to appease her assistant's guilt. *Former* assistant, if she had any say.

Zahra was unlocking her car when her cell phone rang. She didn't recognize the number and thought maybe it was Sam. The day before, she had found the business card he'd given her with his number. She had left a message, but so far she hadn't heard back.

"Hello," she said, her tone higher than she intended. So much for playing it cool, she thought.

"Zahra? Oh good, you kept your old number. I took a chance." She gripped the phone, stunned into silence. "It's Jake, by the way."

"Oh, hi," she said, finally finding her voice. She leaned against the car as a chilled breeze blew in from the ocean, heavy with the scent of brine.

"Wow, don't sound so excited."

She could picture the corner of Jake's lip hitching up in a half smile. "Sorry, it's been a bad day." She winced. A man was dead and *her* day was bad? Something was very wrong with her.

"I was hoping we could meet for that drink," Jake said.

What Zahra really wanted was to collapse on her couch with comfy sweats, a bottle of wine, and a good book. Alexis was at a conference and wouldn't return until the following day, and being in the apartment by herself after hearing of Brandon's torture made her skin crawl.

"You there?" Jake's voice drifted through the phone.

"Yes, sorry." She pinched the bridge of her nose. She didn't want to be alone and thought about going to the shooting range, but it was too far away, plus her mindset wasn't ideal for handling a deadly weapon. Visiting her mom would only depress her, especially with the news of her dad missing. "Sure," she finally said. "But just one drink."

They made plans to meet at the Wayward Tavern—a local bar close to her apartment and one she and Alexis frequented often during happy hour on Fridays. Wayward was famous for its margaritas, which she desperately needed.

Thirty minutes later, Zahra arrived at the bar chastising herself. "This is a bad idea," she said for the hundredth time as she locked her car and walked to the entrance. Maybe if Jake was running late, she could bail on their date. *No, not a date*, she thought—simply old friends catching up.

The sound of rock ballads filled her ears along with clinking glasses and laughter. A waitress sauntered past with a heaping plate of nachos, making Zahra's mouth water. She hadn't had much of an appetite with the news of Brandon and had survived on lollipops and caffeine all day—not a healthy combination.

Her heart skipped a beat when Jake waved from a booth in the corner. A very secluded booth. He rose to his feet and her breath caught. The man could wear the hell out of a pair of jeans, and his forest-green henley stretched across muscles he definitely didn't have in college.

"Just friends catching up," she mumbled as she wove through the crowded tables. When she arrived at the table, a frozen margarita, salt clinging to the rim of the glass, waited for her.

"I thought I'd order for you. I remembered bad days usually equaled tequila," he said, sitting after she slid into the booth.

"Thank you." The beats her heart skipped earlier seemed to return, launching into a pulsating rhythm. She'd forgotten Jake's uncanny ability to sense what she needed, sometimes before she even knew. She sipped the tangy drink, licking the salt off her lips, and sighed. "Just what the doctor ordered."

Jake's gray eyes darkened as his gaze drifted to her mouth. He lifted his bottle of beer and took a long pull.

They talked for a while—safe, mundane topics, and with each sip of her margarita, her tongue loosened. Without any food in her stomach, the buzz hit fast.

"You've let your hair grow," she said, tightening her hand into a fist and restraining herself from touching strands that reminded her of molten chocolate. If she ran her fingers through it, it would be as silky as she remembered.

The corner of his lips quirked. "You like it?"

She shrugged. "It's okay."

He chuckled and scanned the bar. "You hungry? I saw you drooling over the nachos when you came in."

"Aren't you the observant one? But yes, I'm starving. All I've had today are lollipops and coffee."

He shook his head and signaled the server, surprising her when he ordered a large plate of nachos. Jake had always been a bit of a health nut and hadn't approved of her smoking or eating choices. After he placed the order, he said, "You quit smoking, I assume."

"How did you know?"

"The lollipops. Replace one habit with another."

She finished her drink. "Yeah, I might need to get another bad habit, as my teeth aren't appreciating the amount of sugar."

He laughed and the sound sent electric shocks to her stomach. She loved his laugh, and even more, loved making him laugh. When they had first met, he didn't smile, let alone laugh. By the end of their four years together, his countenance had changed. Unfortunately, once she ended their relationship, the laughter in her life had disappeared, especially with her mom's declining health. Thankfully, she'd met Alexis and had found herself smiling more and enjoying life again.

"Hey, what's wrong?" he asked, leaning forward, taking her hand and interlocking their fingers.

She forced a smile, unwilling to reveal the thoughts bouncing around in her head like a pinball machine. "My coworker, Brandon Hayes—I believe you met him at the gala." Jake nodded and she continued, "He was found dead in his apartment. Although the museum staff aren't suspects, I have a feeling that might change." And her fear was she would be at the top of that list.

"Dead? That's awful. I'm so sorry." He released her hand when the waitress brought another round of drinks. "But why would you be a suspect?"

"I sort of lost my temper during the investigation and mentioned how Brandon had intentionally removed my name from the program."

A wrinkle formed between his brows. "What an ass."

"My thoughts exactly, although I feel wretched thinking poorly of the dead. No matter what a sleazeball he was, I'd never wanted him hurt."

The nachos came, and to Zahra's relief, they ate in silence, despite a few groans of pleasure escaping her lips. Jake had almost choked at the first moan she'd let slip. When she made the fourth indecent sound—on purpose—he placed his beer heavily on the table.

"Zahra, I really need you to stop making those noises."

She smiled, enjoying the lightness of her head and the food in her belly. "Whatever do you mean?"

He practically growled at her. "You know exactly what I mean. The last time I heard those sounds, I was inside of you, and unless you want me to take advantage of the tequila replacing the blood in your veins, then I need you to stop."

Heat coiled through her core at his words. The idea of escaping into his touch, his arms around her, his naked body pressed to hers, had her waving to the waitress for another drink. "These nachos definitely rank up there with sex, possibly even top it."

Jake leaned back in the booth, his eyes resembling granite. "Then you haven't had good sex in a long time."

"And I suppose you have," she said, and immediately wanted to recall her statement. "Never mind. Do not elaborate."

The smirk on his face developed into a furrowed brow. He tapped a finger on the table as his gaze darted across her face. "Why did you keep the ring?"

The tortilla chip covered in gooey cheese froze halfway to her mouth. She lowered it slowly and glanced around the bar, trying to avoid his intense stare.

"Zahra, why?"

She huffed out a breath. "It's pretty. And you know lapis is my favorite stone. It practically goes with my entire wardrobe, so naturally I kept it." She winced as the vomit of babbling words exited her mouth. He arched a brow and the corner of his lips quirked, causing her to assume her rambling hadn't convinced him in the slightest.

She tore her napkin to pieces, making a mess on the table. "You were the first man I ever loved, okay."

He tilted his head. "And what about now?"

"Now?"

He leaned forward, and the muscle in his jaw pulsed. "Are you involved with someone?"

"Why do you want to know?"

"Let's just say I'm trying to figure some things out and the answer to this question is important."

She shook her head; the breath lodged in her chest. "No," she finally said. She stood and rested a hand on the table, waiting for her wobbly legs to stop shaking. He reached forward, but dropped his hand when she waved him off. "Need to pee."

His eyes bored into her back as she carefully made her way to the bathroom. She needed space from Jake, and some cold water on her face since her blood was boiling. It was the margaritas—how many *had* she consumed?—that were making it hard to breathe. Why was he so interested in the ring he'd given her? Why did he care if she was with someone else, and what was he trying to figure out? Surely he resented her for what she'd done to him, and to herself.

She cupped her hands, letting the cool water fill them, and patted her cheeks and the back of her neck. Once her heart rate settled, she stepped out of the bathroom, stopping short as she nearly ran into Jake leaning against the wall.

"What are you doing here?" she asked, taking a small step back. She recognized the look in his eyes, a look of hunger as if he were a lion and she was his next meal.

"Making sure you're okay. You seemed a little unsteady." He closed the distance between them, backing her into the wall. He rested his hand beside her head. "*Are* you okay?"

She licked her lips and nodded.

His Adam's apple bobbed as he tracked the movement. "Seeing you again, talking with you—I've really missed you."

She squeezed her thighs together. "This is a bad idea," she whispered, needing to walk away, but her feet weren't responding to the signals from her brain.

"Is it?" Jake leaned closer, and the smell of his cologne made desire ignite in her core.

She grabbed his shirt and pulled him toward her, closing the distance, craving the feel of his mouth on hers and casting her doubts aside. He groaned and pressed his hips against hers while deepening the kiss.

Memories crashed through her as their tongues participated in a dance they had both memorized. The first time he'd kissed her, the first time they'd made love, the crushing weight on her heart when she walked away from him, rain mixing with her tears.

"No," she gasped, and pushed him back, logic finally overcoming her desire. "I can't do this."

He removed his hands from her and placed them on the wall, lowering his head. The pulse throbbing on his neck beat in time with hers. "Just like I remember..." His voice was hoarse, and he lifted his gaze to hers.

"I have to go." She ducked under his arm and walked out of the hallway. The noise from the bar assaulted her, turning her buzz into a screaming headache.

"Zee, wait."

She shook her head, stumbling at the nickname he had given her, and yanked the door open, relishing the chilly night air brushing across her heated cheeks. Thankfully, she was close to her apartment since she was in no shape to drive.

Jake grabbed her arm. "Wait, please."

She spun to face him. "No, Jake. That was a mistake. You can't waltz back into my life and turn everything upside down."

"That's not what I'm trying to do." His jaw clenched as his grip tightened when she tried to break free.

"Oh really? And when do you leave for Vegas?"

He frowned and released her arm. "I'm not..."

She cut him off before he could finish whatever he'd been about to say. "You have your life and I have mine. There's no reason to dig up the past again." Tears filled her eyes, but she wouldn't let them fall, not in front of him. She focused on her shoes. "After what I did, why would you even want me?" Not waiting to hear his answer, she turned from the shock widening his eyes, the hurt flashing across his face, and walked down the empty sidewalk.

Keep it together. Keep it together, until you get to the corner. She didn't look back as she hurried to the end of the block, and when she turned down her street, a sob finally broke free.

Chapter Eleven

Kyden

Kyden leaned against the lamppost across from Zahra's apartment, tapping a bouquet of flowers against his thigh while waiting for her to return home. After discovering Dr. Neeman had mailed a package to her, the fight against Raghav, and finding the archaeologist dead, he'd flown back to Boston and fell into a deep sleep for a day and a half. He needed a lot more than donuts and coffee to restore his power.

He wasn't sure how Zahra fit into this mess, but he was positive she was keeping secrets. He wanted Titus to conduct a more extensive background check on her because something wasn't adding up. Unfortunately, Titus was helping another Slayer across the country and wouldn't return until tonight.

Kyden had noticed she had called him while he was gone. He'd texted her, asking if they could meet up, and then passed out. When he finally woke up Friday morning, he found a message from her saying she was available that night.

Before meeting her, he did a little digging on his own. The museum offices were closed despite the building remaining open to the public, which created the perfect opportunity to snoop. He stayed within the spiritual realm, slipping through walls and doors until he finally located Zahra's office.

Down the hall he noticed yellow police tape across a closed door, which he assumed was Hayes's office. Titus hadn't briefed him on what he'd found on the man's laptop, but he was fairly certain Raghav had orchestrated Hayes's and Dr. Neeman's deaths.

Kyden walked around Zahra's office, a small smile forming at her eclectic decorating scheme. The desk was clear of clutter, but the rest of the room was organized chaos. Of what he knew of the assistant curator, the mess seemed to fit her personality.

He sat in her chair and opened the drawers, quickly rifling through papers and odd knickknacks. There was no sign of a package, but he discovered an industrial-size bag of lollipops lying in the bottom drawer, practically empty. *How many does that woman consume a day?* He rummaged through more drawers until he found a balled-up piece of paper. He opened it and frowned.

I'm sorry. For everything.
Love, Dad.

He thought back to the information Titus had discovered about Zahra. Obviously, she had a father, but based on what they had learned, there had been little interaction through the years.

More questions without any answers.

And so now he leaned against a lamppost with flowers, waiting for her to arrive home. He glanced at his watch. He hated waiting.

He remained in the spiritual realm, monitoring the demon activity on the streets of Boston. For a Friday night, things were pretty calm. Only a few grunts lurked in the alleys, clinging to unsuspecting humans.

A young woman passed by, tears streaming down her face, while a demon lumbered beside her, whispering in her ear.

"You're worthless. No one could ever love you," the demon said in its gravelly voice, causing the woman to choke down a sob. "Ending your life is the only way to experience peace." The demon trailed its black nails along her wrist in a seductive suggestion.

Not on my watch, he thought. He dropped the flowers, his sword appearing in his hand as he materialized in front of the demon and blocked its path. The grunt narrowed its gaze and released the woman. A shuddering breath left her lips.

"You'll torment her no more," Kyden said.

"She will soon be Apollyon's. There's nothing you can do now." The demon smiled, revealing sharp yellow teeth.

The woman walked slowly by, and Kyden reached out, gently touching her shoulder. She shivered and glanced around her. The peace and grace flowing through him slid out from his fingers and encompassed her in an encouraging embrace.

Movement out of the corner of his eye had him dodging. Air brushed his face as the demon's axe sailed past his head.

"You're either very brave or very stupid." Kyden set his feet and raised his sword, the silver blade reflecting the light from the streetlights. "I'm going with stupid."

The grunt screamed and charged. Kyden parried, blocking the demon's strike. He pivoted and turned, slashing the demon through its spine. The grunt dropped to its knees. With another mighty swing, the demon's head fell to the ground. In seconds, the body ignited, leaving behind a cloud of green mist and the smell of sulfur.

Kyden sheathed his blade and jogged after the woman. She had stopped crying but her shoulders remained hunched. He pulled out his phone and sent a quick text, then walked by her side, speaking encouraging words.

Within minutes, a Protector Angel appeared.

"Kyden. Good to see you again," Reya said with a dip of her chin.

"You too." He then pointed to the woman. "She's defeated, and I worry for her safety."

The angel looked over her shoulder at the woman rounding a corner. "I'll make sure she's taken care of."

"Thank you," he said, and watched Reya shift into a human female and follow the woman.

The sound of a car door closing caused him to turn. Zahra locked the door and jogged up the steps to her apartment. He returned to the lamppost where the bouquet lay on the sidewalk. Thankfully, they hadn't been crushed.

Remaining in the spiritual realm, he walked through the doors and up a flight of stairs. He waited a few minutes before heading down the hallway to Zahra's apartment. He quickly checked his appearance before knocking on the door. His Guns N' Roses T-shirt was a little wrinkled, but at least demon blood hadn't stained his clothes.

"Coming," Zahra said from inside, making him shake his head. Nothing like letting someone know she was home.

He waved through the peephole. "Hi." He raised the flowers when she opened the door.

She leaned against the doorframe and folded her arms. "Hi."

He lowered his arm. "Apology flowers for leaving you with your ex. There was an emergency."

"Is everything okay?"

"For the most part, yes. I'd love to buy you a drink to apologize." He offered the bouquet again and smiled.

She narrowed her eyes and then took the flowers, bringing them to her nose. "I just opened a bottle of wine. How about you apologize in my kitchen instead?" She pushed away from the doorframe and walked inside. Her apartment was small but decorated with an eclectic mix of furniture and art.

She wore jeans and a T-shirt, and her bare feet padded against the tile floor. He glanced at his boots and winced at the dirt and who knew what else covering them. He quickly untied the laces and left the boots near the door.

Zahra pulled out another wineglass. She stood on her tiptoes and reached for the top shelf for a vase.

"Here, let me," Kyden said.

Her gaze drifted from his arms down to his black socks. "How tall *are* you?"

"Six-five. Why?" He grabbed the vase and handed it to her.

"Just wondering." After putting the flowers in water and pouring him a glass of wine, she pointed to the couch in the living room, where another vase overflowed with daisies.

He glanced at his assorted bouquet and then at the much larger one and shrugged. "Looks like I'm not the only one giving you flowers."

She curled her legs under her and took a sip of wine. "Yeah, those are apology flowers from Jake. I guess that's the thing these days."

"Pretty sure that's a man's go-to when trying to make amends."

She huffed out a breath and took another drink from her wine. Dark circles lined the skin under her eyes.

He had contemplated remaining in the spiritual realm to search for the package, but he also needed answers. His plan of demanding those answers dissolved when he noticed the fatigue and sadness etched along her face. He inwardly shook his head. When had he become so soft?

"Are you all right?" he asked.

"It's been a rough week, in all honesty."

He set his glass on the table. "Want to talk about it?"

"My coworker was found dead in his home, which is why he didn't show up for dinner at The Indulgence. The police searched his office at the museum and asked us some questions."

"Do they have any suspects?" He already knew they didn't because Titus had hacked into Detective Flores's computer.

"Well, I was on their list, but thankfully I had an alibi. They think his murder might have to do with a gambling debt."

"Hmm," Kyden said, stroking his lip. Zahra's eyes tracked the movement and her cheeks blushed. He quickly lowered his hand. "I can see why that would be stressful."

"Yeah, and my mom isn't doing well, and I feel guilty for not being able to take care of her. And then Jake..." She waved a hand and drained her glass. "You don't want to hear all of this."

"I'm happy to be a sounding board. It's the least I can do after leaving you with him. I hope that wasn't too awkward for you."

She bit her lip and looked as if she wanted to say something but then seemed to change her mind. "I still haven't received the Atar'zul."

He frowned. "What?"

She tilted her head. "Remember, you pretend to be my date, and I let you know when I get it?"

"Oh right. Sorry, long week for me too." Kyden inwardly grimaced at his mistake, obviously not fully recuperated from his flight across the Atlantic. "So you haven't received anything from the dig site in Baghdad?" He needed to press her, plus he wanted to see how proficient of a liar she was.

"No. And Dr. Neeman is still missing. The company he works for filed a missing person report. I haven't heard anything yet." She absent-mindedly chewed on the side of her thumb while her eyes focused on the floor, tension flowing off her like ripples on a pond.

Kyden was about to tell her about the dead archaeologist when her phone rang. She frowned at the number and said, "Will you excuse me for a moment?"

"No problem. Could I use your restroom?"

She pointed toward the bedrooms and answered the call, walking onto the balcony and shutting the door behind her.

He quickly strode down the hall and disappeared, passing the bathroom and picking the bedroom on the east side of the apartment. Time was not in his favor; he was thankful he'd scoped the place out earlier.

Using his enhanced hearing, he kept tabs on Zahra's conversation with someone at the nursing home as he rummaged through her dresser drawers. After finding nothing of interest, he moved to the nightstand.

"Bingo." Inside was a package the size of a jewelry box with the return address from Baghdad. He opened it and found a velvet bag. His stomach clenched as magic pulsed across his fingertips. Tucked inside the bag was a silver feather twisted in a spiral about two inches long—the talisman of a Vaelatori, a guardian of the Atar'zul.

Why had Dr. Neeman sent the talisman to Zahra? A thought entered his head, and he quickly typed a message to Titus.

To keep her safe, he removed the necklace and slipped it into his pocket. The pendant would get her captured and most likely killed if a Fallen discovered she had it. He returned the box and the velvet pouch back into the drawer.

The door to the patio opened, and he used his supernatural speed to sneak into the bathroom. He flushed the toilet and washed his hands.

Zahra stood in the kitchen, pouring another glass of wine.

"Everything okay?" Kyden asked.

"It's my mom. They had to sedate her again."

"I'm so sorry."

She shrugged. "You said you were out of the country? What exactly do you do?"

"I invest in different companies. It's really quite boring."

She sipped her wine as her gaze traveled across his T-shirt. Thankfully, his phone beeped, saving him from lying to her any further. He pulled it from his pocket and saw Titus's number. *That was fast*, he thought.

Titus: Meet me at the church now.

Kyden released a breath and forced a smile before facing Zahra. "I need to run. Thanks for the wine and for accepting my apology."

Her brows furrowed. "No need to hurry off."

"It's been a long day for both of us." He walked to where he'd left his boots and slid them on, quickly retying the laces. "I'll be in touch."

She opened the door for him. "Thanks for the flowers."

He dipped his head. "Lock the door," he said before leaving the apartment, trying to ignore the disappointment and confusion etched onto her face. He couldn't afford distractions—he was chasing answers, not the unpredictability of human emotion. Hopefully, she'd be safe now that he had the talisman.

Kyden jogged down the hallway and slipped into the spiritual realm. His wings unfurled and with a mighty flap, he shot up through the apartments overhead and out into the cool night air

Chapter Twelve

Zahra

The zombie trembled as three holes appeared in quick succession in its head. Zahra adjusted her safety glasses before lining up her next shot. She widened her stance, extended her arms, and aimed. Her finger slid to the trigger and she emptied the magazine. The zombie, now full of holes, slid toward her on the target carrier.

"When the zombie apocalypse happens, I want to be with you," Alexis said loudly so Zahra could hear her through the headphones.

Zahra chuckled. "Head shots are the only way to go with zombies. I've seen *The Walking Dead*."

Champion Gun Range was a place where she could clear her mind as easily as she emptied the magazine into cartoon images of zombies or robbers. As a teenager, she'd joined the American League Junior Shooting Sports program where she not only learned gun safety but also discovered she had a natural talent. She had participated in competitions until the demands of life made competing impossible. She continued to hone her skills and help other women learn how to properly handle such a powerful weapon.

Alexis had been one of her students, and as her friend shot the cartoon bank robber, Zahra smiled with pride. Alexis had improved greatly with her aim and, more importantly, with her confidence.

An hour later and with many zombies put out of their misery, Zahra and Alexis sat at a nearby café, the weather warm enough to sit outside despite the leaves changing with the approaching fall.

"So do you want to tell me what's got you so ruffled? Is it Brandon?" Alexis asked, swirling a french fry into her ketchup and mayonnaise mixture.

Zahra scrunched her nose at her friend's concoction. She and Alexis had talked for hours regarding the murder and her traitorous assistant sleeping with Brandon. Mr. Rousseau had given the staff Thursday and Friday off, but Zahra would have rather worked to keep her mind off things.

"Brandon's death is definitely weighing heavily on me. It's weird that the police don't have any leads."

"But?" Alexis asked.

She figured she needed to confess. After all, that's what best friends were for, and she trusted Alexis completely. She hadn't had many close girlfriends in the past, and with managing work and her mom's health, hadn't made any meaningful connections until Alexis.

"I kissed Jake," Zahra muttered.

Alexis, who'd been sipping from her soda, choked. After patting her chest, she said, "I'm sorry. Did you say you kissed Jake? The ex-boyfriend?"

Zahra winced. "Tavern's margaritas are partly to blame."

"Yeah, that drink has led to a few bad choices on my part too, but you're way more responsible than I am. What made you cave?"

"I don't know. Brandon's death was freaking me out. I didn't want to be alone and I was slightly intoxicated. And he was wearing jeans and a henley." Zahra held her head in her hands. Her excuses for kissing him sounded lame, even to her.

Jake had called and texted a few times in the past couple of days, but she'd ignored them. The flowers had almost broken her resolve since he'd remembered daisies were her favorite. But why rekindle something with him, especially when he lived across the country? She couldn't deny her attraction to him nor how good his lips had felt against hers. A part of her wished she'd been drunk enough to forget how her body betrayed her with just one kiss.

"And what about the goddess?" Alexis asked.

"I guess they were never a couple."

Alexis's brows rose. "Well, I'd say he's definitely interested in you. He also seems like a good guy. Maybe exploring this would be good for you."

"You're supposed to be on my side, scolding me for being stupid and letting tequila have its way with me."

"Sounds like you're scolding yourself enough. I'm just playing devil's advocate. What harm is there in seeing him again?"

Zahra sighed and watched the traffic go by. "All my reasons are slowly crumbling."

"Food for thought," Alexis said, finishing her fries and thankfully switching the subject, recounting her visit to New Jersey with her family. Zahra absorbed her words, wanting to escape into someone else's life for the time being.

Not only was Brandon's death unnerving her more than she cared to admit, but her mom had suffered another episode just before she'd visited the other day. She had wanted to ask if her mom had heard from her father, but she was lost within her own mind. With still no news of his whereabouts, the worry knotted in Zahra's stomach and refused to let go.

Unfortunately, the doctor had sedated her mom before she arrived at the home. The nurse explained that her mom had tried to hurt her neighbor and then threatened to harm herself. Zahra's heart had broken when the nurse told her.

Alexis was sharing details about her latest date when Zahra's phone dinged. She picked it up and frowned at the number.

"Who is it?" Alexis asked.

"Mr. Tall, Dark, and Broody." She opened the messaging app.

Sam: Hi Zahra, this is Sam. We need to talk. When are you free?

His sudden shift in behavior last night confused her. One minute he was charming and the next, he couldn't get his boots on fast enough. After the visit with her mom, she would have enjoyed the distraction, especially when her roommate had been on a date and hadn't come home until late and she found herself once again alone. The temptation to call Jake had almost made her pick up her phone, but she escaped into a book instead.

"Now *that* is a good-looking man. Don't get me wrong, Jake is handsome too, but that guy? He's got the broody hotness down. I'd like to figure out how to make him smile," Alexis said with a wink.

Zahra laughed. Secretly, she agreed with her friend. Sam was very attractive in that "I don't give a shit" brooding attitude way. The one time his lips had curved into a partial smile had made her heart flutter. A full grin on that man might bring her to her knees.

"He actually came over last night with flowers to apologize for leaving me alone with Jake at the restaurant," Zahra said.

"How thoughtful. If I wanted to get over my ex, I'd definitely rebound with him." Alexis wiggled her eyebrows and then slurped down her soda. "Any kissing, or was there not enough tequila?"

She rolled her eyes. "No kissing and no tequila." She glanced at his message, still unsure of her reply, and not wanting to admit his sudden departure stung. Appearing too eager was a definite no, so she pocketed her phone without responding. A few days of waiting wouldn't kill him.

The hairs on the back of her neck tingled and she turned, scanning the crowded café. Families and couples drank coffee and ate pastries while taking advantage of the beautiful weather. A man wearing sunglasses and a tailored dark blue suit typed on his laptop while a college-aged kid appeared to be studying.

She glanced across the street, barely hearing Alexis talk about the latest book she'd read, and rubbed her neck. Shaking her head, she focused on her friend. She chalked it up to nerves—after the week she'd endured, who wouldn't be jumpy?

On Sunday, Zahra spent the morning cleaning her apartment and delaying the visit with her mother for as long as she could. Guilt made her gut churn. She missed her mom, or who her mom used to be. The deadly disease held the woman who had once been Nancy Jenkins hostage, hijacking her mind.

She received a call from the home saying Nancy was stable and the restrictions lifted, and that she wanted to see her. The doctors were slowly introducing a new antianxiety medicine that would hopefully keep the aggressive mood swings at bay.

Finally, when the apartment was spotless, she changed into her favorite T-shirt and jeans and drove to Glendale Home. Nancy sat at the small table in her room, staring out the window into a charming courtyard. Terra-cotta pots brimming with life occupied the space along with a fountain bubbling a soothing rhythm.

"Hi, Mom," Zahra said, bending down to kiss her cheek. Nancy had aged since the last time she'd visited, the lines carving deeper into her sallow skin. Guilt took up residence in her stomach and constricted, causing a sharp pain.

Zahra sat and took hold of her mom's fisted hand. "How are you feeling today?"

Nancy tore her gaze from the window. Her blue eyes were clear and her lips curled into a smile. "Feeling good. How are you?"

"I'm fine." She'd decided on the way over not to bring up her father nor that he was missing. Her mom's mental state was fragile and she didn't want to disrupt that sensitive balance. Instead, she told her about shooting with Alexis and running into Jake, although she didn't share any specific details. Try as she might to get that kiss out of her mind, she couldn't.

"Ah, Jake. He was a good boy. Always liked him."

"He lives in Las Vegas now. Works for a company called Durand Enterprises."

Her mother's brow furrowed. "Durand?"

"Yes, why?" Zahra asked, scooting forward on her seat.

She could tell her mom was searching for some information hidden in her brain. She shook her head and returned her gaze to the window.

"They're out there. Always there," Nancy said, rocking slowly in her chair.

Zahra frowned and stared from her mother to the courtyard. A nurse walked by, pushing an old man in a wheelchair. Birds flittered in the fountain, but other than that, the area seemed peaceful. "Who's out there?"

"Horrible things," Nancy whispered. She rubbed her forehead and squeezed her eyes shut as she rocked back and forth.

Zahra raced to the window and closed the blinds. Whatever her mom was seeing was obviously upsetting her. "It's okay, Mom. You're safe."

Nancy stopped rocking and glanced from the blinds to Zahra. "You're a good girl. Didn't deserve what your dad and I did. I'm sorry."

Zahra tilted her head, not understanding her mother's words. Her dad was the one who left, not her mom. "Have you heard from him recently?" So much for her plan of not bringing him up.

"Your father? Quite the protector." She stood and walked toward her chest of drawers. Zahra rose halfway from her chair, just in case her mom stumbled as she rummaged through a wooden jewelry box. "Here it is! Hugh sent me this weeks ago, but I kept forgetting to give it to you. He said you'd know what to do with it." Nancy unfurled her fingers and revealed a silver key.

Zahra took the key. "Why would he send you this?"

Nancy opened her mouth to speak, but her gaze caught on the open door leading toward the common room. She stumbled back and pointed. "You are not welcome here. Get out!"

Zahra jumped from her chair, an apology on the tip of her tongue to whoever stood near the door, but no one was there.

"Get out now!" her mother shouted again.

Zahra peeked into the hall. A few residents lounged in their wheelchairs, and the sound of forks scraping plates came from the dining room. She shut the door and returned to her mom's side. "How about a nap?"

Her mom's eyes, which had been clear earlier, were now unfocused as if she was trapped inside her own mind. Zahra would need to ask the doctor if the new medication caused hallucinations.

Nancy gave a watery smile and allowed Zahra to lead her back to the bed. After getting her settled, she placed another kiss on her cheek. "I love you, Mom."

Nancy looked up at her and rested her hand on Zahra's face. "Don't be mad at your father. He's a protector. He needed to go."

Zahra glanced at a picture of her parents on one of their trips overseas on some grand adventure. The pyramids of Giza stood majestically behind them. Her father was gazing at her mom, while she smiled at the camera. Zahra squinted and noticed a silver chain around her father's neck. She didn't remember him wearing any sort of jewelry.

"Mom, what's..."

A soft snore escaped her mother's lips. Zahra sighed. "Rest easy." As she left her room, she looked once more at the key her mother had given her. The cryptic clue from her father tempted her to throw it in the trash, but her curiosity won her over, and she shoved it into her purse.

Zahra's nose scrunched at the smell of chemically enhanced lemon floor cleaner as she walked down the long hallway. A whisper of unease brushed along the back of her neck. The unsettling sensation of someone watching her resurfaced, but when she glanced behind her, the hallway was empty. She picked up her pace while trying to ignore the shiver running down her spine and hurried toward the exit.

CHAPTER THIRTEEN

KYDEN

Kyden glanced once again at his phone and gritted his teeth. He wasn't used to being ignored or brushed off, which was exactly what Zahra was doing. She was in danger and the pieces were aligning, all pointing to her, except for the missing halo. He'd spent enough time in the museum searching for the bloody artifact, hoping Zahra was hiding it in plain sight.

As he followed her through the museum, his mind kept returning to the discovery Titus had made. After leaving Zahra's apartment, Kyden had flown to the Sacred Path Church, the steeple cutting through the evening sky like a blade. He landed on the top balcony leading into an abandoned attic where he and Titus had taken up residence. Titus had rigged the area with sensors able to detect trespassers, demonic or otherwise. He'd also placed a glamour on the room to hide their equipment, including the three monitors occupying a large desk.

Titus turned in his chair as Kyden tucked in his wings and stepped inside.

"I can't believe I missed this," Titus said, the muscle in his jaw twitching.

"Missed what?" Kyden sensed the truth circling, and he wasn't sure he was ready for the revelation to land.

"Thirty-five years ago, Zahra's mother, Nancy Jenkins, a professor at the University of New Hampshire, attended an archaeological summit. One guess who she met."

"Dr. Hugh Neeman?"

"Yep. But he wasn't a doctor yet. Just starting out in his career. And soon after, they got married."

Kyden leaned forward, studying the computer screen. "Married?"

Titus nodded. "And five years later, after what seemed a happy marriage with a baby on the way, Dr. Neeman filed for divorce. Nancy never took his last name, which is one reason I missed it. Plus, until recently, Zahra wasn't a person of interest."

"So, you're telling me—"

"Dr. Neeman is Zahra's father."

Frustration had Kyden squeezing his fists until the pain from his nails registered in his brain. "Which means, despite her being a complete liar, she's also a Vaelatori."

"That about sums it up," Titus said, having found a bag of licorice and chomping down on a red strand. "Do you think she knows?"

He removed the talisman from his pocket. The silver feather shimmered with supernatural power as it lay in his palm. "I don't think so; otherwise, she wouldn't have left this in her nightstand." He passed it to Titus, who held it up to the light.

"I wonder which angel this feather belonged to."

Kyden shrugged. "We don't even know how many talismans were created or how many Vaelatori are still alive."

"Whoever they are, they've definitely gone underground. I haven't seen one of these in ages." Titus handed the necklace back to him.

Kyden stood and paced, raking his fingers through his hair. "What are the chances the demons have discovered Dr. Neeman is Zahra's father?"

"Pretty high."

Did he make a mistake in taking the talisman? He didn't believe she was aware of the significance, and based on the letter he'd found in her office, her father had explained nothing. Dr. Neeman must have realized the demons were after him if he sent such a cryptic note.

"Then she isn't safe," Kyden said, his eyes gazing along the Boston skyline.

He'd texted her on Saturday saying they needed to talk, and she still hadn't responded. Over the weekend, he'd monitored her, remaining in the spiritual realm, and so far no demons trailed her. Hopefully, whichever Fallen was involved hadn't learned Zahra's secret yet. It was a gamble he wasn't willing to bet on.

Titus worked with Adinah to discover the identity of the Fallen searching for the halo. Many grunts had earned a fate of dissolving into a green mist by not answering their questions, but still, nothing. Whoever this Fallen was, the grunts were very loyal or very afraid.

Tasked with following Zahra around like a lost dog, Kyden once again found himself in ancient Babylon, or rather the museum's recreation of that time period, staring up at the statue of King Nebuchadnezzar II, a gold circlet around his head. Whoever created the statue knew their history and legends, showcasing the crack on one side of the crown—the exact spot where Michael's and Apollyon's blood had mixed.

No one knew how long Mammon, the Prince of Greed, had possessed the unsuspecting king, but it couldn't have been long since the halo drained power from both angels and demons. Maybe the magic of the halo caused the man to go insane?

He shook his head and turned away from the statue. Zahra, oblivious to his presence, had spent most of the morning at her desk and skipped her lunch break to find solitude in the throne room.

She stood in front of the replica of the magical Atar'zul while sucking on one of her lollipops. Her phone vibrated in her pocket but she ignored it. A wrinkle of thought carved a line through her eyebrows as she stared at the fake relic. What would she think if she learned the magic of the halo was real—forged from the blood of two powerful angels, one loyal and one forsaken?

Familiar voices tore them both from their contemplations. Jake Callahan and his boss, Laurent Durand, strode through the lobby to where a waiting Mr. Rousseau stood with his hands behind his back.

Zahra's eyes narrowed as Mr. Rousseau shook both men's hands. Although they remained on the other side of the expansive lobby, Kyden, with his enhanced hearing, had no problem listening to them. Zahra, on the other hand, hedged closer.

"Thank you for taking this meeting," Mr. Durand said, his eyes harder than what Kyden remembered from the dinner a week ago.

"I was surprised to get your call. And as I explained on the phone, we still have not received the Atar'zul," Mr. Rousseau said.

"Let's take this conversation somewhere private," Jake said, scanning the area. He paused when he noticed Zahra walking toward them.

"What's going on?" she asked. "I didn't know of any meeting."

Mr. Rousseau looked guilty as he straightened his suit jacket. He opened his mouth to speak but Durand interrupted.

"We were in the neighborhood, and I wanted to check in on my investment." Durand's face remained expressionless as he watched her.

"Let's go to the conference room, shall we?" Mr. Rousseau said, pointing Durand in the right direction.

Jake hung back, holding Zahra's arm. "You wouldn't take my calls."

"I have a lot going on right now."

Jake arched a brow. "I certainly don't want to add to your stress, but I need to talk to you."

She paused and faced him. "Why, Jake? There's no point in this."

"I beg to differ. You felt the connection when we kissed. Don't deny it."

Kyden tore his gaze from Durand and focused on Zahra. She hadn't mentioned kissing the man, but then again, why would she?

"I blame that on the tequila." She pulled free from his grasp and moved toward the doors leading to the offices. Kyden walked behind them, observing Jake, who attempted to keep his temper at bay. It seemed Zahra didn't just irritate angels.

Jake pinched the bridge of his nose and breathed deeply. "I tried to warn you that Mr. Durand was on his way."

"No, you didn't," she said over her shoulder.

"Yes, I did. Check your phone."

She pulled it from her pocket and swore. "I haven't heard anything except that Dr. Neeman and the Atar'zul are still missing." She shook her head and marched toward the conference room where her boss and Durand waited.

"I still want to talk to you about the other night," Jake whispered.

"There's nothing to discuss."

Kyden slid through the walls to stand near the window. Mr. Rousseau looked up as Zahra and Jake entered, whispering, while Durand's shoulders stiffened slightly. His gaze drifted from Jake and paused on a map of ancient Mesopotamia next to where Kyden stood.

"Is everything all right?" Mr. Rousseau asked Zahra, who yanked her chair away from the table.

She forced a smile. "Yes, sir. Everything is fine."

Mr. Rousseau glanced between her and Jake. Anyone with eyes could see the tension flowing between those two, but the elderly man simply nodded.

Zahra seemed to regain her composure. "Mr. Durand, I'm sorry about the delay regarding the Atar'zul. It seems to have gone missing along with Dr. Neeman."

Kyden watched her closely, recognizing the tightness around her eyes and the firm set to her jaw.

Durand leaned back in his chair, crossing his ankle over his knee. "I guess you haven't heard."

"Heard what?" Mr. Rousseau asked.

"My sources in the Middle East have confirmed the most dreadful news. It seems Dr. Neeman was killed in an alleyway in Kuwait. A senseless mugging." Durand studied Zahra as if trying to sort out a puzzle.

Jake leaned forward. "He was killed? Why hasn't this information been on the news?"

Kyden ignored whatever Durand said. Zahra had moved her hands to her lap, which he could only assume were clenched into fists. Her nostrils flared, and she blinked rapidly. He was impressed at how well she kept her emotions under control, but she was about to lose it, and then her secret would be out. For reasons he couldn't explain, the need to protect her fluttered to the surface. Plus, he didn't trust any of the men in this room, not where her safety was concerned.

He whipped out his phone and sent her a text. When her phone vibrated on the table, Kyden hoped she'd take the escape he'd given her. He then waved his hand as someone walked by, making them trip and drop all their files, causing everyone to turn.

Zahra quickly grabbed her phone and stood. "Would you excuse me for a moment?"

Mr. Rousseau turned from the chaos in the hallway. "Miss Jenkins, I don't think now is the time..."

"It's from Glendale. It might be an emergency." She gave a quick nod to everyone and hurried from the room.

Kyden released a sigh while both Callahan and Durand watched her, one with a frown and the other with a curious expression.

"I can't believe Dr. Neeman is dead. His death will impact the archaeological world as we know it," Mr. Rousseau said, sadness etched along his face.

Jake drummed his fingers on the table, finally tearing his gaze away from the closed door. "I'm assuming the Atar'zul wasn't found on Dr. Neeman's body."

"No," Durand said. His dark eyes drifted to Zahra's boss. "And you have heard nothing regarding its whereabouts?"

Mr. Rousseau shook his head. "We've received no word. According to Excavate International, they didn't know Dr. Neeman planned to send the relic here. Their contract with Neeman stipulates they retain control over the fates of the artifacts he finds."

Kyden, who'd been about to follow Zahra, stopped. Dr. Neeman seemed to have misled many people regarding the halo. So where was it now? Not at the dig site and obviously not here at the museum. The archaeologist had to have sent it somewhere to keep it safe. He assumed that because Neeman had mailed Zahra the talisman, he intended for her to find the relic as well, but he wouldn't want to put her in danger. So where was the halo?

However, in Neeman's desire to protect his daughter, he may have painted a target on her back. If the demons discovered the connection between Zahra and Dr. Neeman, then her life was even more at risk.

As he moved through the walls, the hairs on his neck stood at attention, but when he glanced over his shoulder, the billionaire was facing Mr. Rousseau and Jake was checking his phone. The room dissolved as Kyden searched for Zahra, a sense of foreboding causing him to quicken his pace.

CHAPTER FOURTEEN

ZAHRA

Zahra stared out the window, willing the tears not to fall, but the persistent bastards ignored her and trickled down her cheeks.

Her father was dead.

She hadn't been close to the man, thinking of him as more of a colleague than her dad, but the remorse flowing through her threatened to suffocate her. Her hand shook as she clicked on her laptop and typed her father's name to see if any reports showed up. The latest image was of him at the dig site, taken a few weeks ago. There was mention of his invitation to the gala but nothing else.

How could the death of one of the most famous archaeologists not have made the news anywhere? Was Excavate International aware?

She shut her laptop and closed her eyes as bile crept up her throat. Someone had murdered her father in an alley. Alone and probably scared. Mr. Durand had said a senseless mugging, but her thoughts drifted back to the note he'd sent, the one she'd crumpled and thrown carelessly into her desk drawer. She found the wrinkled piece of paper and smoothed it out. He had apologized for everything. At first she assumed it was for failing to deliver the Atar'zul, but maybe the apology meant more. Had he known his life was in danger? Was that why he sent the necklace? And for what purpose?

She covered her mouth as a choked sob escaped her lips. Any chance of resolution between them disappeared like smoke on the wind. Regret wrapped its spindly fingers around her throat and squeezed, making it hard to breathe.

How was she going to tell her mother? Or should she? What good would it do? Her mom was barely holding on to reality. Not telling her would be a kindness in the end, wouldn't it?

She closed her eyes as if she could block out the grief. The sensation of hands on her shoulders and a sense of calm encompassed her like a warm blanket on a frigid night. She gasped and spun around. Of course, no one was there, but she shivered nonetheless. The rapid beating of her heart settled into a gentle rhythm, and she was able to inhale a full breath.

"Weird," she said to the empty room as she pressed a hand against her sternum.

A knock sounded on the door.

"Just a minute." She quickly grabbed a tissue and dried her eyes. She checked her reflection in a compact mirror and pinched some color into her cheeks. "Come in."

Jake peeked his head in. "Hey, I wanted to..." His gaze zeroed in on her face. If anyone had the skill to see through her fake expression, it would be him. "What's wrong?"

She forced a smile. "I'm fine. What can I help you with?"

He pointed his thumb over his shoulder. "Laurent and I were leaving, but I wanted to check on you."

"I'll call you if the Atar'zul shows up, okay?"

He walked into her office and shut the door behind him. "I don't care about some ancient artifact. I'm worried about you."

"Why?" That one word dragged like a heavy stone, as if she didn't have the strength for anything else.

He sat in the chair across from her desk and crossed an ankle over his knee. His perceptive eyes examined her face. "You aren't sleeping well, are you?"

"How I'm sleeping is none of your business."

He held up both palms as if in surrender. "Retract the claws, Zee. You look tired. And I can tell you've been crying." He leaned forward. "You can talk to me."

When Jake used her nickname, something soft stirred inside her. A part of her wanted to open up to him. After all, when they dated, he had always been a safe place to land during difficult times. And he was right, of course.

She hadn't been sleeping well. Worry about her mom's health and her dad's whereabouts plagued her. The concealer she'd caked under her eyes didn't come close to masking the dark circles.

"There's just a lot going on. But thanks for checking on me."

He nodded, then stared at his shoes for a minute before lifting his head. "About the other night..."

"No. I don't want to talk about it," she said with a note of finality.

Sadness forced his lips to turn downward. "I have two major regrets in my life."

"Only two?" She crossed her arms.

The corner of his lip curved into a sad smile, but he continued, "Regret number one was how I left things between us." His eyes resembled stone. Not cold, but hard and unyielding, as if the past continued to haunt him.

"And regret two?" Her voice tightened like a string going taut.

"Regret two was not fighting harder for you, waiting for you."

She swallowed past the lump in her throat. She couldn't go there, not now, not with vulnerability circling her like a vulture searching for its next meal. The news of her father's death had left her raw, and she felt too exposed. Panic mixed with sadness in a toxic sludge, and she was close to breaking. The desire for his muscular arms to wrap around her almost had her rising from her chair. Instead, she closed her eyes to escape the possibility of what might have been.

"I can't do this, Jake. Not right now."

His chair squeaked, and then his hand was holding hers. He knelt before her and turned her to face him. "Zahra, I'm so sorry for everything that's going on, and I don't want to cause you more heartache. I came to Boston for closure."

She lifted her gaze to his. "What do you mean, closure?"

He sighed. "I needed to be free of you. I kept holding out, thinking maybe you'd call, maybe you'd change your mind. But after four years, it was time for me to move on. But then I saw you wearing the ring, and thought maybe..." He shrugged his shoulders.

The tears she'd been able to hold back broke forth. She tried to cover her face, but Jake grabbed her hands and pulled her toward him. His heart thumped against her cheek as his arms held her close.

"Shhh, Zee. Everything is going to be okay." His soft voice was like a balm to her fractured soul.

She allowed the tears to fall in earnest in the safety of his embrace. All the stress from the gala, the promotion, Brandon's death and now her father's, plus her mother's failing health had reached a boiling point. Not to mention, the love of her life kneeling before her with only care and concern staring back at her.

He continued to hold her until she finally inhaled a cleansing breath and pushed away.

"Sorry about your shirt," she said, patting the wet mark she'd left.

He smiled, swiping a stray tear with his thumb. "I have more."

She ran her hands through her hair, attempting to gain some form of composure.

Jake stood, pulling her with him. His fingers intertwined with hers. "I'd love to take you to dinner sometime. Or go shooting, see a movie, whatever you'd like." He lifted her chin so she had no choice but to look at him. "Please don't say no."

The part of her focused on self-preservation should say no. But she longed to be held again and perhaps he was right. She'd subconsciously worn the ring like a symbol of hope and hadn't even known it.

Another knock sounded at the door, but before she could say anything, Alexis barged in.

"I heard Jake was here," she said, and then came to a halt. "Is here," she amended with a sheepish smile.

Jake chuckled. "And that's my cue." He gently kissed her on the cheek. "This time when I call, answer, okay?" He dipped his chin at a gaping Alexis and then left the room.

Zahra tucked a strand of hair behind her ear. "Okay," she said as he shut the door behind him.

"It's a little hot in here." Alexis fanned herself. "What was that all about?" She frowned as her eyes darted across her face. "Have you been crying? Did he make you cry? Oh, I'm going to kick his ass."

Zahra laughed quietly, the tension easing enough to allow her to breathe. She loved Alexis; that's all there was to it. "He didn't make me cry. Well, he made me cry harder." She then recapped the last thirty minutes, ending with the news about her father.

Zahra's tears had finally dried, but she handed Alexis a tissue so she could wipe her eyes. "Oh, friend, I'm so sorry," Alexis said with a sniffle.

She shook her head. "My dad was a stranger to me. I think what makes me so sad is we didn't get the chance to reconcile. I honestly didn't know I even wanted to until the option was taken from me."

"Yeah, that's rough." She tilted her head. "Do you need a hug? Or I can go fetch Jake, and he can hug you."

Zahra snorted. "No, I'm better now. The tears were a good release."

"You know what's a better release?" Alexis wiggled her eyebrows.

"Knock it off," she said, laughing. Human emotions were as erratic as a summer storm—sudden rain pounding on a window, followed by a beautiful rainbow. One minute she was sobbing and the next laughing. Allowing Jake to hold her, to share her moment of grief, had taken a load off her shoulders to where she felt like she could stand up straight.

Alexis's phone chirped. "Well, now my other class canceled too. It seems the entire elementary school has come down with pink eye." She rose to her feet. "I'm gonna head out early. How about Thai food for dinner?"

"Sounds good. See you tonight."

Alexis blew her a kiss and sauntered out of her office.

Zahra stared at the note her father had sent. The last words he would ever say to her didn't deserve to be so haphazardly discarded. She rubbed out the creases and then placed it in the top drawer of her desk.

She worked for a few more hours and was about to pack up her things when Meredith buzzed her. "What is it?" She hadn't spoken to her assistant regarding Brandon, aiming to keep things professional, if a little cold.

"A gentleman from A1 Storage is on line two."

"Okay, thanks." Zahra frowned. *I don't have anything in storage*, she thought before pressing the button.

"This is Zahra Jenkins."

"Hello, Miss Jenkins, my name is Clyde Walker. I have your name and number as an emergency contact for storage unit number twelve. We can't get ahold of the renter, and their payments are past due. We'll have to auction off the stuff unless you empty it by this weekend."

"I'm sorry, but you must be mistaken. The only emergency contact list I'm on is for my mother. Her name is Nancy Jenkins. Is it her storage unit?"

"The name I have on file is H. Neeman."

Her stomach tightened. "What did you say?"

"H. Neeman. Does that sound familiar?"

"Yes," she said, confused. She told the man she'd be there within the week, and after writing down the address, hung up the phone. She leaned back in her chair and stared at the ceiling. Why did her father have a storage unit in Boston?

Her head whipped to the side and she grabbed her purse, digging through it until she found the silver key her mother had given her. What was it she had said?

Hugh sent me this weeks ago, but I kept forgetting to give it to you. He said you'd know what to do with it.

First the note with the necklace, then this key. He'd promised to bring the Atar'zul, but then had been killed. The knot in her stomach tightened and swelled. What the hell had her father gotten himself into? And for that matter, what had he gotten *her* into?

She glanced at the clock. It was after five and the sun had already sunk below the horizon. The storage unit would have to wait until tomorrow; besides, she didn't want to go alone. Who knew what she'd find?

Zahra left her office and drove to her apartment. She'd texted Alexis that she was on her way but hadn't heard back. After parking the car, she jogged up the steps. A chill crept up her spine and she turned, bracing for what she wasn't sure. Other than an older lady walking her dog, the street was empty. She rubbed her neck and entered the building.

She frowned at her phone as she walked down the hall and then froze mid-step. Her apartment door was ajar with splinters of wood lying near the entryway. She dropped her phone and yanked her gun from her purse. Clicking off the safety, she slowly crossed the threshold.

Furniture lay on its side, broken glass was strewn on the ground, cabinet doors hung open. She desperately wanted to call out for Alexis, but just in case the perpetrator was still here, she didn't want to alert them to her presence.

Please be getting Thai food, she thought as she silently crept into the room. She rounded the couch and screamed.

Alexis lay on the floor, a pool of blood seeping from under her back.

CHAPTER FIFTEEN

KYDEN

Kyden had followed Zahra the entire day, except when Jake had entered her office. Once he decided she wasn't in danger, he gave them some privacy and returned to the lobby where he watched Durand enter the Babylonian exhibit. Kyden kept his distance, but trailed the man as he stopped at each historic piece. He paused in front of King Nebuchadnezzar's statue; the one Kyden had been examining earlier.

Durand smiled up at the king's harsh face. "Hello, old friend," he said, flicking the golden toe with his finger. A metallic ding echoed through the cavernous hall.

Kyden couldn't get an accurate read on the billionaire. He was charming and friendly, if not a little strange, but that was expected from someone who had enough money to buy a small country. His love of antiquities was well known and his collection enviable.

Kyden followed him into the parking lot and scanned the area for demons, but the lot was empty.

He watched the limousine drive down the street as he called Adinah.

"Hey, Kyden," Adinah said.

"I need you to check out a Laurent Durand. See if he's involved with anything having to do with Baghdad and the surrounding area."

"Isn't this a job for Titus?"

Kyden walked back into the museum. "He's already done a background check on him and nothing flagged, but Durand knew about Neeman's death, and his interest in the halo seems more than just your normal collector."

"Yeah, okay. I'll see what I can find out."

"Thanks," Kyden said, and hung up the phone. By the time he returned to Zahra's office, she was gone.

He took to the skies and flew straight to her apartment. Her car was parked on the street. He canvassed the surrounding neighborhood to see if there was any demonic activity. He was circling back when a scream echoed through the darkness.

He soared through the window of Zahra's apartment. The smell of sulfur and blood had Kyden immediately drawing his sword.

Zahra ran toward Alexis's body and slid next to it. She gently rolled her over. "Be alive," she whispered as she put two fingers on her neck. Her shoulders sagged.

Kyden's ears picked up her roommate's faint pulse. Closing his eyes, he concentrated on the air and sounds, but he didn't sense any demonic presence—whatever they'd been doing, they'd obviously left. He wanted to check the apartment to be sure, but Zahra remained frozen next to her friend as if the sight of blood had short-circuited her brain.

"Call 911," Kyden said, pushing the thought to her.

Zahra stiffened, and then frantically searched for her phone. "Where the hell is it?" she said, patting down her pockets.

He gave her a mental nudge. "Hallway."

She jumped to her feet and ran to the hallway where she'd dropped her phone and bag. She grabbed both and dialed. Her hands shook as she raised the phone to her ear. Kyden placed his hand on her shoulder. She shivered but her voice was calm when the operator answered.

"Please help. My friend has been shot. She's alive but bleeding badly," Zahra said as she ran to the kitchen counter, frowning at the towels lying there. She grabbed them while giving her address. "I think the apartment's empty." She pressed a towel to Alexis's shoulder and nodded. "Yes, I'll stay on the line until they get here."

Zahra put the phone on speaker and set it on the floor. "Alexis, can you hear me?"

Kyden knelt on the other side of Alexis's body and rested his hand on her chest. He closed his eyes and focused on the slow beat of the woman's heart, keeping the rhythm steady until the EMTs arrived. A feather dropped from his wing as his power slowly drained. He needed the EMTs to hurry, just in case the demons returned to the apartment.

Minutes later, a chorus of sirens pierced the night, growing louder with each second.

"Alexis, stay with me now," Zahra said, checking her pulse again and sighing when she felt the steady beat.

Leaving Zahra's side, Kyden explored the bedrooms. Her room contained a high concentration of demon spawn and the velvet bag that had held the talisman lay in tatters on the floor near her bed. He ran the pieces of the bag through his fingers and gritted his teeth. He could still sense a residual trace of magic from the talisman on the fabric, which meant the demons could too.

He had made a mistake in leaving the bag containing the necklace. He'd hoped Zahra wouldn't check inside if everything was in its proper place. That hope could have gotten someone killed.

He returned to the living room when two police officers rushed in, followed by a man and a woman in EMT uniforms. Pulling his phone from his jacket pocket, he called Titus.

"Demons ransacked Zahra's apartment and someone shot her roommate," he said as a way of greeting.

"Is she okay?" Titus asked.

He watched the officer question Zahra. "She will be. I need you to do me a favor."

While the EMTs worked on stabilizing Alexis, he remained by Zahra's side. Her hands, covered in her best friend's blood, were shaking again and the color had yet to return to her face.

An officer brought her a glass of water and led her to the kitchen table.

"We'll bring someone in to dust for prints, but do you have any idea who would have done this?"

"No," she said, taking a drink of water, her wide eyes never leaving Alexis's body.

"What about valuables? Anything missing?"

"I haven't had a chance to look yet."

The other officer walked down the hallway, his gloved hands holding a gun. "Found this in the nightstand in one of the bedrooms."

"That's mine. I have my concealed carry license and a permit."

"How many guns do you currently own?" the other officer asked, his brows hitched.

"Just two. I keep a .22 in my purse, and the Smith & Wesson in my bedroom."

The officer frowned. "Strange that the burglars didn't take the gun."

The paramedics finally loaded Alexis onto the gurney. Zahra ran to her when she groaned and her eyes fluttered opened.

"You're going to be fine. I'm here, okay," she said, gripping her hand.

Alexis gave a slight nod, her face twisted in pain.

"We're taking her to MGH. You can meet us there," one of the EMTs said, her warm smile instantly causing Zahra's shoulders to lower. She wrapped her arms around herself as the EMTs wheeled the gurney out of the apartment.

Kyden rested a hand on her shoulder, giving her strength. "Hold on. Help is coming."

Zahra inhaled a shuddering breath.

Voices drifted from the hallway, a man's voice she'd recognize any-where drowning out the others.

"I need to see her immediately."

"And who might you be? This is a crime scene."

"A friend," Jake said.

Zahra walked to the door, her eyes widening when she saw him. "Jake?"

"Are you okay?" He ran his hand through his hair for what must have been the hundredth time based on the mussed strands sticking up at different angles.

She looked at the officer, who'd placed an arm across Jake's chest. "It's all right. He can come in."

The officer scowled and stepped out of the way. "Don't touch any-thing."

Jake pushed past the man and gripped her shoulders, examining her from head to toe. Kyden moved closer to the window to have a clear view of the streets and alleys, searching the shadows for demons.

"What are you doing here?" she asked as they walked to the kitchen, side-stepping the puddle of blood by the couch. "And how do you know where I live?"

"Honestly, I have no idea. I was working on a project and this unexplainable feeling rushed through me. All I knew was that I needed to see you—that something was wrong. I followed the sirens, and when I saw the ambulance and police cars..." He pressed his lips together and shook his head, and then pulled her into a hug. "I feared something terrible had happened to you."

"Alexis was shot," Zahra said, wiping tears from her face, leaving a bloody streak on her cheek.

Jake noticed the towels on the counter and grabbed one, walking to the sink and wetting it. He gently helped her into a chair and knelt before her. He dabbed the cloth on her face and removed the blood.

Kyden returned to staring out the window while texting Titus.

Kyden: Nice job. He's here.
Titus: Good. Now do you want to tell me what's going on?
Kyden: I think the demons figured out Zahra was Dr. Neeman's daughter. And she knows he's dead.

Kyden dragged his palm down his face. Guilt twisted his stomach into knots as his mistakes continued to pile up. He'd left the velvet bag in her nightstand, putting her in danger, but he should have told her about her father before she learned about his murder from Durand.

Titus: Dang. She's had a day.

Kyden huffed as he typed.

Kyden: No kidding. I'll meet you at the church later.
Titus: What are you going to do?

He glanced over his shoulder to where Jake and Zahra talked, his arm wrapped around her. Once the police finished their investigation, she would go to the hospital and, based on Jake's protective behavior, he'd be with her every step of the way. She was in good hands.

Kyden: My job.

He returned his phone to his pocket and walked through the glass door onto the balcony. He unfurled his wings and launched into the sky.

Now that everyone was safe and taken care of, he allowed the anger to build as he searched for any grunts lingering near the apartment. Demons needed to die, and he was just the angel to do it.

Kyden roamed the streets of Boston, following a pack of grunts that had been near Zahra's apartment. As the grunts maneuvered through the alleyways and streets, they tormented the humans in their path, causing violence, oppression, and lust. Kyden kept his distance while remaining in his human form, not wanting to alert the demons of his presence.

The unsuspecting grunts finally turned down an alley, passing a group of people waiting to get into Club Nyx. The popular nightclub had a line wrapping around the corner of the building, and music pumped from the open door where two bouncers stood guard.

He toned down his enhanced hearing to lessen the volume of the music and followed the demons. Desperation flowed from the humans waiting for admittance into the club. They wanted sex, power, money, or simply to forget their problems for a while. Kyden wished to help each person in line, giving hope, showing a different way, but many had chosen their current path.

Besides, he was on a mission.

Finding the halo and whichever Fallen was behind the murders and attacking Zahra's roommate was a priority. History could not repeat itself as it had during King Nebuchadnezzar's reign, where the balance between good and evil had tipped, leaving only chaos and destruction in its wake—a literal hell on earth.

The grunts disappeared through the wall of the two-story building. Kyden waited a few minutes and then slipped inside. The smells immediately accosted him once he entered the main establishment. Alcohol, perfume, smoke, and drugs, all laced with sulfur from the demonic influence, made him wince. He lingered in the dark hallway, giving himself a chance to acclimate before moving forward.

The nightclub resembled any other with a large dance floor, flashing lights, and a DJ conducting the dancers gyrating with the pounding music. A stainless steel bar lined the entire length of the room, giving off an industrial feel amongst the wall of mirrors and sparkling bottles.

A stairway led to the second floor, blocked by a red velvet rope and two more bouncers. Three of the demons he'd followed scuttled up the brass railing. Kyden remained in the spiritual realm to sneak past the guards and slowly made his way up the stairs.

Scantily dressed women and men roamed between the tables and booths, serving drinks and drugs. The green mist was almost suffocating with the number of demons clinging to their prey. There were also some daemonkin in the room, and since these humans willingly served the Fallen, there must be one nearby.

Kyden shifted into his human form and glamoured his outfit into jeans and a black Bon Jovi T-shirt. He adjusted his tinted glasses, concealing the color of his eyes, and sat at the bar. Through the mirror he observed four Fallen, varying in their appearances from suits to leather jackets. Club Nyx must have been a usual hangout for the demons, as they appeared content to stay in the human realm, unconcerned with revealing their true form. Their skin was still pale and if someone looked closely enough, they'd see nubs on their backs protruding through their clothing.

Kyden shivered, unable to imagine that fate. The Fallen deserved the grace being ripped away from them for choosing Apollyon, but to lose the ability to fly or the protection his wings provided was something he couldn't fathom.

A waitress wearing a skin-tight silver dress walked past the table of demons. He focused on the group, re-engaging his enhanced hearing. A Fallen whispering to a woman sitting on his lap straightened and looked around. The demon had his back to him, but his profile seemed familiar.

Before he turned, Kyden reached for the waitress as he swiveled on the stool. "What's your name?" He pulled her between his legs, gripping her waist with both hands.

"Shayla," she said with a smile, her hand trailing down his arm. "What's yours?"

"Sam," Kyden said.

"What can I get you?" Shayla asked.

"Besides you? How about a bourbon?" He snuck a glance to his side. The Fallen who'd been scanning the room resumed his conversation with the demons at the table.

She licked her lips and a blush filled her cheeks. The woman, or rather girl now that Kyden was closer, was pretty and probably made excellent money working at the Nyx, but he sensed she was miserable. Hopelessness lingered in her eyes, darkened by the heavy makeup.

Kyden removed a card from his jacket's inside pocket. "If you ever want out, call this number."

She frowned and was about to shake her head but then looked into his eyes. Her lips parted. She swallowed and her gaze darted around the room, then she took the card, slid it into her dress, and walked off.

The ruse seemed to have worked as the demons weren't drawing their weapons or threatening to kill him. Four Fallen against one angel, even one as deadly as him—well, he didn't think he'd come out victorious.

One of the Fallen rubbed a hand along his stubbled jaw. "So what happened tonight? I heard the assignment was a failure."

The Fallen with the girl on his lap stiffened slightly while another one—Bakal, if Kyden remembered correctly—snarled.

"She wasn't home, but our men shot the roommate for good measure. Hopefully she didn't survive," Bakal said with a chuckle, the scar tugging on his lip twisting his smile into something sinister. His leather jacket creaked when he lifted his arms as he threaded his hands behind his head. Kyden nearly launched himself off the barstool to punch the demon in the face.

A female Fallen named Arya frowned at Bakal. "You're lucky you're not in the Abyss after tonight's failure. You didn't get the woman or the halo. Shooting her roommate isn't going to please Raghav."

"Nothing pleases him these days," the one with his back to Kyden said.

Arya chuckled, revealing pointed teeth. She donned a red leather jacket and jeans with knee-high boots. She wore her dark hair short, almost to the scalp, and a half-circle ring pierced her nose.

"You better watch yourself, Gael. Raghav wasn't happy with you after what happened in Baghdad," the last Fallen said. He leaned back in his chair with an air of boredom on his pale face. He wore sunglasses and a tailored suit. A server walked by and the demon smiled, running his hand along the server's thigh.

"Well aware, Cree," the demon named Gael said, draining his glass.

"Can I get you anything else?"

Kyden startled, having forgotten about the drink he had ordered. He took the glass and smiled. "No, thank you."

Shayla nodded and walked past the table with the four Fallen—all who seemed to be involved with the missing halo. They had discovered who Zahra was and would hunt her until they had retrieved the relic. By their conversation, Raghav was leader of the group, but that didn't make sense. Kyden could admit the demon was a skilled warrior, but he wasn't a mastermind in any stretch of the imagination. Someone else had to be calling the shots.

"We're close. That's all that matters. The target is clueless and won't be a threat," the Fallen named Gael said, trailing his hand down the woman's bare back.

"She's a Vaelatori and could definitely be a threat," Cree said, his upper lip curling. "But the halo is the priority right now."

Kyden had heard all he needed to, and had lingered long enough. At least he'd learned which demons were involved in this mess. He pushed away from the bar.

A sultry deep voice sent a shiver down Kyden's back.

"Don't run off, little cherub."

Chapter Sixteen

Zahra

The smell of cleaning solution stung Zahra's nose while she sat in a hard plastic chair in the waiting room of the Massachusetts General Hospital and waited for the surgeon to report on Alexis. While Jake drove her to the hospital, Zahra had called Alexis's parents, who were currently on their way from New Jersey.

She thought back over the hour as she watched Jake pace along the tile floor. He talked on the phone, continually running his hands through his already messed-up hair, sporadically glancing at her and offering her a soft smile.

The timing of him showing up when she had felt so alone had been perfect. He had tried to explain again how he had sensed she needed him, but he made little sense. Nor did the peace she'd experienced when waiting for the paramedics to arrive. It was as if someone had been alongside her, encouraging her to call 911 and reminding her where she'd left her phone. All things she would have eventually done on her own, but it was as if a calming presence had surrounded her, clearing her mind and spurring her into action. She longed for that sensation again as the clock on the opposite wall ticked.

She huffed out a breath and shook her head. A calming presence? Exhaustion and worry were causing her imagination to go wild.

Jake finally pocketed his phone and returned to the seat next to hers, leaning back and staring at the ceiling.

"Everything okay?" she asked.

"Work stuff—nothing important."

"Seemed important. Your hair is a mess." She flattened the strands sticking up.

He closed his eyes and leaned toward her.

"I'm sure your coworkers in Vegas miss you," she said.

"Not really. Just tying up some loose ends."

While his eyes were shut, she gave herself permission to study his profile; the angle of his strong jaw, the slightly crooked nose, the long eyelashes that she'd always envied. Her stomach flipped at how gorgeous he was. He had once been hers, and she'd given him up. She had turned from love and all that remained was a loneliness that ached into the depths of her soul.

She lowered her hand and peered down the hallway, wishing the doctor would bring some news. "What a shitty day. First my father and now this."

Jake's brows furrowed. "Your father?"

She sighed and spun her ring around her finger. "We never talked about my dad when we were dating, did we?"

He shook his head. "I just assumed he was out of your life, and you made it pretty clear you didn't want to talk about him."

"Yeah, I did, didn't I?" Shards of grief knifed through her heart. She'd successfully kept her father at a distance, for protection against being disappointed but also for the sake of her career. But those reasons seemed trivial now. Although she wasn't totally comfortable telling Jake everything, the need to share her burden and honor her father's memory had her lowering her defenses and allowing him a peek into her soul.

He wiped a tear from her cheek. "Hey, what's going on?"

"I found out today that my dad was murdered in the streets of Kuwait."

Jake's eyes widened. "What the hell was he doing there?" He cleared his throat and reached for her hand. "Sorry, those don't need to be the first words out of my mouth."

"It's okay." The comfort of his firm hand wrapped around hers relaxed her shoulders. "My father divorced my mom before I was born, but he was still a part of my life, if not really ever present. Once I graduated high school, I basically had nothing to do with him until recently."

"What brought you back together again?"

"The Atar'zul."

Jake frowned, and then his brows rose. "The artifact my boss wants?"

"The very one."

"Why would your dad know about that? Does he work in a museum too?"

Zahra almost laughed, though the emotion was tinged with bitterness. "No. My father is the archaeologist who found it. Dr. Hugh Neeman."

Jake's mouth fell open, and then he quickly snapped it shut. His eyes scanned her face as if trying to make sense of everything she was saying. "Why...?"

She traced their interlocking fingers. "Why wouldn't I tell anyone?" He nodded and she continued, "Because I wanted my career based on my merit, not his reputation. It was just easier that way—to treat him like a colleague instead of my own flesh and blood. He was supposed to come to the gala but never made it. Which didn't surprise me—I'd grown accustomed to him disappointing me, so I thought nothing of it."

"That would explain your reaction when Laurent broke the news. What an awful way to find out. I'm so sorry."

Tears threatened to choke her, and she forced herself to swallow them down before she completely fell apart in the waiting room. Jake released her hand and wrapped his arm around her shoulder, pulling her toward him. He kissed her gently on the temple.

She gripped his shirt as if he were an anchor keeping her grounded while the storm raged around her. "I just feel so guilty. Maybe if I had tried harder to find him, to actually give a damn, then he'd still be alive."

"I'm assuming my boss isn't privy to this information," Jake said, running his hand up and down her arm.

"Only you and Alexis know."

"I have to say—you have a stellar poker face." He squeezed her. "I'm sure staying at work, acting as if everything was okay, was horrible for you. And then to walk into your apartment being trashed and your best friend shot. Definitely a shitty day."

She looked into his gray eyes; the edges crinkled slightly, and gave a small smile. "The shittiest."

The squeak of rubber soles made her turn. A woman wearing scrubs walked toward her, her hair tied back and covered with a surgical cap.

"Zahra Jenkins?" the doctor asked.

She rose to her feet and wiped her sweaty palms on her jeans. "That's me."

"I'm Doctor Galvez. We were able to remove the bullet from Alexis's shoulder and thankfully it didn't cause too much damage. She'll be awake soon and ready for visitors."

Zahra covered her mouth with both hands, and tears welled in her eyes as relief coursed through her. "Thank you so much."

The doctor smiled. "Of course." She disappeared behind the sliding doors.

"That's great news," Jake said.

"I was so worried." She let out a relieved breath. "Thank you for being here."

He traced his thumb along her jaw, sending a shiver down her spine. "There's no place I'd rather be."

"Oh sure. Hanging out at the emergency room is your kind of fun, is it?"

"It's my usual go-to for a good time." He winked and pulled her to him, enclosing her in his arms.

His chest was warm and safe, and she allowed herself a few seconds to enjoy the sensation. She would forever be in his debt for being there for her, but the habit of protecting her heart caused her to retreat. Falling in love with him again would be as easy as breathing, but what was the point? He'd come to Boston for closure and even though she still wore the ring he'd given her, it wouldn't be fair to him to lead him on. Besides, he had a life, a career, a future in Vegas. She had nothing to offer him.

She escaped from the embrace and ran her hands through her hair, putting distance between them. "Yes, well, thanks again. Alexis's parents will be here soon, so..." She glanced at the sliding doors leading to the parking lot, not sure what else to say.

He crossed his arms, his eyes like granite. "What are you doing?"

She shook her head. "Nothing. I appreciate you being here, but you don't need to stick around."

He chewed the inside of his cheek as he scanned her face, and it took everything in her to hold his gaze.

"You're pushing me away, but you've had a nightmare of a day so I'll let it slide. But Zee, I need you to understand something."

She wrapped her arms around herself. "And what's that?"

"I'm in your life and plan on staying here. So get used to me sticking around." He placed a gentle kiss on her cheek, his eyes dipping to her lips. "I'll go find you some coffee," he said, and walked toward the elevator.

She inhaled deeply and tried to control her pounding heart.

"Wow, that was really sweet."

Zahra jumped and spun around. A nurse observed Jake, her gaze soft and a dreamy smile brightening her face.

"You scared the hell out of me," Zahra said, pressing a hand against her chest.

"Sorry about that. I just wanted to let you know Alexis is in recovery. But honey, I wouldn't let that one go so easily."

"It's never been easy," she said with a sigh, glancing at the empty hallway as a familiar loneliness hollowed out her heart.

Zahra sat with Alexis, who was still drowsy from the surgery. Jake had brought her a cup of coffee and soon after, Alexis's parents arrived. Her roommate was safe and protected, and she gave herself permission to leave. The grit in her eyes and the ache in her jaw from yawning were clear indicators she needed some sleep.

She sighed when she glanced at her phone. It was only ten o'clock, but her body acted as if she'd been awake for days.

As she walked through the lobby of the hospital, she thought of returning to her apartment. Immediately, blood pulsed through her ears and nausea swirled in her gut. There was no way she could return after the violation. She couldn't stand to look at more yellow tape or the bloodstain that would forever mar the floor. Maybe she could stay at a hotel for a few days, get a cleaning crew...

The cool night air laced with the smell of the ocean caressed her face as she exited the hospital. She came to a stop and despite her exhaustion, her heart fluttered in her chest. Jake sat on a bench, his ankle crossed over his knee, his gaze unfocused as if he was lost in the past.

He seemed to sense her presence and rose to his feet. "I had a hunch you'd need a place to stay tonight."

She narrowed her eyes. *How does he do that?* she thought. He had a gift for knowing what she needed. Or did he simply understand her so deeply? The notion ignited a spark of hope in her chest, one she was too afraid to fan to life.

"I was going to get a hotel room."

He shoved his hands into his pockets. "I have a two-bedroom suite at the Marriott. It's close by."

Bad idea, she thought, especially in her vulnerable state. But being alone? Despite scrubbing her hands raw, the phantom touch of Alexis's blood clung to her skin. And the terror of seeing her on the floor, wondering if she was dead... Zahra swallowed and glanced at the parking lot.

"Okay, but just for the night until I figure something out."

Jake smiled and nodded toward his car. They drove in comfortable silence to his hotel, and when he opened the door, she whistled.

"Wow" was all she said as her Converse shoes sank into the lush carpet of his suite. "This place is bigger than my apartment." A leather couch and matching chairs sat in the middle of the room, with a fireplace to one side and floor-to-ceiling windows providing a view of the harbor.

Jake dropped his keycard, wallet, and keys on the granite countertop and walked to the small bar. He poured them both a drink. "Durand Enterprises has a hefty expense account." He handed her the glass of amber liquid.

"Must be nice," she said, taking a sip. The bourbon burned her throat but she welcomed the comforting warmth. Her last real meal was breakfast, and the alcohol went immediately to her head. She sat on the couch, rolling her glass between her palms.

He stared at her, his eyes dancing across her face. "Why don't I call up some food? You look about ready to fall over."

She forced a smile. "That'll be great."

He walked to the phone. "Your room is that one," he said, pointing down the hall.

She took another sip and then investigated where she'd be sleeping tonight. The king-size bed looked so inviting with the clean white comforter, soft sheets, and mounds of pillows reminding her of clouds that she almost collapsed right there. But a hot shower to wash away the day took priority.

Shower.

Food.

Sleep.

All while trying to avoid Jake, which was becoming more and more challenging. Having him by her side, telling him the truth about her father, was a comfortable familiarity, like slipping on her favorite sweatshirt.

She stripped out of her stained clothes, leaving them in a heap by the door, and stepped into the steaming mist. The hot water should have soothed her frayed nerves but all she saw when she closed her eyes was blood: Alexis's, and then her father's. Thoughts of him lying dead in the street made her knees buckle.

The next thing she knew, she was on the cold tile sobbing. She couldn't remember the last time she'd cried this much and wasn't sure she could stop. The floodgates had opened and there was no containing the tears of grief and guilt. The water poured down as she wrapped her arms around her knees and cried.

She didn't hear the knock, and jerked when Jake's voice sounded through the foggy glass. He'd opened the door, but kept his back to her, offering some privacy.

"Your dinner is here."

"I'll be right out," she said, unable to calm the trembling in her voice.

"Zee?" The glass door slid open and she turned her head, resting her cheek on her knees and staring at the black and white tiles.

The water turned off and she was surrounded by him as he wove an arm under her legs and placed her onto his lap, wrapping a towel around her. He kissed the side of her head. "I've got you. You're safe."

She collapsed against his chest and allowed the tears to continue to fall.

"Zee, you're going to be okay. You're one of the strongest women I know."

She wasn't sure how long she stayed in his arms while absorbing the comfort he gave. The ice flowing through her veins finally melted, replaced by hunger and heat as his muscular chest pressed against her and strong arms wrapped around her. His warm hand rubbed up and down her back, a movement that soothed while stoking the flames of longing.

She looked into his gray eyes, and his pupils darkened as his gaze drifted to her mouth. Where she sat, she felt how much he wanted her. Granted, she was naked and wet, despite the towel covering her. The desire to forget, to get lost in his touch, his warmth, made her lean forward, pressing her lips to his, soft and welcoming. He tightened his hold on her and deepened the kiss, their tongues slipping into a familiar dance. He groaned, his hands framing her face and tilting her head so he could explore deeper, being thorough with every swipe of his tongue.

She whimpered and wrapped her arms around his neck, weaving her fingers through his hair.

"Jake, please," she said, arching her back and begging for more.

He pulled away, his eyes darting between hers, and inhaled a calming breath. "When you look at me like that, you make it very difficult for me to be a gentleman."

"I don't need a gentleman right now."

"No, you need food and sleep."

She swallowed and looked away, focusing on the cold black-and-white tiles to escape the rejection clawing at her insides.

He gently touched her chin, making her look at him. "Zahra, I want you desperately, and it's taking every ounce of self-control I have right now not to worship every inch of you. But when we finally have sex, and we will, I don't want you broken. Okay?"

In the morning, she would be grateful that one of them was responsible, but in this moment of heat and steam, all she wanted was him.

He helped her to her feet, grabbing another towel for her hair. He wiped away a droplet of water from her collarbone, and any chill inside her evaporated with the way his gaze smoldered when he stared at her body, as if the longing was torturing him. He led her to the bed and pulled the covers up to her chin.

"I'm going to change, and then I'll be back, okay?"

She nodded and tried to swallow past the lump in her throat. His tenderness was enough to make her cry again, but she held the tears at bay. The door snicked shut and within seconds, she was asleep.

Chapter Seventeen

Kyden

Kyden slowly turned toward the demons. His sword appeared along his back, another hung at his hip, and a baldric of knives was draped across his chest. He drew his weapon as his bronze gorget materialized around his neck.

"Easy there," the Fallen named Cree said with a malicious smile on his ugly face. "You wouldn't want to cause a scene, would you?"

Kyden scanned the table. Arya and Bakal both removed their guns from their holsters and pointed them at him. The demon named Gael whispered to the woman on his lap, who shot a glance over her shoulder and then scurried away. He then rotated in his chair to face him, his green eyes widening slightly.

Bakal sneered. "You're in over your head, Kyden. You can't defeat all of us."

Kyden arched a brow. Technically, he didn't need to beat any of them. He simply needed to distract them so he could get out of this mess unscathed. He was a talented warrior, one of the best, but Fallen also knew how to fight, and they didn't care about safeguarding human lives.

Cree pulled up a vacant chair. "Why don't you join us?"

"I don't think so," Kyden said, extending his hand, causing the humans in the room to freeze, and stepped toward the balcony. "Besides, I've learned everything I need to from you degenerates."

Cree's upper lip curled, revealing pointy teeth. His eyes glowed as he stood. "You're not walking out of here."

"Wasn't planning on walking," Kyden said, unfurling his wings.

Arya and Bakal raised their guns. Gael, whose gaze had been locked on Kyden's, shifted, staring at something behind Kyden.

Kyden ducked and spun, slicing his blade through a large grunt. A loud screech sounded, followed by green sulfur exploding from the two halves of the demonic body. Gunshots blasted and he immediately wrapped his wings around himself, protecting his body from the bullets and ricocheting them back toward the demons.

Gael and Arya dove to the side to avoid the rogue bullets. Bakal wasn't smart enough to move and caught one in the chest. Cree flipped the table and ducked behind it.

Now or never, Kyden thought as a hoard of grunts charged him. He flared his wings and was about to launch through the roof when a burning pain cut through his side. He grunted and flapped his wings, sending a rush of air toward the demons. Cree threw another blade, but Kyden swiped it with his sword, altering its trajectory. He disappeared through the ceiling and into the night sky. An eerie yell trailed after him.

He winced as he soared amid the clouds and glanced at his side. Blood trickled from below his ribs where a dagger remained lodged in his flesh.

Titus was going to kill him.

He arrived seconds later on the balcony of the church, grunting at his not-so-perfect landing.

Titus spun around in his chair, and his eyes widened. "What have you gotten yourself into now?"

Kyden sheathed his sword, trying not to grimace, as he limped into the room. "Long story."

Titus stood and pointed at the hilt of the blade sticking out of him. "Is that demon steel?"

"Yes, but the intense burning is new." He sat on the edge of the bed, frowning at the golden blood staining his damaged Bon Jovi T-shirt. "This is my favorite shirt," he muttered.

Titus returned with a first aid kit, which consisted of bandages and holy water. "This is going to hurt."

"Just get it over with," Kyden said through gritted teeth. He tried to breathe through the fiery pain as the poison from the demon steel coursed through him.

"On the count of three." Titus gripped the hilt with one hand and held the bandages in the other. "One, two…" With a sickening squelch, he yanked the dagger free and covered the wound with a gauze pad.

Kyden bit back a few choice swear words he remembered Zahra using and instead focused on his breathing.

Titus dropped the knife on the floor, smoke drifting up from the partially melted blade. "Well, that's different," he said.

Kyden had thought the pain felt strange. "It seems our adversaries have improved their weapons."

"It seems so. I'll have to examine that later to see. It almost looks like acid is coating it." Titus tore his gaze from the smoking blade and shook the bottle of holy water. "This is going to burn too." He poured the liquid into Kyden's wound.

Kyden hissed through his teeth. "Holy hell, that hurts."

Titus pressed the bandage soaked with holy water onto the wound. "Holy hell?"

"That's all I could come up with."

"Want to tell me how you got yourself into this mess?"

"Not really." But he did anyway, starting from when he left Zahra's apartment to arriving at Club Nyx, finding the four Fallen.

Titus listened as he taped a clean bandage onto his skin. He washed his hands and, using a rag, picked up the blade and slid it into a plastic bag without saying a word, which was a dead giveaway the angel was pissed.

Once Kyden finished with his update, he said, "Go ahead and let it out."

Titus kept his back to him, resting his hands on his work chair, his head lowered. "You should have called me. I would've gone with you." He turned, his eyes sad. "You take unnecessary risks. Why is that?"

"I wasn't planning on getting caught. Besides, I'm a Slayer. Risk is part of our job description."

"I'm a Slayer too, as are Adinah and Oz and countless others. But we don't go off half-cocked. You're always looking for a fight and don't give a damn about the consequences or who may be affected if something happens to you. It's like you want to die."

Kyden's mouth dropped. In the millennia that he had known the angel, he'd never heard him swear nor act this serious. With Titus, there was always a joke to be had, a situation to make light of.

"First of all, I can't die," Kyden said. "Well, at least it would be very difficult." For a demon to accomplish ending an angel's existence, they'd have to cut off their head. Except all the angels wore a bronze gorget around their necks to prevent a horrible end.

Titus pointed to the melted blade. "This weapon might say otherwise."

Kyden ran his hands through his hair. "Don't you ever tire of the constant battle, always watching over the humans, Elohim's greatest creation?" The sarcasm dripped from his lips like venom.

Titus frowned as he sat in his chair. "Where is this coming from?"

For centuries, Kyden had fought one war after the other, killing so many demons he'd lost count, all to protect people who were weak and easily led astray. "They're not worthy of our sacrifice."

Titus leaned forward, resting his forearms on his thighs. "Elohim's grace isn't about worth. None of us deserves it."

"I know." Kyden sighed and hung his head. The silence pressed in on him, as did the weight of his vitriolic thoughts.

"So Raghav is leading them?" Titus asked, thankfully changing the subject.

Kyden removed his soiled shirt, threw it into the corner of the room, and fell back on the bed. "That's what they said, but there's no way that idiot is in charge. He has to be answering to someone else."

His friend grimaced at the growing pile of dirty clothes. With a wave of his hand, they disappeared. "One of the princes, I'd wager."

"Me too. I'm just not sure which one. Apollyon might want his halo back, but why now? Mammon is also high on my list."

Titus hummed. "This is something the Prince of Greed would do, especially since he's used the halo before. Adinah also heard that Marach was increasing his activity in Russia."

"So we potentially have Pride, Greed, and Wrath after the halo?" Kyden draped his arm over his eyes, exhaustion turning his thoughts into a tumultuous mess. "What's the status of Zahra and her roommate?"

"Alexis is out of surgery and her parents are with her. Zahra left the hospital with Jake and is currently at his hotel."

Kyden pushed up on his elbows. "Really?"

Titus tilted his head. "Really."

Kyden frowned. He was too tired to contemplate Zahra's actions. And why did it bother him she was with Jake? Where else would she go, knowing her apartment wasn't safe? He covered his eyes again and attempted to focus on the demons instead of a certain headstrong woman.

Kyden leaned against the balcony, closing his eyes to the warmth of the rising sun. He'd slept fitfully, but thanks to the healing powers in his angelic blood and the holy water, his body had recovered. Only a small scar remained, the spot still tender to the touch. As he sipped his coffee, he thought back to his conversation and confession to Titus.

His friend had a right to be angry with him for hunting the demons alone. But that's what he did. Titus worked with computers and technology while he wielded a sword. And maybe he had lost his way a little. He would never fully understand the preferential treatment of humans. They were easily tempted, driven by their own selfish desires, and yet still loved.

He drained the contents of his mug. He didn't have the energy for deep theological reflection, and going down that rabbit hole would simply give him a headache. Plus, he had a mission and her name was Zahra. The gloves were coming off because he needed answers—time was running out and the demons were closing in.

An hour later, he knocked on the door to Jake's suite despite Titus warning him that might not be a good idea.

Kyden was through being polite.

The door opened, and Jake stood in a pair of gray sweats, no shirt, his hair mussed from sleep, and his eyes resembling stone.

"Are you lost?" Jake asked, crossing his arms and leaning against the doorjamb.

"I'm looking for Zahra." Kyden glanced past him to check the main living area of the hotel room. "And don't tell me she isn't here."

Jake chewed on the inside of cheek as if processing his options, one of which was probably punching him in the nose, and then nodded. "Wait here."

The door shut in Kyden's face. He had half a mind to knock it down but twisted his neck, hearing a satisfying crack.

He glanced up at the ceiling. "Give me patience."

A few minutes later, the door opened with a frazzled-looking Zahra dressed in a T-shirt and boxers. Her lips parted, and she shook her head. "I'm actually at a loss for words."

"Good, then I'll do the talking." He pushed past her into the lush interior. "Nice outfit, by the way." He inwardly sighed. Why did it matter that she was wearing Jake's clothes? *Get your priorities straight*, he scolded himself.

"You should talk," she said, pointing to his Def Leppard shirt.

He looked down and frowned. "What's wrong with my shirt?"

"It's practically vintage."

He narrowed his eyes, about to argue with her about the famous band but remembered his plea for patience.

"Anyway, my other clothes are being laundered. Not that it's any of your business." She tied her hair aggressively into a messy topknot. She glanced at Jake, who leaned against the kitchen counter, holding a coffee cup. At least he'd put on a shirt.

"Why are you here? And better yet, how did you find me?" She pointed at him. "And how did you know this was Jake's room?"

"Breathe, Zahra," Kyden said.

Her mouth gaped. She shook her head again and marched over to Jake and stole his coffee. He smirked as she took a long drink, wincing at the heat.

"Would you like your own?" Jake asked as she handed back the empty mug.

Kyden didn't have time for their, well, whatever this was between them. "I need to talk to you." He shot a look at Jake. "Alone."

"This is my hotel room. I'm not leaving," he said, crossing a bare foot over the other, looking completely at ease, but the fire in his eyes betrayed his nonchalant appearance.

"What is this about?" Zahra asked, pulling out a barstool and sitting on it. Her cheeks had more color, but the evidence of dark circles under her eyes made him at least attempt to soften his tone. After all, she had lost her father, her roommate had been shot, and demons were to blame for both events.

"The Atar'zul. Where is it?"

Jake slid another cup of coffee across the bar to her, his brows inching up his forehead.

She narrowed her eyes. "The Atar'zul? Why would I know where it is?"

His gaze slid to Jake's then back to Zahra's. He didn't want to expose her to the man standing by her side. "Because I know you've been keeping secrets. I need the halo, now."

Her eyes flared as her knuckles whitened where she gripped the mug of coffee.

Jake shook his head and chuckled. "Bad move, buddy."

She glared at Jake and then turned her aggression onto him. "Secrets? I don't think I'm the one keeping secrets here. You're not some museum donor, are you? What do you want with the Atar'zul anyway?"

"Who I am and why I want it are irrelevant. You aren't safe, and the only way you will be is if you hand over the halo." His plan of attempting gentleness withered away like grass on a hot day.

"What do you mean she's not safe?" Jake asked, walking around the counter and placing himself between him and Zahra.

Kyden crossed his arms and waited. He could practically hear the gears turning in Jake's mind.

Jake faced Zahra. "Your coworker was murdered, as was your father, and your roommate shot. Does this all have to do with an ancient relic?"

Her face paled as she caught sight of Kyden's glare.

"He knows Dr. Neeman is your father?" Kyden asked through clenched teeth.

Her mouth opened again. If she kept it up, she'd resemble a dying fish.

"How the hell do you know that?" she asked, getting to her feet and shifting her anger toward Jake. "And that was a secret!"

Jake winced, but remained silent.

"I have my sources," Kyden said. "But yes, in answer to your boyfriend's question—"

"He's not my boyfriend," she said, resting her hands on her hips.

Jake shrugged. "Trying to remedy that," he murmured behind his mug.

"Either way," Kyden said, quickly losing whatever patience he had. "I believe all these events are connected. Therefore, you are in danger until I have the halo. Dr. Neeman found it and since he's mailed you other items, it's safe to assume he'd send you the halo."

"Other items?" Zahra licked her lips. "Who are you?"

"What other items?" Jake asked.

The thin thread connecting him to his patience unraveled. With a wave of his hand, Jake froze, his face expressionless.

CHAPTER EIGHTEEN

ZAHRA

Zahra stumbled back, her hand shaking as she pointed to the immobile Jake. "How...how did you do that? Is he okay?" One minute, he'd been speaking, and the next he was catatonic, yet standing up as if frozen in time.

"He's fine," Kyden said, walking toward the floor-to-ceiling windows overlooking the harbor. Sailboats glided on the water, stalked by flocks of seagulls.

She placed her mug on the side table and ran a hand down her face. "All right. You need to come clean. Who the hell are you and how..." She inched closer to Jake, waving in front of his face. Spinning around, she found Kyden watching her with his unique amber eyes. "How?"

"Obviously, I'm not who you thought I was, but I don't have time to explain everything. If I found you, then those hunting the halo will be able to as well."

She crossed her arms. "Well make time, dammit. You just barged in here, telling me you knew about my father, and I'm assuming knew about the necklace he sent, since you said 'other things.' Then did that," she said, indicating the Jake statue.

Kyden huffed out a breath, pulled out his phone, and held it to his ear. "This is going to take a little longer than I'd planned. Keep an eye out." He paused and then rolled his eyes. "Yes, you were right." He snapped the device shut and slid it into his pocket.

"Who was that?"

"My friend, Titus. He's how I found you."

Zahra frowned. Was there an edge in his voice that hadn't been there before? *Whatever*, she thought. She needed to focus. "So is this Titus stalking me?"

"Not really. We're able to track your phone."

Her mouth dropped again. She held up a hand and took a deep breath, trying to gather her thoughts. "Okay, Sam, let's start..." She paused when he winced. "Your name isn't Sam, is it?"

He pressed his lips together and shook his head.

She couldn't remember ever being this blindsided before as her gaze flicked between the liar in front of her and her frozen ex-boyfriend. She examined him, and a relieved breath escaped through her lips when she placed her fingers on his neck and felt a strong pulse.

Her feelings regarding Jake were changing, especially after the tenderness he showed last night, waking up in the security of his arms after such a terrible day. How he held her in the shower, letting her break, and then helped put her back together. He'd even implied he wanted to be her boyfriend again. Her stomach had clenched when he'd confessed that.

She shook her head. *Focus on the impostor in front of you, albeit a magical one who can force people into catatonic states.*

"What is your name?" she asked, facing him with her hands on her hips.

"Kyden."

She lifted her brows. "Kyden? No last name?"

"No."

"And who are you, really?" Her eyes darted to Jake. "Or what are you? And turn him back to his, you know, unfrozen self."

He chewed the inside of his cheek. "I can't tell you, nor will I turn him back yet."

"Why not?"

"For your protection. Please, you just have to trust me."

He took a step toward her, but she held her ground. "It seems you've lied to me from the beginning, *Sam*, so why would I trust you?"

He mumbled under his breath and paced while glancing at the ceiling. He finally sighed and said, "Evil men have searched for the Atar'zul for hundreds of years. Your father was part of a group sworn to protect it, but finding the halo got him killed and literally brought these men to your doorstep."

"It's just a relic and not worth murdering someone over." But she had to admit there were too many connecting links in the recent chain of events. First Brandon, then her father. Would she be dead too if she'd been home when Alexis was shot? Guilt twisted in her gut at the idea of her best friend standing in the literal line of fire.

"What if I told you the legends surrounding the halo are true?" Kyden asked.

She snorted. "You mean it has magical powers? Come on, surely you don't believe that."

"There are forces in this world you don't understand. The halo is the key to all of this," he said.

"Key," she whispered, frantically searching for her purse.

Kyden frowned. "What?"

She shot a glare at him as she threw pillows from the couch onto the floor. "I'm extremely pissed at you, but that can wait. My mom gave me a key the other day. She said my dad mailed it to her weeks ago." She dug through her purse. "Ah ha!"

"Did she tell you what it unlocks?"

Kyden tried to grab the key, but she yanked her hand back, the ridges digging into her palm. "No way, Mr. Liar Liar Pants on Fire."

He arched a brow. "Seriously?"

"And no, my mom didn't tell me what it unlocks, only that I would know what to do with it." Which she did. She hadn't forgotten the call from the man at A1 Storage. Her father must have a unit there, and this key would get her in.

A buzz sounded from Kyden's phone. He frowned at the screen. "Some men just showed up at your apartment. It won't be long before they find you here."

A chill had her wrapping her arms around herself. "Shouldn't we call the cops?"

"It won't do any good."

"What is that supposed to mean?"

The muscle in his jaw ticked and she could tell he was losing his patience. But she couldn't care less.

"This isn't a battle between flesh and blood. Please, I need you to trust me. I won't let anything happen to you, but I need you to tell me everything, and I need to find the halo."

"Getting awfully needy, aren't you?"

She stepped back, putting space between her and the man before her. Was it a trick of the light, or had his eyes glowed? Despite his lying to her, she didn't think he would cause her harm. He obviously knew more than he was telling her, especially with that flesh-and-blood comment, whatever the hell that meant. But she could use him to discover who murdered her father.

"I got a call from a storage company. Supposedly my dad rented a unit there," she finally confessed. Kyden opened his mouth to respond but she cut him off. "Don't even think it. I'm going there, and I'll let you tag along, but first I need to get some things from my place."

"Like what?"

She tapped her chin. "Hmm, let's see—how about my own clothes? And my gun."

He sighed. "You can't go there. Someone will be watching."

"Well, what do you expect me to do?"

He narrowed his eyes. "Give me a minute." And with that, he walked out the door.

She stared from the closed door to Jake. She rose on her tiptoes to look into his eyes. "Jake?" she whispered. Nothing. She paced back and forth along the plush carpet, not sure exactly what to do with herself. None of what she'd witnessed made any sense. "What an absolute cluster—ah!"

Kyden opened the door carrying a familiar-looking duffle bag and tossed it to her. "Get ready. We need to go."

She stared from Kyden to the bag in her arms, unable to wrap her mind around his sudden appearance. She unzipped the bag and saw her T-shirt and jeans, plus her Smith & Wesson she kept by the bed. "How? I thought the police took my gun..."

"Please don't ask. Just get dressed."

The Uber ride to A1 Storage had been relatively quiet. Kyden—what kind of name was that?—hadn't said much but kept his gaze on the side mirrors.

After a few minutes of silence, she simply couldn't stand it. "Is Jake okay? Did you return him to"—she glanced at the driver—"normal?" She had left a note on the kitchen bar explaining she needed to go but would be in touch soon. They had a lot to discuss.

"Yes."

She waited for him to expound. "And?"

Kyden turned toward her with a frown. "What?"

"Will he remember anything?" she asked.

"The human brain is adept at filling holes. He might be a little confused, but will convince himself everything is fine."

She crossed her arms and glared out the window. It was still early and the traffic was light. A1 Storage was on the north side of the city, thankfully only a short drive away.

"How did you do that?" she asked again, facing him.

"Magic," he said, baring his teeth in an icy smile.

"I don't believe in that sort of thing."

Kyden glanced once again at the side mirror. "You might want to start."

They soon arrived at the storage place. Kyden, after telling the driver to wait for them, lingered near the car while she talked with the manager. When she exited the office, she said, "My father's unit is down this row. The owner said a package arrived a few weeks ago."

"How long did your dad have this?"

"I wasn't even aware he did. Supposedly, he's rented it for a few months, but the manager had never met him."

They walked down the row until coming up to unit twelve. "This is it." She dug inside her purse, retrieving the key, and released a sigh when it slid into the lock. Kyden yanked open the door and his shoulders stiffened.

The unit was empty except for a cardboard shipping box lying on the ground in the center of the dark room.

She walked in, the only light inside cast by the open door, and glared down at the box. According to the owner, her father had only paid for a short-term lease, which had come to term a few days ago, and if it wasn't renewed, the instructions were to call her.

Kyden remained near the doorway, his eyes continuing to scan the street and parking lot. She wasn't sure what to make of him, especially after what he'd done to Jake and how he'd retrieved her things from her apartment so quickly. He had told her it was magic, but was that even possible? Currently, she had no other explanation.

He had lied to her about pretty much everything, which stung more than she wanted to admit. She was still angry with him and needed to know the truth, and it seemed her bargaining chip was tucked away inside a cardboard box.

Zahra retrieved her keys from her purse and was going to use one to slice open the tape when Kyden appeared with a wicked-looking pocketknife.

"Here," he said, holding it hilt-first.

Her brows rose. "Where have you been hiding that?"

He rolled his eyes and handed it to her. "Careful, it's sharp."

"I certainly hope so." She took the knife, sliced through the tape, and returned the blade to him. He snapped it shut and placed it in the back pocket of his jeans.

Inside the package was a metal box with a combination lock.

"Please tell me you know the combination," he said, taking a small step back.

She sat on the floor and rested the box on her lap. It was a six-number combination lock. She entered her father's birthday and yanked on the lock, but nothing. She tried her mom's birthday, but that didn't work either. Finally, she tried hers and the lock snapped open.

So he did know when her birthday was. He'd always been days or weeks late with his email messages, and she'd figured he wasn't sure of the actual date. She clenched her teeth, forcing the rising tide of grief to a place where she wouldn't have to be reminded of the guilt.

Indifference and resentment had been bulwarks of support for her over the years when it came to her feelings toward her dad. She didn't want to consider the alternative—that possibly he actually cared for her as his daughter and not as some mutual academic.

She lifted the lid. "This is it." Her hands shook as she unwrapped the paper and ran a finger over the tarnished and cracked crown. An electric shock traveled up her hand and arm as if she had touched an exposed wire.

"Give it to me," Kyden said, moving toward her, his eyes narrowed on the Atar'zul.

"I need to run tests, make sure it's authentic. And tell Mr. Rousseau we finally have it." Holding it up to the light, she moved it from side to side. "Why would Dad send it here, though?"

"To keep you safe. Now give it to me, please." He lunged to grab it, but she yanked back her hand.

"What is your problem?" she asked, getting to her feet.

"Currently, you are."

"Hey!" One second, he was standing five feet away. The next, he stood right in front of her, his fingers wrapped around the halo. She hadn't even seen him move.

She stumbled as his body arched, his head tossed back, teeth bared. His face paled and he groaned, falling to his knees as sweat broke out on his forehead.

She grabbed the halo and had to rip it from his grasp. He immediately collapsed onto his hands and hung his head, inhaling deep breaths.

"What the hell just happened?" she asked, her gaze shifting from the halo to Kyden, who slowly rose to his feet.

He swayed slightly and rubbed a hand over his mouth. "I didn't think it would be that powerful."

She retrieved the box, noticing a dusty journal on the bottom along with a flash drive. She slid the drive into her pocket—she'd have to look at that later. Right now, she needed answers.

Closing the box and locking it, she said, "Start talking."

He wiped the sweat from his forehead and took one last deep breath. "I'm not sure you can handle the truth."

She jutted her hip out. "Oh really? Maybe I should wave this thing at you again, because *you* obviously couldn't handle that."

He rose to his full height, which was rather intimidating if she was being honest, and glared at her, an unnatural glow in his eyes. "Why are you being so stubborn?"

"Stubborn? How's this for stubborn? I'm out of here and taking this with me unless you answer my questions."

He paced in front of the open doorway, mumbling to himself and peering outside into the empty parking lot. She removed her phone from her back pocket just in case she needed to call the cops. Even though he said to trust him, she'd be a fool not to be prepared for the worst.

"Fine," he finally said. He strode toward her, and she forced herself not to retreat. "Put this on. It will be easier and faster than my having to explain everything." He reached into his jacket pocket and removed the necklace her father had sent her.

"You didn't," Zahra said, ripping the chain from his hand. "You stole this from my apartment?"

"To keep you safe. Put it on."

She set the box at her feet and slipped the chain over her head. She chewed the inside of her cheek. "Well?"

"It needs to touch your skin." His voice was clipped but also lined with resignation.

She looked down at the silver feather, twisted into a perfect spiral. She scowled at Kyden and then grabbed the pendant.

Stumbling backward, almost tripping over the box, she backed into the wall. "Holy shit!"

The man before her was no longer wearing jeans and a T-shirt, but rather a skin-tight black shirt with a leather chest piece and leather pants. A sword peeked over his shoulder while his amber eyes glowed and an aura of golden light surrounded him.

She immediately released the pendant to dial 911. With a speed she couldn't fathom, he was in front of her. A loud crunch filled the silence as he crushed the device in his hand, her phone disintegrating into metal bits. Her mouth dropped as she watched the particles drift to the floor.

His face remained expressionless. "That necklace enables you to see into the spiritual realm."

She touched her finger again to the pendant, the ice-cold feeling returning as the image of Kyden flickered from what looked like an ordinary man to a leather-clad warrior.

"What are you?" she whispered, her anger at him destroying her phone disappearing as she stared at the hilt of his sword and the golden light surrounding him.

"An angel."

She waited for more of an explanation, but he'd pressed his lips into a flat line. "Since when do angels wear black leather?"

The corner of his mouth lifted. She blinked against a flash of light and huge silver wings unfolded from his back. Chain mail had replaced the shirt and bronze armor covered him from his neck to his shins. A gold crown circled his forehead, and instead of one sword, he had two: the one on his back and another on his hip. A leather belt wrapped around his hips with a silver emblem in the middle.

"Is this more to your liking?" he asked with a smirk.

She squeezed her eyes shut. She could be hallucinating like her mother did, although that prospect didn't calm her any more than the man before her.

"Zahra, open your eyes."

His voice, a lethal combination of silk and steel, sent a shiver down her spine, and she automatically obeyed. If she thought he was handsome before, now he was stunning and intimidating as hell.

"Explain, right now." She was proud of the confidence emanating from her voice. Inside, her heart raced and her legs wobbled, seconds away from collapsing.

"I'm a Slayer Angel. I kill demons."

She shook her head. "Demons? Are you kidding me? There's no such thing."

"There is. And they are hunting you."

Releasing the pendant, she pushed off the wall, keeping her distance from the ang— Nope. She couldn't even think the word.

Questions ricocheted through her mind like a rubber ball set loose. "Why do you keep changing forms?"

He nodded at the metallic feather lying against her shirt. "The talisman allows you to see me as my true self."

"True self," she murmured, staring past him to the parking lot. The image of glorious yet frightening wings, swords, and armor made her chest tighten to where she found it difficult to breathe. The walls of the storage unit felt like they were closing in on her. She needed to get out of here and away from the crazy man in front of her.

She picked up the box and held it against her, using it like a shield. "Stay away from me."

"I can't do that. You're not safe, especially now that you have the halo."

She walked toward him, and he crossed his arms. "Move," she said, thankful her voice continued to sound strong.

"Zahra, please."

"Don't 'Zahra, please' me. Get the hell out of my way. You've lied to me from the beginning. Nothing about you is true."

The skin around his eyes tightened. "I never lied. Well, except for my name."

"You're an angel!" She shoved past him, blinking as the sun blinded her briefly.

He grabbed her arm, his touch gentle and firm at the same time. A sense of peace washed over her, the sensation familiar, followed by a shiver down her spine. She gasped as she stared at his hand and then into his eyes, while the memory of the calmness she experienced when her best friend lay on the floor surrounded by blood washed through her.

"It was you?" she whispered.

CHAPTER NINETEEN

KYDEN

Kyden stared into Zahra's eyes, trying to convey peace, something he currently didn't feel as he struggled with the lingering effects of the halo. He had known the relic was powerful, but had no idea of its magnitude. When the cold metal had adhered to his skin, his magic, the very essence of him, had dimmed. Once Zahra forced it from his hands, the pain had stopped; his power, however, still hadn't returned to full strength.

"You were with me and Alexis, weren't you? In my apartment?" she asked.

He released her arm and nodded.

She covered her mouth and walked backward to the waiting car. "This is just...too much."

He followed her. "Zahra, please. You're not safe."

"How do I know *you* didn't kill my father or Brandon? You've been after the Atar'zul from the beginning." Her knuckles whitened as she gripped the box tighter. If he wanted, he could use his magic and take it. At least, he thought he could. He wasn't sure of the lasting damage caused by the halo to his power. Or was it his soul? He'd have to process that later. Right now, Zahra looked like she was readying herself to run.

He tilted his head. "You know nothing of angels, do you? I'd never hurt a human."

She stopped retreating, her eyes narrowing as she approached him and poked him in the chest. "News flash, asshole. Being lied to hurts."

He stared down at her finger and arched a brow. Angry Zahra was better than scared Zahra, but now wasn't the time for games. If Titus had the ability to track her phone, then so did the demons. "Let me explain something to you, and I really need you to keep up."

Her mouth dropped and her cheeks flushed, but thankfully she remained silent and didn't run screaming for the waiting car.

"Your father was a Vaelatori, a guardian of the Atar'zul, and that talisman gave him sight into the spiritual realm. And because your father was a Vaelatori, that means you are too. There is evil out there, Zahra, and it's eager to kill for what it wants, and it wants the Atar'zul." He nodded at the box in her hand.

"This can't be happening," she said to herself, staring off into the distance.

"I realize it's a lot to take in, and I'm sorry you found out the way you did." He shoved his hands in his pockets. "But I need to get you off the streets. You're not safe here."

She stared at where he'd hidden his hands and frowned. She then patted down her pockets as if looking for something. "I wish I had a cigarette." She reached into her pocket and pulled out the flash drive.

"I have to look at this," she said.

"Agreed. But not at your apartment or your office."

"Yeah, no kidding." A choked laugh escaped her lips.

"You're about to lose it, aren't you?" he asked, examining her face.

"Yup."

He didn't need her breaking down in the middle of the parking lot. Plus, the driver of the Uber had lowered his sunglasses, not hiding the suspicion narrowing his eyes. He wasn't sure who was ready to bolt first, Zahra or the driver.

"Let me get you somewhere safe and then you can ask me whatever you want, or yell at me if you so desire." He walked to the passenger side of the car. "Honestly. You *can* trust me."

"Not so sure about that. But I bet ditching you would be impossible since you can"—she pointed to his back—"you know, fly."

"Well, there is that." He gave her a full grin.

They rode in silence as the driver swerved through morning traffic to the Sacred Path Church. Kyden had texted Titus, telling him they were on the way.

Zahra sat with her back leaning on the car door, her arms crossed as she examined him, a deep groove carved between her eyebrows.

"What?" he asked, sliding his phone into his pocket.

"You look so normal."

"That's the idea."

"You don't get to be sarcastic with me. Is that clear?"

He arched a brow but decided silence was best. At least until they arrived at the church. He practically heard the gears in her mind grinding as she chewed on her thumbnail. Relief coursed through him at finally having the halo in his possession. The next step was throwing the demons off Zahra's scent. Once she was no longer a target, he'd decide what to do with the cursed relic.

He held off reporting to Raphael, his archangel and a general in Elohim's army, but based on the events of the last couple of days, he figured another long flight was in his immediate future. According to Adinah, Raphael was fighting demons somewhere in Russia.

They drove for a few more minutes until they pulled into a parking lot behind the church.

Zahra leaned over and stared up at the steeple. "What are we doing here?"

"This is where I'm temporarily living."

"Figures," she said under her breath, grabbing the box and getting out of the car.

He shook his head and opened the back door of the church. They climbed four flights of stairs before finally stopping in front of a large metal door.

She pointed to the cameras. "This seems slightly obvious."

A click sounded, and the door unlocked. He pulled it open. "After you."

"How do I know you're not luring me into your evil lair?" She peeked past him to peer into the room.

"Think of it as the Batcave," he said, gently placing his hand on her lower back and giving her a little nudge.

"Let me guess. You're Batman."

He snorted. "Sure, and this is Robin, also known as Titus."

"Why am I Robin?" Titus snapped a piece of red licorice off between his teeth.

Kyden rubbed the skin between his eyebrows. Ever since holding the halo, a headache had lingered in his skull. "Zahra, meet Titus. Titus, this is Zahra Jenkins."

"Hello," Zahra said, extending her hand and then yanking it back. "Wait, are you an angel too?"

"You have the talisman," he said, nodding at the necklace.

When she wrapped her hand around the pendant, her face paled, and she wobbled slightly. Kyden led her to a chair near the balcony.

He knelt next to her. "Just breathe, okay?"

"I'm fine, just need a minute."

"You're actually handling this pretty well. Most people scream or faint," Titus said, returning to his seat and examining a slew of mug shots. "Granted, all you're seeing is our aura. Wait until you see the armor and wings."

"Seen it," she said, taking deep breaths, her head still hanging between her knees.

Titus shook his head. "Subtle, Kyden."

Kyden ignored his friend and spoke to Zahra. "I can make coffee, or how about some water?" He rose to his feet. "Or I have some leftover donuts."

She looked up, a frown marring her face, then shook her head.

"How come you never offer me coffee or snacks?" Titus asked, another piece of licorice hanging from the corner of his mouth and a mischievous glint in his eye.

"Shut up," Kyden grumbled, stomping across the floor to where they had set up their small kitchen and grabbing a bottle of water. They had little in the way of food. "Titus, I need you to grab some groceries for Zahra."

"Do you see DoorDash written on my forehead?" he asked, pointing to his face. "I'm not a delivery boy."

"Titus, please. Zahra and I need to talk." Kyden widened his eyes at his friend, hoping he'd pick up on the hint.

Titus huffed out a breath. "Fine." He strode to the balcony and jumped.

Zahra screamed and ran to the edge. "Oh my god!" She peered at the street below.

Kyden tapped the talisman hanging from her neck.

She wrapped her shaking fingers around the pendant. "Holy shh...oot." She glanced at him with a sheepish smile.

The sun glinted off Titus's wings as he flew toward downtown Boston, banking to the left and disappearing behind a building. Seeing angels fly wasn't anything new to him, but witnessing the wonder in Zahra's eyes made him smile.

He hated wiping that grin off her face, but they needed to talk, find a place for her to hide, and get the halo as far from her as possible.

"How are you holding up?" he asked, handing her a bottle of water.

She tore her gaze from the line of skyscrapers and leaned against the railing. "I think shock and adrenaline, along with exhaustion, are keeping me from throwing myself over the ledge."

"I'd just catch you if you did." He walked back inside and sat on the edge of the bed, pointing at the chair she'd occupied earlier. "Now's your opportunity to ask your questions." His gaze flicked to where she'd put the box on the wooden side table. He'd known the minute she opened the metal case containing the halo his secret would be revealed. He had seriously contemplated taking the relic and leaving her, but he couldn't abandon her, not with the demons actively hunting her.

She sipped the water as she stared at him, her eyes narrowed while her thumb rubbed the silver feather hanging around her neck. "Why can't I see your wings and armor?"

"Because I don't need them right now."

"Is this your normal form?"

He glanced down at his jeans and boots. "Mostly. I can glamour my clothing or appearance whenever I want."

"So if you wanted to pretend to be a cat, you could?"

"Why would I ever pretend to be a cat?" he asked, wondering if maybe she *was* losing her mind.

She shrugged. "Just a hypothetical." She rolled the water bottle between her palms. "So, I've seen you freeze people and, based on your wings and Titus's leap from the balcony, you can obviously fly. What else can angels do?"

"Strength, speed, excellent hearing."

"So, like Superman?"

Kyden chuckled. "Yes, but without the capes or shooting rays of light from our eyes."

"Well, that's unfortunate."

"We can also warp reality, make the weaker-minded people see what we want them to. We can be injured but not killed, well at least not easily."

Her leg bounced up and down as she stared out the window, processing everything he'd said so far. He shot off a quick text to Titus asking him to buy lollipops to help settle her nerves.

"You mentioned evil earlier and something about demons," she said.

"How well do you know your Bible?"

"Historically, I would do pretty well on *Jeopardy!*, but I've never studied the spiritual realm."

He rested his arms on his thighs. "Before humans existed, Elohim created angels. Apollyon wanted to be as mighty and powerful as Elohim, so he led a rebellion, which caused the Celestial War. Those who betrayed Elohim were cast down and their wings destroyed." He scrutinized her face, satisfied to see her eyes clear and focused on him. "The demons who rebelled are called Fallen. They have human forms, and mostly the same powers as an angel, besides flying of course. There are also grunts—smaller demons that can only influence people's emotions and behavior. These are all ruled by the seven princes of hell."

She rubbed her eyes and then stood, pacing in front of him. Her brow furrowed as she absorbed everything he'd revealed so far.

"Elohim? I'm not familiar with that term."

"Most humans call him God."

"And Apollyon?"

"Lucifer is a more common name."

She stopped pacing and whirled toward him. "Did demons kill my father?"

He scratched the stubble on his jaw. "In a way. They didn't physically pull the trigger but they were involved. The same with your coworker. Fallen can possess a person and have them do their bidding. There are also daemonkin. They willingly serve the demons."

He probably should have told her all this when he'd discovered Dr. Neeman had been killed. But at the time, he hadn't known of her connection to the archaeologist. He'd never been more wrong, and now they were stuck in this mess together until he found and destroyed the demons seeking the halo. And if the culprit was a prince of hell, well, he'd need reinforcements.

Zahra folded her arms around herself. "You called yourself a Slayer Angel. What does that mean?"

"There are three types of angels. Archangels, who are the most powerful and serve as intermediaries between Elohim and humans. Essentially, they maintain order. Protectors are what your kind call guardian angels. They are messengers and help people." He stared at his interlocking fingers.

"And the Slayers?" she asked, scanning his face as if trying to read his thoughts.

"We hunt and kill demons."

She bit her lip and returned her gaze toward the skyline. The circles under her eyes had grown darker and her skin drained of color. Whether or not she wanted to admit it, she needed rest and food.

"I think that's enough for now," he said, rising to his feet. She confirmed his thoughts as she simply nodded and plopped down into the chair.

He busied himself at the computer, staring at the mug shots of the men who had gone into her apartment. One looked somewhat familiar, but he couldn't say from where.

"Do you recognize this guy?" he asked her, pointing to the bearded man with a military-style haircut.

She stood and walked over to Titus's U-shaped desk, bending forward to get a closer look. Her hair grazed his cheek, and a shiver coursed through him. He subtly put more space between them.

"I think I've seen him before, but I'm not sure where."

"Yeah, me too." They both stared at the image.

"Is this one of the men who broke into my apartment?"

"Yes."

"Is he a demon?"

"No, although he might be possessed. I'd have to be near him to know."

She straightened and a giggle slipped between her lips. "Do angels drink because, honestly, I really need something stronger than water."

He rose to his feet and walked to the refrigerator. "Alcohol doesn't affect us the way it does humans. But every now and then, I like the taste of beer." He grabbed one and handed it to her.

She popped open the beer. He was about to offer her a glass when his brows shot up as she chugged from the can.

"No glass, then," he mumbled as he placed it back on the shelf. He had to admit, she was stronger than he had assumed and seemed to handle the revelation of the spiritual realm fairly well. Of course, it might be only a matter of time before she completely lost it. He had seen it before and hoped she could keep it together, because somehow he needed to convince her to go into hiding and give him the Atar'zul.

CHAPTER TWENTY

ZAHRA

"I'll take that donut now," Zahra said, rubbing her temple. The beer had calmed her nerves but had also gone straight to her head, since her last meal was the previous night with Jake.

She hadn't had a moment to think about him since Kyden had barged into his hotel room. Jake had been wonderful, just as she remembered him, and it made her heart ache. If he'd been aloof or even rude, then the wall protecting her heart would have remained solid. But the way he'd treasured her, holding her while she slept and keeping the nightmares away, had shattered her defenses.

She needed to call him to see if he was okay, and walked toward her bag before remembering Kyden had crushed her phone. Her hands clenched into fists. "Give me your phone. I need to call someone."

"Who?"

"Jake, and before you ask why, to make sure he's not still catatonic."

"He's fine."

"You don't know that." She crossed her arms and then lowered them to her side. "Please, I just need to talk to him."

Kyden removed his phone from his pocket and typed a quick text, then put it away.

She'd opened her palm, expecting him to hand over his archaic device. As if he would be that accommodating.

"Before you rip my head off, I asked Titus to pick you up a burner phone, one the demons can't track."

She focused on the cobwebs clinging to the rafters. "Demons. Right." She had officially slipped down Alice's hole into Wonderland, but instead of Mad Hatters and smoking caterpillars, she had stumbled into a world with technologically advanced demons.

Perfect.

She slid her hands into her pockets, trying to hide her shaking fingers, and they brushed against the flash drive. Closing her eyes, she squeezed the drive until it dug into her palm, suspecting a message from her father. Did she want to hear what he had to say? Her curiosity would win out but the grumbling in her stomach had her striding to the small kitchen. She found the donuts, all the chocolate ones missing based on the frosting smudging the bottom of the box. Grabbing a plain glazed one and another beer—liquid courage was necessary for what she was about to do—she placed the flash drive on the desk and raised her brows at Kyden.

"Titus is on his way. I'd like him to make a copy, if that's all right with you."

"Why not?" She took a bite of her donut and chased it with a gulp of beer. Not the best combination, but she'd tasted worse.

She studied the large desk and monitors, along with stacks of files. The scene before her seemed completely normal, nothing spiritual or magical here. Her brow furrowed when she spotted a small rectangular box with an old set of headphones attached to it.

Wiping the sugar from her fingers, she picked it up. "Is this what I think it is?"

Kyden reached for it but she took a step back. He crossed his arms and scowled at her. "Give me my Walkman."

She turned the device over, her fingers skimming the buttons, and pushed Eject. "I saw one of these on eBay. They're ancient."

Before she could remove the Billy Idol tape inside, Kyden snatched it from her hand. "I'd hardly consider the eighties ancient." He wrapped the cord around the device and placed it on the other side of the room.

"Aren't we testy," she said with a laugh that morphed into a gasp as a rush of wind and wings shoved her heart from her chest and up her throat. The necklace warmed against her skin as Titus approached at an alarming speed.

What had seemed completely normal minutes ago flew out the window as a warrior with wings landed on the balcony carrying grocery bags.

His long blond hair had fallen loose from its tie and his amber eyes glowed. A frown marred his beautiful face. "Next time, you go shopping," Titus said, shoving the food at Kyden.

Kyden rolled his eyes and unpacked the items. He handed her the burner phone along with a bag of her favorite lollipops.

Her stomach tightened at the gesture. "Thank you."

He dipped his chin and carried the rest of the groceries to the small kitchen.

She was about to unwrap a lollipop when she stopped. How had he known she liked these? She racked her brain, trying to remember if she'd eaten the candy in his presence.

Titus walked toward his desk and picked up the flash drive. "What's this?"

Zahra bit into a root beer–flavored lollipop. Titus grimaced and rubbed his ear. "I'm assuming it's a message from my father," she said. Ready or not, her time was up.

Kyden pulled up a chair and sat next to her as Titus inserted the drive into his computer.

Zahra's father cleared his throat. He sat behind a desk, and based on the canvas wall behind him, he must have been in a tent at a dig site. He licked his lips and stared at the screen.

Her shoulders stiffened as her dad spoke.

"Hello, Zahra. Not to sound cliché, but if you're watching this, then I'm most likely dead."

She felt the weight of Kyden's gaze but her eyes stayed glued to the monitor. Besides a few pictures of him in archaeology magazines, she hadn't seen her father in years. He'd aged, the lines on his face deeper, and his dark hair peppered with gray. He wore his usual tan button-down shirt, and against his neck was a familiar-looking silver chain. She ran her finger along the necklace as the beer and donuts churned in her stomach.

"I discovered soon after I married Nancy that my family tree wasn't your typical heritage. I was approached by a man who was in the line of Branok and was called a Vaelatori, a guardian of the Atar'zul. He revealed to me the history of Apollyon's halo, and my responsibilities, first to locate the halo and then to protect it at all costs. I tried to forget this man and the news he brought, but a calling deep in my soul lured me toward the Atar'zul. This calling I later learned was the favor of God, and all Vaelatori have it. Which means you do too."

She absently scanned her body, and as if her father could see her, he continued, "It's not an external mark, but one on our soul. Because of this mark, evil is drawn to us, putting us and those we love at risk. The repercussions of what I learned meant abandoning the woman I loved and the daughter I so terribly wanted." Her dad closed his eyes briefly and cleared his throat again. "The most precious things in my life would be in danger if the enemy made the connection between us."

Her hand covered her mouth, the monitor turning blurry with unshed tears clouding her vision.

"As you're aware, I spent most of my career searching for historical and biblical artifacts—the more mystery behind them, the better. My journal, which contains my notes, has led me to the Atar'zul."

She caught both Kyden and Titus staring at the side table where the box storing the journal and halo sat.

"Zahra, darling. I'm so sorry this burden has come to you. I ran out of time to do what you must now do. There is a prophecy regarding the halo. The Vaelatori have collected bits and pieces of it over the years. At the dig site in Baghdad, I found the final piece, but it still needs to be translated. It is imperative that the enemy does not get the halo."

The wheels on Titus's chair squeaked as he faced Kyden. "Do you know anything about a prophecy?"

Kyden stared at the screen, his expression carved from stone. "No."

"Shhh," she said, waving at the angels.

Her father looked over his shoulder and frowned. He pulled the necklace free from his shirt. "I'm sending you this talisman. It's made from an actual angel feather, you know." His eyes sparkled as he gave a small smile. "Wear it all the time for your protection against those who will hunt you and the halo. You should receive it before the event." Sadness pulled the corners of his lips down. "I'm sorry I can't be there in person. I couldn't bring that kind of danger to your doorstep. But I think they've learned I found the Atar'zul, and time is a luxury I no longer have."

As her father leaned forward, she instinctively moved closer, as though a magnet tugged at her from the monitor to her chest.

"I've followed your career, and I'm so proud of you, honey. You're brilliant, and I trust you'll figure out the prophecy. And hopefully, you'll get some help. As there is darkness, there is also light. The talisman will allow you to see the angelic warriors who will protect you." He rubbed his hands together and a gold band around his ring finger sparkled. "And please tell your mother I never stopped loving her."

The image dissolved into a blank screen.

She quickly swiped at a tear trailing down her cheek. Kyden signaled to Titus, and they both stood, walking onto the balcony to give her some privacy.

She leaned back and stared at the computer. What the hell had her father gotten himself into? And now he'd dragged her into his nightmare. He had dumped this whole mess in her lap and shifted her entire reality. Her mother's words from the other day made a little more sense.

"Don't be mad at your father. He's a protector. He had to go."

Her mom must have known he hadn't just abandoned her and their unborn daughter but had left once he'd discovered he was a Vaelatori. Which meant Zahra was too. Were there others? Maybe she could pass the burden on to them.

She shook her head. If her father had known of anyone else, he would have kept all of this away from her. Of that, she was certain. Plus, he had faith in her to translate this prophecy. She drew herself up in quiet affirmation of her worth—a sensation she hadn't realized she desperately needed. Her dad was proud of her and had followed her career. The notion soothed the resentment that had hardened her heart for so many years.

She removed the journal from under the silver box containing the halo and ran her fingers over the dusty cover. Her breath hitched when she saw her father's familiar scrawl detailing the history of the Atar'zul on the first few pages. As she flipped through the book, anger simmered, overshadowing the pride she'd been feeling.

Her knuckles whitened on the journal. "Stupid, arrogant, son of a bitch. I could have helped you, you idiot."

Kyden cleared his throat and she jumped. He and Titus both stood in the room, arms crossed and brows raised.

"I probably shouldn't swear in front of you two, should I?" she said, wincing.

"Well, you're smart enough to come up with better adjectives, but..." Kyden shrugged.

"Sometimes dropping a good curse word feels more satisfying," she said, tamping down her anger. She'd need to deal with the muddled emotions of guilt, love, and anger at another time, preferably not around angelic warriors.

Titus chuckled. "You find anything so far?"

"No. I started flipping through it, and then I got mad. Of course, I figured his job would one day get him killed. He always took risks, but I never would have thought something like this would happen." She closed the journal and rose to her feet, unable to focus on the words. Despite sleeping soundly last night, she was exhausted, but there were a few things she needed to do first.

She removed the burner phone from its packaging. After sending a quick text to Alexis, checking in on her, and one to Meredith with the new number, claiming she lost hers, she started to call Jake.

"Dammit. I don't know his number," she said, staring at the phone.

Titus walked to his desk and scrawled the number on a piece of paper.

"Do I even want to know how you have this? Or why, for that matter?" she asked, entering the number into her contacts.

"Probably not," Titus said.

She was about to call Jake when Kyden touched her arm.

"It's best not to reveal what you've learned."

She frowned at the gravity in his tone. "You don't think he's involved with any of this, do you?"

He crossed his arms. "Right now, I don't trust anyone, and you shouldn't either. Demons are clever."

"I think I'd be able to tell if a demon had possessed Jake," she said, the phone digging into her palm.

Kyden's eyes narrowed. How had she not seen his warrior tendencies when she first met him? The man—angel, she corrected herself—was intimidating as hell.

"Just guard what you've learned for now, okay?"

She sighed. "Fine."

"I'm leaving in a little while. There are some things I need to check. While I'm gone, Titus is in charge." He pointed at her, which made her want to yank on his finger. "You cannot leave this room."

Blood rushed through her ears. She resisted the urge to flip him off and stepped outside. "Bossy fricking angel," she said under her breath.

Titus chuckled and said, "You certainly have a way with women."

She shut the door, blocking out Kyden's reply. Dusk approached, and she breathed in the cool fall air before making a quick call to the nursing home, giving them her number in case they needed to reach her. Finally, she called Jake, trying to ignore the butterflies in her stomach.

He picked up on the third ring. "This is Jake Callahan."

His voice sent a shiver down her spine. "Jake, it's me."

"Zahra? What the hell? I've been trying to reach you all day. Where are you? Are you all right?"

"I'm fine. My phone was damaged." Not a lie. "And I'm staying with a friend for a few days." Also not a lie, sort of.

He released a breath. "I was so worried. In the future, maybe not leave such a vague note."

"That's the whole purpose of a note. Short and sweet."

"Knock it off, smartass."

She chuckled, imagining his smirk and gray eyes wrinkling at the corners. "Sorry I worried you. I had some urgent things I needed to take care of."

"But you're okay?"

"I'm good. How about you?" She had no idea what the side effects of an angel freezing someone were and she really hoped Jake was his normal self.

"The weirdest thing happened. It's like when you're really drunk, and you're missing parts of your memory. Except I wasn't drunk. Anyway, I remember drinking coffee with you and the next thing I knew, I was going about my normal routine. I wasn't even aware you'd left." He huffed out a laugh. "I don't think I'm making any sense."

She obviously couldn't tell him that a warrior angel had busted into his hotel room and frozen him. In fact, she really couldn't tell him much without him admitting her into a rehab facility. *Keep it simple*, she thought.

"Thank you for taking care of me last night," she finally said.

"It was my pleasure." He paused for a moment. "I'd love to see you again. No nachos and margaritas this time. Just coffee?"

She laughed and her chest warmed, realizing she wanted to see him too, but with everything going on, how could she? Plus, she didn't want to put him in danger. Kyden's words filtered through her thoughts.

"Right now, I don't trust anyone, and you shouldn't either. Demons are clever."

She didn't believe Jake was involved in this nightmare, but if she was honest with herself, she wasn't one hundred percent sure.

"I can't right now. I have some things that need my attention. Besides, you'll be leaving for Vegas soon."

"I've been meaning to talk with you about—"

"Look, Jake," she interrupted, not wanting to crumble under his powers of persuasion. "It's best not to rekindle anything."

A sigh sounded through the line. She pictured his furrowed brows and the muscle in his jaw pulsing. "Zee, that flame has been lit, and I intend to throw gasoline on the fire. But in the meantime, you've had a hellish couple of days. Get some rest and we'll talk later."

She hung up the phone and closed her eyes. Hellish couple of days was an understatement.

Chapter Twenty-One

Kyden

Kyden flew across the Atlantic Ocean, again, in search of the archangel Raphael. Titus wasn't thrilled to be watching over Zahra, but he'd grimaced when Kyden suggested he report to one of the seven generals of Elohim's army.

"Raphael likes you better," Titus had said when they'd stood on the balcony of the church while Zahra rested.

Kyden wasn't so sure about Titus's statement, but Kyden had served under Raphael the longest and both had the propensity to slash first, ask questions later. He supposed they were similar in that regard.

The seven archangels were extremely powerful, but the most fearsome was Michael, who'd single-handedly fought off Apollyon and triumphed. Next came Gabriel, with Raphael close behind. They flew faster, wielded stronger healing power, and didn't lose strength when they utilized their Divine Light, unlike the Protectors and Slayers. Their powers and abilities demanded more of them and the burdens they bore were ones Kyden would never choose.

The last Kyden had heard, Raphael was near Kiev, and based on the demon carnage, sulfur clogging the air, and blasts of Divine Light, he'd located the battle where the demons and angels were fighting. Screams from disintegrating grunts combined with the clashing of steel, creating a symphony of chaos that echoed across the battlefield.

Kyden landed and immediately marched toward the fray, drawing the sword off his back while his armor appeared. A grunt spun toward him and Kyden slashed through its neck, sending its head flying and leaving a puff of green smoke in its wake.

He found a fellow Slayer, Celina, as she battled three grunts. A rope of braided brown hair hung to the middle of her back, and by the amount of demon blood speckled on her olive skin and armor, she'd been busy.

He joined her, slashing through the remaining grunt.

She whirled but halted her strike as she met his eyes. She arched a brow. "What are you doing here?"

"Looking for Raphael."

She used her forearm to wipe the blood and sweat from her face. "He's on the other side, in the command tent."

Kyden was about to fly off when a Fallen sped toward them, a wicked double-sided axe gripped in his hand.

Celina drew a second weapon and widened her stance.

"Want help with this one?" Kyden asked, twirling his sword.

"I've got it." Her lips curved into a menacing smile. "Good to see you again, Kyden."

He saluted her and shot into the sky as a massive shock wave rocked across the ground from Celina's and the Fallen's colliding weapons.

On the eastern edge of the battlefield, the angels had set up a large white tent next to a human military base. A stained and torn Ukrainian flag fluttered in the breeze.

Kyden nodded to the two angel sentries as he entered the tent. Raphael, half of his long golden-brown hair tied back, leaned over the war table, studying a map. Blood spattered on his armor and a slash across his cheek was slowly healing. The archangel stood a foot taller than Kyden and besides the height difference, the only other outward dissimilarity between the archangels and their subordinates was their eye color. Raphael's glowed gold as he looked up from the papers in front of him.

Kyden laid his palm on his chest and knelt on one knee. "General," he said, keeping his head bowed.

"Kyden. To what do I owe the honor?" Raphael motioned for him to stand. The golden halo resting on his forehead seemed to make the angel's eyes glow brighter.

"What happened to your face?" Kyden asked, approaching a map of the two human armies battling alongside the spiritual war in the overlapping realm.

Raphael's lip curled. "Marach got in a lucky shot."

"Where's the Wrath Prince now?"

"Hiding on the other side of the city. Chamuel joined the fray, giving us a bit of a breather. The demon is smart enough to know he can't defeat two archangels." Raphael walked around the table and leaned against it. "You're a long way from home."

"We found the Atar'zul," Kyden said, getting straight to the point. Raphael was focused on the war, and he didn't want to distract the archangel any more than necessary.

Raphael's brows lifted. "Where is it?"

Kyden didn't trust there weren't grunts nearby. They'd have a death wish coming so close to the command tent, but they weren't known for their intelligence. He waved his hand and the word *Boston* appeared in midair.

Raphael frowned. "That's not what I was expecting."

"The archaeologist who found it mailed it to another interested party." He replaced *Boston* with *daughter*. "She's safe, but two people have already been killed. I ran into a few Fallen, who are involved. They implied Raghav was in charge."

"He reports to Marach, but I don't see the prince making a play for the halo," Raphael said.

Kyden's eyes shifted to another map, one not found in the human world. Alongside the names of the continents were red lines showing the tunnels from the Abyss. These passageways were how the demons traveled so quickly from one location to another. Demons would never have the speed of angels, but until the creation of airplanes, their method had proven effective.

Marach, the Prince of Wrath, claimed Asia as his territory and had caused havoc ever since. Mammon, the Greed Prince, and Leviathan, the Envy Prince, lived in the Americas. The other princes—Asmodeus, Beelzebub, and Belphegor—created chaos throughout Europe and the Middle East.

Apollyon, the Prince of Pride, the most powerful of the princes, ruled the Abyss. He would make his presence known wherever the most destruction was, whether that was wars, famine, or natural disasters.

Raphael tugged on his bottom lip. "Apollyon is our most likely suspect, since it was originally his."

"But why?" Kyden asked. "I've felt its effects. One touch and the thing brought me to my knees."

"The halo is powerful, but it sounds like it's getting stronger."

"The archaeologist, who was a Vaelatori, mentioned a prophecy."

"The Vaelatori are the guardians of the halo and the ancient texts accompanying it. For reasons only Elohim knows, the angels are unaware of the writings regarding the prophecy. In all honesty, we haven't given much thought to Apollyon's crown." Raphael rested his hands on his hips and stared at him as if trying to sift through the thoughts tangled in his brain. "Have you heard the prophecy?"

He shook his head. "No. Supposedly, the information is in his journal. The woman"—he didn't want to say her name aloud—"needs to translate the last section. All he said was the enemy must not get their hands on the halo."

"Agreed." Raphael walked around the table, his golden eyes glowing with an internal fire. "You will protect her and the Atar'zul until she accomplishes her purpose."

His shoulders stiffened as his world shifted beneath his feet. "I'm not a Protector."

"You are now."

"Why can't we destroy the cursed thing? An archangel surely has the power," he said. Destroying the relic seemed like the obvious solution, and would keep him from doing something he vowed never to do again.

"If it was meant to be destroyed, Michael would have after Apollyon was defeated."

Kyden turned away from the archangel. "So we are to be subservient to humans once again." His blood pounded in his ears, drowning out the sounds of battle beyond the canvas walls of the tent.

He'd hoped Raphael would give the order to eradicate the halo, end this battle before it began, all while removing the threat against Zahra. But if her destiny was wrapped up in the Atar'zul, then she was in even more danger. If she wasn't successful in deciphering the prophecy or was killed in the process, who knew what the ramifications would be.

"I cannot fail again." The words, brittle and low, slipped through Kyden's clenched teeth. Fractured memories from long ago forced their way through the cracks in his mental vault. Smoke surrounded him as he fought a Fallen named Phenex while trying to protect the human assigned to him.

He had walked alongside Tamara Wilden early in her life when she struggled with an addiction to laudanum. He'd impersonated a doctor, and they both celebrated her defeat of the drug until her world changed drastically with the death of her husband.

Phenex and his grunts terrorized the growing colony and Tamara and Kyden got caught in the crossfire. Kyden, bleeding and exhausted from fighting for what felt like days in the spiritual realm, lost track of Tamara in the chaos of battle, and his negligence cost him. He'd been unable to rescue her from the pit of hopelessness, and Phenex took advantage of her despair.

Kyden finally found her kneeling on the ground in front of Phenex, who had altered his appearance, and offered her an escape from the pain and grief. Despite his speed, he couldn't get to her in time as she lifted the jagged blade and sliced it across her throat. Phenex's victorious laugh haunted him to this day.

He took his revenge on the Fallen, having tracked him down, waiting patiently until one night his sword severed the demon's head from his body, forever ending him and his evil ways.

But the demon's demise didn't erase Kyden's failure, and in that moment he willingly hardened his heart against humans. He'd lost faith in Elohim's chosen creation but more so in himself, spurning the role of Protector.

For him, slaying demons was instinctive, almost rational. The position didn't require second-guessing—just his blade and the sulfuric mist that followed.

A large hand rested on his shoulder, silencing the past. Kyden shoved the memories back into their vault.

"We've all lost someone we were supposed to protect, Kyden. None of us are perfect. You've closed off your heart ever since Tamara. Your pain has made you a lethal Slayer, but our primary mission has and always will be compassion."

Kyden spun and glared at Raphael, an act that was insubordinate at best. "Compassion is what got me into trouble the first time, and I will not allow that to happen again."

Raphael crossed his arms across his golden chest piece. "Find a way. I don't know what the princes are up to, but I have a feeling their plans could affect the angels in some catastrophic manner."

"Send someone else." He winced when Raphael's eyes flared. Slayers and Protectors didn't order an archangel to do anything. He dipped his chin, keeping his gaze fixed on the floor.

"Does this woman trust you?"

Kyden longed to release a compilation of the swear words he'd witnessed Zahra use so colorfully, but dug deep for his self-control. Even though she still seemed angry at him for lying, he knew she didn't fear him—a fact that somewhat grated on his nerves.

"Based on your reaction, the answer is yes," Raphael said. His face softened. "We can't let our past mistakes define us. The grace we give the humans is also for ourselves." He gave him one last look and then returned to the map. "I have faith in you, Kyden."

Kyden turned to leave when the ground shook. The flaps of the tent burst open, and Zindel, a fellow Slayer, sprinted in, black blood covering his face and armor.

"What is it?" Raphael asked, coming from around the table, the softness in his tone turning to molten steel.

"Apollyon. He's joined Marach and summoned demons from the Abyss," the angel said.

The corner of Raphael's lip lifted. "Well, this just got interesting." He picked up his claymore, the blade shimmering with power, and strode past Kyden and Zindel as the ground shook once again.

Kyden had fought in many battles over the millennia, but ages had passed since he'd been in one with two archangels and two princes of hell. The Fallen, emboldened by Apollyon's appearance, attacked with a newfound fury while the grunts, their numbers in the thousands, shifted from a nuisance into a calamity.

Raphael and Chamuel summoned Slayers and Protectors from nearby regions to join the fray, barking commands at their army. The clash of swords rose to a deafening roar and craters from where Raphael fought Apollyon sizzled in the damaged earth. Chamuel and Marach were in a standoff on the edge of the battlefield, blasts of fire and Divine Light devouring anything that came near.

In the human realm, the war was dire as bombs and missiles flew through the air. Buildings collapsed, silencing the screams of the innocent. Something needed to tip the tide of the battle before any more damage occurred.

Kyden panted, wiping the sweat from his brow as he gathered a group of Slayers. "I have an idea, but it's risky."

Celina scoffed. "When aren't your ideas risky?"

Another angel, Raiel, snorted. "She does have a point."

"True. The Protectors have their hands full keeping the grunts off us as we fight the Fallen. It's time for something drastic, but it will drain our powers."

Adinah, who had flown in for the battle, crossed her arms, her brows lifted. "Are you suggesting using our Divine Light?"

"I am. A concentrated blast would eliminate many of the Fallen and grunts."

Zindel frowned as he stared across the battlefield where green mist covered the ground. "We'll be at a disadvantage if this doesn't work."

"I know," Kyden said. "But only half of us need to do it. The others can clean up the fallout."

Adinah smirked. "I like it. Count me in."

All the other angels nodded their consent for his plan. It was risky and would drain their power considerably, but if it worked, then the battle would be over.

The ground shook again as Raphael and Apollyon fought. Raphael's arms trembled from fighting for days on end, though Kyden had no idea how many. Apollyon was fresh and taking advantage of the archangel's fatigue. It was now or never to level the playing field.

"Let's do this," Kyden said after organizing which Slayers would use their Divine Light and which would hold the line.

He and his fellow warriors attacked with renewed fury as they entered the middle of the battlefield. Kyden lifted his sword, and with a shout to the Heavens, the landscape ignited.

Chapter Twenty-Two

Zahra

Zahra's phone dinged again. She had tried to rest, but images of glowing warriors assaulted her whenever she closed her eyes. Kyden recently asked how well she knew her Bible. She'd attended Sunday School when she was young, but the pictures of angelic beings had never looked like the two angels she'd seen today.

Witnessing Titus fly off to do something as mundane as grocery shopping, and then later watching Kyden flare his wings before shooting into the sky, sent her heart galloping with excitement and trepidation.

"You're a popular person," Titus said, his broad back to her as he hunched over the keyboard. His setup was impressive with the monitors and whirring hardware. His long hair, sharp features, and muscular physique didn't match the image of the computer geeks she had known.

Why are angels so attractive, she thought. Her phone chimed again, proving his point about her popularity.

She and Alexis had been texting on and off. Worry over her friend's safety still gnawed on her frayed nerves, but thankfully, she was healing quickly and would soon be released from the hospital.

This most recent message was from work. Her brows furrowed as she read the text from Meredith.

Meredith: You just received a beautiful bouquet of flowers.
Zahra: Is there a card?

Jake wouldn't have sent flowers to her work, and she couldn't think of anyone else who would. While the three dots bounced with an incoming message, Zahra strode to the fridge to grab a bottle of water. The beer she'd chugged earlier accomplished its purpose, relaxing her enough to attempt to sleep. But a clear head is what she needed now as her father's journal lay unopened on the floor.

Seeing his face on the computer screen had caused a multitude of feelings to ascend to the surface, and knowing she would never talk to him again created a hollowness deep in her soul. Even though they didn't have a strong relationship—hell, even using the word "relationship" was a stretch—she still respected the man and, after all, he was a part of her DNA. Genes that now included being a Vaelatori.

Meredith's message finally came through. Zahra read it two more times before saying, "That son of a bitch."

The squeak of wheels made her look up. Titus faced her, a smirk curving his lips.

"Whose mother are we insulting?" he asked.

She winced, still not comfortable swearing in front of a heavenly being.

"It seems the entire office is now aware that Dr. Neeman was my father."

Titus's eyes widened. He spun and hit a few keys. Meredith's voice drifted through the speakers.

"No, sir. I didn't know—not until the flowers came."

Zahra shot to her feet. "Is that my office? You bugged it?"

"Shh," Titus said, waving at her.

"Did you just shush me?" She fought the urge to smack the angel on the back of the head.

Titus slid her a look from the corner of his eyes but remained quiet.

Mr. Rousseau's voice sounded tense, and she could imagine the purse to his lips. "Read the note again, please."

An audible sigh drifted through the speakers. "Miss Jenkins, I'm so sorry for your loss. Your father, Dr. Neeman, was truly a remarkable man and will be sorely missed."

"The famous archaeologist is, or rather was, Miss Jenkin's father? How was I not aware of this?" Mr. Rousseau asked. "Who are the flowers from anyway?"

"The signature is the letter L. That's it."

Fury vibrated through her as she listened to her future at the museum she loved fall apart. She had purposely deceived her boss and the board of directors for years regarding her relationship with Dr. Neeman. She justified her behavior because his contributions had garnered an increase in interest and money for the museum.

"Meredith, get her on the phone. I need a meeting with her."

"But, sir, she just lost her father and her best friend was shot."

"I don't care. Get her in here now!"

Zahra winced at the anger exploding from her boss, but she shoved the hurt down as her phone rang. She ignored it as she glared at the back of Titus's head.

"Explain," she said to the angel.

Titus's shoulders bunched. "The night of the gala, we thought it best to bug Brandon's, your boss's, and your office. We needed information on Dr. Neeman and the Atar'zul, and..."

"What do you mean, 'we'?" Her nails dug into her hands.

He turned in his chair, his eyes hard. "*We* as in Kyden and me."

Her hand trembled as she pointed at the speaker. "That is a complete violation of my privacy."

He slowly rose to his feet, and she instinctively took a step back. "No offense, Zahra, but we don't care about your privacy. The information your father acquired regarding the halo"—he nodded to the silver box on the chair—"is more important than your simple human feelings."

Her mouth dropped. "My simple human feelings?"

Titus raked his fingers through his hair. "I shouldn't have said that. I'm sorry. This is just bigger than you can imagine. We made the call. If it's any consolation, you never said or did anything compromising."

"Oh, what a relief." She crossed her arms, trying to maintain some semblance of control over her temper.

"Do you know who 'L' is? And how they found out about your father?" Titus asked, walking to the counter in the kitchenette and stealing one of her lollipops.

"Those are mine," she said, ripping it from his hand. He snorted and grabbed another one, popping it into his mouth with a smirk. She suspected who sent her the flowers but if she was right, then not only had Kyden betrayed her trust, so had Jake.

"Well, do you know?"

She held up a finger, and Titus huffed. She dialed Jake's number and waited.

"Zahra. I'm so glad you called. I…"

She cut him off. "Who did you tell?"

"Who did I tell what? What are you talking about?"

"There are only a few people on this planet who knew who my dad was, Jake. Now, who did you tell?"

Silence drifted through the line followed by a long sigh. "Mr. Durand. He kept pushing for a meeting with you when he'd learned the Atar'zul was sent to Boston. When I told him you couldn't meet because your father had died, he sort of put two and two together. I'm sorry."

She bit through the lollipop. "Thanks to you, my entire office knows. You've single-handedly ruined my career." A pounding behind her eyes made her wince. How much more could she take right now? If there was a breaking point, she was teetering on the edge.

"I don't understand. How did they find out?"

"Your boss sent flowers. He didn't simply leave condolences but felt it necessary to tell everyone Dr. Neeman was my dad."

"Shit, Zahra. I'm sorry. I didn't mean—"

"Save it, Jake. I have more important issues to deal with than appeasing your guilt." She stabbed the End button on her phone and tossed it onto the bed. "Laurent Durand, Jake's boss, sent the flowers."

She strode onto the balcony and peered out over the city. Office windows glinted in orange and red as the sun slowly descended toward the horizon. She'd trusted Jake with her secret, and how easily he discarded her trust made her heart ache.

Her phone rang and she stabbed the Decline button. A text came in seconds later.

Jake: I don't understand why Laurent did what he did, but I'm sorry. I shouldn't have said anything. Please call me.

She rubbed the space between her eyes. Had she been wrong to keep her relationship with her father a secret? Pride and bitterness had kept her from revealing who he really was. She knew Jake hadn't meant to harm her, but her emotions mimicked an exposed nerve, raw and reactive.

Titus joined her and leaned over the balcony, his long blond hair blocking his profile. "Were you close to Durand? I mean, I understand he's a donor at the museum, and you all ate dinner with him after the event, but does it seem odd that he'd send flowers?"

She'd been too distracted by Jake and her boss's reaction to really think about Durand's behavior, but Titus made a good point. "Maybe he was just being polite," she said with a shrug.

"Maybe." He lifted his head as his eyes tracked the skyline. "I texted Kyden but haven't heard back. He'd want to know about this."

"Where is my little deceiving angel?"

Titus arched a brow. "I'm so telling him you said that." She rolled her eyes and he chuckled. "He flew to Kiev to speak to an archangel."

"To Kiev? How long will that take him? How far can you guys fly anyway?"

"Far, and before you ask, we're extremely fast. He's probably already on his way back."

Her brows shot up. She'd once flown to London for a conference, and that flight was over seven hours. Kyden would have made it to Kiev in half that time. Her mind simply couldn't wrap around the power or speed it would take to accomplish such a distance.

"Did you say one of the archangels? How many are there?"

"Seven," Titus said.

"And they're more powerful than you?" He nodded and she frowned. "Then why are there demons, if they're so powerful?"

He leaned his hip against the balcony. "There are seven princes of hell too. Apollyon likes to mimic everything Elohim does. He's the ultimate impostor."

"Elohim, as in God, right?" she asked.

"Actually, there are many names for Him. Angels use Elohim since humans have turned His name into a swear word."

She winced. She'd been guilty of that as well.

Titus peered into the darkening sky. "Elohim has His seven archangels, so naturally Apollyon has seven princes of hell."

She rubbed her temples. "Naturally. And let me guess, they coincide with the seven deadly sins?"

"You got it."

"Are there any princes in America?"

"Yes, both Greed, named Mammon, and Envy, named Leviathan, live in North and South America."

"And this Apollyon. Where does he live?"

The angel's face darkened. "Everywhere. The entire earth is his in which to cause chaos and destruction."

"And what does your Elohim have to say about that?" She hadn't meant for her words to sound so clipped.

He faced her, his eyes softening. "Spiritual warfare has been around since the beginning of time. The angels fight for humans, but you have this thing called free will."

"Don't you? Have free will, I mean?"

"In a way. We face the same temptations, but we were created differently. It's hard to explain."

"No kidding." She left the balcony, the ocean air chilling her, and plopped down on the bed.

Titus sat back in his chair. "You're handling this pretty well. I would've thought you'd be freaking out by now."

"Oh, I am. I'm just internalizing it," she said with a humorless laugh. Her gaze drifted to her father's journal. "I need to go to the office, see if I can save my job."

He chewed on the inside of his cheek. "The museum is the first place the demons will search." She opened her mouth to argue, but he held up his finger, copying what she'd done to him a few minutes ago. He smirked and then said, "You understand we can't let you out of our sight now that you've found the halo. And it's a good bet whoever is looking for it knows you have it."

She wanted to scoff at his overprotectiveness, but considering her father and a coworker were dead, her apartment broken into, and her roommate shot, the angel made a convincing argument. She thought back to the gala and how Brandon had bragged about working with her father and expecting the Atar'zul to arrive soon. Was that why he was killed? And whoever had murdered him made the crime appear to be an old gambling debt.

She leaned forward and held her head. "Is my life ever going to be normal again?"

"Is normal what you want?" Titus asked.

She looked at the angel, his amber eyes full of kindness and understanding. She supposed he had a point, and besides, what was normal these days?

Her dad had given her a job and despite her feelings for him, she would figure out the prophecy and the mystery of the Atar'zul.

A loud clunk made Zahra jump. The glow from her phone told her it was after ten. She'd been sitting in the same chair for hours and her neck ached. Titus had left a little while ago to do a quick patrol and stop by her apartment for some clean clothes. She glanced around the room, wondering what had caused that noise.

Suddenly, the balcony doors swung open and Kyden lumbered in. Black liquid spotted his armor and face. Mud, and she wasn't sure what else, covered his boots.

"What happened to you?" she asked, lurching to her feet, and grabbed his arm when he wobbled. Granted, if he fell, the smartest thing would be to get out of the way.

"Battle" was all he said before his wings disappeared, along with his armor, replaced by gray sweatpants and a T-shirt, but the splatters still covered his face.

"You look like you're about to pass out."

His gaze shifted toward her, his amber eyes dull with dark shadows underneath. "Just need rest and food. I'll be fine."

She led him to the bed and forced him to sit, then retrieved a bottle of water and a soda. "Which one?"

He chose the soda and chugged half of the contents of the can.

"Sugar it is," she said, and returned to the kitchenette. Titus had bought an assortment of junk food, along with some fresh fruit and a bag of carrots. She picked up the box of donuts and placed it on his lap.

"Thank you," he said, his voice hoarse.

"Don't take this the wrong way, but you're kind of a mess."

He nodded and shoved half a donut into his mouth. She walked to the small bathroom and held a towel under the faucet. He shied away when she approached, but she knelt on the bed next to him.

"Do I want to know what's all over you?" she asked, gently wiping off the grime.

"Demon blood."

Her hand paused. "Demon blood is black?"

He grunted, finishing the donut, and grabbed another. *Must be nice to eat a box of pastries and not worry about the consequences*, she thought as she resumed cleaning his face. His eyes closed and he leaned slightly toward her.

"What color is your blood?"

"Gold," he said, his head beginning to droop.

Flying to Russia and back, and, it seemed, fighting a battle against demons, had left him way past exhausted. He started to fall backward, so she guided his body to the bed, seizing a pillow for his head. The constant furrow on his brow smoothed out as he slept, his lips slightly parted. She wished she could draw, for his face was perfect, an artist's masterpiece.

"What have we gotten ourselves into?" Her sigh morphed into a jaw-cracking yawn. She lay next to the sleeping angel, maintaining an appropriate distance between them, assuming spooning with an angelic warrior was not acceptable behavior.

CHAPTER TWENTY-THREE

KYDEN

Kyden stood on the balcony with his wings flared as the morning sun shone red through his closed eyes. He barely remembered the flight home and had been surprised to wake up with a blanket over him and a woman snuggled beside him. Even more surprising was how his arm had rested over her hip. Thankfully, her back had been to him, and she slept like the dead. He had extricated himself from the bed without waking her.

Titus was still asleep on the smaller bed in the corner of the room, his soft snores drifting onto the balcony. Kyden shook his head at the ribbing he'd get from his friend—there'd be no end to his teasing remarks.

Even with the chaos of battle and flying across the ocean, the frustration of Raphael ordering him into the role of Protector still rankled him. There were other angels more capable than him of keeping Zahra alive. Raphael easily could have summoned one of them to protect her. He had accomplished his mission—he'd found Apollyon's halo. His time would be better spent hunting down the demons involved instead of babysitting.

His jaw ached from clenching his teeth. He lifted his chin, letting the rising sun soothe him.

A shiver ran down his spine, and he spun, his wing almost knocking Zahra backward.

"What are you doing?" he asked, scowling down at her.

Her hazel eyes widened as she gripped a cup of coffee. "I wanted to see how soft they were."

He tucked in his wings and then made them disappear completely. Better safe than sorry with her around. "Never touch my wings again without asking. Is that clear?"

She arched a brow. "Didn't realize angelic warriors were such babies about their wings."

He crossed his arms and glared at her. "Just don't touch them."

"Fine, geez—What side of the bed did you wake up on?" She sipped her coffee, her eyes darting across his face.

Definitely the wrong side, not to mention the wrong bed, he thought, turning from her inspection. Waking up next to her and then her stroking his feathers created an influx of sensations he wasn't currently equipped to handle.

He attempted to soften his tone, remembering Raphael's words. *Our primary mission has and always will be compassion.* "How are you feeling?"

"Me? I'm not the one who was covered with blood and passed out from exhaustion."

He forced a small smile. "True, but that's normal for me. What you've gone through...well, it's a lot."

She sipped her coffee while they watched seagulls drift effortlessly in the breeze. He envied their freedom, to ride the wind without a care.

"What did you find out about the Atar'zul?" she asked.

"It looks like you're stuck with me until you figure out the prophecy."

She tilted her head. "Why do you sound so frustrated?"

"Because Raphael demoted me from Slayer to Protector until this is done." He kept his gaze on the horizon.

"Look, I didn't ask for this to happen, nor did I ask for you to get involved. You did that all on your own."

"Well aware," he growled, turning from the sunrise, the warmth no longer comforting. He stepped toward her, slightly annoyed that she didn't retreat in fear. "We're doing this my way, you understand? And the quicker you translate the prophecy, the better."

She closed the distance and glared up at him. "I see the considerate man bringing flowers and apologizing for his behavior was an act. Instead, you're simply a rude, grumpy angel. Glad we got that cleared up."

He inwardly grimaced. She had a point there, and he was being unfair. None of this was her fault. Before he could apologize, she stormed off the balcony and slammed the glass door behind her.

Titus shot up from the cot with a dagger drawn. "What's going on?"

"Ask him."

Titus raised his brows at him when he entered the room and beelined for the kitchenette. He would need more coffee to deal with the swirling emotions right now. As he poured himself a cup, he noticed her shoving her feet into her shoes. After twisting her hair into a knot, she gathered her father's journal and the box containing the halo and stuffed them inside a backpack she'd found by the closet door. "I don't need your help with this, and I'm sorry you're involved."

Her voice hitched, and he lowered his head as shame swept over him. "Zahra, I'm sorry. I shouldn't have growled at you."

"You growled at her?" Titus asked, his amber eyes sparkling.

"Shut up," Kyden said to Titus, and addressed Zahra. Her phone rang before he could salvage the mess he had caused.

She pulled it from her purse. "Hello."

Titus grunted as he got out of bed and walked past him. "Growling? Seriously?"

He pondered throwing his friend off the balcony if he wasn't going to be helpful.

The color drained from Zahra's face. "But I don't have an uncle," she said, her words trembling in the air. She shook her head. "No, I'm on my way."

He took a step toward her. "What's going on?"

"Where's my purse?"

He closed the distance and held her arms. "Zahra, tell me."

Panic caused her movements to become jerky as she pulled out of his grasp and searched for her belongings. "The nursing home called and said my uncle had left some papers."

"Okay, what's the big deal?" he asked.

"She doesn't have an uncle," Titus said, finding her purse near the chair and handing it to her.

Whose side is he on, anyway? "You can't visit your mother. That's one of the first places the demons would go," Kyden said.

Her wide eyes darted across his face. "It sounds like they've already been there. I'm going, Kyden, so help me god."

His shoulders automatically stiffened at her use of one of Elohim's names. He forgave the slight and raised his palms. "You're not going—"

She shoved the end of her phone into his chest. "Don't you dare tell me what I can and cannot do."

"You didn't let me finish. You're not going alone."

"Fine. Titus can join me."

Titus's brows inched up his forehead. "Yeah, no. Keep me out of this."

She glared at him, strode for the door, and yanked on the handle, but the door wouldn't budge. "How the hell do I get out of here?"

He focused on the ceiling. "Give me patience," he whispered, then grabbed a set of keys from the hooks on the wall and pressed his palm against the door. When it opened, he waved her through. "After you." He then looked back at Titus. "And I want you trailing us in the van just in case."

Zahra muttered curses under her breath, each one landing in time with her footsteps down the stairs, until they reached the bottom and walked into the parking lot.

"We're taking that." He pointed to his motorcycle.

"And you think a metallic beast of leather and chrome is safe?"

"You'll be fine. I won't let anything happen to you." He strode to the bike and straddled it. Her gaze danced between the motorcycle and the parking lot. The only other vehicle was Titus's van.

He arched a brow. "You coming or not?"

Releasing a sigh, she slowly approached the bike. "This is such a bad idea."

The wind blowing through Kyden's hair soothed his frustration as they wove through traffic on their way to the nursing home. He glanced in his side mirror and saw the van a few miles back. If demons attacked them while

Zahra visited her mother, at least they would have a warning. The thought gave him little peace since he was fairly certain they were walking into a trap.

The demons would know as much about Zahra as he and Titus did. Going to the nursing home was one of the first places he would have gone if he'd been searching for her. But Zahra was stubborn. She'd made up her mind the second she'd hung up her phone.

He swerved past a car, barely missing the bumper, feeling her arms tighten around his waist. A general of Elohim's army had given him orders, orders he would obey, which now meant he was tethered to her path. The thought made him grind his teeth.

Slaying demons, although messy and sometimes painful, didn't require any emotion from him, not like being a Protector. An angel naturally empathized with the human they guarded, often enduring their burdens and feelings, and he couldn't venture down the same path he had centuries ago with Tamara. He'd grown to care for her as he tried to alleviate her pain and struggles. And he had failed.

Blaring sirens jerked him from the past. He pulled the bike over and waited for a cop car to speed by, its lights flashing. The car pulled into a familiar parking lot.

"Oh no," Zahra said, rising from the bike to get a better look.

The parking lot of A1 Storage teemed with cop cars and an ambulance. A body lay on the ground, covered with a sheet, but the green mist surrounding the man removed any doubt the demons were tracking them with relentless purpose.

Kyden scanned the street but didn't see any grunts in the vicinity.

"What's that green stuff?" she asked as they drove past the storage facility.

"It's a residue left behind by grunt demons." Worry burned through him like acid at how closely the enemy hunted them. Despite the protective measures Titus had placed around the church, they needed to get out of Boston. "You're wearing the talisman?" he asked when they stopped at a traffic signal.

"Yes. You told me not to take it off."

He huffed out a laugh. "That's surprising."

She leaned past him, her brow furrowed. "And why is that?"

"You rarely do what I ask of you."

She rolled her eyes and tightened her grip as he revved the engine and shot down the street. They soon pulled up at the nursing home. He scanned the gardens and parking lot, but no demons lingered in the vicinity; however, that didn't mean they weren't hiding in the shadows.

They walked toward the entrance while he continued to search their surroundings. "Keep the necklace hidden, just in case someone here is working for a Fallen. And if I say run, you run. Got it?"

Her knuckles whitened where she gripped the straps of the backpack. "Are you staying visible or...?" She waved a hand up and down his frame.

"I suppose that"—he mimicked her gesture—"means spiritual realm," he said with a smirk. "And no, I'll be in my human form."

They entered the building and Zahra stopped at the reception desk while he hung back, examining every person who walked through the lobby.

A nurse stood near a hallway, texting on her cell phone. She slipped it into her pocket and approached Zahra, her white sneakers squeaking on the tile. "Hello, Zahra. It's good to see you again, and what a pleasure meeting your uncle."

Kyden edged closer to Zahra.

"As I told you earlier, I don't have an uncle," she said. She pushed past the nurse and jogged toward her mother's room. Kyden used his speed and beat her there, bracing an arm across her chest before opening the door.

"I go first." He drew his sword and stepped into the room.

Nancy Jenkins sat in a chair by the table, paging through a magazine.

"Mom?" Zahra said, shoving past him and dropping to her knees. "Are you all right?"

Nancy's eyes narrowed slightly before the wrinkles on her face deepened. "Zahra, dear. How are you?" she asked with a smile.

Zahra's gaze traveled across her mother's body. "I'm fine. The nurse said a man came to visit you. Do you remember him?"

"Oh yes, he was strange but had lovely brown eyes. He was conducting a survey or something. I can't quite remember all the details. But he's single. If he's still here, you should find him." She winked, and then finally noticed Kyden leaning against the wall.

She seemed fairly lucid but with her disease, that could change at any moment. He sensed she didn't have long on this earth and wondered where her soul was headed.

"Oh, and who are you?" Nancy asked.

Zahra glanced over her shoulder at him before answering. "He's just a friend. Mom, can you remember anything else about this man?"

Nancy's gaze shifted out the window to the courtyard. She blinked and noticed Zahra, who still knelt at her feet.

"Zahra, dear, how are you?"

Her shoulders sagged. "I'm good, Mom. How are you?"

Kyden moved to the window. Dead leaves skirted along the ground while storm clouds gathered in the west. He wondered if the man impersonating Zahra's uncle was a Fallen or a daemonkin, and if they were still on the premises.

Nancy fidgeted with the hem of her shirt. "The nurse won't give me my pudding. It's rather rude of her."

Zahra forced a smile and stood. She stacked some papers on the nearby table and an envelope fell to the floor.

She picked it up and gasped.

"What is it?" he asked, immediately rushing to her side.

Her hand shook as she showed him three photos. One was of Alexis in her hospital room and the other was of Jake, buying coffee at a local bakery downtown. The third was of Nancy sleeping in her bed. He flipped the photo over to find writing on the back and read it aloud. "*We know who you are and what you have.*"

Zahra covered her mouth and turned away from her mother's inquisitive stare. "That bastard," she said through clenched teeth.

He opened the backpack and handed Zahra her gun. "Stay here and lock the door. I'm going to search the grounds." He strode down the hall, shifting out of his human form and stepping into the spiritual realm. The demons had located Zahra's mother faster than he'd expected, and they'd done their homework, knowing the three most valuable people to her. They were taunting her, since they left no instructions. Causing crippling fear was a tactic the demons used to the fullest extent.

After twenty minutes of searching, he returned to the room, stopping in the hallway. He pulled his phone from his pocket and dialed a number he had tried to forget. His last confrontation with the head of the Protector Angels hadn't gone well, and they'd almost come to blows.

"Elias, this is Kyden."

Silence greeted him, and then the angel on the line spoke. "Haven't talked to you in ages."

"Yeah, well, I don't have time to catch up now. Three humans need Protectors."

An unfriendly laugh filled Kyden's ears. "You have some nerve ordering me around, Slayer."

"I'm not a Slayer, not anymore. Raphael assigned me as Protector of Zahra Jenkins. It's too long of a story, but her loved ones are in danger."

"A lot of loved ones are in danger these days. Why is she so special?"

"She has Apollyon's halo and the demons are hunting her." He raked his fingers through his hair. "They've already killed two people."

"Hmm" was all Elias said.

"Zahra is in danger, and I need to get her and the Atar'zul out of town." He leaned his forehead against the wall and shut his eyes. Zahra wouldn't leave her mother's side, not after seeing those pictures, and they needed to get out of Boston before the demons harmed any more humans. "Please, Elias."

The line was silent for so long that he checked his phone to make sure he still had a signal.

"Give me the names. I'll have someone there in less than an hour."

His shoulders lowered as he gave the specifics, hung up the phone, and knocked on the door. "Zahra, it's me."

The lock clicked and she opened the door. "What's going on?"

"Time to go." He raised his hand, stopping whatever she was about to say. "Protectors are arriving soon for your mom, Alexis, and Jake. They'll be safe, but I need to get you and the halo out of here."

She bit her lip and glanced over her shoulder to stare at her mom. Her chin dipped in a ghost of a nod before returning to her mother's side.

He waited by the door as Zahra draped a blanket over Nancy's legs. She hugged the older woman and whispered in her ear, discreetly wiping away a tear from her cheek. She slid on her backpack as they walked down the hall.

On the way out of the nursing home, she once again stopped to talk to the receptionist.

"Did the man who visited my mom leave a name?"

The woman's brows disappeared behind her brown bangs. "No, Miss Jenkins. Is there a problem?"

"Yeah, I don't have an uncle."

Kyden leaned forward. "We'd like to see the security footage from earlier today. Please." He added as an afterthought.

The receptionist licked her lips. "I don't believe I can do that unless you're with the police."

"You let some strange man visit my mother. He might have stopped by another resident's room," Zahra said.

"I'll need to talk with my supervisor. Wait here, please."

The hair on Kyden's neck stood at attention. They were running out of time. "Titus can get the information faster." He dialed his number. "Come on, pick up," he said after the fourth ring and his voicemail message answered. He entered the number again, and a sinking feeling tightened in his gut. He scanned the empty lobby. Something wasn't right.

"Let's go." He grabbed Zahra's arm and dragged her across the tiled floor.

"Zahra, is everything okay?" The nurse from earlier exited a side door and walked toward them with an eerie smile on her face, her eyes dark. He sensed the Fallen skulking inside the woman.

Zahra gasped and stumbled, drawing her gun from the waistband of her jeans.

Kyden walked backward, keeping his body between Zahra and the Fallen. He slid one of his knives from the baldric across his chest and handed it to her.

"Where are you going, little cherub?" the nurse said, her voice distorted. "All we want is the halo. Hand it over, and no harm will come to your human."

Kyden figured it was the same demon from the nightclub. He just needed to get outside, and then he could fly Zahra to safety. Angels had no problem disappearing through walls or ceilings. Humans, on the other hand...well, that would get messy.

He unfurled his wings as they drew closer to the sliding doors. "Stay close to me," he said to Zahra, who nodded, her weapon trained on the woman slowly approaching while she gripped the knife in her other hand.

His shoulders stiffened, and he pivoted. Yellow eyes and teeth flashed as a grunt demon landed on him with a swarm of more in its wake. He yanked the keys from his pocket and threw them to Zahra. "Get to the bike!"

CHAPTER TWENTY-FOUR

ZAHRA

"What the actual...!" Zahra couldn't believe her eyes as the necklace against her chest burned and the veil parted, revealing the most horrific creatures. Demons appeared all around them, their skin leathery, with fangs protruding from their mouths and hanging past their jaws. They carried in their sharp claws wicked-looking weapons and their yellow eyes zeroed in on Kyden.

Bronze armor covered the angel from his neck to the metal bracers protecting his shins. A gold halo wrapped around his forehead, and his amber eyes glowed as he drew his second sword. If she hadn't been so frightened, she would have watched him for hours, entranced by his fierce beauty.

The nurse, shrouded in an ebony aura, laughed as she emerged from the building. A black SUV idled near the entrance to the parking lot, its tinted windows blocking whoever sat inside. Zahra gauged the distance between the SUV and Kyden's motorcycle, wondering if she could make it to the bike in time.

"Stop or I'll shoot." Zahra raised the gun and the demon-possessed nurse laughed again as she stalked toward her.

"Your weapon can't hurt me."

She remembered briefly what Kyden had said about demons and mortal weapons, but if the demon needed a body to harm her, then her bullets would at least slow them down.

Kyden's voice sounded from the middle of the horde of grunts he was fighting. "Go!"

She aimed at the nurse, wincing, not wanting to injure an innocent person, and squeezed the trigger. The woman screamed, falling to the ground, gripping her thigh as blood seeped through her scrubs.

Zahra didn't wait to see what happened next as she sprinted for the motorcycle.

A larger demon, about her height, lumbered after her. The scrape of its clawed feet against the pavement sent a trickle of sweat down her back, where her pack bounced. The cacophony of clashing swords rang in her ears as she neared the motorcycle.

The smell of sulfur and death wafted through the air, and hot, putrid breath whispered against her neck. She dove to the side as the demon attacked, its claws barely missing her shoulder. The grunt spun around and charged again. She raised Kyden's dagger and sliced it across its belly. The demon screamed and sulfuric green smoke covered her.

She ran, not daring to look behind her as she closed in on the motorcycle. The roar of an engine caused her to pivot. The SUV raced in front of her and slammed the bike into another car.

She jumped to the side, tripped over a curb, and fell hard.

The back door opened.

"Zahra, move!" Kyden's voice jolted her into action.

She scrambled backward and quickly rose to her feet. Her hands ached from clinging to her gun and Kyden's dagger.

A man dressed in a suit appeared from the back seat. When his head lifted, Zahra swore. *Not human*, she thought as sickly green eyes glared at her from deathly pale skin. A dark aura, the opposite of the angels, surrounded the thing she assumed was a Fallen.

"Give me the halo, Zahra Jenkins," said the demon, sounding as if its throat was scorched, each word trying to claw its way out.

"Stay the hell away from me." She retreated another step as she pointed the gun at the demon's chest.

Green mist slithered around her feet and sulfur burned her nose. The only thing silencing the scream building up her throat was Kyden telling her that demons couldn't kill a human without dire consequences.

Another man emerged from the car. "Use me, Master."

She cursed, unsure where to aim her gun. Her jaw dropped as the demon grabbed the man by the neck. The demon's body flickered as he entered the man, causing his back to arch and a horrific scream to escape his mouth. His chest rose and fell at an alarming rate until he shivered. When he lifted his head, a malicious grin split his face, and dark, empty pits where eyes should have been glared at her.

The possessed man stalked toward her. "Give me the halo," he said, his voice sounding like two people speaking at the same time.

She inhaled, trying to calm her racing heart, and squeezed the trigger. The bullet hit true, striking the demon in its chest. The impact sent him shuffling backward, giving her a second to locate Kyden. A swarm of demons surrounded him. The nurse she'd shot struggled to her feet, her face twisted in pain as her dark aura flickered. Zahra glanced back at the demon-possessed man, who looked down at the blood pouring from his chest. His eyes flashed green and then the bleeding stopped.

"You must know your mortal weapon can't hurt me."

"But it can slow you down, you ugly son of a bitch." She released four more shots. Two at the demon's knees, and the other two at the tires of the SUV.

She turned to run when a force knocked her off her feet. The pavement dug into her cheek as she wriggled away from the demon who clung to her back. Fabric ripped when she twisted while swiping her dagger at the grunt. Metal clinked and the silver case containing the Atar'zul bounced along the ground.

Zahra swore and scurried to her feet. The grunt had torn her backpack, and the ancient relic lay between her and the possessed man. His thin lips curled into a smile.

She tightened her grip on the dagger and lunged for the box. Her progress stopped when a demon appeared at her side and sank its claws into her. She was about to scream from the pain but instead of nails piercing flesh, an oppressive despair crushed her. A moan escaped her lips while she clung to her bag, tears blurring her vision.

The man limped forward and retrieved the metal case. He addressed the demon whispering in her ear. "Don't let her go. She'll break soon."

The man's back arched again, and then he collapsed in a puddle of his own blood. The Fallen stared down at the discarded body and smiled as he held the silver case in his hands.

Deep in the corners of her mind, she knew she needed to stop the demon, to grab the box, but the menacing presence attacking her left her immobilized.

She heard her name being called through the shadows of oppression but was unable to pick herself up off the ground, to stop the shaking. The handle of the gun warmed in her hand. She could end her misery—the stress, the loneliness, the grief—the suffering would disappear with the squeeze of a trigger.

A sharp pain burned against her chest. She tried to break free of the demon clinging to her but a stronger wave of helplessness crashed over her, drowning her in despair.

"Do it. End your misery. Only peace lies on the other side," a voice like dead leaves scraping across the ground whispered in her ear.

"Zahra, fight it!" someone yelled from a distance.

The pendant lying against her skin flashed and burned. Intense pain removed the haze until she recognized these feelings weren't hers. The hilt of Kyden's dagger dug into her palm.

"Give in and let go. Just pull the trigger," whispered the demon.

She wrapped her fingers around the dagger. "No!" She twisted and came face-to-face with the grunt, whose claws had embedded in her neck and back. With a scream, she stabbed the demon in the throat. Black blood sprayed her face and green haze surrounded her. The rush of sulfur caused her to wretch.

A car door opened, and a wave of evil wafted over her, assaulting her senses. Her gaze focused on the box the Fallen held. She couldn't let it take the halo. It was hers. She could sell it for money and move out of her small apartment, or finally get that promotion and have everyone at the museum acknowledge her success. The power was at her disposal if only she had the Atar'zul. The desires coursing through her made her rise to her feet.

She was about to lunge for the box when a voice forged in shadow, dripping with malice, stopped her cold.

"Raghav, grab her," the eerie voice said from the depths of the car.

The Fallen lurched for her when a blast of light zipped past, throwing the demon against the side of the SUV. The thoughts of power and gain dissipated as the demon, his clothes and skin smoking, retreated toward the car, taking the halo with him.

The grunts surrounding Kyden dissolved into green mist as he exploded from the center, his wings fully extended and shimmering from the sun peeking through the clouds. A sneer curved his mouth and his amber eyes glowed with a fierceness that made her legs wobble. She ran toward him as he dove from the sky.

The cement cracked where he landed. He threw a dagger, impaling the Fallen in the shoulder and knocking him into the partially open door, revealing the occupants inside.

Another man struggled in the back seat, his blond hair familiar. Golden liquid streaked down his face.

She covered her mouth. "No."

"Titus," Kyden whispered, taking a step closer to the car. She grabbed his arm and pointed behind him as another horde of demons charged toward them. The muscles in his jaw twitched, and his knuckles cracked as he clenched his fists. He wrapped one arm around her waist, while the other slid under her legs. "Hold on."

She squeezed her eyes shut while her stomach sank to her toes as the ground quickly disappeared and wind slammed against her face. His mighty wings flapped, putting miles between them and the screaming demons.

"Are you hurt?" he asked once they were a safe distance away.

At a loss for words, all she could do was shake her head. His armor dug into her cheek while she focused on the beat of his wings, counting every flap until her heart rate settled.

"It's gone." Her voice sounded foreign to her, feeble and scared.

He looked down at her. "What's gone?"

"The halo. A demon ripped my bag and it fell out. And...and they have Titus." Tears streamed down her cheeks.

"I know," Kyden said, tightening his grip. "We'll figure it out. Right now, we need to get somewhere safe."

Safe.

The word rattled around in her brain. After what she'd witnessed—creatures that lived among unsuspecting humans causing who knew what kind of emotional and physical destruction. Would she ever feel safe again?

The pendant from her father dug into her palm, and a wave of resentment rushed through her. She would never forget the yellow, burning eyes or the smell of sulfur. She would never stop hearing the screech of demons nor feeling the sting of their claws. The wave of oppression that had almost broken her—she'd never forget the hopelessness nor the desperation to end it all. Her life had forever changed, and she feared she'd never be safe again.

The Boston skyline disappeared, replaced by pine trees jutting from the hillside like ancient sentinels guarding the landscape they clung to. Coldness seeped into Zahra's body, her fingers cramping from gripping Kyden's chest piece. She sneaked glances at the angel's face as they flew. His eyes resembled gemstones, impenetrable and beautiful, while the muscles in his jaw pulsed.

"Where are we going?" she asked as the wind rushed past them while the tips of the trees grew closer.

"There's a cabin in the Blue Ridge Mountains."

They coasted over a quaint town and then dove through the forest toward a lake surrounded by log cabins. If the shock of what she'd been through hadn't left her mind feeling like mush, she would have enjoyed the sensation of flying, the carefree way they glided through the air.

"What did that grunt demon do to me?" Her voice barely carried over the flapping of Kyden's wings.

He circled the area before landing behind a small, dilapidated cabin. The front porch sagged and boards were missing on the steps leading to the door. What appeared to be years of grime and dirt covered the windows. Dread settled in her stomach as she imagined how the inside looked.

"What did you feel?" he finally asked, gently guiding her feet to the ground.

She took a minute to get her bearings. "Like I was drowning in grief and there was only one way out." She shut her eyes. "I've never felt that hopeless."

"It was a demon of oppression. They can influence people to destroy themselves. More and more have evolved as society has grown focused on self."

She followed him to the cabin, her brow furrowed. "What do you mean, evolved?"

"Grunt demons reflect society, and the worse it gets, whether it's more violent or more selfish, more obsessed with possessions or sex, the more demons emerge from the Abyss to torment humans."

"Can't you stop them?" The thought of unsuspecting people battling the emotions she'd experienced was terrifying. Thanks to the talisman around her neck, she'd been aware of the demon whispering seductive thoughts of her demise, even if fighting the deceit had required her to dig deep into her resolve.

"That's what Protectors and Slayers do, while the archangels battle the princes." He trudged up the steps, his wings folded down his back. "Unfortunately, I didn't see the Fallen who stole the halo. Can you remember what he looked like?"

"I was a little distracted by the creepy green eyes and fangs. And then he possessed a man right in front of me." She wrapped her arms around herself. The man had seemed normal besides the black eyes—nothing like what she'd seen in the movies. "But I also heard another voice—a deeper one, and the power and darkness coming from it…" Her hands fell to her side. She had no words for what she had experienced.

Kyden stopped abruptly and faced her. "The power felt different?" She nodded and he continued, "What did the voice say?"

"He said a name, I think. It started with an R. And then he told him to grab me."

He raked his fingers through his already windblown hair. "That must have been a prince of hell. That's why the grunt affected you the way it did. They draw power from the princes."

"Figures," she said, rubbing her hands up and down her arms to remove the chill settling deep inside her.

"The Fallen who attacked you and stole the box must have been Raghav. His name has come up too many times for it to be a coincidence, and I don't believe in coincidences."

She didn't think she could handle any more information about princes, Fallen, or grunts. The knowledge of the spiritual realm was too much. And now she was shacking up in a literal shack. She really hoped the plumbing worked since she desperately needed a shower.

Kyden ran his hand over a loose board by the door. A click sounded and a keypad slid out. Within seconds, the door opened, revealing a small yet cozy living room and kitchen.

"Wow. Based on the outside, I was expecting spiderwebs and broken-down furniture," she said, trailing her fingers on the back of a leather couch.

"Keeps people away." He closed his eyes and his armor and weapons disappeared.

"I don't think I'll ever get used to that." She placed her bag on the table and headed for the kitchen. She needed a drink. A cigarette wouldn't be bad either since her nerves were shot. Unfortunately, there was only bottled water and a few bags of chips in the cupboard.

Kyden rubbed the back of his neck. "I saw a pizza place as we flew over. Give me an hour to get things figured out and then we'll go into town. Sound good?"

"Sure." She spotted a hallway presumably leading to a bathroom and bedroom. "I'm going to hop in the shower. I smell like rotten eggs." She didn't wait for a reply as she meandered toward the back room.

After finding the bathroom and shutting the door, she turned the water on and stripped out of her clothes. The silver pendant shone against her chest, as if lit from inside. Her father said it would protect her. The burn of the talisman and Kyden yelling her name had stayed her hand. Without either, she feared what would have happened.

She stepped into the shower and sighed as the hot water ran down her skin. Images of the battle flooded her mind. When she closed her eyes, the appearance of the Fallen and his malevolent smile haunted her. If it weren't for Kyden, she'd be dead right now, and the thought terrified her.

She finally emerged from the shower when the water cooled and wrapped a towel around herself, using another one to wipe steam from the mirror. Dark circles stained the skin under her eyes, which were widened in fear and possibly shock.

A knock sounded on the door.

"Zahra?"

"Just a minute." She stared at her dirty clothes, refusing to put them on, and tightened the towel around her chest, her wet hair dripping along her back. She opened the door, and Kyden visibly swallowed as his eyes drifted down her body. When they returned to her face, his brow furrowed. "Are you okay?"

The need to feel safe outweighed any rational thought. She didn't think twice before crushing herself against him, burrowing her cheek into his warm chest. He stiffened and his hands remained by his side.

"Please hold me." Her voice wavered, and she hated how pathetic she sounded, but if she had to beg, then so be it.

He slowly wrapped his arms around her. A sense of peace enveloped her and her racing heart settled.

"You'll be all right, Zahra. I won't let anything happen to you," he said, stroking a hand down her wet hair.

A shiver traveled along her spine. She grabbed the back of his shirt, for fear of letting go and once again being alone. Longing replaced the ache in her chest, and her thoughts immediately drifted to Jake. After the time she spent with him recently, she realized what a mistake she'd made ending their relationship—a decision rooted in fear.

The water dripping down her back reminded her too much of that horrible day in the rain when she'd said goodbye. Her mind and emotions were a chaotic mess and if anyone could distract her from the horrors she'd seen today, it was Kyden.

She lifted her chin and gazed into his eyes before settling on his mouth.

His body turned rigid, like a wire pulled taut. Standing on her tiptoes, she pressed her mouth against his. His lips were warm and soft, and she craved more. She traced her tongue along the seam of his lips. His hands briefly tightened around the towel before releasing her.

His eyes were closed as he gently pushed her away, his Adam's apple bobbing. "Zahra, I can't." The sentence trembled in the air between them, causing goose bumps to form on her skin.

"Can't or won't?"

"Does it matter?" He put more distance between them. "Besides, it's not me you really want."

"Don't tell me what I want," she said, wincing. She sounded like a petulant child.

He lifted her chin, his fingers warm and gentle. "I'm telling you what you already know in your heart." His smile didn't reach his eyes as he retreated. "I'll go into town and get us something to eat."

The door slowly closed, and she was left facing her distorted reflection in the foggy mirror. The sting of rejection didn't bite like she thought it would. She remembered the night when she'd kissed Jake at the bar. Granted, the blur of alcohol somewhat dulled the memory, but nothing could touch the fire that ignited when her lips had met his.

Was Kyden simply not attracted to her, or was he correct about her feelings toward Jake?

"Of course he's right—the insufferable man," she said, dragging a comb through her wet hair, and then paused. "Not a man." She groaned and covered her mouth. "I kissed an angel."

CHAPTER TWENTY-FIVE

KYDEN

Kyden paced along the front porch of the cabin, inhaling the scent of pine and listening to the chirp of crickets as he brooded over his complete failure from the past twenty-four hours. A bitter heat had surged up his throat at seeing his best friend, beaten and bleeding, in that SUV, especially when Titus had been there on Kyden's orders. The demons must have spotted the van, and no matter Titus's skill as a warrior, he was no match for a prince of hell.

Based on Zahra's description of the power she'd felt, plus her severe reaction to the grunt's influence, he was certain there was a prince in the car with his friend. The question was, which one?

Once he'd thinned the horde of demons, his past and present merged into a horrific reality. One minute, Zahra was on the ground, holding her gun, with the Fallen standing over her and a grunt clinging to her, and the next, images of Tamara kneeling with a blade in her hand had almost brought him to his knees. Terror had him screaming Zahra's name. Thankfully, history hadn't repeated itself, but Zahra didn't come out of that altercation unscathed.

His dread had shifted to worry when her eyes, usually brimming with resolve, seemed broken and lost. The hopelessness he'd seen when they'd arrived at the cabin compelled him down the hall to knock on the bathroom door when he should have just left well enough alone.

The way she'd clung to him, desperation and longing filling hazel eyes, her lashes wet, had almost broken him. When she'd stared at his mouth, he knew what she wanted and it took every ounce of self-control not to kiss her back.

Deep down, they both knew he wasn't what she needed. And when he said, "I can't," he meant it. Physically, he could, but he wouldn't allow himself to get emotionally or relationally involved. So he retreated before the temptation sank its teeth into him.

To keep his mind off her, he dissected the events from when they first arrived at the nursing home. He hadn't sensed a demon possessing the nurse when they walked toward Nancy's room, but he remembered the nurse on her phone. She must have tipped someone off to Zahra's location. And the way the possessed nurse had called him "little cherub" meant the Fallen was most likely Cree from Club Nyx.

Either way, the fight had been a disaster. Normally, he would have unleashed his fury to rescue Titus. Abandoning his friend made his skin crawl, but his orders were to protect Zahra. He'd already failed at saving the halo—he couldn't fail with her.

Frustration had him grinding his teeth until his jaw ached. If only another angel were around to spar with to release some of the tension coiling through his body. He had faced storms and shadows without flinching, attacking whatever came at him with a confident resolve, but the weight in his chest and the memories he'd buried violently rising to the surface rendered him exposed. He didn't know what to do.

He'd already called Adinah and another Slayer named Oz to help search for Titus. The cabin wasn't equipped with the computers he needed to look for him, plus Adinah was better at sifting through information. And, as he kept reminding himself, Zahra's safety was his priority.

He still had one more call to make. The phone rang once before a deep voice answered.

"Not sure I'm happy to be hearing from you," Raphael said.

"Then you won't want to hear this," Kyden said, dreading what he was about to say. Admitting failure to an archangel had him gritting his teeth. "We were attacked and the halo taken."

"And the woman?"

"Uninjured. She even took out a grunt while shooting a Fallen—two, actually."

"That's impressive," Raphael said, and Kyden could imagine the angel raising his brows. "Who were the two Fallen?"

"I didn't get a chance to identify the first, but I'm pretty sure it was Cree. The other one might have been Raghav. Zahra couldn't remember the actual name, but she said it started with an R." He waited a beat before adding, "They have Titus."

Silence filled the line. Finally, Raphael said, "Why would they take him? Surely, they must realize all of Heaven will fight to get one of theirs back."

"Unclear, sir. Adinah and Oz are working on locating him. Zahra and I are currently at the Virginia safe house."

"Does she still have the journal?"

"Yes." Kyden sighed. "General, I'm sorry I failed…"

"Do *not* finish that sentence." Raphael's voice was sharp enough to cut glass. "Your mission is the safety of Zahra first and foremost."

"But the halo—"

"Deciphering the prophecy is paramount—we must know what the demons are planning. I'll do what I can on this end to find Titus."

"Yes, sir," he said before the line went dead.

He stared toward the Heavens. "Give me the strength to do what I must." His voice was carried away by a gentle breeze rustling through the aspens. The full moon lit up the sky, illuminating the forest surrounding him, and his shoulders lowered as the peaceful babble of a nearby stream played a soothing melody. He remained on the deck as the moon continued its trek across the inky night sky, his head dipped in silent prayer.

The squeak of the screen door made him jerk in his chair. Dawn had arrived, and with it a new day, hopefully better than the last.

"Have you been awake all night?" Zahra asked, wearing the leggings and T-shirt he'd found for her when he'd gone into town. He had also purchased food and another burner phone since her other one was no longer safe.

He rubbed his neck, wincing at the stiffness. "I slept a bit."

She handed him a cup of coffee and plopped down in the chair opposite him, wrapping a blanket around herself to protect from the morning chill. They sat in comfortable silence, listening to the awakening forest.

"It's so peaceful here," she finally said.

The wicker chair creaked as he leaned back and crossed an ankle over his knee. He took a long sip of his coffee, immediately feeling more alert. He remembered what Titus had said about angels being addicted to caffeine, and the thought of his friend in the enemy's hands made his stomach tighten into knots.

Zahra shifted in her chair and faced him. "About last night. I wanted to apologize."

He raised his hand. "No apology necessary. It's a typical reaction, for a human," he added.

"Sometimes I forget you're not human. Like now, you just look so normal."

He lifted a brow, which made her smile. The dark circles under her eyes had lessened and color had returned to her face.

She took another sip of her coffee. "But out of curiosity, when you said you can't, do you mean you really, you know, can't?"

Why was he surprised she'd ask questions? Her curiosity made her excellent at her job, but probably landed her in trouble more times than anything.

"Physically, I can."

"Oh," she said, lowering her gaze and playing with a loose thread on the blanket.

"Angels don't have the same needs as humans."

She nodded pointedly at his coffee cup.

He rolled his eyes. "The same physical needs..."

"Caffeine *is* a physical need."

He practically growled at her. "We don't have the same lust-filled needs as humans. There, is that better?"

The corner of her lip quirked, but she still kept her gaze on the wooden planks of the deck. "What about love? Do you experience that?"

He wanted to groan. It was too early in the morning, and he hadn't had enough sleep for this conversation. "Angels were created differently. Elohim didn't need us to procreate and fill the earth, therefore we don't need sex, therefore we don't crave it like you humans do." He wasn't explaining this properly but it was the best he could do at the moment. "We're just different and need different things."

She finally looked at him. "And what do you need?"

"Oh, for the love of all that's holy." He shot to his feet and glared down at her. "I need you to quit asking me questions."

He was about to walk inside to refill his mug when she laughed. "Come back. I'm just yanking your chain." He turned toward her, and she patted the chair next to her. "I won't ask any more questions about the personal nature of angels, for now," she added with a mischievous smile.

He sat and rubbed a hand down his face, desperate for a change of subject. "I bought you a new burner phone and destroyed the other one just in case it was being tracked. It's a good bet the demons are monitoring Alexis's and Jake's phones."

"What about Mom? The demons have already infiltrated the nursing home once. What's keeping them from attacking again?"

"Her Protector is posted and there's been no other sign of demons. I'll get another update within a few hours."

She chewed her thumbnail. "Any news about Titus?"

Her concern over his friend's well-being softened his heart for a second before he remembered his job. Raphael had preached compassion when he'd reassigned him to the role of Protector, but for both their sakes, maintaining his defenses was the wisest choice, especially after she'd kissed him last night.

"Not yet."

Sadness crept into her eyes. "I read in my father's journal that a demon named Mammon had stolen the Atar'zul during the Babylonian Empire."

"Mammon, the Prince of Greed, possessed King Nebuchadnezzar II when he attacked Jerusalem. The halo had been hidden in the temple, which Mammon desecrated."

"Does the Atar'zul have—and I can't believe I'm saying this—evil magic?"

He drained the last of his coffee and walked inside to refill his cup, motioning for her to follow him. She leaned against the counter, a deep wrinkle between her brows.

"From what I understand, it doesn't have evil magic, so to speak. It drains the powers of both angels and demons," he said.

"And in all your years of existence, you've never heard of the prophecy?"

He frowned. "No. The Vaelatori have kept the prophecy hidden. Raphael said the reason had to do with balance."

"How old are you, anyway?"

"Old."

She huffed out a laugh and dug through the bag of lollipops. She finally picked the flavor she wanted, unwrapped it, and shoved it into her mouth.

"I can practically hear your mind whirling," he said, refilling his mug.

She pointed the candy at him. "Hold that thought." She walked toward the back bedroom, returning with the journal and flipping through the pages. "There's a line in the prophecy that implies the Atar'zul will change."

"Change? How?"

She lifted her head and frowned. "Am I supposed to share this with you? I don't want to upset the 'balance.'"

He scratched his jaw. "If you suspect the halo has changed, then the balance might already be off."

"Good point. I'll just give you a snippet, then."

He snorted behind his mug. "I'm glad to see you taking your Vaelatori role so seriously."

She rolled her eyes. "There's a line here that says, *Of all the sins it was power they craved, and altered the crown for the depraved.* Doesn't that sound like it's been changed, and not in a good way?"

"Yeah, it does, which might explain how it affected me when I first touched it."

"Also, what's keeping the demons from knowing the prophecy? Pretty sure they don't care about balance."

He lowered his mug and stared out the window. A hawk swooped low in search of its prey while sunlight filtered through the trees like long, spindly fingers. "That's a possibility," he said, facing her. "Didn't your dad say he'd found the last part but it still needed to be translated?"

"Mm-hmm," she murmured, flipping through the pages.

"In your father's tent at the dig site, we discovered burnt papers and ashes in a stone pot. They must have been the originals."

She looked up. "What are you getting at?"

"If the demons learned of the prophecy, they would only know the first part. They wouldn't have what your father found. Which gives us an advantage."

She tapped her lip, her eyes narrowed in concentration. "Since you understand the enemy better than I do, it would be shortsighted not to let you read this," she said, pointing to the journal.

A thought drifted through his mind. If he understood the prophecy, then why would he need Zahra? He could make sure she stayed at the cabin, and then he could find Titus and the halo.

Zahra flipped a page and pointed to another line in the journal. "*A mortal must bleed to feed the light*. There are some other words here I'm not familiar with, and then it continues, *to turn the tide against the night*. So a mortal needs to change the magic in the halo back." She scratched her neck. "By bleeding. That sounds ominous."

"What? How could a human be needed?"

"You know, sometimes you say the word *human* the way I would say cockroach," she said, crossing her arms. "You don't think much of us, do you?"

A twinge of guilt tightened his chest. She wasn't wrong, but he thought he was more adept at hiding his feelings. He had never understood Elohim's grace and mercy for humankind, which was why the role of Slayer was better suited for him.

"How long will it take you to translate the rest of the prophecy?" he asked instead of explaining his behavior.

She narrowed her gaze, obviously aware he hadn't answered her question. She shrugged, giving him a reprieve. "A few days, maybe less."

He rubbed his temples. He would go stir-crazy in this cabin with nothing to do besides worry about Titus and listen to Zahra crunch her lollipops.

She surveyed the room. "Does that computer work?"

"Of course it does."

"You're grumpy when you're tired. Drink some more coffee and let me get to work."

The next two days crawled by at a snail's pace. Zahra kicked him out of the cabin after he'd paced in the living room for the first few hours, ordering him to find something productive to do.

He busied himself with manual chores around the cabin. An enormous pile of chopped wood lay in the middle of a clearing, enough for all the residents within five miles to use. He took to the skies, searching the area three times a day for any demon activity, and almost traveled to a nearby city to fight some grunts, but he didn't want to give away their location.

Zahra sent him into town twice for "real" food, more clothing, and a list of toiletries. He wasn't sure if all humans were this high maintenance or if she was extremely skilled at annoying him while sending him on errands. He had never lived with a human for this long, and yes, two days was extremely long. Even with Tamara, he had lived at his own residence while assuming a different identity.

By the third day, he was about to pull out his hair. He'd just finished making breakfast, something other than opening a box of donuts, when his phone buzzed. He removed it from his pocket, expecting an update from Elias regarding the status of the Protectors watching over Alexis and Jake.

He frowned when the name Shane appeared. Why was his snitch texting him? He opened the message.

Shane: The halo is on the move.

Kyden's heart jumped, and he quickly typed a reply.

Kyden: Where?
Shane: Vegas
Kyden: How do you know this?
Shane: Your friend is with it. I'll be in touch.

"What is it?" Zahra asked, blowing on the scrambled eggs he'd made her.

"It seems the Atar'zul and Titus are on their way to Las Vegas."

She sat forward. "Nevada?"

"Yes." How his snitch had this information was beyond him, but the man had yet to lead him astray. Granted, there was a first time for everything.

"I have so many questions right now," she said.

"Why am I not surprised?"

She punched him in the arm. "Ow," she said, shaking her hand. "Who was that? And how do you know Vegas is our destination? And for that matter, why Vegas? And most importantly, what are we going to do?"

He slid a glance at her from the corner of his eye. "That *is* a lot of questions."

She rested her hands on her hips and tapped her toe.

He sighed and leaned against the counter. "The person who texted me is Shane and happens to be my snitch. I've worked with him before, plus he helped me locate the Atar'zul in Baghdad. How he knows all of this is a terrific question, and one I'm determined to get the answer to. I have a suspicion about why Vegas, and as to what we are going to do? My job is to keep you safe, which means staying here."

The thought irked him. Finally, some action after being confined to the cabin, watching Zahra work. But as a Protector, his mission was clear.

She pointed at his white knuckles. "Based on the fact you're splintering the countertop, I'm pretty sure staying here isn't what you want to do."

He pushed away from the counter and flexed his hands. "It doesn't really matter what I want."

She chewed the inside of her cheek. "Okay, we'll table that for a minute. Why Vegas?"

"You mentioned reading about Mammon in your father's journal. Las Vegas would be an ideal place for the Prince of Greed, don't you agree?" He still wasn't sure how Raghav fit into all of this since he reported to the Wrath Prince. And considering the halo originally belonged to Apollyon? He shook his head. The number of unknowns gave him a headache.

"It would. So when are we leaving?" she asked, walking to the kitchen and setting her plate in the sink.

"*We* aren't going anywhere." He sent a message to Adinah relaying what Shane had said.

She rested her hands on her hips. "Nope. We're going to get that halo back and save Titus. It's my fault those demons got the Atar'zul and that Titus is in this situation."

"Technically, it's my fault regarding Titus. I'm the one who dragged him into this mess." The guilt churned the coffee in his stomach.

She waved a hand at him as if he were a pesky mosquito. "Either way, I'm going to Vegas. I only have a few more words to translate, which I can do there. If you want to protect me, then you have to come with me. Just tell your archangel I made you."

"Yeah, you don't *tell* an archangel anything."

She gathered her things and shoved them into a bag. "Come on."

"Zahra, if something happens to you..." He stared down at his boots. "I can't fail again."

She approached him and rested a hand on his jaw. "I trust you. And whether you like it or not, we're a team."

He lifted his gaze and focused on the golden specks in her eyes. "You'll do as I say. If I say run, you run. If I say hide, you hide. If I say—"

"Yeah, yeah. I get it. You're in charge." She gave him a light slap on his cheek. "How long will it take to fly us to Vegas?"

"Flying by myself—minutes. But your human body couldn't handle the stress."

"Right. Well, what are we waiting for?"

Kyden flew as fast as he could while also protecting Zahra. They had to land every few hours to warm her up and let her catch her breath. They made it to Las Vegas by late afternoon and checked in at the Wynn Las Vegas Hotel. Normally, he wouldn't reserve a room in such an elegant place, but he had a feeling staying in the center of the city would prove beneficial.

During the trip, he had received a text from Elias. Alexis and Ms. Jenkins were still safe, but curiously, Jake had left Boston and was currently flying in a private plane. His destination—Las Vegas.

He had asked Zahra during one of their breaks if Jake had seemed interested in her work or ancient relics.

"No. The only interest was because of his boss. Other than that, he never really cared about archaeology." She'd narrowed her gaze. "Do you think he's involved in this?"

"Just keeping options open." He didn't want to worry her, but he also didn't want her to be naive. "Have you heard from Durand?"

"Except for the flowers he sent to my office, no, but he was definitely interested in the Atar'zul. Then again, so were you," she said with a smirk.

Titus had done an extensive search on Laurent Durand and had found nothing worth noting, but maybe he missed something because she was right—the billionaire had seemed almost obsessed with the halo. After they arrived in Las Vegas, he would have another look at Durand and Jake Callahan.

Kyden escorted Zahra to her room and handed her the keycard. "I need to check on something. I'll be back in a little while. Lock the door and don't let anyone in."

Zahra, her cheeks red and circles darkening the skin under her eyes, covered her mouth as she yawned. "Okay. Knock loudly, as I might pass out."

"Pretty sure I can walk through walls and doors."

She clicked her teeth and pointed at him. "Right, oh mighty angelic being." She entered her room and shut the door.

He chuckled and returned to the lobby, moving through the casino onto the Strip where taxis and limos clogged the streets. A few blocks down was an internet café—the perfect spot to do some probing without completely revealing his location to the demons.

He slid behind a computer with a view of the street and performed a search on Jake Callahan. Titus had shown him his research, but at the time, he hadn't been high on their list of suspects. He wanted another look at Zahra's ex-boyfriend.

After thirty minutes of reading up on the man, he sat back in his chair. Nothing stood out to him besides the person he worked for. But Jake didn't work in Durand's antiquities department, so even that connection was weak, except for joining his boss in Boston. Why had he been there?

A group of women stumbled by, the one in front wearing a veil and a tank top that said, *Kiss the Bride-to-Be*. Behind them, a white van rolled past, slowing with the traffic. He was about to look away when he noticed a logo with a blue and green scarab on the side of the van.

He frowned. Why did that seem familiar? His phone vibrated on the desk, and Shane's number lit up the screen. He glanced back at the street, but the van was gone.

"We need to talk," Shane said, his voice muffled.

"Then talk." He wasn't in the mood for games.

"Face-to-face."

His brows rose. Shane never wanted to meet in person. His anonymity was more valuable than the thousands of dollars Kyden had paid his snitch.

"Fine. Where?"

"I'll find you," Shane said, and the connection dropped into silence.

Chapter Twenty-Six

Zahra

Zahra strode straight to the minibar after she left Kyden in the hallway. Even though she was exhausted, she needed something to take the edge off and a bag of lollipops would not cut it. A miniature bottle of whiskey called her name. She twisted the lid and swallowed the contents in a few gulps, relishing the warmth pooling in her stomach.

The sensation of flying with Kyden had affected her more than she had let on. When they'd escaped Boston, they hadn't flown nearly as fast or as high. Flying across the country was another matter entirely. The pressure on her chest and in her head had finally lessened to where she didn't feel like throwing up anymore. Vomiting on an angel ranked high on the humiliation scale.

She peered out the window and onto the Vegas Strip filled with pedestrians and taxis. The talisman resting against her skin warmed slightly as even from this height she spied grunt demons in the street, clinging to oblivious people and leaving behind their eerie green mist.

A shiver ran down her spine. Memories of the emotional torment that grunt had inflicted on her made her reach for another bottle. This time, she mixed it with soda. Kyden wouldn't be pleased to return to the hotel and find her hammered.

"Might as well be useful," she said to the empty room, and opened her father's journal. She still needed to translate a few more lines of the prophecy. But even if she did, would they understand what to do with it?

She worked on the last paragraph while sipping her drink. She'd memorized the code her father had written on a separate page and the words formed faster.

A sacred bond, united and pure, shall cleanse the crown of dark allure. From shadow's grip and sorrow's chains, the angels rise in light's refrain—redeemed through blood and solemn vow, they seek the grace they once let down.

She tapped her lip as she stared at the last stanza, and images of kissing Kyden flooded her brain. The desire to sink through the floor with embarrassment assailed her once again. She had kept her composure the last few days, and thankfully, his explanation of why he didn't reciprocate the kiss had erased some of the sting.

She'd been scared and lonely, and when a warrior angel shows up in your bathroom with only a dingy towel separating you—well, any woman with a fraction of libido would do the same thing.

At least, she kept telling herself that.

Before Jake, the last man she had kissed was her coworker, Brandon. The kiss with Kyden hadn't compared to what Jake had done to her against the wall of the bar the other night. Jake had left her wanting more. A lot more.

She took her phone out of her bag.

Kyden's questions about Jake's interest in the Atar'zul made her uneasy. She hadn't talked to him in a while, and the need to hear his voice had her dialing his number.

"This is Jake Callahan," he said, the connection staticky.

"Jake, it's Zahra."

"Hold on." Muffled words sounded and after a few seconds, he whispered, "Are you all right? I tried calling you."

She frowned at the panic straining his voice. "I...lost my phone, again."

"Again? Zahra, what's going on? You were on the news."

"What? Why?"

"There were reports of you shooting someone at the nursing home. You were with that guy from dinner."

"Shit." She rubbed a hand down her face. Why hadn't she thought of cameras recording her? And of course, they wouldn't pick up the swarm of demons. The need to get to a computer had her turning from the window and grabbing her key card. There would be a computer somewhere in the lobby.

"I don't know what you're involved in, but I can help. I'm about to land in Vegas, but..."

"Vegas?" She stabbed the elevator button harder than she needed to. "Why are you coming here?" Kyden's questions about Jake's interest in the Atar'zul clenched her heart.

"I'm with my boss. There's a business deal he needs my help with but I'm returning to Boston..." His voice trailed off. "Hang on. You said 'coming here.'"

She grimaced, realizing her mistake. "I gotta go." The ding announcing the elevator sounded.

"Zahra, wait. Are you in Vegas?"

She ended the call just as the elevator door clicked shut. She descended toward the lobby in search of a computer, dread hardening into a lead ball in her gut.

Thirty minutes later, she walked through the lobby, inhaling the cigarette smoke as she passed. She had vowed never to smoke again, but she couldn't help it if someone smoked nearby and she just happened to walk through the cloud of nicotine.

After her horrifying search on the internet and witnessing herself shooting the nurse in the leg and running through the parking lot, she'd wanted to throw up. Realizing she hadn't eaten breakfast—and the alcohol from earlier resembled a churning pit of nausea—she decided to grab a sandwich while disregarding Kyden's command to stay in the hotel. Before leaving, she stopped by the gift shop to purchase a hat and sunglasses, just in case someone recognized her from the nursing home shooting.

She slid the keycard into her door and opened it. "Dammit," she mumbled, seeing a very pissed-off angel, wings on display, pacing in her hotel room. She walked around the angry warrior to the small table near the window. "I was hungry."

"Ever heard of room service? I told you to stay here." The words slid through his clenched teeth.

She dropped the bag of sandwiches onto the table. "You're my Protector, not my boss, so back off."

His eyes narrowed. "It's difficult to protect you if I don't know where you are."

She plopped down in the chair. "Since you're already ticked off, I might as well inform you that Jake is on his way to Vegas." She unwrapped her sandwich and took a large bite.

He glanced at his boots, and she stopped chewing. "You don't seem surprised by that tidbit of information."

"Elias told me he was coming here."

"So that's why you asked about his interest in the Atar'zul. Thanks for giving me a heads up." Anger had her shoving another bite of sandwich into her mouth, filling her cheeks.

"I didn't want you to worry until I knew more. I did another search on him and couldn't find anything. I think you can trust him."

"Super. He also knows I'm here."

"And how did he figure that out?" he asked, crossing his arms.

She pointed to the other sandwich. "You want one?" She opened her bag of chips and matched him glare for glare. When it was obvious he wouldn't answer, she sipped her soda and licked her teeth. "I screwed up, okay? I was a little distraught to hear I was on the news, accused of shooting an innocent nurse."

He tapped his finger against his bulging bicep, his eyes still stern, but at least his jaw didn't remind her of a ticking time bomb anymore. He walked to the table and surveyed another sandwich, chips, and a brownie. Picking up the dessert, he arched his brow.

"I got it for you since you're addicted to sugar," she said.

Her heart rate had finally settled. The call with Jake had shaken her up more than she cared to admit. A part of her wanted to tell him everything, but that wouldn't be wise. Seeing Kyden so angry had made her pulse thump loudly in her ears. She'd seen his power and logically knew he'd never hurt her, but the fierceness of his gaze, his stature, and his majestic wings hanging down his back—well, she understood why people in the Bible fainted when they saw angels.

Kyden inhaled the brownie in three bites before unwrapping his sandwich. He removed his phone and opened it to his photos. "Does this look familiar to you?"

A white van with the logo of a scarab beetle filled the screen. She frowned. "It does, but I can't place it." She sipped her soda while staring at the scarab, enlarging the photo to see if there were any words or a company name. Why did the image seem familiar? The ancient Egyptians revered the beetle, which she had seen often in her work at the museum. "Maybe it has something to do with an archaeology company?"

She passed the phone back to Kyden, who had stopped chewing. With an audible swallow, he snapped his fingers. "That's it. I saw the same logo in Baghdad before I went to your father's dig site."

"Is that a happy coincidence?"

"I don't believe in coincidences, happy or otherwise," he said, tapping some numbers on his phone.

"What are you doing?" she asked, finishing her sandwich and scrunching the paper into a ball. She tossed it at the trash can and missed.

His eyes shifted to the discarded sandwich wrapper and then back to his phone. "I'm texting Adinah—asking her to check out any archaeology companies with this logo." Once he finished, he grabbed his sandwich. "Thanks, by the way."

"Don't mention it."

He devoured his meal in a shockingly short amount of time and threw his balled-up paper without looking; of course, it landed perfectly in the trash can. "I should've bought us a laptop..." he mumbled to himself.

"There's a computer in the lobby. That's how I discovered I'm on *America's Most Wanted*." She still couldn't believe the images that had flashed across the screen. And to think, a few weeks ago, her biggest concern was getting a promotion. She had logged in to her email, seeing a notice from her boss terminating her employment. But who needed a job when you were going to prison? That is, if she survived demons and princes of hell.

A frantic giggle escaped her lips, and she smacked a hand over her mouth.

"You look like you're about to freak out." Kyden sipped his drink with a brow raised.

"Super close," she said, her voice higher than normal.

"Well, before you do, I have a feeling Mammon is also in Vegas. Seems the popular place to be."

The sandwich turned to lead in her stomach. "A prince of hell is here? You can feel him?"

"I sensed an increase in evil, plus there's an abnormally large number of grunts in the city. I spotted a few Fallen too," he said with a shrug.

How he could act so cavalier was beyond her. "Have you ever fought a prince?"

"Never alone. Hence why I notified Oz and Adinah."

"Then the Atar'zul must be here, right? Which means Titus is too."

"That's what I'm hoping. The issue is finding them and figuring out what they want with them."

"Let's assume the demons know at least part of the prophecy." She thumbed through her father's journal until she turned to the correct page.

"You translated the whole thing?

"Yep. Say goodbye to the balance," she murmured, and then read the prophecy.

From loyal blood and fallen grace, the
crown was forged from war's cruel
fate. Its form was neither cursed nor
blessed, but watched by eyes that never rest.

Guardians shaped from mortal clay
concealed the relic and held darkness
at bay. Their purpose pure—to guard
the lore, from hands of peace and
those of war.

When halo's gleam was again exposed, it drew the eyes of the op-
posed. Of all the sins it was power
they craved, and altered the crown for
the depraved.

The angels bowed to twisted might,
and shattered all they held as right.
Once steadfast and pure, their will
now bent to shadow's lure.

Yet hope remains, though dim and
slight. A mortal must bleed to feed the
light—bound to an archangel's heavenly might, to turn the tide against
the night.

A sacred bond, united and pure,
shall cleanse the crown of dark allure.
From shadow's grip and sorrow's
chains, the angels rise in light's refrain—redeemed through blood and
solemn vow, they seek the grace they
once let down.

"As far as I can tell, the first two stanzas deal with the past—when the Atar'zul was created and details about the Vaelatori." She pointed to the third stanza. "From here down, I believe, is happening now."

Kyden leaned forward and turned the journal toward him, his eyes scanning the page. "That makes sense."

"One thing I don't understand," she said.

"Only one?" His lips curled into a smirk, but his gaze remained glued to her father's journal.

"Ha, very funny. But what would make an angel's will bend to shadow?"

His shoulders stiffened. "Nothing."

She chewed her thumbnail. "Well, now don't get your wings ruffled, but that's not necessarily true. There was at least one time when the angels had a choice and some chose poorly, right?"

His eyes narrowed but instead of being irritated with her, which was a first, he seemed to be in deep thought.

"Could the demons use the halo as a weapon?" She watched his amber eyes shift across the page, tracking each word of the prophecy.

"Possibly. The prince, whom I suspect is Mammon, may have figured out a way to use the halo against angels."

"You said angels can't die, right?"

"Unless our heads are cut off."

She flinched at his cavalier remark. "Then what does 'divine order fractured' mean?"

"I have no idea." He continued scanning the page.

She walked to the small kitchenette to grab a bottle of water. A knock sounded on the door.

She moved toward it. "Zahra, no!"

The door opened, and she screamed.

Chapter Twenty-Seven

Kyden

Kyden shoved Zahra out of the way and drew his sword before the demon at the door raised his hands.

"Easy, Kyden. It's me." Green eyes stared back at him; the corner of his lip lifted.

Kyden recognized the Fallen and his annoying smirk from Club Nyx. He tightened his grip, ready to strike, but paused. The demon hadn't removed his sword from its scabbard.

"Mind lowering that and letting me in?" the Fallen asked, glancing along the corridor, his ebony hair falling in waves to his shoulders.

The familiar voice caused him to stumble, almost knocking Zahra over. "Shane?"

The demon dipped his chin. "My true name is Gael." He slid past Kyden, who was frozen in shock, into the room. He wondered if the Fallen had used his magic against him, but realized he had full use of his faculties. He scanned the hallway and quickly shut the door while keeping Zahra behind him.

She stood on tiptoe, peeking around his shoulder. "Why in the hell would you let one of those bastards in?"

Gael arched a brow. "Because you need my help."

"Like hell we do," she said.

Kyden slid her a look from the corner of his eye.

"Does she always swear this much?" Gael asked.

"This is actually rather tame." He lowered his sword but refused to put it away. Fallen were deceptive, and it seemed Gael had managed to fool him for years. "Explain."

He grimaced when Gael turned to stare out the window. Bony nubs, where his wings used to be, stuck out from under his suit jacket. He didn't think he'd survive if he'd ever lost his wings. They represented favor and freedom—both of which he needed desperately.

Gael sat in the chair Zahra had vacated and tapped his thumb on the table. "I've been providing intel to your kind for the past hundred years. Not only you, but other angels, even Gabriel."

"You've worked with a general of Elohim's army?" He gently pushed Zahra onto the bed where he could keep an eye on both of them. Knowing her, she'd go for her gun and shoot the demon just for good measure. Depending on how this conversation went, he might even let her.

Gael rolled his eyes. "He's a little high-strung, that one."

"I wonder why," he said, tapping the tip of his sword against his leg.

"You can put that away. If I had wanted to fight you, I would have done it when you exited that internet café. Or back in Boston, even at Club Nyx—I've had plenty of opportunities."

Kyden tilted his head. Gael had a point. He slid his sword into the scabbard on his back.

"No way. You might trust this creep, but I don't," Zahra said, jumping to her feet, grabbing the dagger off his hip, and pointing the blade at the demon.

Gael's lips curved into a smile, his fanged teeth protruding past his bottom lip. "Quite the feisty one, aren't you?"

Kyden sighed. "You have no idea."

"I see she's wearing a talisman."

"I am standing right here, you know," Zahra said.

Kyden pulled her onto the bed and sat next to her. "Why have you been helping me?"

Gael's smile fell. "Because I'm trying to right some wrongs, and I don't want them using the halo. The repercussions would be disastrous."

Kyden frowned. He'd never heard of a demon doing the right thing. He didn't even realize they were capable of making the distinction. "Right some wrongs? That's rather vague, don't you think?"

Gael's lips curved. "Let's just say that information is above your rank."

Kyden fisted his hands. Punching the demon wouldn't get them the answers they needed.

"Are they trying to use the halo as a weapon of some sort?" Zahra asked.

Gael cocked his head. "Why would you ask that?"

"There's information in my father's journal. Demons didn't have the ability the last time your side had the relic, but now I'm assuming they do."

Kyden held up his hand. "First things first. Who is 'they'? I'm assuming Raghav is involved."

"You assume correctly."

"Marach has never shown an interest in the halo, so is Raghav working for a different prince?"

Zahra nudged him and said out of the corner of her mouth, "Who is Marach again?"

"The Prince of Wrath," Kyden said.

"Ah," said Zahra. "And Raghav?"

Gael crossed his leg, resting it on his knee. "He's a Fallen."

"Got it." Her brow furrowed as if she really didn't.

"In answer to your question, Raghav has been secretly working for Mammon," Gael said.

Before Zahra interrupted again, Kyden said, "Prince of Greed."

"Oh, right."

"That's who I figured was behind this, but what I don't understand is that we haven't seen Mammon in centuries."

The demon leaned forward. "He's been playing the long game, one I just figured out recently. Mammon kept to himself, not attracting any unwanted attention. Thirty years ago, he possessed a college student, assumed his identity, and has been passing for a human ever since."

Kyden's mouth dropped. "He's possessed the same person all these years? I didn't think that was possible. A human couldn't survive that."

Gael shrugged. "If the host is willing, then it can be done. But Mammon's possession has been the longest. He's been in the same body for so long, I doubt you'd even sense him."

Kyden stood and walked to the window. Neon lights glowed and traffic moved along the Strip at a snail's pace. The Prince of Greed, hiding in plain sight, had him grinding his teeth.

"Do you know the name of the person?" Zahra asked.

"No, I wasn't privy to that information. Raghav meets with him privately. Only he's aware of the prince's human identity."

Kyden kept his gaze on the horizon. "How are they going to use the halo?"

"I don't know that either," Gael said with an edge to his gravelly voice.

Kyden spun. "What exactly do you know? So far, you've given me nothing I can use. For a spy, you're not very good."

The demon shot to his feet, his green eyes narrowed and fists clenched. "Not very good? You thought I was a mere human only minutes ago, as did many of your kind. I've risked my life helping you angels."

Kyden had never been this close to a Fallen without his sword in his hand swinging for the killing blow. Zahra had slowly risen to her feet and pointed the dagger in their direction. Color drained from her face, and her hand shook slightly. If he and Gael came to blows, she could get caught in the crossfire.

He lifted his palms and retreated a step.

Gael's chest rose and fell rapidly. He glanced toward Zahra, nodded, and returned to his chair.

After taking a deep breath, Gael said, "I might not know who Mammon is impersonating, but I have a good idea where Titus is. I'm sure that's valuable to you."

Kyden stepped forward, his anger lessening with any news of his friend. "Where is he? Is he okay?"

"There are two places where they might hold him. And last I heard, he was okay, for now."

"For now?" Zahra asked. "What does that mean?"

"Whatever they're doing with the halo, they'll need to test it. Time is against us."

A lead ball dropped into Kyden's stomach. Could the halo be used to kill Titus? He didn't see how, but he wouldn't let that happen. The words from the prophecy were ominous regarding the fate of the angels, and Mammon must have figured that out.

He'd have to completely trust the Fallen and combine their information if they had a chance of saving Titus. He removed his phone and showed Gael the picture of the van. "Do you recognize this logo?"

Gael's eyes widened. "Where did you see this?"

"In Baghdad, when you gave me the tip on the dig site, and then recently a few blocks away."

The demon's lip quirked. "I think I've figured out who the human is that Mammon is possessing."

Kyden clenched his hands and resisted strangling the demon while he waited. This was the break they needed. If they found the prince, then they'd find Titus.

"Who the hell is it?" Zahra asked, her patience obviously at an end too.

"Ironically, you've both met him." His gaze shifted to Kyden. "And you even had dinner with him."

He was about to reach across the table to strangle the demon when a memory clicked into place—one where he shook a man's hand and something hadn't seemed quite right. He'd been too occupied with pretending to be Zahra's date and finding information about the Atar'zul.

The need to unleash a litany of swear words had him digging his nails into his palms. "Laurent Durand," he growled.

"What?" Zahra shot to her feet.

Gael nodded. "That scarab is the logo for one of his companies, although it's owned under a different name."

He definitely felt like strangling someone. He'd been in the presence of Mammon, the Prince of Greed, and hadn't even known it.

The background check Titus had done revealed the college Durand had attended and all of his businesses, but they hadn't delved further into his past because never in a million years would he have assumed a demon possession lasting this long. How the human was still alive was beyond him.

Zahra slowly sat on the bed, her face pale.

"What is it?"

She looked up with wide eyes. "Jake's on his jet," she said in a whisper before addressing Gael. "Is he involved in this too?"

Gael shook his head. "I don't think so. But I guarantee that if Mammon is aware of your interest in Jake, then he isn't safe either."

"Where is Mammon?" Kyden asked.

Gael checked his phone. "His plane landed thirty minutes ago at Mc-Carran International Airport, which is my cue to leave."

"What about Titus?" Kyden stood.

Gael reached into his jacket pocket and removed a piece of paper. "He's at one of these locations. If I find out anything more concrete, I'll try to contact you."

"You'll *try*?" Zahra asked, her hands fisted on her hips.

Gael walked to the door, opened it, and turned. "I'm risking more than my life. Please remember that."

Kyden crossed his arms. "Those who lose their life for Elohim's sake will find their life."

The Fallen arched a brow. "Did you just Bible thump me?"

Kyden snorted and reached out his hand. "Stay safe."

Gael stared at his hand and then shook it. "You too."

After Gael left, Kyden walked to the middle of the room, his mind spinning faster than he could fly. "There have been very few instances where I've been so completely shocked. Pretty sure today has topped them all."

Zahra plopped back on the bed, his dagger cradled in her lap. "So your snitch, who you've worked with for years, is a demon."

"Yep. Never saw that coming."

"And Laurent is an alter ego for Mammon?" She rubbed her face. "And I thought he was charming."

"If it makes you feel any better, so did I."

"I have to call Jake." Fear tightened the skin around her eyes.

He sat next to her. "You still love him, don't you?"

Her mouth opened and then she snapped it shut. "I need to know whether I can trust him or not."

He pried the dagger from her hands and slid it into the sheath on his thigh. He fisted the paper Gael had given him and headed for the adjoining room. "I can't answer that for you." He faced her, saddened by the tears welling in her eyes. "I have some calls to make. Adinah and Oz will be here soon. Try to rest."

He chuckled when she mumbled, "Rest my ass," and then he shut the door. He collapsed against it and closed his eyes. What a complete fool he'd been for not recognizing a demon, whether it was Gael pretending to be Shane, his snitch, or Mammon, an actual prince of hell, masquerading as Laurent Durand. How could he have been so blind? He wasn't worthy of the title of Slayer nor Protector if he couldn't even spot evil when it was staring him in the face.

He used the excuse of making calls—he only had one to make regarding this latest information. He needed time to gather his thoughts and sort through the multitude of emotions crashing into him in relentless waves. For Zahra's sake, he'd acted calm, but in reality he was spiraling into a bottomless pit of doubt and rage.

CHAPTER TWENTY-EIGHT

ZAHRA

Zahra stared at the door, anxiety drumming a chaotic rhythm in her chest. She had come face-to-face with a Fallen, again, but at least this one hadn't tried to harm her. She didn't know what to think of Gael and seriously doubted she could trust him. He reminded her of a predator stalking its prey, especially when those sickly green eyes had focused on her, a slight curve to his lips revealing his pointed teeth.

Speaking of predators—Laurent Durand was like a viper, hypnotic and graceful, and based on what Kyden and Gael had said, patient, waiting for the perfect moment to strike. He'd been charming and so poised, nothing like the picture she had of someone possessed.

And then there was Jake. Gael had said he wasn't involved, but what if the demon was wrong? What if everything Jake had done was to manipulate her? She shook her head. No, she had to believe he didn't know his boss was inherently evil because if he did...

Grabbing her phone from the table, she called his number. "Dammit," she mumbled, as his voicemail told her to leave a message. She decided to trust Jake, even if Kyden didn't—she just hoped her plan wouldn't backfire. "Jake, if you get this, I'm at the Wynn Las Vegas. Whatever you do, don't tell your boss."

She flipped the phone shut as Kyden emerged from the other room, his eyes hard and jaw set. "My angel friends are on their way up."

She rose to her feet. "Are you all right?"

"I loathe being duped like this. The fact that I was in Mammon's presence and didn't even know makes me want to unleash hell on earth. So, no, *all right* is not how I'm feeling."

"Did you just swear?" She covered her heart dramatically. She didn't enjoy seeing him so edgy, for she truly believed he could reign down hell if he set his mind to it. The power of angels was beyond her understanding.

He narrowed his gaze, his amber eyes lit with an internal fire. "Technically, hell is a location, so no. But I'm summoning every ounce of my self-control to *not* pull a Zahra."

She snorted and was about to respond when a knock sounded on the door.

"Why do you bother knocking when you can just walk through?" she asked.

"We're being polite," said a deep voice from the other side of the door.

"Oh right, excellent hearing." She rubbed her forehead. "Forgot about that one."

Kyden shook his head and opened the door.

Her jaw dropped as a woman—the words *beautiful* and *badassery* merged into one cohesive adjective in her mind—strode into the room. Her sleek blonde hair hung below her chin, and she wore black cargo pants that somehow looked sexy along with black lace-up boots. The definition of her arms and shoulders was on full display in a formfitting gray tank top. Her amber eyes, similar to Kyden's, narrowed slightly when she noticed her.

Zahra glanced at her plain T-shirt and jeans, and the desire to hide under the bed sent a burning to her cheeks. Compared to this warrior goddess, she resembled the "before" photo during a makeover.

The other man she assumed was Oz. He was tall, like Kyden, and appeared just as powerful in his leather pants, black boots, and a forest-green shirt that clung to the contours of his muscles. Strands of his long brown hair had fallen free from where he'd gathered it at the nape of his neck.

She couldn't fathom how these two warriors looked in the spiritual realm with their armor, wings, and weapons. A truly magnificent—and if she was being honest, scary as hell—sight to behold.

"Adinah, Oz, this is Zahra," Kyden said, making the introductions.

"Hi, Zahra." Oz smiled and shook her hand.

She liked him immediately. Adinah, however, lowered her chin in a ghost of a nod, and then focused on Kyden.

"What's the plan?" she asked, striding toward the table and draining what was left of Zahra's soda.

"I was drinking that," Zahra said, resting her hands on her hips.

"Oops." Adinah took one last sip, crushed the cup, and threw it over her shoulder, where it landed in the trash can.

Kyden pinched the bridge of his nose and sat in a chair. "I've recently discovered my snitch is a Fallen named Gael."

"Are you serious?" Adinah asked at the same time Oz said, "No way."

"I'm totally serious and completely shocked. Supposedly, he's helped the angels for a century, including providing intel to Gabriel," Kyden said. "Anyway, he gave me two locations where Mammon might be holding Titus. And to make matters even worse, it seems the Greed Prince has possessed the same man for thirty years."

"I didn't know that was possible," Oz said, repeating Kyden's earlier words.

"Neither did I, and I had the pleasure of meeting—"

"The bastard," Zahra cut in.

Kyden shook his head. "I was going to say 'Laurent Durand.'"

"I like her version better," said Adinah.

"The billionaire from the gala is a prince of hell?" Oz asked, his eyes darting from Kyden to Zahra.

"Yes, and time is not on our side. We need to split up and search each spot."

Oz crossed his arms. "Splitting up isn't a great idea—not against a prince."

"I'm aware, but Gael mentioned Mammon testing the halo on Titus. We don't have the luxury of exercising caution. I want the two of you to scout the warehouse," he said, handing them a slip of paper. "I'll check out the Imperial Noire Resort."

Zahra cleared her throat. "We'll check it out."

The muscle in his jaw ticked. "I would be a horrible Protector if I brought you within one hundred yards of a prince of hell. You're staying here."

"That's utter bullshit," she said, not caring anymore about swearing in front of angels. "I'm going with you. Besides, the prophecy says you'll need a Vaelatori."

Oz raised his brows. "You figured it out, then?"

Kyden rubbed his temple. "Only partially."

She smirked and strode to her purse, removing her gun and checking the magazine. "You need me, cupid. Best get used to it."

Adinah coughed, attempting to hide her laugh. She finally gave up and released a loud guffaw. "Cupid? That's hilarious."

Kyden sighed and shook his head. "Don't encourage her, Adinah."

"Why? She's got spunk. I like her."

Zahra smiled at the female angel, forgiving her for drinking her soda. At least they had one thing in common—enjoying needling Kyden every chance they got.

Kyden rose to his feet. "Fine. Check out your location, but don't engage. Reconnaissance only, and stay in touch."

Oz and Adinah nodded. They both walked toward the window as their wings exploded from their backs. Zahra shielded her eyes from the sudden flash. When the spots cleared, the two warriors were gliding through the sky, disappearing behind a nearby hotel.

"I suppose we can't do that," she said.

"Unfortunately, no, not until we get somewhere less crowded. Even in Vegas, humans aren't known to fly on their own."

She huffed a laugh and slid her gun into her bag containing her father's journal. A part of her felt guilty for leveraging her knowledge of the Atar'zul, but she also wouldn't be left behind. She may be a mere human, but she could still help.

As they descended in the elevator, her phone chimed.

Jake: In the lobby.

She swallowed at Jake's message.

Kyden frowned at her. "What's up?"

"I'm sure you've heard the saying, 'the shit's about to hit the fan'?"

"I have, even though it doesn't make sense."

The elevator doors opened. "Yeah, well, it's about to."

Jake leaned against a planter filled with tropical flowers. He wore a black suit and gray shirt, his tie loosened and his hair mussed as if he'd been running his fingers through it.

Kyden placed his arm in front of Zahra, and Jake's eyes narrowed.

"Can he see you?" she whispered.

"Yes, I'm in my human form."

"Well, that wasn't part of my plan."

He glared down at her. "You probably should have included me in this plan, don't you think?"

"You said I could trust him." She sidled past the grumpy angel and approached Jake.

He wrapped his arms around her and nuzzled into her neck. "I've been so worried about you. What have you gotten yourself into?"

She breathed in his cologne, the familiar sandalwood scent he'd worn when they had dated, and a sense of calm settled across her shoulders. "There's a lot to discuss, and some of it is going to be hard to swallow."

She pulled back and stared into his gray eyes, eyes that drifted from hers to the angel behind her.

"What's he doing here?" he asked, staring at Kyden.

"Long story. Does Laurent know where you are?"

Jake forced his gaze from Kyden and fixed his attention on her. A shiver trailed down her spine at the intensity of his stare.

"No. I told him I had some errands to run. Why?"

"An even longer story." She winced when she heard Kyden sigh behind her. "Where is he now?"

"I'm assuming his office. He took a separate car from the airport. Now tell me, what the hell is going on?"

Kyden cleared his throat. "We're on a bit of a time crunch, so talk and walk." He didn't wait to hear either of their replies as he strode through the lobby, people instinctively moving out of his way.

"That guy seems different from the last time I saw him," Jake said.

"You could say that." She assumed he only remembered the dinner they'd all shared and not Kyden barging into his hotel room. She had to give it to the angel—he was quite the actor. "I can't tell you all the specifics, but I need you to trust me. A friend was kidnapped, and the Atar'zul stolen. We think your boss is behind it all—Brandon's and my father's deaths, the attack on Alexis at my apartment, everything."

Jake slid to a stop and gaped at her. "Are you serious?"

She yanked him out the door and onto the crowded sidewalk. "Yes. Let's just say we have an inside man who can verify your boss's extracurricular activities."

"And how is he"—Jake nodded at Kyden's back—"Sam, is it? How is he involved?"

She winced. "His name isn't Sam. It's Kyden."

"What kind of name is that?"

Kyden looked over his shoulder, giving a smile that would cut glass. "A holy one."

Jake's brows shot up as he glanced from Kyden to her. She sighed and rubbed the spot between her eyes where a headache had begun its incessant thumping against her skull.

Kyden stopped at the corner and whistled. Immediately, a cab veered toward them, screeching to a stop.

Jake lurched back, swearing.

"After you," Kyden said, opening the door, eyes piercing like a blade across skin.

She grimaced as she ducked her head and slid into the back seat. Her angelic warrior wasn't pleased, but she hoped involving Jake would work to their advantage.

"Where are we going?" Jake asked once Kyden settled into the front seat.

"The Imperial Noire Resort," she said.

Jake frowned. "That's one of Durand's hotels."

"Not surprising." Kyden gave the address to the driver and stared out the window.

"Okay, Zahra. Come clean," Jake said, turning toward her.

She wrung her hands together, her nerves making it difficult to sit still. "The Atar'zul actually has magic, and your boss is going to use it for evil." She winced at Jake's dumbfounded expression.

He chewed the inside of his cheek. "You don't believe in magic."

"Let's just say I've seen the light."

Kyden snorted from the front seat.

"Are you two…" Jake winced, and then finished quietly, "Together?"

It was her turn to snort. Kyden turned his head slightly, sliding a glance from the corner of his eye.

"No," she said. "We're just friends."

Even though Kyden's rejection had stung, she had come to terms with how impossible any sort of romantic relationship would have been between her and an angel who got his kicks slaying demons. And she had also realized her heart still belonged to the man sitting next to her, whether she wanted it to or not.

Jake's shoulders relaxed, and he leaned back into the seat. "I checked on your mom before I left town. She seemed calm, actually remembered my name."

"Really? Why would you do that?" Doubt niggled at the back of her mind. The last person to visit her mother had been a demon. But no, surely Jake wasn't involved in this. She squeezed the talisman, searching for a dark aura surrounding him, and let out a relieved breath. He wasn't possessed, so that was a plus.

"Besides knowing you'd want to know how she is? I'd think the answer would be obvious."

Kyden turned in his seat, his gaze unforgiving. "And what answer is that?"

Jake tilted his head. "Am I missing something?"

The tension in the cab caused a prickling along her neck. "A stranger visited her the other day—the day I became a star on *America's Most Wanted*." She grimaced, and wouldn't be surprised if the man beside her jumped out of the moving car to get as far away from her as possible.

"About that," Jake said, slowly enunciating each word.

"It's not what you think. We were being attacked, but…"

"The video didn't show the complete story. Zahra was only protecting herself," Kyden said.

Jake chewed the inside of his cheek. "I actually had one of my tech guys analyze the recording and even they said something wasn't adding up." He squeezed her hand. "I do trust you and I want you to trust me too. The main reason I visited your mom is because I care about you and, therefore, care about her."

Kyden stared between her and Jake and then said, "Zahra, I want you to stay in the car with Jake. I'll handle it from here."

"We've already talked about this, and I'm going with you. You might need my help."

"No offense, but why would he need your help?" Jake asked.

She raised her brows. "Offense taken."

He sighed. "He seems more than capable of finding his friend without you. Plus, I don't want you in danger."

"I won't be in danger," she said.

Kyden once again looked over his shoulder. "You will be in danger. You should stay with Jake, where it's safe."

For once it seemed the two men, or rather the man and the angel, actually agreed on something, but she wasn't having it. "Both of you alpha-holes need to step back."

Jake arched a brow. "Alpha what?"

Kyden shook his head as they pulled up to the curb of the hotel. "Alpha-hole. Essentially, she's saying we're acting dominant and hyper-masculine with a little arrogance mixed in."

"Try a lot of arrogance," she said, opening the door of the cab and squinting against the flashing lights and electronic signs promising loose slots and free drinks.

Kyden shook his head and slid from the passenger seat, paying the driver. "So, Callahan, where would an evil boss hide his nefarious activities?"

Jake emerged from the car. "Nefarious activities? Who talks like that?"

Zahra grabbed his hand and tried to give him an encouraging smile. He was handling the vague information she'd given him rather well. She hoped his amenable attitude would hold out.

He straightened his suit jacket. "I'll show you, even though I can't imagine Laurent doing what you have accused him of."

Jake led them through the front doors, and she subtly removed her gun from her purse and slid it into the waistband of her jeans, ignoring the sign banning firearms. She wanted her weapon just in case daemonkin were helping the demons. At least bullets would stop them.

"Wait here," Jake said, leaving her and Kyden at the edge of the lobby while he spoke to a large man standing guard at an elevator.

Kyden crossed his arms. "This is time we don't have. I can easily get us past that guy." He looked away from the guard and focused on her. "Why didn't you tell me you'd called him?"

"You had a lot on your plate," she said with a forced smile. When he simply glared at her, she sighed. "What if he were in danger? Or if he *is* involved in all of this, I needed to know, preferably when my guardian angel is around to kick his ass."

He opened his mouth to respond but snapped it shut when Jake joined them. "Come on," Jake said.

The guard arched a brow at her, but his gaze hardened as his eyes roamed over Kyden. The man ran his badge across the scanner and the doors opened.

Jake waved her and Kyden through and pressed a button to the lower levels. She stood between the two, sensing both of their stares boring into her side. If the elevator ride with Jake the other night had been uncomfortable, then this one was downright cringeworthy as the silence squeezed around her.

The doors opened onto a long, gray-tiled hallway. Unlike the lobby and other areas of the resort, there were no cameras, or at least none she could see. She supposed that even if there were, Kyden would magically disarm them.

"What's down here?" Kyden asked.

"The vault and some offices. There is, however, a door only Mr. Durand can enter." They stopped in front of a complicated key pad and retinal scanner.

Jake pointed to it. "I can't get past this unless you have his eyeball in your pocket."

Kyden placed his hand on the scanner. A click sounded and the door opened.

Jake swore. "How did you do that?"

Kyden simply smirked and walked into the secret room.

She grabbed Jake's arm and gave it an encouraging squeeze. "That's one of those *details*."

Jake scowled. "There seems to be a lot of those."

Kyden's sword appeared on his back along with the dagger at his hip. A leather chest piece replaced his Van Halen T-shirt. "You do as I say." His gaze shifted to Jake. "Both of you."

She licked her lips and nodded.

Jake crossed his arms. "Who do you think you are?"

"Let me make something very clear to you. I will protect Zahra with my life—"

"Yeah, well, that makes two of us."

Warmth spread through her chest, but the incessant ticking clock had her stepping between them, hands raised. "We don't have time for this."

Kyden's amber eyes glowed briefly before he nodded.

A large room lay before them, filled with desks and computers. On both sides were smaller rooms with glass doors, reminding her of an emergency room at a hospital.

She walked toward one desk and swore. Kyden was at her side in seconds. A picture of her getting out of her car at the nursing home lay on the desk, along with another picture of her having coffee with Alexis.

"This is definitely his headquarters," Kyden said, shooting off a text, she assumed to Adinah and Oz.

Jake examined the other desks. "There are pictures of Dr. Neeman here."

"What?" She jogged over and gasped. Images of her father at the dig site lay in a pile. One was of him holding a familiar silver box.

Jake continued to search the desks while Kyden pulled her aside. "I don't sense any demonic presence, but just in case." He handed her a dagger, which she gripped tightly. "You two take that side. I'll check this one."

She and Jake walked toward the hallway on the right while Kyden searched the one on the left. The first room they came to was unlocked. They peeked inside and she froze. A medical bed sat in the center of the room, black spots dotting the sheet. An IV stand stood behind the bed with what looked like black tar lining the sides of the clear bag. Her eyes darted back to the soiled sheets, and she remembered Kyden returning covered in the same liquid.

Demon blood.

Jake maneuvered past her to a metal table with an assortment of medical devices on it. "What the hell was he up to?"

"Believe me when I say your boss is not the man you think he is." She exited the room and found the next one just as strange. The space was a combination of a mechanic's garage and an ammunition factory. Welding equipment sat in one corner, and bullets of different calibers lay on a metal table, along with an assortment of weapons, including swords and daggers.

"This keeps getting weirder and weirder. No wonder Laurent didn't let anyone down here," Jake said.

She picked up a bullet and held it to the light. "Does this look odd to you?"

Jake took the bullet from her. "It seems to have some sort of metallic coating."

She confiscated a magazine for her gun's caliber and slid it into her bag before leaving the room.

As they rounded the corner, she froze. Sulfur burned her nose and another underlying scent she couldn't place filled the air. She reached for the knob but it didn't budge.

"Kyden," she whispered, knowing he would hear her, as Jake checked the next room.

"Empty," Jake said, returning to her side.

Kyden jogged toward them. "What did you find?"

"Pretty sure we found demon blood, along with welding equipment and weapons. However, this is the only door that's locked," Zahra said.

Jake's head spun toward her. "Wait. Did you just say, 'demon blood'?"

Kyden arched a brow. "You brought him into this. He might as well see it all."

"Can you do that?" she asked as Jake said, "See what all?"

"Of course I can," Kyden said, his jawline pulsing with impatience.

She winced and said, "Okay, try not to freak out."

Jake's eyes narrowed. "What in god's name are you—"

Kyden pressed a finger against Jake's forehead. "Sight granted."

Jake moved to smack Kyden's hand away and then froze, his eyes wide. "Is that a sword?"

"Welcome to *The Twilight Zone*," she said as Jake continued to gape at Kyden as if he'd grown an extra head.

Kyden held the doorknob. The metal glowed, and a click echoed through the silence.

"Stay behind me," Kyden said and pushed the door open. His back stiffened and his sword fell to his side. "No," he whispered.

She peeked past him and gasped. Jake immediately moved closer to her and swore.

Titus hung from the wall, his arms outstretched, his head dangling to the side. A gash carved along his stomach, and dried golden blood stained the floor. Blood dripped from his chest where three bullet wounds had punctured his skin. His wings, normally silver, had shifted to a dull brown.

"Oh god," Zahra said, covering her mouth.

Kyden dropped his sword and ran toward Titus. "Come on. Be okay."

She slowly approached while Kyden pulled a blade from his boot and cut through the ties securing Titus to the wall.

"Hold him," Kyden said to her when Titus's arm dropped. His muscular bulk nearly brought her to her knees.

Jake, who'd stood frozen at the door, joined her, helping bear the weight of Titus's unconscious body. "What the actual fuck is going on?"

Kyden slashed through the other rope, and a pained groan escaped Titus's lips. Kyden let out a breath as he laid his friend on the ground. "He's still alive."

"Zahra?" Jake grabbed her arm, his eyes wide as they darted across her face.

"They're angels," she explained. "You're now able to see into the spiritual realm."

He shook his head as if trying to dislodge the images from his mind. "The spiritual realm?"

She nodded. "There's too much to explain, but there's a war between angels and demons. One of the demons is after the Atar'zul." She squeezed his arm and then knelt next to Titus.

"Can you heal him?" she asked, pressing her fingers to Titus's neck, his pulse faint. Her gaze drifted across his bloody chest. "Why would they shoot him?"

The golden aura usually clinging to the angel flickered. Wetness glazed her fingers and when she lifted them, she cringed. Titus's blood covered her hand, but the color was darker than the dried blood on the floor. She quickly wiped it on her jeans.

Another groan sounded from Titus. "Kyden, go." His words pained, barely a whisper.

"Not without you."

"I'm in Elohim's hands now." He coughed, and blood dribbled from his lips. "The halo...corrupted..."

"Shh, save your strength. Adinah and Oz are on their way."

Titus shook his head. "Mammon is here."

Kyden's tortured gaze found hers, and wetness lined his eyes.

A noise emanated from the corridor.

He looked at Jake. "Get her out of here, now."

"It's too late for that, I'm afraid," a smooth voice sounded from the doorway.

Zahra quickly turned and bit back a scream. Laurent Durand appeared in the hallway, a malicious grin carving through his face. In his hand was the Atar'zul, the metal no longer silver and cracked, but blackened and whole.

Chapter Twenty-Nine

Kyden

Laurent Durand loomed in the entryway, wearing an expensive-looking suit and a smug smile. Even now, Kyden couldn't sense a demonic presence. The patience and control it must have taken to become completely inconspicuous would have impressed him on a normal day. But today was anything but normal.

He rose to his feet, trying to ignore the cold wetness of Titus's blood oozing through his pants. Immediately his armor covered him from head to toe. His hand tightened on the hilt of his sword, the celestial steel glowing with holy power.

"I'd say you're a tad outmatched," Durand said. Behind him stood Raghav and Gael, the latter with his arms crossed and wearing a bored expression, while scraping claws reverberated off the walls, filling the hallway.

Kyden glared at his former snitch. Had he set them up to get captured?

Titus groaned and tried to push up off the floor, but Zahra rested a hand on his shoulder. "No, stay down."

Jake, now with the ability to see into the spiritual realm, had paled and a sheen of sweat beaded on his forehead. "Mr. Durand?"

"In a manner of speaking. It's a shame they brought you into this. You were a valuable employee," he said.

Kyden twirled his sword and stepped in front of Zahra, Jake, and Titus. He flared his wings, providing them a shield, for if this went down the way he assumed it would, they'd get caught in the crossfire, and he wouldn't allow that to happen.

Where are Oz and Adinah? he thought, praying to the Heavens. He had fought two Fallen in the past and emerged victorious. But a prince of hell? The best he could do was distract the demon long enough to give Zahra and the others a chance to escape.

"You've accomplished quite the feat, Mammon, pretending to be human for so long," he said, stalling for time.

Raghav stepped forward, his teeth bared. "That's Prince Mammon to you."

"He's not my prince," he said, glaring at Raghav. "I'm sure Marach will be interested to learn you've switched allegiances."

Raghav sneered, his sickly green eyes glowing with wickedness. Kyden frowned at the gun holster on the demon's hip.

Durand raised his arm, blocking the Fallen's path. "Now, now. All in due time, Raghav. You'll have your chance." He unbuttoned his suit jacket and draped it over a chair. "Spending thirty years compressed inside this human body has been challenging, but I'm tenacious, and I always get what I want." He lifted the halo, running his thumb along the completed crown.

"You fixed it?" Kyden asked.

"In a manner of speaking. Let's say I made it better. Just ask your friend there."

Kyden glanced out of the corner of his eye to where Titus lay, a sheen of sweat glistening against his pale skin. The blood drying on his chest was no longer gold, but a lackluster brown, and when his friend looked up at him, veins of obsidian webbed through his amber eyes. Ashen feathers mixed with the silver ones on his wings, and the bullet holes had shrunk in size. If Mammon had used the halo on him, then he shouldn't be able to heal.

"What did you do to him?" Kyden asked, a sick feeling settling in his stomach as words from the prophecy pushed to the forefront of his mind: *The angels bowed to twisted might, and shattered all they held as right. Once steadfast and pure, their will now bent to shadow's lure.* Zahra had asked what would make an angel bend toward the shadows. He had a suspicion he was about to find out.

"I've evened the playing field." The corners of Durand's lips pulled into a wicked smile. "Titus, come."

Kyden's spine stiffened as Titus pushed off the floor with a moan and staggered to his feet. He limped past Zahra and glanced at Kyden. His eyes sparked amber. "Run," he whispered.

Durand crossed his arms as Titus stood before him. With a victorious smile, he said, "Kneel."

Kyden's stomach fell to the floor. He couldn't comprehend witnessing his best friend kneeling before the Prince of Greed.

Rage twisted through Kyden's soul. "I'll enjoy sending you to the Abyss, Mammon."

The prince chuckled. "Once again, I believe you're outmatched." He signaled to Titus, who unfolded to his full height and took his place at Mammon's side.

Raghav laughed as Kyden unsheathed a dagger from his baldric. Gael gaped at Titus, horror flashing through his green eyes, the emotion vanishing as quickly as it had appeared.

"Soon, I'll have a legion of angelic warriors at my side and this world will be mine," Durand said, his mouth twisted in an evil smile. "Apollyon and his pawns will have no choice but to bow to me."

The ceiling vibrated, causing Durand to look up. Using the distraction, Kyden flipped his blade, pinching it between his fingers.

A bright light exploded through the room as Adinah and Oz appeared, both landing with a resounding crack.

Kyden flicked his wrist.

Durand's eyes bulged as he stared at the dagger lodged in his chest. Blood seeped through his silk dress shirt. "No!"

Relief flowed through him, and hope filled his chest as Adinah and Oz drew their swords. He peered over his shoulder, his gaze meeting Zahra's eyes and then shifting to Jake's. Giving him a dagger, he said, "Get her out of here."

Zahra shook her head but didn't argue. Jake took the blade and grabbed her arm. They ran to the other side of the room, trying to get to the door, but slid to a stop as a large grunt blocked their escape.

Durand roared and arched his back, the muscles in his neck bulging. Within seconds, the Prince of Greed emerged from Durand's body. The man collapsed like a puppet whose strings had been cut. Blood covered his chest and vacant eyes stared at the ceiling.

Mammon stood almost seven feet tall. His long silver hair hung down his back, and unlike Fallen, whose eyes burned green, the prince's were bottomless pits of swirling shadow. His face resembled white marble, chiseled and lifeless, and he donned armor similar to Kyden's. After all, a millennium ago, Mammon was favored by Elohim, one of his trusted warriors. But he'd chosen greed and power and followed Apollyon into the Abyss.

"That was very foolish." Mammon's lips pulled back into a sneer. He slid the Atar'zul onto his head, and his spine stiffened.

Why isn't the halo draining his power? Kyden raised his sword while Oz and Adinah flanked him.

Adinah edged closer and whispered, "Raphael is coming."

He gave a slight nod.

Mammon extended his palm, and Kyden spun, thrusting out his wings. A blast of energy slammed into his back, almost making his legs buckle as pain shot through his spine. The assault was brief but effective as his power waned.

He turned, his knuckles cracking as his grip tightened on the hilt of his sword. "Is that the best you can do?"

Mammon laughed and signaled to Raghav, Gael, and Titus. With a yell, Raghav charged, and Oz lunged forward and met the attack. Steel collided, sending a shock wave through the room and knocking equipment to the floor. Adinah sprinted toward Gael, wrapping her arms around his waist, and tackling him. They flew through the wall, disappearing into the main room.

Titus approached Kyden, his movements disjointed, pain etched along his face.

"Titus, stop," Kyden said, his stomach rolling. He raised his sword, but retreated a step. How was he supposed to fight his best friend?

Out of the corner of his eye, Zahra and Jake fought off grunts while inching toward the hole Adinah and Gael had crashed through.

Titus's fractured eyes shifted in their direction. He lunged and swung his blade. Kyden flapped his wings and surged forward to block the strike.

"Fight it," Kyden said through gritted teeth, the edges of their swords grinding in a shower of sparks. The torment on Titus's face had disappeared, replaced by a vacant expression as if his thoughts were no longer his own. Only thin streaks of amber lingered in his eyes, and wings that were once a blinding silver were dull and brown.

Mammon laughed. "It's no use. He now belongs to me." The prince unsheathed his sword and advanced. Kyden couldn't fight them both. Instinctively, he spun, cracking his elbow into Titus's face, the impact dropping the angel to the floor.

Shrieks from grunt demons reverberated from the other room as green mist and the smell of sulfur snaked along the floor. Zahra was almost through the hole when she turned. Her eyes widened and terror lined her face as she looked past Mammon toward the door.

"Watch out!"

Kyden spun and stared down the muzzle of a gun.

Raghav squeezed the trigger.

Time slowed.

Gael sprinted across the room.

A flash of light burst from the gun, followed by the acrid smell of burning lead.

Gael had landed on Raghav, and with a yell, he drove his blade through the other demon's neck. Raghav screamed, and his body dissolved, leaving behind a pool of bubbling black blood.

Kyden grimaced from the searing pain. The bullet had created a smoking hole in the armor protecting his shoulder. Whatever power he had left vanished and his armor disappeared. He blinked, his legs failing him, and he dropped to one knee.

Mammon approached and stood above him, victory shimmering in his black eyes. He slashed a blade across Kyden's side. "Welcome to my army." He grabbed him by the neck and yanked him to his feet. He froze, his gaze narrowing at it shifted to the ceiling. "Raphael," he growled.

Kyden twisted out of his grip and fell to the floor, relief coursing through him with the knowledge that the archangel was close.

Adinah and Oz flew through the walls and positioned themselves between him and the demon prince. Their chests heaved and sweat dripped along their brows.

Mammon seized Titus, using him as a shield, and walked backward through the entryway. Grunt demons lurched around him like water parting for a stone. He pointed at Gael. "There is nowhere you can hide, you worthless piece of shit."

With a cruel smile, the Prince of Greed grabbed Titus and disappeared down the hall.

"Titus," Kyden whispered, as blackness crept into the corners of his vision.

Oz helped him to his feet. "Come on, we need to get you out of here."

A blast of Divine Light shot from Adinah's hand, obliterating the demons clogging the entryway. "Hurry," she said, her tone sharp as the sound of claws and screeches echoed from the hallway. Another horde of grunts would be upon them, and Kyden barely had the energy to stand, let alone fight.

Zahra pulled out of Jake's embrace and ran to him, horror tightening her features as she stared at the blood pouring from his wounds.

Oz lifted his hand and light exploded from his palm, carving a hole through the wall into the lower parking garage. "That's going to attract some attention," he said, and then pointed to Jake. "Help him."

Jake ran over and took Kyden's arm, throwing it over his shoulder. Kyden groaned as blood spurted from the wound. Zahra moved to his other side and together they led him toward the exit.

Kyden glanced behind him where Adinah fought a grunt. In a spray of green mist, she turned, her lips in a flat line.

"Find Titus, please," he said.

She nodded, her gaze as sharp as the steel in her blade.

Oz pointed at Gael. "You too. Adinah and I will hold them off."

Kyden wobbled on his feet as Gael sprinted toward a parked car. Gael used his power and unlocked the doors. The engine revved to life. "Get him somewhere safe."

Kyden grabbed Gael's shoulder. "Thank you."

Gael dipped his chin and then addressed Zahra. "Figure out the prophecy. It's the only way to save him."

The sound of screaming demons was deafening as it echoed in the parking garage.

Zahra and Jake led Kyden toward the car and opened the back door. He slid in, grimacing at the pain in his shoulder and stomach, a pain he'd never experienced. He leaned his head back as Jake and Zahra jumped in. Jake stomped on the gas and peeled out of the garage just as the swarm of demons erupted through the hole.

The neon lights of Vegas shone through Kyden's eyelids as they drove across the city. Zahra and Jake whispered softly, but he wasn't listening. Even if he wanted to, his enhanced hearing had disappeared, as had all his power.

A hand touched his knee. "We're almost there." Zahra's eyelashes were wet and her face pale, but she forced a smile.

He simply nodded and shut his eyes again. With the bullet lodged in his shoulder, his armor and wings had been replaced by his street clothes, now stained with blood.

They finally exited the freeway and entered a cozy neighborhood, passing an elementary school and a park. Quaint, cookie-cutter homes lined the streets, and bicycles and toys decorated the neat lawns.

The relief of dawn was still hours away as the darkness of night pressed in on him. He thought about Titus and the changes he'd undergone. Somehow, Mammon had weaponized the halo and now controlled his friend. He swallowed past the lump in his throat as the words from the prophecy once again ran through his jumbled thoughts.

The car pulled into a driveway. "Wait here," Jake said.

Zahra leaned forward as he jogged toward the front door.

"Where are we?" he asked, his voice hoarse from pain.

She turned in her seat. "He said a friend's house, but it's not someone he works with, so Laurent or Mammon—whatever his name is—won't know. I hope," she added.

He gritted his teeth and slid toward the door.

"What are you doing?" she asked.

"Getting out of this car." He grabbed the wound in his side as he opened the door and stepped out, inhaling the warm desert air.

Zahra yanked her door open, practically falling into the driveway. The porch light flicked on, and a woman with auburn hair, wearing a tank top and sleep shorts, answered the door.

Zahra's shoulders stiffened. "Figures."

Kyden leaned against the car as Jake spoke to the woman, pointing at the two of them in the driveway. She nodded and opened the door wider.

Jake jogged back down the steps. "We're all set."

Zahra crossed her arms. "You forgot to mention your *friend* was a beautiful redhead."

Jake arched a brow as he moved to Kyden's side. "I didn't think Harper's hair color was relevant."

"You know what I mean," she said, frowning as Jake helped him toward the door. "And how is she supposed to help him?"

"*She* happens to be a nurse. After everything that has just happened, this is what's got you ruffled?" he asked, scowling back at her.

Kyden sighed. "Leave me out of this lover's brawl. Besides, I can walk on my own."

Zahra's eyes narrowed. "Lover's brawl my ass."

Chapter Thirty

Zahra

Zahra slumped in an old rickety chair and watched Kyden's chest rise and fall. Harper, the beautiful redhead, who was "just a friend" according to Jake, had successfully removed the bullet and given Kyden something to ease the pain.

The lines of his face, usually hard and immovable, now relaxed as he slept. She wondered if he dreamed. He had walked the earth for eons, and she couldn't imagine the horrors he had witnessed, with humans and demons alike. Did he ever sleep peacefully?

Despite not wanting to revisit the scene from earlier, her mind returned to Laurent's strange building and the battle after finding Titus, everything replaying in slow motion. Worry dug its claws into her as she thought about Titus. She'd checked Kyden's phone a few times, but so far no messages from Adinah or Oz had come in.

Watching all three warrior angels fight had left her quivering in fear, but what she'd encountered with the demons was so much worse. The malevolent presence from the prince of hell had covered her like a shroud, and his power seemed stronger now that he had shed his earthly body. A maelstrom of vice had swirled around her, greed and corruption attempting to drag her into its inky depths.

She glanced at the clock. Two hours had passed since they'd arrived, and she wondered how long it took for an angel to heal, especially after enduring the magic from the halo and the tainted bullet.

The Atar'zul, according to legend, drained an angel's power, but eventually they would heal. Or at least they were supposed to. Her thoughts drifted to Titus and how he'd changed, how he'd obeyed the Greed Prince. Something was different about the halo, something Mammon had done when he'd supposedly fixed it.

She pulled her father's journal from her bag on the floor and opened to the page she'd marked. Now that she'd translated the prophecy, she needed to figure out what it all meant.

The angels bowed to twisted might, and shattered all they held as right. Once steadfast and pure, their will now bent to shadow's lure.

Somehow, Greed had altered the halo, warping the angels and making them bow to him. Her eyes focused on the next two stanzas, the word 'hope' shining like a beacon.

Yet hope remains, though dim and slight. A mortal must bleed to feed the light—bound to an archangel's sacred might, to turn the tide against the night.

A sacred bond, united and pure, shall cleanse the crown of dark allure. From shadow's grip and sorrow's chains, the angels rise in light's refrain—redeemed through blood and solemn vow, they seek the grace they once let down.

Was this the way to save Titus? Her gaze drifted from the worn pages of the journal to Kyden's face. She retrieved from her bag a bullet she'd taken from Laurent's lab and examined it.

Based on what she had learned about ammunition, the bullet was armor-piercing, usually used by gang members against the police. But the metal seemed different. It almost reminded her of the halo Mammon had placed on his head.

The room with the hospital bed and IV stand, black blood spatters on the floor and counter. The bullet wounds in Titus. She leaned closer to Kyden and lifted the bandage covering the wound. "Please be gold." She bit her lip at the brown blood on the bandage. Whatever the halo did to Titus would happen to Kyden if she didn't figure out a way to help him.

Jake softly cleared his throat and she turned. He held two cups of what she assumed was coffee and nodded toward the outside.

"Be back soon," she whispered, touching Kyden's hand lightly. Jake handed her the mug and followed her to the porch. In the east, the sky transformed from midnight blue to wisps of pink and orange as dawn approached.

"How's he doing?" Jake asked, taking one of the two rocking chairs.

She shrugged and sat. "I honestly don't know what the Atar'zul did to him."

He blew on his coffee, his eyes fixed on the palm trees lining the street. "I'm not sure I'll ever wrap my head around what I witnessed today."

"Yeah, definitely a mind trip." She rubbed her thumb along the pendant her father had given her. Thankfully, the streets were free of demons.

"Can you explain everything from the beginning, now that I know what I'm dealing with?" He rested his forearms on his thighs and stared at her. His hair fell in soft waves across his forehead, making her fingers itch to brush it back.

She started with receiving the talisman from her father, covering all the events up to the attack on the nursing home. He listened intently, nodding every now and then. When she finished, he reached across the space separating them and took her hand. Their fingers interlocked perfectly.

"I'm so sorry all this has happened to you. I wish I had known who my boss was. Maybe I could have protected you," he said, staring at their joined hands. Although his grip was gentle, the tension in his jaw and the coldness in his eyes indicated a resolve honed by steel.

"I already have one protector, Jake. I don't need another." She wasn't sure why his statement made her angry, but it did.

He slowly lifted his gaze to hers. "Then what do you need?"

She shot to her feet, stress and exhaustion making her irritable. "Hell, I don't know. Let's see—I need sleep, a shower, and a decent meal. I could use a stiff drink and a cigarette, but I don't have those so I have to settle for coffee. I need to figure out this prophecy because if I don't, that angel in there might turn evil. I need you to *not* be nice to me, because I don't deserve it!"

Her breath released from her mouth in strangled gasps as her chest rose and fell like she'd just finished a race. A dog barked down the street, and she winced, realizing she had been yelling. She had finally lost it, but considering all that had happened in the past few days, she'd hung on to her sanity pretty well.

Turning toward the street, she tried to settle her racing heart.

The rocking chair squeaked behind her and then Jake was by her side, resting his forearms on the wooden rail. "So when did you get this needy?"

She spun her head around, lifting her fist to punch him in the arm when she noticed the slight curve to his lips. "Ha. Very funny."

He twisted to face her, tucking a strand of hair behind her ear. "You've been through hell and deserve to let off a little steam. I can take it. But one thing I don't understand is why you want me to be mean to you? Do you think I resent you for saying no?"

"You should." She lifted her hand as he opened his mouth to speak. "I broke both our hearts that day. You were right. I was scared, so I pushed people away. It's safer that way."

"It's really lonely too."

"I thought I was okay with being alone. But then I met Alexis, and she became my best friend. I realized I've been shortchanging myself. And then you waltzed back into my life."

"I'm quite good at dancing, especially the waltz." He smiled and traced her bottom lip with his thumb, sending a wave of heat through her body. His touch was familiar and comforting, and she couldn't keep herself from leaning into it.

Jake slid a hand behind her neck and bent down, his eyes fixed on her mouth. She gripped the material of his shirt and pulled him closer.

His kiss was gentle, as if she were made of glass and would break under the slightest pressure. True, her emotions were frayed, and she'd thrown a minor tantrum, but the last thing she wanted was gentle. She needed the images in her mind erased and the hollowness of her heart filled with something other than a foreboding sense of dread.

He deepened the kiss and she moaned.

"Zee," he whispered as his other hand slid down to her lower back. She gasped when their hips touched and his hardened length pressed against her stomach.

Hearing the desperation in his voice as he uttered her name had her lifting a leg and wrapping it around him, pulling him closer and creating the friction she craved.

The squeak of the screen door brought her to her senses. Her heart raced as she gazed into his eyes darkened with desire.

Harper cleared her throat. "Sorry to interrupt, but your friend is awake."

Zahra maneuvered out of his embrace, her cheeks burning with passion and embarrassment at being caught literally wrapped around Jake. "Thank you, Harper, for everything. We'll be out of your hair soon."

Harper's gaze flicked to Jake. "No rush."

Zahra slipped past her and walked down the hall toward the spare bedroom. She inhaled calming breaths and ran her fingers through her hair. That man had always known how to kiss her, making her lose all sense of self-preservation. She melted under his touch every time while her defenses slipped away.

Kyden sat at the edge of the bed, his head in his hands.

She leaned against the doorframe. "Who knew warrior angels were such babies?"

He arched a dark brow and then shook his head. "How long have I been asleep?"

"A few hours." She entered the room and took a seat. "How are you feeling? Is your power back?"

"Not completely, but something is off." Dark circles stained the skin under his eyes and his face had lost its healthy glow.

"I can bring you coffee or something to eat."

"I need to move around a bit. Just point me to the kitchen." He rose to his feet and stretched.

She swallowed as her gaze moved over his naked chest. His body would give Adonis a run for his money with the carved muscles and tapered hips.

Kyden cleared his throat, and despite the corner of his lip lifting, his eyes had darkened.

"Right," she said, and led him down the hallway to where Jake and Harper sat at the kitchen table, whispering, their heads bent together.

They both stood when Kyden entered the room. "Thank you for your help. All of you," he said, nodding to Jake.

"Now that you're awake, I should check your wound," Harper said, walking toward him.

"No need. I could, however, use some coffee and some food."

"Donuts, if you have them," Zahra said.

"Possibly a shirt," Jake mumbled.

Zahra and Harper smiled at each other and then looked at Kyden. "Nah," they both said.

Jake frowned while Kyden rolled his eyes and took the mug Harper offered him.

"I'll let you three talk. I'm sure there's something I need to be doing somewhere else," Harper said, winking at Jake.

Zahra couldn't help the oily sensation slithering through her at the ease of their relationship. She remembered what it felt like to be comfortable around him, winking at him and making him smile. They seemed to be making progress, especially after their latest exchange, but would they ever go back to how they were? Did she even want that?

"So what's the plan?" Jake asked.

She pressed her palms onto the cool granite countertop as if to center herself. "Jake, you've done enough. I can't put you in any more danger."

His eyes narrowed, hard as flint, then cut to Kyden. "So, *Kyden*, what's the plan?" Her mouth fell open when Kyden chuckled. "If I'm already in danger, might as well stay close to an angel and the woman I love."

She had just snapped her mouth shut when it dropped open again. *The woman he loves.* The declaration made her heart race with excitement and fear.

A muscle twitched in Kyden's jaw. He frowned and shook his head. Taking another sip of coffee, he said, "I need to meet with Raphael. Adinah and Oz should have updated him on what we discovered."

"Mammon altered the halo, didn't he?" she asked, deciding to think on Jake's words later.

"It seems that way, but I'm not sure how. The halo is supposed to drain our magic, but he's figured out a way to wield the magic without harming himself." Kyden shifted in his chair. "You saw more of the space than I did."

She rubbed her temples. "One room looked like a hospital room and there was demon blood. And then another room had welding equipment and bullets. I think Greed used his blood to fix the halo."

"Angelic blood cracked it in the first place, so that tracks," Kyden said, staring into his coffee as if the answers swirled in the rising steam.

"Altered the crown for the depraved," she whispered.

"What was that?" Jake asked.

"The prophecy said the halo would be altered for the depraved, which we can assume is Mammon. His blood now runs through the crown and when he wears it, it's like it answers to him." She shook her head. "I don't know if that makes sense."

Kyden frowned. "The first time I held the halo, my power drained. Not a lot, but enough. This time, when Mammon used the halo against me, combined with his power, the effects were still draining but also...different."

"If this demon prince weaponized the halo, then what's with the bullets and other weapons?" Jake asked.

Zahra took the bullet from her pocket and handed it to Jake. He knew his guns just as well as she did. "What do you think of this?"

He held the bullet up to the light. "Gunsmiths use a powder coating to increase the efficiency of their ammunition. What if this prince coated the bullets and other weapons?"

Kyden rubbed his side. "Like poison."

Jake nodded.

"That's why Titus acted the way he did, why his eyes were different, and his blood..." Kyden stared at the bandage on his shoulder. His hand shook as he removed the tape. Zahra's stomach sank. She knew what he would find.

He sighed and reattached the bandage. "The transformation has already begun."

Jake leaned forward. "Are you saying you're going to turn evil just like your friend?"

Kyden lashed out and grabbed Jake by the throat, spilling his coffee and sending the mug crashing to the floor. His eyes flared. "My friend isn't evil."

Zahra jumped between the two as Jake tried to release Kyden's hold.

"Kyden, look at me," she said as calmly as possible. For once, she was thankful he wasn't at his full strength. She wasn't sure Jake would survive if he were. "Kyden!"

His narrowed eyes widened, and he released his grip, looking at his hand as if it were a snake ready to strike.

"I'm sorry." He lowered his head.

Jake rubbed his throat. "Yeah, no problem," he said after tense seconds ticked by.

"There's a way to reverse this," Zahra said. "At least that's what the prophecy says. I haven't quite figured out how, but I will." She held Kyden's arm, giving it a slight squeeze. He looked up, dread coursing through his expression. She hadn't known the angel long, but the desperation in his eyes strengthened her resolve to decipher the meaning of the prophecy. Based on the dimming glow and webs of onyx forming in his irises, she didn't have much time until she lost her Protector.

Zahra retrieved her father's journal and used Harper's computer while Kyden rested. She didn't know if he was truly tired or simply wanted to be alone with his thoughts. She couldn't imagine what he was feeling. Since the beginning of time, he'd been practically invincible as he fought against the darkness. He wouldn't understand what vulnerability felt like.

She'd have to check on him soon, but the best way to help him was to figure out a way to reverse what Greed had done to him and Titus.

Jake brought her another cup of coffee since she hadn't finished the first. The kiss had sent a jolt to her system that not even the strongest caffeine could match. But that sensation had long worn off, and as the morning sky brightened, fatigue tugged at her shoulders.

She yawned a thank you and sipped from the steaming mug.

"Harper's gone to work and won't be back until her shift is over," Jake said.

She stretched her neck, watching as he paced behind her, a wrinkle forming between his brow. "She didn't seem too fazed by gold blood."

"I gave her a quick rundown of what was happening."

She spun in her chair. "She knows Kyden's an angel?"

"After seeing his blood, she kind of assumed."

"Who would ever assume that?"

He shrugged. "She goes to church. Believing in the spiritual realm seemed natural for her, I suppose."

She crossed her arms and chewed the inside of her cheek as she stared at him.

His brow arched. "I know that look."

"No, you don't."

"Yes, I do."

She huffed and turned back toward the computer. "How did you two meet anyway?" The question had sparked inside her since arriving and grew into an irritating flame when she witnessed the ease with which they interacted.

He turned her chair to face him. "You're not jealous, are you?"

"Me? No, of course not."

He chuckled and poked her scrunched nose. "You're cute when you're jealous."

She slapped his hand away. "Knock it off."

His chuckle morphed into a full laugh. "You have nothing to worry about. Harper's in a serious relationship. I met her at the hospital when I had my appendix removed last year." He lifted the corner of his shirt to show her the small scar.

She swallowed as tan skin and cut abs stared back at her. After the few times he'd held her, she could tell he wasn't the gangly young man she'd dated in college. And the evidence of his workout regime was smacking her in the face, causing her cheeks to heat.

Jake had ditched the suit and tie and now wore jeans and a cream-colored shirt. "I'm assuming the new digs are Harper's boyfriend's?" she asked, attempting to keep her voice light.

"Yeah," he said, smoothing down the shirt. "She left some clean clothes for you too. Unfortunately, she doesn't have anything that would fit Kyden."

The new shirt he wore was a bit small and highlighted his muscular physique. *Focus*, she thought, and turned back to the computer screen. She didn't need to be ogling her ex-boyfriend when Kyden's life was on the line. She loaded images from her research of Babylon and its king. Now that she knew she was dealing with the spiritual realm, maybe she could find something she'd missed earlier.

"Can I help?" he asked, rubbing her shoulders.

She let out an indecent moan, flushing at the sound, as his deft fingers kneaded the tension in her muscles.

His grip stilled. "This definitely isn't the right time, but if you're going to make those noises, I'd rather hear them in my bed."

"Now is definitely not the time," she said, trying to add some seriousness to her tone despite the curve to her lips. She'd rather be making those noises in his bed too.

He sat next to her. "But you're saying there's a chance." His smile made the butterflies in her stomach swarm.

She rolled her eyes and returned her attention to the computer screen.

"So what exactly are you looking for?" he asked.

"A clue, something to make sense of this prophecy." She pointed to the fifth stanza. "There's got to be some ritual somewhere regarding an archangel's blood and a human's."

He raked his fingers through his hair. "Why is it always blood?"

"Blood requires sacrifice. Sacrifice equals power. If the demon's blood can alter it, then it would follow logic that an archangel's and a human's could fix it."

"Why a human's?"

"I've searched a lot of biblical text, and God's greatest creation is humankind. Plus, the Vaelatori…"

"The what?"

"Vaelatori, guardians of the Atar'zul, are charged with holding the darkness at bay—at least that's what this prophecy says."

He edged closer, the warmth of his arm seeping through her sleeve. "So God favors humans more than the angels?"

"Seems so." She clicked on a few more images. One made her pause.

"Isn't that from your exhibit?" he asked, pointing at the screen.

She leaned back and chewed her lower lip. "It sure is." She faced him, warmth settling in her chest. "You remember that from the gala?"

"Of course I remember."

She tilted her head to study him further, surprised that he'd actually paid attention to her exhibit.

He huffed a laugh. "Get it through your thick skull."

She waved him off, but couldn't help smiling as she pointed to an image. "I thought this drawing was of King Nebuchadnezzar and one of his advisers, both holding the crown. It had always confused me since all the other historical drawings were of the king *wearing* the crown, who I recently learned was Mammon possessing the man."

"The guy gets around, doesn't he?"

She chuckled and zoomed in on the image. She pointed to the folds of the robes of the taller man. "What does this look like to you?"

He squinted. "Angel wings?"

"Exactly." She flipped through the pages of the journal and found the prophecy. In the margin was her father's scrawl, causing the warmth she'd experienced earlier to disappear, her blood like ice. "We need to get the halo back. It's the only way to save Kyden."

CHAPTER THIRTY-ONE

KYDEN

*W*elcome to my army.

Mammon's words repeated in Kyden's mind on a never-ending loop as he stared out the window, seeing nothing. The peace he'd relied on, even taken for granted, was nowhere to be found. Instead, chaos flowed through him, and it seemed with every minute, he lost a little more of himself.

Welcome to my army.

Mammon had turned the halo into a weapon and used it against Titus, who had practically changed before his eyes. Because of the three bullets still lodged in his body, along with the wound caused by a tainted blade, the transformation of his friend into a mindless servant of the Greed Prince had seemed to have happened quickly.

Despite Harper removing the bullet from his shoulder, it appeared that the damage was already done. However Mammon had corrupted the halo, twisting its magic to drain an angel's powers and then fill them with something demonic, it was slowly consuming him. He wondered how much time he had before he became an agent of darkness and bowed to a prince of hell.

He flared his wings, and revulsion clawed its ways up his throat at the external evidence of the dark void growing inside him. Ashen feathers mixed with the silver ones as if his tainted soul had seeped into his wings.

He walked to the dresser, where a mirror hung on the wall, knowing what he would see when he opened his eyes. Instead of glowing amber irises, solid and pure, obsidian veins cracked through the surface as Greed's corruption infected him from the inside out.

He squeezed the edge of the dresser, and the wood splintered. At least his power was back, but he wasn't sure that was a good thing, not without Elohim's grace protecting him. He made his wings disappear, and the turbulent thoughts settled from a raging storm to a light rain.

For the first time in his long existence, he hungered, not for righteousness, but for power and vengeance. The attitude and personality of Mammon battled his own, but with his power subdued by staying in the human realm, then maybe he could hold off the transformation until Zahra found a cure.

The thought of her brought another sensation, causing his heart to pound. When she had gazed upon his naked chest, lust had ignited in his core—an ember quickly aflame, threatening to burn him. Earlier, he'd been able to douse the sensation, but as his power slowly returned, so did the temptation, until an unfamiliar craving sank its claws into him. And when Jake professed his love for Zahra, jealousy had caused him to lash out in anger. He had never treated an innocent human like that before, and the lack of self-control terrified him.

A knock sounded on the door. "Kyden?" Zahra's muffled voice said.

"Just a minute." He threw on his shirt, still stiff with blood, and pulled the blinds closed so his changing eyes wouldn't be so noticeable. "Come in."

The door squeaked open, and Zahra entered. "How are you feeling?"

"Fine." He was about to sit on the bed and decided against it. The chair would be a safer option.

She cocked her head as she examined him, probably searching for signs of his demise. She moved toward the window, but he grabbed her wrist.

"Don't."

"Why?" she asked, pausing in front of him.

His fingers twitched with the need to pull her closer. He closed his eyes. "I'm no longer your Protector. It's not safe for you to be around me, for either of us."

She pulled free from his hold and opened the blinds, allowing the morning light to warm his face.

"Open your eyes," she said, placing her hand on his cheek.

He instinctively leaned into her touch and opened his eyes. She'd recently showered, her hair slightly damp, hanging loosely on her shoulders. The flowery scent of the soap lingering on her skin made his nostrils flare. The memory of her with only a towel covering her wet skin as she pressed against him caused an unfamiliar heat to burn in his core.

He groaned and rose to his feet, pushing past her. He needed distance, even though a part of him longed to be closer, to take what he wanted.

He clenched his fists, keeping his back to her. "I'm changing. Not just my appearance, but my very soul. It's tainted, and I...I can't be trusted."

His hearing picked up the scuff of her bare feet on the carpet as she approached him. "I think I've found a way to help you."

He spun around so quickly, she stumbled. "How?"

She fiddled with the hem of her shirt. "We need an archangel. Their blood combined with a human's can reverse the damage the halo caused."

His upper lip curled. "A human's blood mixing with an archangel's?" He raked his fingers through his hair, disgust making his teeth grind together. His fate, his very soul, depended on a human. He released a harsh laugh. Why wasn't he surprised?

"Yes, but we need to get the halo back," she said, eyeing him cautiously.

"Of course we do." And where the halo was, so was Titus. "Can you help Titus too?"

"I think so. How do we contact an archangel?"

He searched the room for his phone and found it on the bedside table. He'd been so caught up in his own pity party he hadn't checked for messages. Adinah had texted three times and called twice, while Oz had texted once. The voicemails increased in intensity as he listened to them. He winced at Adinah's last message, basically threatening to cut off every extremity if he didn't call her back.

She picked up on the first ring. "It's about time."

He rubbed his neck while monitoring Zahra, who'd sat in the chair, her gaze narrowing as she watched him. "Sorry, I was recuperating. Any news on Titus?"

She started to talk, but he interrupted. "Hold on, I'm putting you on speakerphone. Zahra's here."

"Oh, goodie," Adinah said.

Zahra raised her brows, and he shrugged while sitting on the bed.

"Raphael met Oz and me at Mammon's creepy laboratory. I haven't seen him this angry since the flood."

"What flood?" Zahra asked.

"Noah's flood," Adinah said, her tone impatient. Zahra's mouth dropped. "Anyway, we took what we needed and moved it to an abandoned warehouse on the edge of town. Then we did damage control to make it look like nothing happened."

"Why?" he asked, his eyes shifting to Zahra, who chewed her thumbnail.

"We don't want the cops involved again," she added. "I already had a mess to clean up outside the nursing home and didn't want another one."

"What do you mean, mess to clean up?" Zahra asked, abandoning her thumb.

"Congratulations, you're no longer a wanted woman," Adinah said.

Zahra's eyes widened as she gazed at him. He shrugged again. Altering video footage and making humans believe a different reality wasn't that difficult. He wasn't sure how Adinah had fixed the incident in the nursing home's parking lot but trusted she'd been thorough. She was the best, next to Titus. Remembering his friend made him dig his nails into his palm.

"And Titus?" he asked, his voice hoarse.

"I'm getting to that," Adinah said. "We have a pretty good idea of where he is. Durand owned another resort off the Strip. The arrogant narcissist's private office is the top floor of the building. The *entire* top floor."

"What's Raphael's plan?"

"Zahra, have you figured out the prophecy?" Adinah asked.

She moved next to Kyden and took the phone from his hand. Her arm brushed against his, and a chill traveled down his spine.

"I believe so, but to help Kyden, we need the Atar'zul and an archangel."

"What do you mean, help Kyden? What's wrong with him?" Adinah asked, her tone sharp.

"I've been compromised," he said. Uttering the words twisted his stomach with dread.

Zahra grabbed his hand and squeezed. "I'll explain when we get there, but we need the halo." Her gaze darted across his face. "Time is of the essence."

"Copy that. I'll let Raphael know."

The phone went dead, and she handed it back to him, still holding his hand. The dread in his stomach shifted into hunger. Her smell, the sound of her heartbeat, the shape of her mouth all called to him in a way he'd never experienced, and he craved more.

His eyes moved from their joined hands, up her body, to the pulsing along her throat. He wove his free hand through her hair and grabbed the back of her neck.

She pressed against his chest, her eyes wide. "What are you doing?"

"What you've wanted since you first met me." He didn't recognize the huskiness in his own voice.

"You said you couldn't."

Her breath caressed his mouth, and his mission to get the halo back—to find Titus—dissolved into the background of his mind. The memory of when she'd kissed him at the cabin flooded his thoughts, silencing the warning bells in his head.

He pulled her against him, feeling her soft curves, and crushed his mouth against hers. He couldn't hold back his groan at the taste of her. Sliding his tongue along the seam of her lips, needing to explore every part of her mouth, caused his body to react in a way he'd never experienced.

He'd spent his entire life fighting and bleeding for humans. For the first time in his eternal existence, maybe he could take something instead...

Zahra's body stiffened and she yanked her head to the side while trying to push him away. "Kyden, stop. You don't want to do this."

The voice screaming in his mind finally broke through. In less than a heartbeat, he launched himself away from her and pressed his back against the wall. He panted, his breath bursting from his mouth in rapid succession.

What had he just done? He wiped his mouth as shame flooded him. "Zahra, I'm..." He had never had to apologize to a human for his behavior, ever. And now he'd apologized twice within a few hours. The damage Mammon and the halo had done to him made him want to scream in rage.

The bed squeaked as she rose to her feet, straightening her shirt. Her lips were swollen and tear tracks lined her cheeks. Her eyes brimmed with sadness, or was it disappointment?

"I'm sorry," he said, dropping his gaze, focusing on the tan carpet.

A heavy silence filled the room until she finally broke it. "Deep down, that wasn't you. It's the effect of the Atar'zul."

"Still, I should be stronger." His hands shook as he raised them to his face. "Why aren't I stronger?" His words slipped between his clenched teeth.

Zahra wrapped her arms around herself and gave him a soft smile. "You're one of the strongest angels I know."

He frowned. "You really don't know that many."

"True." She took a small step closer and his spine stiffened. As if noticing his discomfort, she stopped. "Keep fighting, okay? I need my Protector. I can't do this without you."

She walked past him, opened the door, and quickly slipped out. With his enhanced hearing, he could hear the rapid beat of her pulse as she leaned against the door. Despite her understanding words or the forgiveness on her face, she feared him, or at least what he was becoming.

"Remember this," he commanded himself. All the guilt and disappointment wrapped around him like chains, chains he needed as an anchor keeping him steady in the approaching storm. He glanced in the mirror again. Amber eyes fractured by black veins stared back at him.

Chapter Thirty-Two

Zahra

Zahra fell back against the door, pressing against her chest as if that would calm her pounding heart. She had never feared Kyden, even the first time she'd witnessed his glory as a majestic warrior.

Not until now.

Obsidian veins wove throughout his amber eyes like spiderwebs, and the peace she experienced in his presence had unraveled, replaced by a rising tide of panic and fear.

Her attraction to him from the beginning had been real—what sane woman wouldn't desire Kyden?—and naturally she'd entertained the fantasy of kissing him. But that attraction had deepened into something more profound when he assumed the role of Protector. And now that Jake was back in her life, she could distinctly separate her feelings for the angel and for her ex-boyfriend.

When Kyden had kissed her, the lust shrouding him loomed over her like a predator's shadow with the sole purpose of conquest and domination. Thankfully, there was enough of the angel stopping him from going further. She shuddered at what could have happened.

She valued his friendship. Based on how quickly he was changing, they needed to hurry before she lost him forever to the Prince of Greed.

She walked down the hall, attempting to cool the blush in her cheeks while wiping away any trace of the tears clinging to her face. Jake would lose his shit if he learned what had happened in that bedroom. He wouldn't be upset with her, but despite his physical strength, he was no match for an angel, especially one who was slowly losing pieces of his soul.

Her throat worked around a tight swallow. She hated Greed for what he'd done to Titus and Kyden. She wasn't one to ask favors from Heaven, but she mumbled a quick prayer to this Elohim for help in saving her friends.

Jake waited for her in the kitchen, reading the journal entries her father had written. He looked up when she entered. "So you're really one of the Vaelatori?"

She slid onto a barstool next to him. "Seems so."

"Do you know how many there are?"

"No, Dad wasn't very clear on that in his message." She traced a tan streak of marble in the countertop. "If he had trusted me with this knowledge, I could've helped him. He might even still be alive."

Jake wove his fingers through hers. "This isn't your fault, Zee. Your dad did what he thought best to protect you, and I don't blame him. What I witnessed..." He shook his head. "Never in my wildest dreams would I have imagined demons and princes of hell."

"Yeah, it's definitely a mind fu..." Just then Kyden emerged from the hallway. She scanned his face, breathing a sigh of relief that the black streaks in his eyes had lessened.

"We need to go. Normally, I'd fly us to the warehouse, but I don't want to use my powers unless I have to." His gaze drifted to their joined hands. "I assume Jake is coming with us?"

Jake bared his teeth in an icy smile. "Good assumption."

She sighed. "Is there any way I can convince you—"

"Don't even finish that sentence." Jake pushed off his stool. "I may not be built for battles in the spiritual realm, but there's no way I'm standing on the sidelines."

His piercing gaze silenced her argument, locking her words behind her teeth. She closed the journal and slipped it into her bag alongside her gun. No longer believing in coincidences, she was glad she'd had the forethought to take a magazine with the bullets Greed had altered that fit her gun's caliber. She shot a look at the ceiling and mumbled a quick thank you to whoever was listening.

Thirty minutes later, they parked near the front door of the warehouse Adinah had mentioned. Zahra slid out of the car and scanned the street. The talisman lay cool against her skin, and thankfully she didn't see any demons. Glancing over her shoulder, she asked Kyden, "Does Jake still have the sight?"

"Yes." He shut his door and led them to the entrance.

Jake came alongside her, eyeing the angel, then whispered, "A man of many words, I see."

Her chuckle faded as Adinah strode out the door. She'd donned her armor and her silver wings draped down her back. Her golden halo rested against her forehead like elegant coiling vines, and she'd twisted her hair off her face into small braids. The effect was beautifully frightening.

"Damn," Jake said, appreciation lining his voice.

Zahra elbowed him in the side, but couldn't hold back her smile, which vanished as they entered the warehouse. At least twenty angels occupied the space. A few sparred in the corner while others strapped on blades, their heads bent together in quiet conversation. All had their wings on display along with their halos resting on their foreheads.

Casually lounging in a chair, wearing a suit instead of armor, his dark hair falling in loose waves, sat Gael. He wore sunglasses, probably to hide the strangeness of his eyes. He was in enemy territory, a fact confirmed by the narrowed glances of the angels near him, including Oz, whose hand rested on the hilt of his sword.

Jake caught her when she stumbled at the majestic warrior standing in the center of the room. He stood over seven feet tall, with armor covering his body, and his wings the color of freshly fallen snow. His golden eyes glowed as his gaze met Kyden's.

Kyden left her and Jake and approached Raphael. At least, she assumed this was the archangel. A part of her didn't want her Protector to leave her side in the presence of one of the seven most powerful beings alive. She struggled to swallow; her mouth now as dry as the desert.

Kyden knelt and bowed his head.

What happened next was not what she expected. Raphael lowered himself to Kyden's level and lifted his chin. He whispered to the angel, a sad smile lining his beautiful yet fierce face.

Kyden's shoulders stiffened, but then he nodded, and they both stood.

Raphael's piercing gaze met hers. "Greetings, Vaelatori."

She took a hesitant step forward, not sure if she should bow. Considering how weak her legs were, bowing might be better than crumpling in a heap. "Hi. I'm Zahra."

"Yes, I'm well aware." The archangel's lips curved into a smile, his gaze shifting to Jake. "And you must be Mr. Callahan."

"Jake," he said, dipping his chin.

She approached the table, peeking over her shoulder to find Adinah trailing them. She smiled at Oz and then Gael. "Good to see you both are all right."

Oz nodded. Gael smirked and said, "You as well."

Kyden stood next to her and crossed his arms. Despite the battle for his soul, he was still protecting her, even against the Fallen. Gael appeared to be on their side, but it was clear no one completely trusted the demon.

"So what's our next move?" Kyden asked, staring at the table covered with blueprints.

Raphael laced his hands behind his back. "From what Gael has told us, Mammon's main office is on the top floor. He's most likely holding Titus there. My sentries did a flyby, but they can't see anything because the windows are tinted with privacy film."

"That's clever," Kyden said, his eyes narrowing as he scanned the blueprints. "Is there a way in besides the obvious?"

All eyes shifted to Gael, who raised his palms. "As important as I might seem, Mammon never invited me to his office."

"Then why are you here?" Kyden asked.

"Self-preservation, of course. Surrounded by angelic warriors is the safest place for me."

Raphael continued staring at the papers on the table. "I asked him here. He has intel on Mammon we might need."

Gael crossed an ankle over his knee. "Besides, there *is* someone in here who probably has visited Prince Mammon's throne room."

"Who?" Adinah asked.

Gael pointed at Jake.

Zahra's head spun in his direction, and Jake winced.

He rubbed the back of his neck. "Laurent conducted most of his business in his office on the other side of town. The times he met here were special meetings."

"What kind of special meetings?" Oz asked.

Jake glanced at Zahra from the corner of his eye. "The kind with powerful leaders: presidents, sheiks, dignitaries. It's where he'd entertain them to get their support and money."

"Entertain?" she asked, pretty sure she understood the hidden meaning behind the word. An oily sensation writhed in her gut as she imagined Jake involved in a prince of hell's type of entertainment. She unconsciously retreated a step, moving closer to Kyden, and didn't miss the hurt that flashed in Jake's eyes.

He held her gaze and then approached the table. "There's a private elevator not listed in the original blueprints."

As Jake explained the layout to Raphael, Oz, and Adinah, Kyden gently nudged her.

"You okay?" he whispered.

She licked her lips and nodded. "You?"

His hand trembled as he ran his fingers through his hair. "Hanging in there."

She squeezed his arm and stepped toward the other angels. "Sorry to interrupt, but we need to get the Atar'zul from Greed if we're going to save Kyden and Titus."

"Can't we just destroy the thing?" Oz asked.

"Not if we want to fix the damage it's done." She grabbed her journal and opened it to the marked page. "It says here, *a sacred bond, united and pure, shall cleanse the crown of dark allure*. It goes on to mention the angels rising in light's refrain and redeemed through blood. I believe this is about the angels who've been turned by the corrupted halo."

Raphael frowned. "And how did he accomplish this?"

"Based on what Jake and I saw, he used his own blood to mend the halo, and because of his blood, the halo no longer drains his power. But we also found bullets and other weapons. I believe he siphoned his blood while wearing the halo and then coated the bullets and weapons."

Raphael crossed his arms. "Like a poison?"

"Exactly." She pulled the magazine from her purse and laid it on the table alongside a single bullet. "He shot Titus and left the bullets inside him, which is why he changed so quickly. At least that's my guess. Jake's friend removed the bullet from Kyden, but..."

"The transformation is slower, but the more I tap into my power, the quicker the change," Kyden said, his brow furrowed.

"Is that why you're still in human form?" Adinah asked.

His jaw muscle clenched as he nodded.

"And how do you reverse the effect?" Gael asked, the nonchalant attitude disappearing as he leaned forward, examining the bullets.

She glanced at Raphael. "Your blood combined with mine."

The silence in the room was deafening as the angels stopped sparring and edged closer. The others pressed in with varying expressions of anger and worry.

Adinah fisted her hands on her hips. "An archangel's blood? You've got to be kidding me?"

She tried not to bristle at the statement. *Her* blood was important too. At least, she thought it was, but she assumed the angels thought otherwise based on the wary expressions aimed her way. All except Gael, who raised his brows while a smile tugged at the corner of his mouth.

She wasn't sure what to think of the Fallen who had betrayed his own kind to save Kyden, for that's what he'd done when he tackled the other demon. If not for Gael, that bullet would have ended up in Kyden's head, making it impossible to get out. Was there enough grace for a fallen angel?

Kyden nudged her again and interrupted her thoughts. She realized the angels were staring at her, as was Jake, whose expression revealed nothing. He'd always had a superior poker face, unlike her.

"What?" she asked.

Raphael smiled. "You and I need to discuss a few things." His eyes shifted to Kyden. "Privately."

She felt Kyden stiffen beside her. She swallowed audibly, the dryness of her mouth making the simple act difficult. Nothing like a one-on-one meeting with an archangel.

Hotel Decadence, created from glass and ambition, rose from the pavement and shimmered in the desert heat. Based on the information from Jake, the hotel included a casino and luxury boutiques. The top floor, practically the size of a football field, had been used for Durand's personal pleasures and special guests.

Shielding the sun from her eyes, Zahra stared at the sparkling windows, tinted to protect from the sun's harsh rays and prying eyes. She choked down the nausea of imagining Jake taking part in activities instigated by a prince of hell.

She followed Kyden inside the hotel, sensing Jake's stare between her shoulder blades. After her meeting with Raphael, she and Jake had chosen weapons from the stash stolen from Durand's secret laboratory. Adinah also gave them celestial daggers.

"Use the pointy end," she had said, handing over the blades and winking at them before walking away.

The angels prepared for the battle, and she and Jake were finally alone. As she chose a pistol that felt comfortable in her hand, Jake had cleared his throat.

"If I could erase the things I did early in my career, I would," he said, palms resting on the table, his eyes focused on the weapons.

"You don't need to explain." Her clipped words shut the door to his divulging the details.

"But I don't want you thinking less of me. I saw the look in your eyes, how you leaned away from my touch." He choked out a humorless laugh. "Just when I was finally making progress with you, with us, my past made a reappearance and ruined everything."

Was everything ruined between them? Who was she to hold grudges for things he'd done or how he'd behaved when they weren't together? After all, she was the one who had walked away from their relationship. She might not have lived the life of luxury he had, but she'd made her fair share of mistakes. Images of her one-night stand with Brandon filtered through her thoughts.

She clicked the magazine into the barrel of the gun and slid on the safety, placing it in the holster. "Everything isn't ruined, Jake."

He slowly lifted his head, his beautiful gray eyes dancing across her face. "It's not?"

"No, but now isn't the time to talk about it. And I don't know if I really want to."

The frosty air and the chimes of slot machines snapped her back to the present. She slid a look at Jake, whose face remained expressionless.

"How do you do that?" she asked, stepping around a server carrying a tray of drinks.

His brow furrowed. "Do what?"

"Make your face, you know, blank."

He chuckled. "Years of practice, especially when you're involved in million-dollar deals."

"You need to teach me that trick," she said, having always wanted a poker face.

He stopped walking and turned toward her, his gaze intense. "I'll never teach you that. I love your face and every emotion that flickers across it."

He ran his thumb along her jaw, and heat curled through her core. The man she knew from college and the one standing before her were so different, and yet so similar. The biggest change was his transparency, especially toward her. He displayed a confidence in his convictions that she envied.

Someone cleared their throat. Kyden stood between Adinah and Oz with his arms crossed, his brow arched, and the muscle in his jaw pulsing. His eyes, revealing more of the black spiderweb lines, followed Jake's hand as it left her face.

"This is your last chance to bow out, Callahan," Kyden said.

"You can't get rid of me that easily." Jake winked at her and then faced the angels.

"Shame." Kyden turned and strode toward the elevators.

Adinah frowned as she stared after him. "What's going to happen when he shifts into his angelic form?" she asked, siding up to Zahra.

Zahra allowed the other angels to walk past, all disguised as humans. Several patrons—men and women alike—paused their gambling to gawk at the procession as if Vegas had suddenly hosted a runway event and these were the models.

"I don't know, but I suspect we won't have much time when he does."

Adinah nodded, determination tightening the skin around her eyes. The amount of information they had wasn't enough to set Zahra's mind at ease.

Based on the prophecy, she wasn't sure if there was a certain point in the transformation where the angel was beyond redemption. Could Titus be saved? Was there still a part of his soul remaining that could rise above the damage done by Greed? And Kyden? How much time would they have once he stepped into the spiritual realm, shredding his humanity? None of the other angels, especially Adinah and Oz, would be able to stomach fighting him.

The number of unknowns created a snake of anxiety curling inside her, making her pulse race. The fate of two angels, and possibly more, rested on her shoulders. Well, hers and an archangel's. She had revealed the prophecy to Raphael and showed him the image she had found in her search, the one she'd assumed had been King Nebuchadnezzar. His eyes had closed briefly, and she had wondered if she was wrong. When he opened them again, he had vowed to help her with the ritual.

She had spent little time with the archangel, but from what she gathered, he cared greatly for the human race and for his fellow angels—a thought that encouraged her to put one foot in front of the other.

Jake led them toward the service elevator and slid his card into the slot. "Let's hope it still works."

The elevator dinged and the doors opened.

"That's either a good sign or a bad one," Kyden said, pushing the button to the top floor.

"Why a bad one?" Oz asked.

"It means he's expecting us."

"I have a bad feeling about this plan." Oz leaned against the mirrored wall with his arms crossed.

"You always say that," Adinah said.

Oz scowled at her. "Explain to me again why Raphael isn't with us?"

Kyden sighed. "Because Mammon would target him instead of me. We wouldn't stand a chance if Raphael took a hit from the halo."

Oz chewed on the inside of his cheek. "I still don't like it."

Zahra agreed with the angel but also understood the reasoning. If Raphael fell to the power of the halo, then their chances of saving Titus and Kyden decreased considerably. She couldn't fathom the power Mammon would wield with a turned archangel by his side.

"Just be ready to give the signal," Kyden said to Oz and turned toward her and Jake. "Remember, the demons can't physically harm you unless they want to sacrifice themselves, which they rarely do. But if Mammon has daemonkin, then you need to be careful. They're humans, therefore we can't kill them no matter where their loyalty lies."

"And don't waste those bullets on grunts," Adinah said. "Focus on the Fallen or Mammon himself."

Zahra nodded, attempting to swallow the lump of fear caught in her throat. Jake squeezed her hand.

"We've got this," he whispered in her ear.

"And one more thing," Kyden said as the elevator reached the top.

"What?" she asked, gritting her teeth from all the last-minute instructions they'd already gone over a hundred times before.

"Once the halo is cleansed, I want both of you to get the hell out of here."

Oz's brows lifted, and Adinah smirked. Zahra figured they hadn't heard their fellow Slayer swear before. Of course, according to Kyden, hell wasn't a swear word but a location.

The elevator slowed to a stop, and the doors slid open.

Speaking of hell, she thought as the office space spread out before them like a labyrinth of nightmares. Green mist swirled along the black marble floors, where grunts of every size lingered in packs throughout the cavernous room. Men and women, whom she assumed were daemonkin, lounged on the crimson couches, participating in sins she'd only ever read about. Fallen demons presided over them, their pale faces and green eyes unblinking as they entered the room.

Zahra peeked over her shoulder, a sense of foreboding tightening her chest when the elevator doors slid shut. She scanned the skies through the floor-to-ceiling windows, hoping to catch a glimmer of silver wings. A bar lined one wall, the mirror behind it reflecting the jeweled chandeliers hanging from the vaulted ceiling.

"Kyden." Mammon's deep voice echoed throughout the space. "I see you brought friends. How delightful."

A raised platform sat on the opposite side of the room. The Prince of Greed lounged on an onyx and gold throne while more Fallen and grunts stood guard.

The angels fanned out, keeping Zahra and Jake in the center behind Kyden, Adinah, and Oz.

"All we want is Titus," Kyden said, planting his feet, his back rigid.

Greed smiled, revealing pointed teeth. "You can have him."

Zahra frowned. She couldn't have heard him correctly. Three Fallen, who stood near the platform, moved, and her heart hit the floor.

"That is if he wants to go with you. He seems quite happy where he is."

"No," Kyden whispered.

Titus lounged on a leather settee, his arms wrapped around a woman sitting on his lap, her hips gyrating in time with the music. She kissed along the skin of his neck—skin that once had a healthy glow, now sallow. His wings, now completely brown, draped on the floor. Zahra knew if she looked in his eyes, the obsidian cracks would obscure the beautiful amber color.

"You bastard," she said, stepping around Kyden and lifting her gun.

Within seconds, the daemonkin, who had seemed uninterested in their arrival, moved to the center of the room, blocking her shot. Grunt demons scurried forward with their weapons drawn.

Greed laughed. "You're on the losing side, my dear. Are you sure you don't want to switch? Ask your former lover. He was quite satisfied when he worked for me."

"Zahra, get behind me," Kyden said through gritted teeth.

"I have a better idea." Greed rose to his feet, eyeing the other angels who maneuvered along the edges of the room. "Kyden, come here."

Kyden's shoulders stiffened, and he moved forward as if drawn by an unseen force. Adinah grabbed his arm and pulled him back. He resisted at first, then shook his head.

"I'm fine," he said, looking over his shoulder.

Zahra sucked in a breath at the black webbing covering his irises. He was losing the battle, faster now that he was in Greed's presence. She hadn't considered the effect the prince of hell would have on Kyden. Her stomach fell to the floor—it was a mistake to bring him.

She glanced at Jake, whose knuckles whitened as he gripped the dagger. He held his gun in the other hand while grunts prowled toward him.

Greed sighed. "I guess we'll do it the hard way." He signaled to Titus, who pushed the woman off him and rose to his feet. Drawing his sword, he joined the other Fallen.

"Titus?" Kyden said, his face twisted in pain.

Greed raised his palm, and black sparks swirled around the halo. A flash of darkness erupted from the demon's hand, hitting an angel in the chest. He cried out as he fell to the floor, smoke flowing from his armored chest piece.

"That's another angel added to my army. How many more is up to you, Kyden."

Kyden drew his sword. "You'll have to kill me before I join you."

Mammon laughed. "Based on your eyes, you'll be fighting by my side soon." He nodded to the Fallen and they raised their weapons. With a yell, they charged, the grunts and daemonkin following close behind.

As a swarm of grunts veered toward her and Jake, she slid her gun into her holster. She only had so many bullets and those were meant for Greed and his Fallen. She and Jake stood back-to-back, slicing through any demon that maneuvered within their range.

"Don't let them latch onto you!" she yelled over her shoulder to Jake.

Another blast of energy filled the room, followed by an angel's scream.

A ding sounded behind her.

She turned as the doors slid open, and drew her gun.

"Jake!"

The warning was barely out of her mouth by the time a Fallen sprinted through the sulfuric mist toward Jake.

The other one ran at her. She squeezed the trigger, hitting the Fallen in the throat. Black blood spilled as the demon fell. It writhed on the ground until its body dissolved into an oily film, disappearing against the black marble.

A yell had her spinning.

"No!" Within seconds, Kyden was by her side but it was too late. Jake stood and dusted off his jeans. When he lifted his head, an evil smile twisted his face and his beautiful gray eyes turned a sickly green.

His gaze traveled down her body, and he licked his lips. "He's a strong one," a gravelly voice said as Jake's hand trailed over the muscles in his chest.

She looked away, unable to stomach watching a demon possess the man she loved.

Chapter Thirty-Three

Kyden

Kyden wrapped his arm around Zahra's waist and pulled her from Jake. He'd seen the Fallen exit the elevator but hadn't been fast enough to warn them.

Darsh, the Fallen Adinah had fought in Kuwait, seemed to have regenerated faster than he thought possible. She fought to control Jake's mind and body as pain twisted his face and he grabbed his chest. Eyes like flint replaced the green as Jake continued to wrestle against the demon infecting his soul.

"Get Zahra away from me!" His voice had returned to his own, but he wouldn't be able to hold on much longer.

"Jake!" Zahra struggled against Kyden's arms.

"You can't help him," he said, putting more distance between them. Movement from the corner of his eye made him raise his sword as a grunt leaped through the air, its axe aimed at Kyden's head. With a slash, the lesser demon disintegrated, and more mist billowed around their feet.

He gritted his teeth and waged war against the evil force within him. The incessant lure of Mammon pulling on his soul grew stronger the longer he remained in the prince of hell's presence. The tightening against his chest reminded him of chains, making it difficult to breathe.

"We need to help him," Zahra said as the possessed Jake strode slowly toward them, a malicious smile on his face.

"We will, but we have to stick to the plan." Which, he didn't want to admit, had completely fallen apart. Adinah or Oz were to steal the halo while he and the other angels distracted Mammon. Zahra and Jake were to remain close and grab the halo.

Darsh possessing Jake wasn't part of the plan. Despite Kyden giving him a hard time about joining them, he was secretly glad he was here to help Zahra complete her mission. But now, he had a sinking feeling she was on her own. He didn't know how long he could withstand Mammon's seduction.

Kyden scanned the chaos, needing Adinah's help, and when he found her, his heart sank. Adinah clashed with Titus, their blades a silver blur through the sulfuric haze. He had fought alongside the female warrior enough times to know she was holding back, but how long could she keep that up?

"On your right!" Zahra said.

He pivoted and sparks flew as his sword crashed against a Fallen's blade. Black leather, spattered with gold, and the telling scar puckering the corner of the demon's mouth made him all too familiar.

"I owe you one," Bakal said, sliding his weapon along Kyden's.

Kyden frowned as the lights from overhead shimmered on the sword, revealing a dark film coating the steel. He had assumed they'd retrieved all the tainted weapons from Durand's laboratory, but obviously he'd been wrong.

"It's not my fault your aim sucks," Kyden said, sidestepping and swinging his blade for the space between the metal band wrapped around his neck and his chin. Cutting off Bakal's head would be so satisfying.

The Fallen parried Kyden's attack and lunged. The cursed blade swiped through the air, forcing him to step back. Darkness encroached on the edge of his thoughts as he kept Zahra behind him while holding off Bakal. He was running out of time.

A scream sounded behind him, followed by the sound of a gunshot.

Bakal's eyes widened, and he lowered his sword. "That's my gun," he growled, his gaze focused on Zahra.

"Come and get it," she said, aiming the weapon at the demon's head.

"You'll both get yours soon enough," Bakal said with a sneer, and retreated into the swirling mist.

Kyden turned. Zahra's gun smoked and what was left of another Fallen lay on the floor in a bubbling mess.

"Nice shot," he said.

"Thanks." She wiped sweat off her brow. "You do realize our plan has gone to hell, right?"

"I do. And to make matters worse, the demons' weapons are tainted with Mammon's blood."

Cries of pain and smoke permeated the air as another angel succumbed to the power of the Atar'zul. Celestial steel crashed against the demons' blades as Fallen streaked across the black marble, engaging the angels, taking advantage of the ones who'd been hit by the halo's power. Grunts scurried like vermin, making focusing on the Fallen chaotic and dangerous.

The angels were at a disadvantage as daemonkin fought alongside the grunts. And if an angel could get free of the swarming demons, Mammon would hit them with the magic of the halo.

They needed to shift the balance if they were to have any chance of winning this battle. Kyden found Oz slicing through a grunt while elbowing a human in the face, dropping them to the floor.

"Oz! Now!" Kyden yelled.

Oz turned and raised his palm. With a yell, a blast of light exploded from his hand, shattering the windows. He cried out as Cree slid by him, dragging his blade through the angel's thigh. Smoke and golden blood oozed from the wound.

"No!" Kyden grabbed Zahra and pulled her with him toward Oz, who barely dodged another attack from Cree. Oz fell to one knee, pain etched along his face.

The Fallen circled Oz, victory making his sinister eyes sparkle. He raised his sword for the killing blow.

Kyden shoved her behind a couch. "Stay hidden." Without waiting for her reply, he risked using a small amount of his power and tapped into his speed.

Cree's blade arched through the air.

Kyden's sword caught Cree's inches from Oz's neck. Cree swore, and Kyden tightened his grip, stepping into a fighting stance. The desire to hack the demon to pieces brought a smile to his face.

Cree retreated a step. "You'll soon be one of us. That's the only reason you're still alive." He turned, streaked across the room, and attacked another angel.

Kyden grabbed Oz's upper arm and helped him to his feet. "Are you all right?"

Oz gaped at the smoking wound. "The blade..."

"It's tainted," Kyden said, searching the horizon. Mist and smoke billowed from the shattered windows but there was still no sign of angelic wings.

Oz grimaced, tying a piece of his torn shirt around his leg. "Something's wrong."

"No kidding." His spine straightened as the sudden desire to use his blade against his friend entered his mind. He shook his head, trying to purge the image. As if pulled by a thread, his gaze met Mammon's. The prince smiled, his silver hair shimmering and black eyes sparkling in victory. Kyden turned away and shoved down the dread that twisted low in his gut. "Oz, get in your human form. It'll slow down the transformation."

Zahra hedged out from behind the couch. "Where's Raphael?"

"Good question." Oz, his wings and armor gone, shook his head. "I told you I had a bad feeling about this."

"I know," Kyden said. He wiped sweat from his brow, trying to keep his hands from shaking. "Warn the other angels about the demons' blades and tell them to fight in their human form if they've been injured."

"We don't stand a chance like that."

"Raphael will be here." His blood burned as if fire coursed through his veins, causing him to bend over and groan.

A small hand touched his shoulder. "Hold on, okay."

He lifted his chin, clenching his jaw so tight it cracked. "We still need to get the halo."

Another wave of power washed over him and the urge to fight against his brothers and sisters made it difficult to breathe. Oz and who knew how many more were infected with Mammon's magic, and Raphael and his soldiers were nowhere in sight. His body shook with rage as he continued to resist Mammon's enthrallment.

He breathed deeply and stood, forcing a smile, and gripped Zahra's hand. "I'm all right. Let's move. Oz, warn the others."

"On it," the angel said, picking up his sword and limping away from them as they maneuvered through the enemy forces.

The smell of sulfur made his eyes water as more grunts spewed from the stairway on the far side of the room. Thankfully, the few angels still fighting cut them down.

He needed to get Zahra closer to the halo if she had any chance of reversing the magic. They were almost to the middle of the room when a fierce tug on his mind made him stumble.

Mammon's voice echoed through the chamber. "Kyden! Come."

As if pulled by an invisible chain, he released Zahra's hand and walked toward the prince of hell, his feet moving of their own accord. His mind emptied, the only thought was pleasing the voice beckoning him closer. The emptiness, the one simple command, made his shoulders relax and his sword lower to his side. He was so tired of fighting.

Why was he carrying it in the first place? The presence urging him closer would not harm him.

Golden-blonde hair flashed before him, and two hands pressed against his chest.

"Look at me, Kyden." Hazel eyes shone up at him.

He focused, trying to remember her name, but the presence compelled him, and he shoved her away.

She scurried around him, blocking his way. "Fight it, dammit!"

He frowned at the familiarity in her voice. Her palm struck, and a sharp sting burned through his cheek.

The haze lifted, and he shook his head. The blissful emptiness in his mind roared back to life with the sounds of battle. Everything from the past few minutes surged into him: Jake possessed, Adinah and Titus fighting one another, Oz hurt and now cursed. And still no sign of Raphael.

"Did you just slap me?" he asked, rubbing his cheek.

A relieved smile unfurled across her lips. Focused on her presence and the clarity of his thoughts, he didn't notice Jake slinking up behind her until he wrapped an arm around her throat and yanked her backward.

"Zahra!" He reached for her, but Jake pressed his gun into her ribs.

"Ah, ah. You stay right there. We can't harm you, but her?" The green in Jake's eyes darkened as his tongue slid along her neck.

Zahra shuddered. "Jake, please stop."

He pinned her arms to her side and smiled. "Oh, I like how you beg." Zahra screamed as Jake's teeth sank into the soft skin of her neck. Blood dripped along her collarbone, disappearing beneath her shirt.

"Darsh, I will kill you," Kyden said between clenched teeth, raising his sword.

The demon laughed. "Soon, you will bow before Prince Mammon. And after I've had my way with her, you'll make her beg for death.

She tried to twist away from Jake, but the demon lurking within him was too strong.

Helplessness threatened to swallow him whole. Darsh had taken root inside Jake, and the only way to purge the demon and save Jake was to flood his soul with Divine Light. The act would require him to step into the spiritual realm, making him more vulnerable to Mammon's seductive pull. He was steadily losing his soul moment by moment, and he wasn't sure how long he had before he completely lost himself.

Zahra's nails dug into Jake's arm, and blood trickled down her neck. Evil intent shone in Jake's eyes as he pressed his gun into her side. There was only one way to save them. As her Protector, he knew what needed to be done.

Daylight shone through the broken windows. *Raphael, hurry*, he thought as his wings exploded from his back.

Chapter Thirty-Four

Zahra

"Kyden, no!" Zahra struggled against Jake as Kyden's armor appeared across his body and his silver-and-brown wings flared out behind him. By using his power and weakening his resolve to fight Mammon's magic, he was sacrificing himself to save her—an act she couldn't allow no matter the cost. Fear wrapped around her throat, steadily strangling her.

Kyden lifted his hand but only black sparks twined through his fingers.

"Finally." Mammon's deep voice resonated through the green mist and smoke. The prince of hell pushed past the throng of grunts and angels, victory swirling in his eyes. "Well done, Darsh."

The Fallen inside Jake dipped her chin in reverence but didn't release her grip. Revulsion coursed through Zahra alongside the pain from where the demon had bitten her neck. Blood dripped under her collar, and if it weren't for the precious body and mind the demon controlled, she'd stab it in the throat and return the favor.

"Kneel," Mammon said, his merciless gaze fixed on Kyden.

The muscles in Kyden's neck bulged as he tried to resist the command.

Zahra forgot about the demon at her back as her heart hit the floor when her Protector disjointedly lowered himself to one knee. The room had grown silent as his armor clanked against the marble.

"I knew you wouldn't be able to hold out for long. Once you used your power, you'd be mine," Mammon said.

Jake chuckled against her ear. Fear had gripped her like steel talons, but now those claws twisted into fury. Years of self-defense classes kicked in as she bit down on Jake's arm while stomping on his foot. He cursed at her when she slid out of his arms.

Blood coated her tongue, almost causing her to retch, but she was free of his grasp. Her eyes darted between Kyden, still kneeling on the ground, and Jake, his face twisted while black shadows writhed around his aura.

Had she lost them both to the fires of hell?

Suddenly, a bright light exploded into the room, followed by a rush of power, knocking her to the ground. Raphael shot through the broken windows, the floor cracking from the impact. In his wake flew the remaining squad of angels. He rose to his full height, golden eyes glowing with unspeakable power, his face carved into stone.

Relief coursed through her as she steadied her legs under her. Darsh, still possessing Jake, had scrambled away once the archangel had arrived.

"You're late," she said, noticing the black blood splattered across his armor.

Raphael's gaze slid to hers, and he arched a brow. He lifted his hand and blinding white light erupted from his palm. A horde of grunts disintegrated in seconds.

Raphael scanned the room and anger flashed in his molten eyes when he noticed Kyden kneeling in front of Mammon. Kyden's body trembled as if every cell inside him fought against the demon's hold.

The smirk on Greed's face made her want to lash out in rage.

"Raphael," Mammon said with a sneer. "Your timing couldn't be more inconvenient. Either way, you failed. Your angels will soon join me and fight by my side. As will you."

Raphael withdrew his sword. "What you have done is an abomination."

"Of course it is. That's what we princes of hell do, after all." Greed roared as his body contorted, followed by the sound of ripping fabric. Leathery black wings erupted from his back, twisted and misshapen.

Zahra gasped as black ichor dripped from the unnatural wings. Shock and anger radiated from the angels near her, like the smell of ozone after a lightning storm.

"That's not possible," Raphael whispered, disbelief widening his eyes.

Greed winced as he flared his deformed wings. "Your reign of power has come to an end, Raphael. No longer will your wings give you an advantage.

Thanks to my new pet"—he pointed to Titus, who stood rigid, his gaze fixed on Raphael—"I've just leveled the playing field."

"You will pay the price for stealing what does not belong to you," Raphael said through clenched teeth.

Zahra slowly moved to Kyden's side. Greed's unholy eyes trailed her movement.

"It's no use. My blood flows through his veins, just like his friend here. Just like the angels you brought into this. I will have the power of demons and angels at my disposal. Not even the archangels will defeat me."

"We shall see." Raphael raised his sword as his soldiers approached, creating a wall of armor, wings, and blades while Greed's demons did the same.

The tension in the room ticked like a bomb ready to explode, and somehow Zahra found herself in the middle of the blast zone. A gentle touch skimmed across her hand. Kyden's head was still bowed, but he was no longer hunched over.

"Be ready," he whispered.

She slowly dragged herself away from him until she stood next to Adinah.

Greed lifted his palm, an evil smile twisting his face, and lit the fuse.

The room exploded into pandemonium.

Divine Light and dark bursts of energy collided, along with clashing steel and screeches from the demons.

A daemonkin raised his weapon, aiming at Raphael. Zahra drew her gun, slid off the safety, and fired. The bullet spun the man around. She didn't wait for him to fall as she targeted another person loyal to the demons. She shot again, hitting a woman in the chest—the one who'd been writhing on Titus.

"Zahra!" Adinah pointed at Jake, who lurched toward her, a dagger in his hand, malevolence lining his face.

She had less than a second to decide what to do before he would be on top of her. Releasing a breath, she squeezed the trigger. Jake's body twisted, and he fell to his knees.

"Please work," she whispered, the gun aimed at his heart despite her shaking hands.

Jake looked up, his eyes narrowed. Blood oozed through his fingers as he clutched his upper arm.

"You bitch," the gravelly voice said as the Fallen struggled to her feet.

Zahra's finger rested on the trigger as Jake took a step toward her. He frowned, staring at his body, and then the muscles in his neck bulged and his back arched. With a scream, the Fallen slithered out of Jake. His hands and knees hit the ground with a painful crack.

The demon, no longer in Jake's body, coiled low to the ground, green eyes flashing with menace. She bared her teeth as she lunged for him.

Zahra emptied the magazine into the Fallen's chest. Greed's tainted bullets smoked from her body as she roared. Out of nowhere, Adinah flew past, her sword drawn. A sickening thunk sounded, and the Fallen fell, her head rolling across the black marble before dissolving among the smoke.

Jake lifted his head, and she breathed a sigh of relief at seeing familiar gray eyes staring back at her.

She ran to him and helped him stand. "Are you all right?"

"I can't believe you shot me," he said, the corner of his mouth quirking upward despite the pain tightening the skin around his eyes.

"Sorry. I was out of options." She used the dagger and ripped his shirt to make a bandage to control the bleeding.

He wrapped his arm around her and pulled her close. "If I'm going to be shot by anyone, it might as well be you." He pressed his lips to hers and gave her a hard kiss. "I've got your back. Go." He nodded to where Raphael crossed blades with Mammon.

How am I going to get the halo off him? she thought as she maneuvered through the chaos.

A grunt demon lunged for her but she dodged and swiped Kyden's blade across its neck. Most of the Fallen were preoccupied with Raphael's soldiers, but one reached for her. A bullet whizzed by and hit the demon between the eyes.

She glanced over her shoulder to where Jake stood. He winked and aimed his gun at another Fallen.

She searched for Kyden among the calamity. Her heart lodged in her throat when she found him fighting Titus. Only a few white feathers were visible in Kyden's wings. She couldn't see his eyes from this distance, but the countdown ticking in her head was nearing zero at a sickening pace.

The two angels fought behind Mammon, who'd retreated to the raised platform. He shot another energy blast toward Raphael, who battled three Fallen. One of his soldiers leaped in front of him and blocked the strike. She cried out in pain as the warped magic from the halo slammed her in the back. Mammon raised his palm again and another angel took the full weight of the cursed magic while protecting the archangel.

It was now or never, she thought as she ran toward the prince of hell, her fingers wrapped around the gun's handle. She cried out as excruciating pain whipped her head back.

Titus stared at the blonde strands of hair in his hand. He tilted his head as he looked her up and down. Tears blurred her vision, the back of her skull throbbing. Her heart sank when she saw Kyden on his knees, grabbing his head. His sword lay at his feet and bronze-colored blood dripped down his side.

"Titus, please," she said, focusing on the angel threatening her.

His face revealed nothing, as if there wasn't any part of his personality or soul remaining inside of him. He raised his blade.

She retreated a step and lifted her gun, not wanting to shoot Kyden's best friend, but if she had to, she would. A blur of bronze streaked past her. Kyden hit the ground in a kneel, his gauntleted arm rising just in time to block Titus's sword.

The Prince of Greed appeared through the smoke like death personified, his unholy wings flaring, dark and bat-like within the gloom. He lifted his hand.

"No!" She reached for Kyden but had to jump back from the heat of the blast.

Black energy shot from Mammon's palm and hit Kyden between the shoulder blades. His back arched as he yelled. Any silver remaining in his wings turned brown and feathers drifted to the floor. Mammon's face twisted with power as he continued to use the halo against Kyden, who'd fallen once again to his knees.

Anger replaced her fear as she slapped a new magazine of tainted bullets into her gun and aimed at the prince of hell. She released a breath and squeezed the trigger. Mammon screamed and lurched to the side as the bullet pierced his hand, the movement causing the halo to slide off his head. She lunged for it, the metal slipping past her fingertips as the halo clinked away from her along the marble floor.

"Get her," the prince yelled, holding his arm as black blood poured from the hole in his hand.

She was almost to the halo when a Fallen stepped into her path, causing her to slip on blood and gore. She skidded to a stop and stared down the barrel of a gun.

Raising her weapon, she aimed at the demon's head. "I wonder if your aim is as good as mine," she said, keeping her gaze fixed on the Fallen while Oz limped toward them, his sword ready to strike.

"Care to find out?" the demon's gravelly voice said.

Celestial silver flashed and the Fallen yelled. It gaped at its arm lying on the ground. Zahra didn't hesitate, not wanting to waste the advantage she had, and squeezed the trigger.

All those hours targeting paper zombies paid off as a hole burned into the demon's forehead.

Oz picked up the halo and handed it to her. "Run."

She headed straight for the archangel, who was battling a horde of grunts. Raphael's angels increased their attack on the demons, creating a safe path for her to sprint through. She glanced briefly at Jake, who held his own against a daemonkin. Another blast of light erupted from Raphael, exterminating a swarm of demons around him.

She finally reached the archangel, her heart pounding and sweat dripping down her back.

"Quickly," Raphael said, removing a knife from the baldric on his chest and sliding the blade across his palm. Gold blood pooled in his hand while he handed her the dagger.

She winced when the blade pierced her flesh. "Join hands," she said, glancing at Kyden, who lay on the ground, his wings smoking and his body twitching while Titus stood over him, his brow furrowed. Her Protector had sacrificed himself over and over to save her, and she prayed this ritual would work.

Raphael pressed his palm into hers while she held the Atar'zul below their joined hands. Gold and red blood, holy and human, mixed and dripped onto the halo, the black metal sizzling as their blood coated the crown.

A roaring wind blew through the room, almost dragging her away from Raphael. He grabbed her as lightning flashed and the ground trembled.

The smoke cleared and the halo gleamed, the tarnish removed, where only pure silver remained.

Raphael gripped the halo and closed his eyes. His shoulders lowered and a smile pulled at the corner of his mouth. His fiery gaze found Mammon.

Chapter Thirty-Five

Kyden

Darkness swirled around him like smoke, and death reached for him with spindly fingers, tempting him to succumb to its embrace. He stood at the edge of an endless chasm with screams spewing from its depths.

Or was he screaming?

Pain burned along his spine while an emptiness so consuming suffocated what little of him was left. Only a small ember of light glowed, an ember he assumed was the remaining piece of his soul. But that too slowly dimmed.

Bitterness and anger beckoned him, and he longed to give in to their tempting call. An eerie blackness seeped from the chasm and into the void growing in his heart, gradually swallowing the light of his essence.

He tried to grab on to the ember, to protect it from the encroaching darkness, but his body wouldn't cooperate. The pain was crippling, making it impossible to move, to fight.

What was he fighting for anyway? Exhaustion pressed him on all sides. His entire existence seemed to be one constant war—against what, he couldn't recall.

Smoke the color of midnight oozed from the chasm, snaking toward him and seeping into his chest where darkness promised an end to his suffering, an end to servitude. It promised power. All he had to do was step off the rim of the chasm, and he'd be free.

He wouldn't be missed, for he was just one of many.

His foot slid forward, his toes hanging over the edge. From the corner of his eye, the diminished ember of light pulsed.

A majestic voice whispered through the gloom like a refreshing breeze across his face.

Kyden.

He teetered on the edge, ready to surrender, wanting to give up. And then the voice called again, louder.

Kyden!

Kyden—the name was familiar. A holy name piercing the darkness inside of him. The small ember pulsed brighter and warmth touched his skin. His pain lessened.

The voice spoke again—a calming balm wrapping around him.

Kyden, my faithful warrior, my beloved.

He knew that voice, had loved that voice since the beginning of his existence. The ember grew into a flame and drove back the darkness within.

Kyden was his name. He was an angelic warrior of Elohim, a Protector of humans and a Slayer of demons. He was valued. He was loved.

Hope bloomed in his chest, and he stepped back from the chasm. The ground shook and the edges of the ravine grew closer together, shutting out the dark and silencing the screams. Light swirled around him, filling every dark crevice of his heart until the pain disappeared.

Another voice drifted into his mind, this one softer—a woman's voice.

Kyden, can you hear me?

Images rushed through his thoughts, memories from long ago. Golden crowns reflecting the light and silver wings outstretched in a glorious arch. Faces of friends he held close to his heart. Another face, one with hazel eyes, filtered through the haze, and an urgent need to protect her filled him. Power, pure and sacred, coursed through him, strengthening him.

Her mouth moved. *Kyden? Please come back to me.*

The flame of his soul ignited, and the darkness retreated. He turned from the narrowing chasm and faced a glorious light. Finally, his hand reached for the fire burning with purpose, alight with hope, his soul bright and whole once more.

He slowly blinked open his eyes. A warm hand pressed against his side, and as he turned his head, familiar eyes wet with tears stared back at him.

"Welcome back," Zahra said.

"It's good to be back." His voice sounded as if he'd swallowed sandpaper. He frowned. "Why are your eyes glowing?"

She smiled, and more light filled his soul.

Another hand wrapped around his arm. "Kyden, look at me."

He tore his gaze from Zahra. "Adinah?"

The angel nodded. Black blood spotted her face and armor and her amber eyes burned from within. Her gaze darted across his face as if searching for something hidden. "Raphael used the halo on you. How do you feel?"

He sat up. All the pain he'd suffered was gone, as was any lure toward Mammon. "It worked." He inhaled deeply and sensed his power growing—his divine power, not the evil magic of Mammon.

Adinah helped him to his feet and handed him his sword. "This isn't over yet."

He scanned the room. Green mist swirled out of the broken windows while grunts continued to fight, sacrificing themselves to allow the remaining Fallen to escape through the exit where someone had blasted a hole. Metal glowed and wires sparked from the jagged edges.

The angels who'd escaped the power of the Atar'zul fought the grunts, while Raphael used the mended halo to heal the cursed angels.

"Where's Mammon?" he asked, his grip tightening on the hilt of his sword as more of his power renewed itself.

Adinah shook her head. "He created a portal and disappeared."

"Coward," he said through clenched teeth.

A swarm of grunts charged them, and he flared his wings, relieved to see mostly silver feathers. As his armor formed along his body, he quickly glanced over his shoulder. "Zahra, get to safety."

He didn't wait for her to respond as the grunts attacked with renewed vigor. He and Adinah fought back-to-back, their swords a blur as grunts disintegrated with screams and sulfur. More angelic warriors joined them and as if sensing a losing battle, the remaining demons scurried toward the exit.

Kyden moved to follow but a pair of brown wings caught his attention, and a sinking sensation grew in the pit of his stomach. "Titus," he whispered, and ran to his friend, who lay on his side with his wings draped behind him. His sword skidded along the marble as he dropped to his knees and pressed his fingers to Titus's neck. He released a sigh when he felt a pulse but wondered why he was unconscious and his wings still ashen.

"Did the halo not work on him?" he asked.

"We need to get him home to heal properly," Adinah said as Zahra and Jake approached, a blood-soaked bandage wrapped around his shoulder. Kyden shot to his feet, grabbed Zahra, and pulled her behind him.

"Hey," she said, smacking his arm.

Jake raised his hands. "It's me, and only me."

Kyden frowned, not remembering much of the last minutes of the battle. His mind had been too focused on resisting the prince of hell. "How?"

Jake smiled, his gaze drifting to Zahra, who had moved back to his side. "You finally got your wish. She shot me."

The corner of Kyden's lip lifted. "You don't say." His gaze returned to Zahra's. "And how are you holding up?" Tears filled her eyes, which were in fact still glowing. He thought maybe he'd imagined that.

"I'll be fine," she said, forcing a smile.

He arched a brow and was about to call her bluff when her eyes widened and the color leached from her face.

Time seemed to slow as Adinah yelled while Jake grabbed Zahra and pulled her to his side. She ripped her gun from its holster.

Cold blackness swirled around him but before he could turn, steel pressed against his throat, and the smell of demon blood washed over him.

"You thought you could defeat me?" The black and green mist parted as Mammon appeared. The hand holding the demon steel had a charred hole in it, and ichor oozed from the wound.

Kyden's stomach dropped. In Mammon's other hand was a gun, which he pointed at Zahra.

"You dared to use my weapons, my blood against me?" the prince asked, his voice gravelly and strained. "You will join me in hell."

She held her gun with both hands and aimed the muzzle at Mammon's head. "I don't think so."

Jake and Adinah flanked her, both holding weapons, targeting the prince of hell, but Zahra was still in the line of fire and he was helpless as Mammon's blade dug into his neck.

The majestic whisper of a voice brushed across his mind, and peace settled through his soul.

"You've lost, Mammon. Apollyon will know of your betrayal, and if you harm me or those I care about, you won't only have to deal with Raphael, but all of Heaven." Kyden's gaze darted between Zahra, Jake, and Adinah—all poised to attack, if only he wasn't in their way.

The blade dug in deeper as Mammon hissed in his ear. "If I go to the Abyss, I'm taking her with me." The demon's finger slid to the trigger of the gun.

Zahra's eyes flicked to something behind him, and suddenly a blast of holy power encompassed him.

Mammon screamed.

Zahra dropped to one knee and squeezed the trigger while Adinah flicked her wrist. A silver dagger flew toward his head, and Kyden lunged to the side, grimacing against the sting in his neck from Mammon's sword.

Another shot fired and the demon stumbled, his eyes wide and mouth open in shock. One hole burned through the prince's forehead, another through his chest, and Adinah's dagger was lodged in his throat. Kyden twisted Mammon's wrist, palmed his sword, and pivoted, the blade cutting through the air. The sword sliced through his neck, and Mammon's body hit the ground with a resounding thunk.

Kyden dropped the demon's blade and staggered back. Zahra's eyes narrowed at the body, her gun smoking but still aimed at the prince. He gently touched her arm.

"Nice shot," he said.

She swallowed and finally tore her gaze from Mammon. "Thanks."

"Nice? That was amazing," Jake said, pulling her into a hug.

Raphael approached, his hand still raised and brow furrowed as he stared at the headless body of the prince of hell. Between the archangel's Divine Light, Adinah's dagger, bullets to the brain and heart, and a sword through the neck, Mammon was no more. The Prince of Greed was only a memory.

Kyden noticed the Atar'zul in Raphael's other hand. "Thank you for saving me," he said, and dipped his chin.

Raphael arched a brow. "It was a team effort. Zahra's blood mixed with mine mended the halo, reversing the effects."

Adinah crossed her arms. "Not bad for a human, even with the glowing eyes," she said with a wink, and sauntered across the room. She knelt next to Oz, who quickly slapped her hand away when she tried to help him stand.

"Why *are* my eyes glowing?" Zahra asked, rubbing them as if she could erase the unusual brightness.

"I assume it's the lingering effect of my blood mixed with yours," Raphael said. "It will fade."

She gave Kyden a Cheshire-cat grin. "So I'm as powerful as you?"

Kyden rolled his eyes while Raphael and Jake laughed.

"Not quite," Raphael said, and glanced toward the windows. "I need to take the halo to Michael and see what we should do with it now."

"What about Titus?" Kyden asked.

"He will need some time and healing to find his way back," Raphael said.

Kyden's gaze drifted to his friend, who still lay unmoving on the floor. "And the other angels? Are they cured?"

Raphael lifted his hand. "They seem back to normal, but will need to return home again for healing. As will you."

"I'm Zahra's Protector. I'm not going anywhere."

She rested her hand on his arm, smiling up at him. "You did protect me, more than you could ever know."

He frowned. "But..."

"It's over, Kyden. We won—this battle at least. Mammon may have been working alone, but Apollyon will need to replace his prince," the archangel said. He nudged the leathery wing lying listlessly on the floor. "And we need to figure out how he accomplished this."

"But what about the Fallen who escaped?" He hated the idea of those demons running free, causing destruction wherever they went.

"There will be opportunities in the future to hunt them down. For now, we need to tend to our own."

Kyden stared around the room. All the demons were gone, either having escaped, been destroyed, or returned to the Abyss to regenerate. Except for Mammon, whose headless body haunted the room with its evil presence. To his knowledge, a prince of hell had never been killed.

"What about him?" Jake asked, nodding toward the fallen prince.

Raphael pointed his palm at the body and Divine Light emerged once again, engulfing what remained of Mammon until nothing but acrid smoke drifted through the air.

Zahra sagged against Jake, a relieved smile curling her lips. He pulled her closer and kissed her temple. The man had proven himself today, and as he held Zahra, keeping her tight at his side, Kyden knew she'd be safe. She wouldn't need a Protector anymore.

She wouldn't need him.

CHAPTER THIRTY-SIX

ZAHRA

Sirens blared from fire trucks as news of the explosion in Durand's office spread. Zahra and Jake needed to get out of there before someone arrived asking questions she wouldn't have a clue how to answer. She'd overheard Adinah spreading a rumor that a gas leak had caused the blast, but that wouldn't hold off the police for long.

Jake seemed to have the same opinion. "We need to go."

She squeezed his arm. "I'll be right back."

She walked across the destroyed room and past the bodies of the dae-monkin. In the distance, emergency vehicles wove their way through traffic, and once again, time ticked by faster than she wanted it to.

Raphael stood before the blown-out window, his wings flared, as his angels took to the skies. His features remained fierce, but relief shone in his golden eyes.

He turned toward her and held out his hand. "Thank you, Zahra. You've proven yourself loyal by sacrificing your blood and saving my angels."

She shook his hand, hers bandaged, his already healed. "What happens now?" Her gaze automatically drifted to Kyden, who spoke with Adinah, while Oz rewrapped Jake's arm. Kyden's eyes, returned to their beautiful amber color, met hers, and his lips formed a tight smile.

Raphael still held the Atar'zul. "I'll meet with Gabriel and Michael to destroy Apollyon's halo. He would have learned by now what Mammon had done. I'm sure he's not happy."

She stared longingly at the halo. "Yeah, I guess it's not safe in a museum, is it?"

Raphael chuckled. "Not really." He squeezed her shoulder and with a flap of his wings, flew into the sky.

"And there goes my promotion," she mumbled. If anything could have convinced her boss to give her job back, returning to the museum with the Atar'zul in hand would have done it.

Kyden, Adinah, and Oz approached. Oz, not having been infected long with Greed's tainted blood, seemed back to normal, but Raphael had ordered all angels affected by the halo to return to their home.

Oz pulled her into a hug. "See you around. Maybe." He winked and flew out the window.

Adinah rested her hands on her hips. Black blood splattered her armor and face, but Zahra still thought she was beautiful.

"You did good," Adinah said, a sparkle in her eyes. She glanced at Kyden and nodded. With a flash, she too disappeared among the clouds.

An awkward silence wedged between her and Kyden until she cleared her throat. "How are you feeling?"

He focused on the sky, his eyes slightly narrowed. "Okay. There's still some lingering effects, but I will heal." He forced a smile and faced her. "How about you?"

She crossed her arms. "I'm sure I'll have nightmares for months, but I'll be fine."

Kyden's eyes drifted to Jake, who sat in a torn leather chair, his eyes fixed on his shoes. "You're in good hands now." He tilted his head. "Angels can't detect if humans are lying, but we are excellent judges of character. He loves you, Zahra."

She smiled as warmth filled her chest. She didn't need an angel to tell her that. Jake had proven himself over the last few days, and if she was certain of one thing, it was that he was here to stay. And now that any chance of her getting her job back had literally flown out the window, the only reasons to stay in Boston were Alexis and her mother.

Guilt pressed her from every side. She hadn't worried about her mother since leaving the nursing home. Granted, the events from the last few days had been a little crazy as she had been fighting for her life and possibly humanity. She now had a small understanding of what her father must have experienced after he'd discovered he was a Vaelatori. Knowing what he did about the spiritual realm, he had fought the battle alone.

She glanced at Jake again. Could she do the same? Would she even have to? The Atar'zul was no longer on this earth, the prophecy fulfilled. The purpose of the Vaelatori was complete.

Her gaze shifted to Kyden. "After you heal, will you return?" She couldn't keep her voice from trembling.

He tore his gaze from the clouds. "No. My role as Protector is finished."

"Back to slaying demons, then." She tried to smile but was sure her mouth formed more of a grimace than anything.

He sighed. "It *is* what I do best."

"I don't know. You're pretty handy to have around. I mean, who else will fetch me lollipops?" She tucked a strand of hair behind her ear, focusing on everywhere but his beautiful face as she held back the tears.

A brief flash made her blink and his armor disappeared. He wore a Whitesnake T-shirt and jeans. "Come here," he said, opening his arms and pulling her close.

She pressed her cheek to his chest, content to listen to the soothing rhythm of his heart. "Thank you for everything, Kyden, even for pretending to be my fake date."

He chuckled, and the sound both warmed her and made her want to collapse into sobs. He was leaving, and she had a depressing premonition she would never see him again.

He leaned away and wiped a tear from her cheek. "Lay off the lollipops. Your teeth will thank you." The muscle in his jaw twitched. He turned to face the sky and tilted his head as if listening to a voice she couldn't hear. "I have to go now."

She nodded. Words escaped her as he flared his wings, the feathers mostly returned back to silver, though some remained brown.

Jake had risen to his feet and approached them, his eyes darting between her and Kyden. Kyden held out his hand and Jake took it. No words were spoken, just a simple understanding.

Kyden walked to where Titus still lay unconscious and picked him up. He looked at her one last time and smiled. "Be good."

With a flap of his wings, he and Titus shot into the sky and disappeared behind the clouds.

Zahra stood at the window overlooking the Vegas skyline with her arms wrapped tightly around herself. Her gaze drifted to the clouds, hoping to see a flash of silver wings, but the sky was clear of any supernatural beings. The talisman on her neck had cooled since the battle, and she'd washed off the blood—angelic, demonic, and human.

She almost felt normal.

Almost.

The closing of the door drew her attention from the window. Jake entered with to-go cartons of Chinese food.

"Hey," he said, placing them on the table.

"Hey."

His gaze traveled the length of her. "Your glowing eyes are gone."

"Don't you know how to charm a girl," she said, giving him a playful slap on the cheek.

When she and Jake had returned to her hotel room, she had stared in the mirror as the glow in her eyes faded. Raphael had said she'd had the blood of an archangel flowing through her veins. Her hand still stung from the celestial blade that had sliced across her palm, and her body hummed with energy, but the electric charge coursing through her had lessened with every passing minute. She knew once the effects of Raphael's blood wore off, she would pass out from exhaustion.

But food first.

After they finished eating, Jake leaned back in his chair and took a long pull from his beer. "I finally understand the saying, 'Ignorance is bliss.'"

She snorted. "No kidding. For years, I'd chosen not to believe in anything supernatural or spiritual. I definitely have a different outlook on life." She remembered back to the dinner where Kyden had pretended to be her date and Laurent had questioned their belief in magic. Kyden had said, *faith is to believe what we do not see.*

How ironic that two powerful beings, one evil and one holy, had sat at a table eating dinner discussing magical artifacts and faith.

"What are you thinking about?" Jake asked.

Her eyes drifted to the window as the sun began its descent. "Faith."

Jake gathered the empty containers and threw them away. "Yeah, it seems I have a lot to learn."

She agreed with him but was too tired to delve into that now, especially when her jaw cracked as she yawned. "I'm going to book a flight home and then call it a night."

He nodded. "I have a few things I need to wrap up. The movers come in two days..."

She frowned. "What do you mean, movers?"

"I've been trying to tell you, but I never seemed to get the sentence out." He rubbed the back of his neck. "I'm moving to Boston."

Her mouth dropped, and she quickly snapped it shut. "Why? Isn't your job here?"

"Not anymore. I had come to Boston for closure between us, but then I saw you again, and you were wearing my ring. I realized it wasn't closure I wanted, but you in my life. So I'm moving to Boston. I want to give us a chance."

Tears welled in her eyes, making his face blur. "You'd do that for me?"

He closed the distance between them and traced her bottom lip with his thumb. "For the woman I love, of course I would." Smile lines wrinkled the corners of his eyes. "Also, I'm sick of this desert heat. Don't think too highly of me, though. I simply transferred my job to Boston. Of course, I'm not sure who my boss will be." He shrugged as if moving across the country was no big deal.

She ran her hands through her hair. Excitement flared inside her, but doubt still clung to the recesses of her heart. What if he regretted changing jobs and moving for her? What if he realized he didn't love her enough to stay? She closed her eyes and mentally shut down the what-ifs. Fear of the unknown wouldn't control her life. "I...I don't know what to say."

He kissed the tip of her nose. "How about, 'Jake, you're simply amazing.'" He then kissed her cheek. "And so gorgeous." His lips found her other cheek. "I simply can't keep my hands off you." He finally pressed his mouth against hers in a gentle, deliciously slow kiss that made her knees weak. "Or how about, 'I love you, Jake.'"

She laughed and wrapped her arms around his neck. "I love you, Jake."

He smiled and held the back of her neck while his other hand gripped her waist. "I love you too, Zee."

Just as she'd expected, once the food settled, Zahra crashed, not even bothering to turn the lights off before crawling into bed. A deep sleep found her quickly, as did the nightmares.

Green, sickly eyes glared through the darkness while pointed teeth snapped at her. The scraping of claws skittering on the floor almost drowned out her scream. Jake stood before her, his gray eyes black and his lips twisted into an evil grin. Blood dripped down his chin as he called her name.

"Zahra!"

Strong hands gripped her shoulders, and she struggled to get away.

"Zahra, sweetheart, wake up."

Her eyes flicked open and the warm glow from the bedside lamp illuminated Jake, his lips pressed into a flat line. He gently brushed the wet hair off her forehead.

"Just a dream. You're safe," he said.

She sat up and inhaled a shaky breath. "I'm pretty sure my nights are going to be plagued by nightmares." Glancing at the clock, she sighed having only slept for two hours.

Jake had changed from his bloody clothes into a T-shirt and sweat-pants with the hotel's logo on them. He followed her gaze and smiled. "It was this or a sequined speedo."

She chuckled. "That might be interesting."

He tucked another strand of hair behind her ear. "You okay?"

She trembled, and goose bumps formed along her arms. She was about to say she was fine but if this fledging relationship was going to last, honesty needed to be its foundation. "No," she finally said, the words sharp against her tongue. "No, Jake, I'm not."

She couldn't help the tears welling in her eyes. His face softened. He rose from the bed, and at first she thought he was leaving, but he walked to the other side and crawled onto the mattress.

"Lie down."

She slid back between the sheets. He settled in behind her and wrapped his arms around her, pulling her close. "I've got you. You're safe now."

His forearm draped over her chest, and she absent-mindedly trailed her fingers along the corded muscle.

"I don't remember these feeling like this," she said.

"What?" His breath tickled her ear.

"Your arms. Were they like this in college?"

He chuckled and a shiver raced down her spine. "No. I started lifting a few years ago—a way to manage my stress."

"Well, it's productive, that's for sure."

The ice in her veins the nightmare had left behind melted as his body pressed against hers, sending delicious heat to her core. She was no longer tired, nor did she want to sleep. What she needed was him.

She rolled over and stared into his eyes.

He arched a brow. "What's going on in that head of yours?"

She leaned close and licked his bottom lip, dragging it into her mouth. She'd always loved his lips, how the bottom one was fuller than the top.

His body turned rigid. "Zahra?"

"Jake?" She trailed her hand from his collarbone, along his sculpted chest to his abdomen that trembled under her touch. "I remember your uncanny ability to distract me."

He groaned when she slid her tongue up the column of his neck. But then he grabbed her wrists, halting the progress of her curious hands. "Babe, as much as I'd love to distract you, I think maybe..."

She stopped his words with a kiss and rolled him onto his back while she straddled him. "Stop thinking and make love to me."

His eyes traveled down her body, his Adam's apple bobbing at her tight tank top and pink panties. A wrinkle formed between his brows. "Are you sure?"

"Always the gentleman." She smiled and smoothed out the crease of worry with a kiss, her breasts scraping against his T-shirt. "Yes, I'm sure."

The corner of his lip lifted. "Then I'd be more than happy to distract you. How about I start here?" He ran his thumb over her nipple, and she arched into his touch. His other hand skimmed down her side until he found the hem of her shirt.

He slowly raised the material. "Do you know how long I've wanted to see you like this?" he asked, his voice husky.

She couldn't find the words as his fingers teased the skin below her breasts. The need building between her legs had her moving her hips along his hard length. He tipped his head back and closed his eyes as she rubbed against him.

She gasped as his hands finally cupped her breasts. Her impatience snapped, and she ripped her tank top off, baring herself to him. He sat up, pulling her legs around his waist and swirled his tongue along her sensitive flesh, tasting, teasing.

Needing his skin against hers, she removed his shirt and pulled him against her as her lips found his once more. The kiss was like coming home, welcoming and safe. He tilted her head and drove the kiss deeper. Longing ignited as his tongue explored every corner of her mouth, and still she wanted more.

He seemed to have the same idea as he flipped her over onto her back and stared down at her.

"You are so damn beautiful." His hand ran down her body until he stopped at the top of her underwear. He slid the material to the side and dragged a finger down her center. His eyes darkened at how wet she already was for him.

Her hips automatically jerked as he continued to explore, first with his hands and then with his mouth. Her thoughts melted away as he had his way with her until her entire body shook and she cried out his name.

"That's my girl," he said as he rose to his feet and removed his sweatpants. She couldn't help but admire his sleek muscles, the sexy V at his hips, his tan skin with a light dusting of hair.

He was beautiful, and he was hers.

"Jake, please." She couldn't remember the last truly fabulous orgasm she'd had, but he'd just given her one of the best, and she craved more.

His body slid over hers, and he kissed her as he paused at her entrance.

"Open your eyes," he said.

She hadn't realized they were closed but when she opened them, he thrust home. His groan tangled with her gasps as he drove them both higher and higher. He filled her, not just her body, but her heart and her soul. Whatever darkness had tainted her thoughts dissipated as he made love to her.

Her toes curled, and her entire body resembled a live wire as he moved, her hips matching his with every stroke. She threw her head back and stars exploded as she clenched around him, her body rigid with pleasure. He groaned, his rhythm hurried and uneven until he finally fell with her over the edge.

He collapsed on top of her, his weight a comforting balm as their breaths slowed. Rolling her over, he snuggled behind her, holding her close.

"Are you thoroughly distracted, love?" he asked, his words tickling her ear.

She smiled and wove her fingers through his. Exhaustion crept into the corners of her mind, but before sleep overtook her, she said. "Quite thoroughly."

He kissed her temple. "Go to sleep. I'll distract you more in the morning."

And she did, with a smile on her face, wrapped in the security of his arms and the assurance of his love.

CHAPTER THIRTY-SEVEN

KYDEN

Kyden leaned against the railing of a three-story building overlooking Sanctaria, the city of the angels. The streets, made of carnelian quartz, sparkled, reminding him of vibrant sunsets on earth where the reds and oranges painted the sky with broad brushstrokes. Sanctaria, a realm between Heaven and earth, was the angels' home, a place of refuge and rest, where they stayed to heal if necessary.

Titus, Oz, and all the angels affected by the cursed halo had flown to Sanctaria immediately after the battle. All experienced complete healing except for Titus. Raphael had put Titus in a state of hypnorestoration to allow his body and mind to mend itself where nightmares would not haunt him.

Time worked differently in Sanctaria, but Kyden felt like he'd been in the city for at least a week, and he was getting antsy—the need for an assignment, to wield his sword and track demons, made him pace the length of the balcony of the home he and Titus shared.

The space was a comfortable two-story dwelling, containing all the accommodations one needed for rest. He likened it to the humans' idea of an AirBnB, only brimming with magic.

The bedroom door squeaked open, and Kyden turned from the view of white buildings giving off an ethereal glow. Jophiel, one of the seven archangels, entered the room. He wore his blond hair short, like Kyden's, and a scar cut a jagged line through his cheek—an injury from the Celestial War, but Kyden wasn't sure which prince of hell had inflicted the damage.

He nodded at Kyden, and then knelt next to Titus to examine him, running a hand along the brown feathers still marring his wings. Jophiel opened one of Titus's eyes and then shut it, moving to the various wounds along his chest and side. Kyden was relieved to see the injuries caused by Mammon had healed, but scars remained. Jophiel finished his examination and then signaled for Kyden to follow him.

He left the balcony doors open, allowing the breeze to flutter the silk curtains and air out the room. He wasn't sure if his friend heard him while in his magical sleep, but he hoped the sounds of chirping birds and laughter from the streets below would bring Titus comfort.

Kyden stepped into the hall where Jophiel waited.

"Good to see you. Again," the archangel said, a faint smile on his lips. He had donned the customary white robe that all angels wore in the city, tied with a golden sash, and leather sandals covering his feet. Angels visiting Sanctaria carried no weapons and wore no armor. There was no need after all.

"You too." He rubbed his neck. "How's he doing?"

"His blood is clear of the demon's contamination, but his wings and eyes still show the effects, although they are improving."

"Will he ever be back to his old self?"

"I'm not sure."

Kyden crossed his arms, his thumb tapping along his bicep as he remembered the last line of the prophecy: *...the angels rise in light's refrain—redeemed through blood and solemn vow, they seek the grace they once let down.*

The halo, mended from Mammon's demonic blood, had healed the angels—they were redeemed, so why wasn't Titus already healed?

"I realize that's not the answer you want. The damage caused by the halo might have lasting effects. Once he awakens from his healing sleep, I believe his battle will be more mental than physical. Whether Titus returns to his former self will be completely up to him."

"What's that supposed to mean?" He winced at his gruff tone, reminding himself he was addressing an archangel, not a fellow Slayer.

"Walk with me," Jophiel said, and headed toward the front door of their home. Palm trees arched gracefully over the sparkling streets, and flowers spilled from the planters, saturating the air with a sweet fragrance. A breeze fluttered through Kyden's wings and rustled his robe.

"Raphael told me about Mammon's wings," Jophiel said, "mentioning something about stolen grace. I can only assume the prince took some of Titus's essence to create a serum, which he used to give himself wings."

Kyden raked his hand through his hair. "But what does that have to do with Titus returning to his true self?"

"Until he wakes up, I won't know for sure, but Titus's very soul was violated. How he rebounds from that—time will tell."

They walked in silence beside the Elyndra River, which flowed through the center of the city. He pondered the archangel's words regarding the journey Titus would have to travel, and wondered about his own.

As if sensing his thoughts, which was annoying, Jophiel asked, "Is there something else on your mind?"

He sighed, not one to divulge his emotions to anyone, except Elohim, who already knew everything anyway. He hadn't told anyone how close he'd been to giving up, to having his essence forever removed. Sensing a nudge in his spirit, he stopped walking, his gaze fixed on the magical sky, where no sun, moon, or stars could be found.

"When I was under the enthrallment of Mammon, I'd almost surrendered everything I am, my soul, my identity—everything." He swallowed past the lump in his throat. "And for that, I am ashamed."

A large hand rested on his shoulder, and when Kyden glanced up at Jophiel, only understanding shimmered in his golden eyes.

"All of us have struggled with our faith, some more than others. What you experienced would have brought many an angel to their knees."

"But I almost failed. How am I not stronger?" He remembered uttering those words to Zahra in Las Vegas as he slowly transitioned into something he never dreamed he'd become. "If it weren't for Elohim calling me back to him..." He shuddered, unable to finish the sentence.

"Elohim never once gave up on you. We are all proud of you, Kyden."

He huffed out a bitter laugh, shaking his head. "Proud?"

Jophiel chewed the inside of his cheek. "Elohim may have gotten your attention, but your free will was still intact. You chose the right path, the harder path. That is why we are proud."

Kyden shoved his hands into the pockets of his robe, secretly longing for his jeans and T-shirts. The archangel's encouragement was a balm to his soul—one he hadn't realized he needed. A weight lifted from his shoulders and the air seemed a little sweeter, the sky a little brighter.

"Come on," Jophiel said, and led him to an outdoor café overlooking the Elyndra River flowing through the city.

Kyden and Jophiel sat and two steaming mugs magically appeared on the table, one with coffee, and by the earthy, floral scent tickling his nose, the other was some variety of black tea.

Even in Sanctaria, angels needed their caffeine.

Kyden crossed his ankle over his knee and leaned back in his chair, fiddling with the lip of the mug as he observed the other angels going about their lives. He never spent much time in the city—his body seemed to crave action, and too much relaxation made him twitchy. He was ready for another mission. Unfortunately, he no longer had a snitch providing him intel on demonic activity.

"Any news on Gael?" he asked. The last time he'd seen the demon was before the battle with Mammon.

"He's still being monitored, or as the humans say, under house arrest," Jophiel said.

"What angel got assigned to that job?" He couldn't imagine any of his brothers or sisters wanting that responsibility. Apollyon would have heard of his betrayal by now and who knew how many Fallen were hunting him.

"Not an angel," Jophiel said.

He was about to sip his coffee but stopped. Had he heard the archangel correctly? "Are you saying a human is protecting him?"

The angel chuckled. "Is that so hard to believe, especially after what you've been through over the last few weeks?"

He shrugged and stared down the street. An angel with golden-blonde hair, similar to Zahra's, stopped to smell some flowers at one of the many shops along the avenue. Humans and their determination, abilities, and even sacrifice had proven him wrong, but he couldn't help the knee-jerk reaction. Something he vowed to work on.

"What's going to happen to Gael?" he asked, returning to the subject of the interesting Fallen.

"I'm not sure. That's between him, Gabriel, and Elohim."

He arched a brow. "Have you ever heard of a Fallen obtaining redemption?"

"No, I haven't, but I've also never witnessed a Fallen accomplishing what Gael has." Jophiel added sugar to his tea and sipped the hot brew. His golden eyes drifted to Kyden's bouncing knee. "Raphael wanted me to ask you if you're ready for your next mission. Based on how fidgety you are, I'd say yes."

He stilled his leg. "I'm definitely ready."

The corner of Jophiel's lips curved upward. "Good. As you're aware, some of the Fallen escaped with the weapons Mammon had made. Also, we couldn't find any evidence of the serum Mammon used for his forbidden wings. We can't assume he used it all or didn't make extra."

Kyden's knuckles whitened as he gripped the handle of his mug. With the inner war he'd been fighting, he hadn't paid attention to which demons had met their end and which had fled.

"Let me guess. Cree is one of the cowards who fled?" he asked.

Jophiel nodded. "And I believe another named Bakal."

"I loathe them both. Where were they last spotted?"

"Unclear. They're in hiding, probably in the Abyss, although I'm not sure Apollyon is pleased with them either. When you're ready, Raphael wants you to meet him in Turkey."

"I'd like to stay until Titus wakes up, if possible." The need for action made him feel as if spiders crawled along his skin, but he wanted to be there when his best friend awoke.

"Raphael figured you'd say that." Jophiel waved at two angels crossing the street. They smiled and returned the gesture. "He said to take as long as you need. The war isn't going anywhere anytime soon, although I do sense the end is near. But before you go..."

Kyden was sipping his coffee and almost spit it out when Jophiel laid the halo on the table. His heart immediately pounded in his ears. He didn't think he'd ever forget the controlling power of the halo—the black void, the desperation that had dug its claws into his throat.

"Why do you have that?"

Jophiel ran his finger along the metal, which was no longer a shiny silver but tarnished and dented as if the halo had rested in the ground for thousands of years. "Michael figured out a way to remove the magic. It's now simply a piece of history. I believe you know what to do with it."

He slowly reached for the halo, trying not to allow his hand to shake. When his fingers wrapped around it, he sensed nothing. Breathing a sigh of relief, he took the halo, holding it up to the light. What used to contain immense power was now a powerless relic. Jophiel was right—he absolutely knew what to do with it.

CHAPTER THIRTY-EIGHT

ZAHRA

The cold nipped at Zahra's cheeks as she walked up the steps to the Gallery of Time Museum. On her flight back to Boston, she'd received an email from Mr. Rousseau, requesting her presence at her earliest convenience. A part of her wanted to drive straight from the airport to the museum, but she'd had someone very important to check on first.

She had been a little worried when she visited her mother at the nursing home, half expecting a squad of cop cars to be waiting for her, but everything was back to normal, including the nurse she'd shot.

The talisman rested against her skin and thankfully no demons were present and the nurse's aura was clean. The nurse said she'd taken a tumble and accidentally stabbed herself in the leg. She walked with a slight limp but otherwise seemed oblivious to the fact that she'd been possessed or that Zahra had shot her. Whatever Adinah had done was mind-boggling.

Nancy Jenkins slept in her bed with heavy blankets cocooning her. Zahra sat next to her and found the picture of her parents. A sense of pride washed over her for completing the job given to her by her father, and she longed to tell her mother everything: curing the halo and how archangel blood had momentarily flowed through her veins, the battles, her helping to defeat a prince of hell, and the angel who had been her protector.

Her phone dinged, and she smiled when she glanced at the text from Alexis. Her best friend, completely healed and going stir crazy with her parents hovering over her, had returned to Boston. Zahra and Alexis decided that a new apartment was in the future as neither wanted to stay in the place where

Alexis had been shot. They'd found a cute two-story condo that was close to work and in a safe neighborhood. They planned to move after Thanksgiving.

"Zahra?"

She lifted her head and smiled at her mom. The nurse taking care of her mother warned her that Nancy spent most of the day sleeping and that if she woke up, it was only for short periods. "Hi, Mom. How are you feeling?"

Nancy smiled and then drifted off to sleep again. She held her frail hand and blinked away the tears. She'd studied this disease enough to accept that her mom's suffering would soon end. Having never thought much about life after death, her thoughts returned to the spiritual realm. After all she'd experienced, along with witnessing the creatures living in the Abyss, she planned to visit the church where her mom had attended for so many years. She craved answers and figured church was the best place to get them.

Zahra sat with her mom for a while longer, telling her about Jake and how they were getting back together. She didn't, however, go into the details of the night and morning they'd shared—Jake had taken the task of distracting her seriously and done a phenomenal job.

Thoughts of Jake brought a smile to her face, one she needed as she'd left her mother at the nursing home and drove to the museum. She found Mr. Rousseau at the Information Center, holding a package and talking with a volunteer. When he saw her, he straightened his tie and gave her a welcoming smile.

"Miss Jenkins. Thank you for coming in so quickly."

She inhaled a calming breath, trying to suppress the butterflies swarming in her stomach. She'd never taken her job for granted, but after reading the email with her termination, she realized that working in the museum was what she wanted more than anything. Well, that and a certain someone with silky brown hair and gray eyes.

"Hello, Mr. Rousseau. I wanted to apologize..."

Mr. Rousseau held up a hand. "There's no need. Yes, I was upset about you keeping your relationship with Dr. Neeman a secret, but I also understand why you did." They walked by the entrance to the Babylonian exhibit where King Nebuchadnezzar II stood, and a shiver trailed down her spine. A tour group meandered past while the guide spoke about one of the most famous kings in Mesopotamian history.

"Your work has been exemplary, and the board and I agree that you'd be a wonderful curator at this museum."

She almost stumbled at his words but thankfully didn't fall flat on her face. "What are you saying?"

"Your work ethic alone makes you the perfect person for the job, but after receiving this..." He handed her the package, which she noticed he'd opened. The lines around his eyes crinkled. "I don't know how you did it, but your exhibit is now complete."

She gasped when she lifted the lid.

"It was addressed to the museum, but your name is on the card inside," Mr. Rousseau said, a slight blush reddening his cheeks.

Her hands shook as she removed the Atar'zul from the packaging. The halo, which had once shone pure silver, now resembled the other relics from the exhibit. She'd assumed the angels had destroyed it, but instead they'd given it to her.

"When did you get this?" she asked, swallowing past the lump in her throat.

"It arrived an hour ago by courier."

The hair on her neck stood at attention. She glanced around the crowded museum and her stomach hit the floor as a shock of black hair and a Bon Jovi T-shirt drew her gaze.

"Kyden," she whispered, taking a step forward. A group of tourists walked in front of her, blocking her view. By the time she maneuvered around them, he was gone.

"Miss Jenkins, are you all right?" Mr. Rousseau touched her shoulder, a look of concern lining his eyes.

She licked her lips and glanced around the crowded lobby again. "I'm fine. Just thought I saw someone I knew." She took the note out of the package.

Zahra,

Here's a little something for all your hard work and sacrifice—don't worry, it's safe.

Kyden

She couldn't help the laugh that escaped her lips.

Mr. Rousseau cleared his throat. "Yes, well, I expect your application for my job on my desk within the week. Formalities and all that," he said with a wave of his hand. He turned and strode toward the offices, leaving her with the Atar'zul and, by the sounds of it, her promotion.

Zahra rubbed her thumb along the silver feather pendant as the sun warmed her shoulders. Birds chirped in the cool morning air and a light dusting of snow covered the ground. Jake's warm hand wrapped around hers, offering a comfort and assurance she didn't realize she needed.

She couldn't believe one month had passed since the confrontation with a prince of hell, since she'd seen angels and demons fight, since she'd seen Kyden.

Jake squeezed her hand and kissed her temple. "I'll meet you in the car. Take as long as you need."

She nodded, her gaze fixed on the two headstones as tears streamed down her cheeks. Her mom passed away soon after Zahra returned to Boston. She would miss her mother, the woman she'd been before the disease changed her, but she treasured the relationship they had shared. As for her father, she would rest easily knowing he had loved her and everything he did had been to protect his family. She'd always regret the time lost between them, but also understood the reasons behind his absence.

Her mind drifted to Kyden and wondered if she'd really seen him that day in the museum, the day she received the Atar'zul. Now that the halo was no longer magical and simply a piece of the past, her ability to see into the spiritual realm was gone. The role of Vaelatori was complete, but the war still raged on.

She couldn't help imagining where Kyden veis, off fighting demons somewhere, or wondering how her other angelic friends were doing.

She huffed out a laugh. "Did you two know I have angelic friends? Who would have thought? Oh, and Mom, Jake and I are together again. I know you've always liked him. Plus, I've broken my lollipop habit."

Jake, being the health-conscious person he was, had introduced her to working out, "a healthier form of stress relief," or so he claimed. She still wasn't convinced.

"Dad, you'll be happy to know I got my promotion at the museum and the Atar'zul is safely behind glass. Granted, it no longer has any power, but better safe than sorry. Anyway, I'll visit again soon." Her voice wavered and she cleared her throat. She removed the talisman from her neck and draped it over her father's headstone. After all, she wouldn't be needing it anymore. "I love you both."

She was about to wipe the tears away when a shiver ran down her spine and the whisper of a breeze caressed her cheek. Peace enveloped her, and she smiled.

An hour later, Jake pulled up to the curb at the museum, since she still had some work to catch up on with her boss's retirement party and with Christmas right around the corner.

Jake's fingers drummed on the steering wheel as she unbuckled her seatbelt. Over the last couple of days, he had seemed more jittery than normal. She wasn't sure if it was his new job at a prestigious company in Boston or if it was something else.

"How about dinner tonight?" Jake asked. "The Indulgence is under new ownership. I thought we might give it a go."

She arched her brow. "How did you get reservations? That place is booked out for months."

The corner of his lip lifted into an adoring smirk. "I have my ways."

"Sounds good. Pick me up at six?"

When she leaned in to give him a quick kiss, he held the back of her neck, and trailed his tongue along the seam of her lips. She opened for him, unable to stifle a moan. She loved how he kissed her, like the meeting of their mouths was as essential as breathing. A horn honked and they pulled apart, both breathing heavily.

"Gonna have a hard time focusing on work now," she said, fixing her hair.

"Hard is an understatement."

She snorted and got out of the car. "See you in a couple of hours."

When she arrived in her office, her new assistant, Roger, waved, the phone tucked neatly between his ear and neck. While she had been gone,

Meredith had found another job, which had saved her the awkward task of firing her former assistant.

"A package came for you, Miss Jenkins," Roger said, hanging up the phone.

"Roger, please call me Zahra. You make me sound old."

He chuckled and resumed typing on his computer.

She dropped her bag by her desk and sat in her comfortable leather chair. Most of her belongings had already been boxed up, and she'd soon be unpacking them into a much larger office. She couldn't help the smile spreading until her cheeks ached. Finally, the promotion she'd worked so hard for was hers for the taking. And take it, she would.

Her eyes drifted to a small rectangular box on her desk. The packaging seemed familiar. When she lifted the lid, her heart skipped a beat at the velvet bag laying in the center of the box. With shaking fingers, she pulled the necklace from the bag. A silver feather, twisted into a beautiful spiral, sparkled in the waning light drifting in from her office window.

Zahra,

I wanted you to have something to remember me by. Don't worry, there's no magic in it—just a simple feather, but I thought you could have your own.

All is well on the home front, and Titus sends his regards. He's still battling some inner demons, but is almost back to his old self. I'm doing what I do best, but my protective instincts can't help but check in from time to time. Tell Jake hello for me.

Kyden.
P.S. Glad you gave up the lollipops.

She tilted her head back and stared at the ceiling. "Thank you," she whispered.

A peace settled deep in her soul, and despite the loss of her parents, joy took root in her heart. Kyden may no longer be her official Protector, but he was still looking out for her. The promotion she'd always wanted would soon be hers, and if her hunch was correct regarding Jake, she'd have a new ring on her finger by tonight. For the first time in a long while, her life finally felt like it was falling into place.

Epilogue

No one at the bar knew an angel sat among them. A heavenly host, who nursed a beer, his gaze transfixed on a football game yet seeing nothing.

No one at the bar would know the angel battled sensations and feelings he hadn't learned to control—that at one point in his eternal existence, his soul had hung in the balance. And even though he'd won the battle, a darkness tainted his being where unholy images haunted his dreams.

Titus's phone vibrated on the bar, revealing a text message from Kyden, a message he chose to ignore. Other angels had reached out, like Adinah and Oz, but he wasn't ready yet. They couldn't understand or help him more than they already had.

Mammon's blood had run through Titus's veins and his essence stolen, and he had yet to figure out where he belonged. After waking up in Sanctaria, he hadn't felt like himself, and until he discovered his purpose, the wise course of action was to keep a low profile and stay out of the spiritual realm.

Especially with the desire for revenge pressing in on all sides, squeezing the breath out of him.

A cheer rang out as the home team scored a touchdown.

The barstool next to him squeaked as a man sat down, and Titus rolled his eyes. He'd chosen this spot to be alone, frowning at all the unoccupied seats the stranger could have taken.

The man signaled the bartender. "Whiskey, neat."

Titus slid a gaze from the corner of his eye and found the man smiling at him.

"Can I help you?" Titus asked, not bothering to hide the irritation edging his voice.

"I think we can help each other."

Titus swiveled on his stool, figuring intimidating the stranger would make him leave, but the man's lips curved into a smirk.

The hairs on his neck bristled. "Who are you?" Titus asked, reaching for the dagger hidden at his waist.

The man slid his glasses off and green eyes glinting with mischief stared back. "The name's Gael."

A Note to My Readers

If you've made it this far, you've walked through the shadows, chased the light, and survived the chaos right alongside my characters. Thank you for reading and for believing in this world with me.

If you enjoyed this book, leaving a review would mean the world. It helps other readers discover my books and keeps this indie author fueled with caffeine and hope.

Leave a review here

Want more magic, sneak peeks, and behind-the-scened mischief? Join the Light & Shadow Guild by signing up at **cassiesanchez.com.**

And if you want to hang out between books, come find me online: Instagram, Facebook, TikTok: **@cassiesanchezauthor.**

Acknowledgements

Before anyone else, I thank God—the source of every spark, every whisper of imagination, and every bit of courage that carried me through the shadows and into the light of this story. His presence has been my compass.

A huge thanks to my beta readers, whose constructive criticism and encouragement helped shape this book in what it needed to be.

Alyssa, I hope you no longer want to off Jake. Thank you for pushing me to make him a more likable, green-flag character.

Linda, you're excitement helped keep my butt in the chair and your expertise in mythology pointed me in the right direction.

Ginger, thank you for making sure I stayed on track biblically— while still allowing room for creative license.

And Janine—thank you for always being thrilled for my books and catching all those lovely repeated words.

To my editor, Rachel—one of these days I'll figure out where the heck to put those commas. Thank you for your guidance and for helping this story become its best version.

Laurissa, thank you for proofreading with such a keen eye. You found the tiny mistakes I somehow missed a hundred times, and I appreciate you more than you know.

None of this would be possible without the constant support, love, and encouragement from my husband. Thank you for always being in my corner, for being my number one fan—and let's be honest—for footing the bill.

Lastly, to my readers who have accompanied me on this journey: You keep the magic alive and for that, I'm eternally grateful.

Also by Cassie Sanchez

The Darkness Trilogy
Chasing the Darkness
Embracing the Darkness
Conquering the Darkness

About the Author

Cassie Sanchez is an award-winning author of fast-paced fantasy romance where danger dances with desire and magic always has a price. Based in the enchanting Southwest, she lives with her husband and two crazy labs, Bullet and Scout. When she's not writing happily-ever-afters, she can be found wielding a Pickleball paddle or cuddling with her dogs for an afternoon nap.

At the heart of Cassie's stories are characters who stumble, fall, and rise again—wrestling with forgiveness and searching for redemption. Step into her world, where every story casts a spell and love conquers all, even the shadows.

www.ingramcontent.com/pod-product-compliance
Lightning Source LLC
Chambersburg PA
CBHW031117160726
47991CB00004B/1425